Unra [illegible] nan

By

Fi Whyms

ISBN: 9791041522927

Chapter One

When he found out about my deception, D'Artagnan was – well, he was many things. And all of them were synonymous with the word 'destroyed'.

He was:

- broken
- crushed
- demolished
- devastated
- ruined
- shattered
- wrecked.

D'Artagnan was all of those things.

I tried so hard to make him understand why I could not tell him that his business partner Guillaume had raped me twelve years ago. Why I thought it essential that I brought Guillaume to justice without him knowing about it.

I reminded him of what he'd said. 'If he ever touch you, Nicole, I kill him.' He'd smiled that lazy half-smile at me as we'd sat together on the sofa in the hotel in Bordeaux, the voile curtains billowing gently into the room. His tone of voice had been mild, matter-of-fact, and his soft brown eyes were filled with the early evening light from the French windows.

But I knew D'Artagnan quite well by then, and I knew that he meant what he said. We'd argued many times about toxic levels of masculinity no longer being appropriate in modern-day France and he'd been unmoved by my robust denunciation of his alpha-male sensibilities. 'You cannot change what I think, Nicole! You cannot change how I feel! If Guillaume touch you, I kill him. It's very simple.'

I reminded him of this while we were sitting side by side in the Duchess's salon. I repeated it to him, I even copied his French-accented English, which usually annoys him, but he still would not look at me. He was leaning forward with his forearms on his thighs, staring at the floor.

'So I kind of assumed that where the touching in question was rape, you would instantly go all Terminator. I mean, I'm sorry if I was wrong – I'm really, really sorry – but you've got to see it from my point of view.'

I put my hand on his arm, willing him to look at me. He did not.

'Guy,' I pleaded. 'Please. Please try to understand. I have every reason to believe you when you say things like that. I sat here, in this room, right there—' I pointed to the oak floorboards in front of the sofa where there was still a slight stain despite the floor having been scrubbed, sanded and repolished '—I sat in a pool of your blood with your head in my lap, watching you nearly die because you decided it was better that I finish talking to Karl rather than call an ambulance!'

I paused, conscious that my eyes had filled with tears. I hated having to summon that image.

'So I don't think it was unreasonable for me to think that you would go after Guillaume if you found out what he'd done. And I couldn't bear that. I couldn't bear the thought of you ending up in prison or worse, ending up in hospital.' Or ending up in a graveyard. Because Guillaume (or Satan, as he was known to me) carried a gold-handled, pearl-embossed flick-knife. I knew this because he had put it against my neck and told me that he wouldn't hesitate to use it if I ever told Guy about what had happened.

D'Artagnan still did not move. I leaned forward to try to get him to look at me and saw that his eyes were glassy with tears. My heart felt like a lump of cold, wet dough being tightly squeezed. 'Guy, please! Try to understand why I didn't tell you. Please, I'm begging you!'

He didn't move. He blinked, and a tear splashed onto the floor.

I slipped my arms around his shoulders, laid my forehead in the curve of his neck, breathed in his scent. I realised that I was crying too – and still he didn't move.

I sat back and wiped the tears from my face with the back of my hand. This was not going to plan. My husband was supposed to get angry and then he was supposed to see that, actually, what I'd done made sense. Then he was supposed to forgive me.

'If you're worried about the financial consequences, don't be. Xavier looked into it carefully. Neither you nor Francesca will suffer any—' *That* got a reaction.

Guy turned to me, his eyes livid, absolutely livid. 'I don't *care* about the money, Nicole! *Mon dieu*, how the fuck can you think I care about the money?!' He expelled the words with such force that I actually recoiled from him.

Then it started to sink in; I had underestimated what deceiving D'Artagnan would cost me. It turned out that the price was very high, so high that it was priceless. It couldn't be paid. It seemed I didn't have the right currency.

That realisation was very difficult to bear.

***

So Guy left. D'Artagnan left the château, his château. He left quietly the same night, New Year's Eve. There was no customary wheelspin, no sprayed gravel from the tyres of his car as he drove off. He stood at the bottom of the staircase with his overnight bag in his hand, the expression in his eyes... The only word I can think of is destroyed. He blinked his beautiful brown eyes as I sat there in the salon, hollow inside, my face soaked with tears.

'I just... I can't, Nicole, *je ne peux plus*. I don't know any more how to be with you when there is no trust between us. *Tu m'as brisé le cœur*.'

You've broken my heart.

And then he left.

***

'*Bah,* Nicole, I am not surprised he leave.' Xavier leaned against his desk and held the box of tissues out to me as if they were chocolates.

I glared up at him from under my naked eyelashes; I had given up wearing mascara for the foreseeable future. 'Gosh, you too, Xavier? It's fascinating, all these people with a PhD in hindsight telling me they knew that Guy would leave.' I paused. 'Perhaps it would have been useful to share that little nugget of wisdom with me before he left?'

Xavier rolled his eyes in exasperation and thrust the box of tissues into my hand. He went around to his side of the desk and sat down. He picked up the file in front of him, shook his head and muttered something under his breath.

I blew my nose again. 'What? What did you say?'

He looked annoyed. Today, he had 5pm stubble at the 8pm mark, and one of the cuffs of his shirt – the one with the wine/ink stain on the breast pocket – was even more frayed than it had been at our last meeting in December.

He cleared his throat. 'I say, Nicole, that I did tell you about this, that I tell you this will happen! I warn you that you must tell Guy about this, that you cannot do this on your own without telling your husband what happen!'

I glared at him and blew my nose again. 'No, Xavier, you never tell me that "zis will 'appen, Nicole". You never said Guy would *leave* me.'

He did an enormous Gallic shrug, all hands in the air, eyes rolled to the ceiling, full-lipped pout and expulsion of air. '*Pffff! Mon dieu,* Nicole, I cannot tell you exactly what will happen, but I tell you many, many times to tell Guy about this. And every time you say "*non, Xavier*, I know what I am doing. I will tell zis to Guy layder".'

Parodying me, he did a little wriggle in his chair and raised the tone of his voice. He regarded me crossly. 'Do not try to blame me for this, Nicole. I am only your lawyer, I can only tell you what I think is the best thing for you to do. I cannot force you to do it!'

I stared at him angrily for a while then I asked, 'Is it very badly paid, Xavier, being a criminal lawyer?'

'Why do you ask me this?' He frowned.

'Only because your shirt is a bit – knackered. Can't you afford a new one?'

His cheeks coloured. He tilted his head to one side and said stiffly. 'I am sorry, Nicole, if my clothes—' he pronounced this *cloth-izz* '—if my clothes offend you.'

I immediately felt ashamed. 'No, I'm sorry, Xavier,' I said meekly. 'That was horrible of me. I didn't mean to say it, I was just angry. I'm just so angry and so sad and so upset that Guy has left. I don't mean to take it out on you.'

When I dared to look back at him he was watching me closely, but the expression on his face was a little softer.

He sighed. 'It's okay, Nicole. I am also sorry. I am maybe not as ... *bah, sympathique* as I should be. *Je suis désolé.*' He paused and glanced at his watch. 'It is nearly lunchtime. Will you like to come with me? We go have some lunch and we talk about the next step for the case, okay?'

We went to a busy bistro near his office and were shown quickly to a table. He invited me to sit on the red-leather banquette and took the chair opposite. His untidy dark curls might possibly have been brushed that morning because they didn't look quite as 'fighting aliens all night' as they normally did.

Not for the first time, I wondered if Xavier was married or had a girlfriend and, if so, whether she was also sight-impaired. It was a shame because he was sort of good-looking if one disregarded the NHS glasses held together with Sellotape, the wild hair and the frayed, off-white shirts customised with food, drink and ink.

The waiter, wearing a knee-length apron, presented us brusquely with the menus and proceeded to rattle off the day's specials in indecipherably fast French before whirling away again.

'*Bah*, you should try this Nicole, the *menu du jour*.' Xavier smiled. 'Today, it is *pâté de foie gras*, braised rabbit for the *plat du jour*, and *crème brûlée*. It is very good here – I can recommend this.'

I sighed. There was still quite a lot that Xavier didn't know about me, starting with the fact that I'm vegetarian. And I don't do sugar; sugar and size 36 Chanel are not compatible, a fact that had been hammered into me relentlessly from the tender age of seventeen.

I opened the menu and scanned it. 'I'll have a *salade César*. Do you think you could ask the waiter to leave out the chicken, though?'

Xavier frowned at me. 'A *salade César*? With no chicken? It is January, Nicole. It is cold outside. You need to eat hot food.'

I frowned back at him. 'I'm thirty-eight years old, Xavier. I think I know by now what I need to eat.'

His eyelashes swept over his eyes several times, then he shrugged. 'Okay. Do you want some wine?'

I nodded and tried to smile. 'Yes, please.' I glanced at the menu again. 'A glass of white – the *Pessac-Léognan*, please.'

As I said it, I felt despondent again. Françoise, D'Artagnan's sister, produces a wonderful white *Pessac-Léognan* from her vineyards. Françoise also has a PhD in hindsight.

***

She'd stared at me, her brown eyes so similar to D'Artagnan's and yet never quite as deep, never as intense, never as mesmerising. But they were very wide when I told her about Satan, about what Satan had done in the Marble Villa in Hell outside Milan all those years ago.

We were sitting side by side on the sofa in her elegantly furnished salon. One of Pascal's vibrantly colourful paintings was hanging above the carved stone fireplace. Seeing it there had made me smile briefly; it made me happy to think that I was the link that had brought Françoise and Pascal together.

I explained the whole sordid story in my bad French, interjecting the occasional English word where I really couldn't retrieve the French one. Françoise took my hand while I was talking and held onto it. Her lips were pressed tightly together and, by the time I'd finished talking, her eyes were shut tightly too.

'I am so sorry this happened to you, Nicole,' she said when I'd finished. She opened her eyes and they were full of sorrow. 'I always knew he was a bad man, but I never knew how bad he really was.' She squeezed my hand. 'I am so angry with my brother – I told him that Guillaume was bad, that he shouldn't go into business with him. I told him! You heard me tell him, but he wouldn't listen!'

I gave a big shrug. 'Guy has many talents, Françoise, but unfortunately judging character isn't one of them. It's not his fault. It's partly because he's a very loyal person and that he's known Sa— Guillaume all his life. He's unable to look at him critically.'

She continued slowly shaking her head. 'When did you tell him about this?' she asked.

'On New Year's Eve. Two days after Sa— after Guillaume was arrested and taken into custody.'

She frowned at me. 'Last week?' I nodded. The frown did not clear. 'Last week?' she asked again, then started to cough. I could see that she was still suffering with the bronchitis they'd all had over the New Year.

I nodded again. I wondered if my French was really so bad that I hadn't understood her question.

She stopped coughing and reached for the glass of water on the table in front of her. 'You waited until last week to tell my brother about this?' she asked after she'd taken a sip.

I gazed at her. I'd thought that Françoise was pretty smart, but I was starting to wonder whether D'Artagnan wasn't the only bad judge of character in our marriage. 'Yes?'

Her eyes opened wide and her eyebrows arched. 'And how did he react when you finally told him?'

I gave a deep sigh. 'Er, badly. That's kind of why I'm here. I wondered if you'd seen him or heard from him in the last week.'

She looked bemused. 'He's left? You don't know where he is?'

I shook my head and pressed my lips together, willing my eyes not to fill yet again. 'No. I wondered if maybe you knew because he's not answering his phone. Have you heard from him? Have you spoken to him?'

She shook her head slowly, still without taking her eyes from me. 'No.' She paused. 'Why didn't you tell him about this earlier, Nicole? You say you realised last year in the spring that it was Guillaume who raped you – but you waited until now to tell Guy?'

I took a deep breath as I wondered how to translate 'toxic masculinity' and 'reckless disregard for his own life' and 'apeshit, Bruce Willis-style' into French.

'Uh, let's just say your brother has a tendency to over-react, Françoise. I decided it was probably better not to tell him until Guillaume was in custody and out of Guy's reach.'

She was *still* frowning. 'But you say this happened to you a long time ago, Nicole.'

'Twelve years ago this year.'

She nodded slowly. 'But still you decide not to tell my brother about this thing that happened many years ago.' She paused. 'I don't think that was the right thing to do, Nicole.'

'Well, I do, Françoise.' I tried not to be too snappy. 'Do you know what Guy is like, Françoise? I mean, really like?'

Slightly withering eyes. 'He's my little brother, Nicole. I've known him for fifty-one years, so yes, I do think I know what he is like.'

It came out in a rush. 'Well, maybe you don't know this but the reason why Guy nearly died when he accidentally tried to remove the lower half of his leg with a chainsaw was because he just sat quietly in the salon and waited while I spoke to my ex-boyfriend who had scheduled a surprise visit. He thought *that* was more important than suggesting that it might be an idea to call an ambulance.'

I blinked at her a few times. She blinked back.

'Yes,' she said finally. 'He mentioned that your ex-boyfriend came back. He thought you were going to leave him.'

I stared at her. 'He told you about that?'

She shrugged. 'Yes. But you didn't leave. I told him he was stupid to think that you would. It's obvious how much you love him, how much he loves you.' She paused. 'But you should have told him about Guillaume as soon as you knew, Nicole.'

I widened my eyes. 'Oh my God, Françoise! Surely even you can see that Guy would have gone straight to Guillaume and attacked him! I mean, he *categorically* told me that was what he'd do if Guillaume ever touched me!'

She frowned. 'In what context?'

'In the context of my having an affair with Guillaume.' I gave a bitter laugh. 'As if that was *ever* on my fucking radar.'

She carried on staring at me. 'But that wasn't what happened, was it, Nicole? What Guillaume did was many years ago. It's not the same thing.' Her voice was very serious. 'You should have told my brother about this, Nicole. I'm very sorry that he left, but I am not very surprised.'

It seemed that, so far, I had two exceptionally bright PhD students.

***

Fortunately, Xavier had moved on from 'I told you so' mode.

I picked the bits of chicken out of my salad and put them on the side (apparently it is impossible to serve *salade César* without the chicken) while he expertly de-boned the dead rabbit.

'So, Nicole. The *juge d'instruction* ask to meet with you and with Léa in three weeks. Tuesday the—' he picked up his phone and scrolled through the calendar, peering at it through his glasses which had slipped down his nose '—seven February. Can you do this?'

I thought for a minute and mentally flicked through my busy social calendar which only had three things in it: weekends and Wednesday afternoons/evenings with Nina; Thursday morning French lessons with Bérengère, and the rest of the time gazing at Espiritu and trying not to think about how much I missed D'Artagnan.

I nodded. 'Yup, I can do Tuesday the seventh. Here in Bordeaux?'

He nodded. He put another mouthful of braised Mrs Flopsy into his mouth and took a sip of his wine, spilling a little onto the white tablecloth as he simultaneously set the glass down and pushed his glasses back up his nose. I opened my mouth to ask why he didn't just get his glasses fixed, then shut it firmly. Xavier had had more than enough sartorial criticism from me for one day.

He carried on chewing, swallowed and drew a deep breath before speaking again. '*Bah*, but Nicole, I think I must warn you that this *juge*, the *juge d'instruction*, she is quite a – *comment dire* – a hard person? Quite aggressive. She is very good, she is a good *juge*, but it will not be the same as the meeting we have with the *procureur* in December. She will ask a lot of question because she need to decide if she can believe you. She will not be very *gentille,* I think. This is my experience with her, anyway.'

***

Xavier and I had met with the *procureur* in his chambers in Bordeaux at the end of the previous year. He was a kind, elderly man, and he'd questioned me slowly and carefully in French after reviewing the very thorough dossier that Xavier had prepared. He'd also reviewed the excellent quality video-evidence that I'd obtained by tricking Satan into confessing to what he'd done. Xavier had been angry about that and had spent the last three months warning me that the *procureur* would probably reject it.

In late November, however, Satan's sweet ex-girlfriend, Léa, had admitted to me what Satan had done to her and had forced her to do. She'd agreed to join the criminal case for rape and sexual abuse and at that point Xavier had felt a little more confident that the procureur would not be able to reject the video-evidence. And he hadn't.

***

I frowned. 'What do you mean she needs to decide if she can believe me? That's the whole reason why the *procureur* referred the case to her. It's the whole reason why Guillaume is in custody, isn't it?'

Xavier nodded. 'Yes, that is why he is in custody. And it is not that she doesn't believe you, but now she want to be very sure that you are telling her everything. That you are being completely honest, that you are not hiding anything.'

I continued to frown. 'What would I have to hide, Xavier? It happened – Guillaume raped me and repeatedly abused Léa. The *procureur* interviewed us both and accepted the video where Guillaume admitted that he drugged and raped me. Surely the case has been established?'

'Yes, Nicole,' he said patiently. 'But the *juge* must prepare the dossier to go in front of another *juge,* and the dossier must be very strong. It must present a strong case when it go in front of the *Cour d'Assises*. I explain this to you in the beginning.'

I rolled my eyes and ate some lettuce after deftly removing two croutons and placing them alongside the bits of chicken on the side plate. Xavier watched me, looking slightly puzzled.

'So basically we have to convince a whole series of judges that Satan is an evil bastard before they'll let us go in front of a jury in order to convince *them* that Satan is an evil bastard who needs to be locked up?' I said.

Xavier is more or less up to speed on the cast of characters in my head – at least, he knows who Satan and D'Artagnan are. He gave a slightly apologetic shrug.

I shook my head slowly. 'Wow. It's hardly surprising that the percentage of convictions for rape is so low in France.'

'It is not just in France, Nicole.'

I picked up my water glass and took a sip. 'That's hardly reassuring, is it, Xavier?' I gazed at him glumly then sighed. 'Anyway. Whatever. Let's go and convince the *juge d'instruction* on the seventh.' I speared another lettuce leaf and removed yet another carefully hidden crouton.

Xavier frowned. 'You don't eat chicken and you don't eat croutons? Why do you order the *salade César* if you don't like *salade César*, Nicole?'

'I like the lettuce and the boiled egg and the parmesan cheese,' I protested. 'And the dressing is nice as long as there's not too much of it. Is that okay?'

He made a face and finished mopping up the last of Mrs Flopsy with some bread. 'It must be very boring.'

I raised an eyebrow. 'What? Not eating dead animals?'

He shrugged. 'Or bread. How can you live in France and not eat bread?'

'I do eat bread sometimes, but it has to be really good bread not deep-fried bits of crap, which is what croutons are.'

Xavier grinned a little. He had a nice smile. 'You have a lot of *robuste* opinions about everything, don't you, Nicole?'

'Have you met my husband?'

He looked confused. 'Of course I meet Guy. I meet him at Emma's wedding last year when I meet you, and I meet him many years ago when Laurent was my boss.'

'It was a rhetorical question. It means the reason why I have *robuste* opinions about everything is because I've learned that I have to with Guy, otherwise he'll trample over everything I believe in.' It had taken D'Artagnan the better part of a year to accept that being vegetarian did *not* mean that I ate fish.

He grinned. 'Yes, he have quite a ... big personality, your husband.'

I did not say what was on the tip of my tongue. Instead I said, 'That's one way of describing it.' I finally managed to catch the last sliver of parmesan cheese with my fork and had barely let go of it when the waiter swooped out of nowhere and snatched away our plates.

Xavier took off his glasses and began moving around the smudges on them with the end of his shirt, which was now untucked.

'What about you?' I asked. 'Are you married? Or do you have a girlfriend?' *And does she also dress in the dark*? I didn't ask.

He looked away from me, his pale-grey eyes slightly hooded beneath his long, dark eyelashes. 'No, I am not married. And no,

I don't have a girlfriend any more. Last year we finally accept that we do not want the same things.'

He hadn't put his glasses back on; he was actually rather good-looking without them. His face was kind of – classically sculpted.

'I'm so sorry,' I said gently. 'It's really hard when relationships end.'

He gave a little shrug, put his glasses on again. '*Bah*... I just wish maybe that she have not taken so long to decide she does not want to have children, to have a family. Now I am already thirty-eight and I wait ten years for her to decide, and then finally she say no. She say it is bad for the planet to have children, that she cannot do this.' He continued to look down and his shoulders drooped.

'I'm so sorry,' I said again. 'But increasingly it's the reason a lot of people are choosing not to have children. It's such an enormous decision to have a family nowadays. There's so much to consider.'

He shrugged a shoulder. 'Yes, I know this. But I did not want a big family, I only want Amelie and me to have two children.' He seemed so dejected that I automatically started to reach for his hand. I stopped myself just in time.

He glanced up at me. 'What about you and Guy? Don't you want children?'

I stared at him, wondering if the phrase 'Pandora's Box' had the same meaning in French. Finally, I said. 'Yes, I did want children but I can't have them. Well, I *couldn't* have them. Well, once I *could* have had one, but then I – uh – had a bad fall. I didn't know I was pregnant. So that didn't last either.'

I shook my head, cross with myself that I'd imparted that information to Xavier whom I didn't know very well. I'd only ever told D'Artagnan about what had happened in Ireland when I'd fallen and miscarried, and it had taken five years for me to form those words and speak them out loud. It had been very emotional and we'd both cried, but it had also been cathartic to unlock that tightly sealed, festering box of misery.

I took a deep breath. 'And besides, D'Artagnan had a vasectomy before I met him, so we can't.'

Xavier frowned deeply. 'I'm so sorry Nicole. That must have been very difficult for you.'

I shrugged. 'It was, but it's in the past now. And now we're going to adopt Nina – I told you about Nina, didn't I?'

He smiled warmly. 'Yes, you tell me about Nina in December. I am very happy for you. How long will this adoption take?'

The clammy, insidious hand of fear slipped around my heart. 'Normally the psychiatric evaluation is about five or six months after we've submitted the dossier, and Guy did that in December.' I pressed my lips together to stop my eyes filling before I continued to speak.

'But I'm a bit worried now. I mean ... he's left. He's not talking to me, he's not talking to anyone. What if – I mean, I know I'm maybe being overdramatic, but what if he doesn't want to be married to me anymore? What about Nina?' Despite my best efforts, my eyes filled with tears again and I started scrabbling about in my handbag for a tissue.

'*Bah*, Nicole.' Xavier's voice was gentle. 'It is only a few days since Guy go away. I am sure he will come back soon. He is just a bit angry.'

I blinked at him and wiped my eyes. 'It's been two weeks, Xavier.'

The waiter deftly deposited Xavier's *crème brûlée* in front of him and the cheese that I'd ordered in front of me.

Xavier smiled reassuringly and repeated, 'I am sure he will come back soon.'

***

I drove home from Bordeaux that afternoon under a leaden winter sky. The light was fading fast as I arrived back at the Duchess and stopped on the gravelled forecourt. I turned the engine off and continued to sit in the car, gazing up at the sixteen perfectly symmetrical windows of her main façade framed between the two graceful, fairy-tale stone towers.

She's rather beautiful, the early seventeenth-century château that D'Artagnan is the latest in a long, unbroken line to inherit. She wasn't beautiful when I first set eyes on her nearly two years previously. Her roof had leaked, the single-glazed windows were ill-fitting and draughty, and the interior decoration she'd been subjected to by previous generations of the illustrious Du Beauchamp dynasty was – well, horrifying in places.

I had immediately set about dragging her kicking and screaming, into the twenty-first century, which had infuriated her. In revenge, she had exploded toilets full of shit at me, regularly turned off all the electricity at the most inconvenient times, and she often spat the washing machine hose from its housing so that the laundry room was flooded. She rained maggot-ridden dead birds onto my head when I was cleaning out the vast, Hogwarts-style fireplace in the dining hall, and she turned the stairs down to the wine cellar into a moist, green slipway, down which she contrived to make me fall.

The Duchess occasionally manifests herself in human form in my peripheral vision; I've never been able to look at her directly but I know she's there. I reckon she spent time at Versailles at some point in her prime because I think she wears one of those preposterous wigs and a tightly-corseted ballgown with her boobs bulging out. But her prime has long passed and now she's a little bit tatty around the edges.

She hates me for thinking that.

***

The Muffins were channelling *The Shining* when I pushed open the heavy oak door and switched on the hall light. They were sitting side by side on the bottom stair at the end of the hallway, two round pairs of yellow-green eyes wide with malice. If he'd been wearing a watch, Mr Muffin would almost certainly have been tapping it in annoyance at my sloppy attitude towards the running of their hotel and, more importantly, the hotel restaurant.

They followed me into the kitchen, both shouting loudly about their brush with near-death by starvation, a claim somewhat difficult to believe given the untouched biscuits in their bowls. After I'd served their preferred choice of dinner from that week's expensive little gourmet tins, I went into the library in the opposite tower and cleaned out the wood-burner, laid new kindling and coaxed it alight.

While I was waiting for the kindling to catch properly, I sat down on the cracked leather chesterfield. Unable to help myself for the fourteenth time that day, probably the hundred-and-forty-fourth time since he'd left, I dialled D'Artagnan's number. It was the same as ever: it went straight to voicemail.

I did not leave a message. We were beyond messages, him and I. I sat on the sofa and stared into the flames, now burning brightly. I had no idea how to find him.

I knew he wasn't with his elder brother Stephane, because Stephane had developed late-onset wanderlust after his thirty-five-year marriage had imploded the previous year and he'd headed off to South East Asia in December. And I knew Guy wasn't with Antoine, his thick, racist brother who lived in Nice, because he detested Antoine.

Although I hadn't yet plucked up the courage to call his children, I was almost certain that Guy would not be with them either. They were in their early twenties, they lived in Paris and had busy social lives, and I was fairly sure he was not in Paris.

I had contemplated calling his ex-wife, Isabelle. Having been married to him for twenty years she knew Guy better than I did, and she might have had an idea where he would go if he was feeling angry and devastated. But I chickened out of that, too; it felt too much of an airing of our dirty laundry to contact her and Guy would be really annoyed if I did that.

Because I wasn't feeling miserable enough already, I clicked on Photos on my phone and gazed at the picture I'd taken of him in the Maldives just six weeks earlier. He'd been on the deck of our cabin, the cabin in which we'd spent several hours every afternoon on the vast bed underneath the rhythmic whirr of the ceiling fan having very slow, achingly exquisite sex. The deck was suspended over the aquamarine atoll that we swam in several times a day and Guy was sitting, knees bent, his deeply suntanned arms resting on them. Drops of water were glistening on his muscular body, in his hair, his beard, his chest-hair. He looked so gorgeous in that photograph and I had to bite my bottom lip very hard as I gazed at my beautiful, strong musketeer. I missed him so much and I had no idea where he was. D'Artagnan was missing; deceived, angry and missing.

I rose from the sofa and crossed the length of the château to the kitchen in the opposite tower, took a bottle of wine out of the wine rack, opened it and poured myself a glass. I opened the fridge and stared at its meagre contents for a while, then shut it again because nothing took my fancy.

I retraced my steps to the library. The Muffins followed me and had a brief dispute about who was going to occupy the suede bean-bag in front of the wood burner. Mrs Muffin won and Mr Muffin started having a very thorough wash to show just how unbothered he was by that.

I picked up my phone again. I really wanted to call Jules but I didn't want to burden her with the whole epic, seething saga. Then, as I sipped my wine and stared at my phone, it started buzzing. I smiled; our telepathic skills *did* still work, even though she was hundreds of kilometres away in Buckinghamshire.

***

Jules blinked at me repeatedly and took another sip of her wine. I took a sip of mine and blinked back at her.

'Is this why you were so out of it last year when we met in Paris for the dress fitting? Because you were *really* on one, babe. And you were so skinny! I could tell something was wrong but I couldn't figure out what or why.'

I nodded slowly. 'Yeah, it was. After I found out – after that sick bastard Satan mentioned that he'd preferred me when I was *younger* – I kind of flipped for a while.'

'I'm so sorry, Nicky. Finding that out must have been so difficult to deal with.' She frowned. 'What were you taking, anyway? I remember thinking you were exactly the same as when you were doing smack with Karl.'

I looked away, ashamed. 'Effectively it *was* smack, Jules. Do you remember Annabelle, the vile wedding planner?'

She started laughing, which made me smile. I love it when Jules laughs because it's so infectious. 'Oh God, yeah, I remember Annabelle the wedding planner! She hated you, Nicky! You made her life hell!'

'Well, Annabelle was getting me oxycodone, which is basically heroin in tablet form. It was the only way I could focus on all the sparkly, fluffy stuff that she wanted me to make decisions about.'

Jules' eyes widened. 'You were doing smack again?'

'Yes,' I said, very quietly. 'But not for long. Maybe only six weeks.' I took a deep breath. 'And then, once I'd decided that I was going to get Bastard Satan, I stopped. And you know, Jules, I hardly even have to take diazepam any more. I'm just not so ... anxious about stuff. Finding out that it was Satan that drugged me, that it was Satan and his little fuckwit friends in that villa— It's been weirdly helpful. I don't feel as frightened now that I know what happened.'

Although Jules was frowning, she was also nodding slowly. 'Yes, I can see that. This is what we're currently learning about at uni, that facing the traumatic event is empowering. It allows the patient to feel in control, to realise that what happened was *outside* of their control but that how they deal with it is *within* their control.'

Jules was studying part time for her masters in psychology. She wanted to change career from business analyst to human analyst, and I knew she'd be brilliant at it.

'Yes. That's exactly how it feels. Empowering.' I smiled at her.

She smiled back and then her smile gradually faded. 'You really don't know where Guy's gone?' she asked quietly.

I shook my head. 'No. No idea. Even Françoise doesn't know. He hasn't talked to her either.'

Long pause. 'What about Nina?'

My eyes closed involuntarily, and it felt as if my heart was being crushed. 'Obviously, I'm hoping that Guy being angry with me isn't going to change anything about our decision to adopt Nina.'

Nina had already asked where D'Artagnan was.

***

The weekend after he'd left, Nina had been there on the Saturday morning as usual, all silky dark hair and big green eyes and skinny arms. She'd let herself in and picked up Mr Muffin on the way upstairs to our room. I'd woken abruptly when Mr Muffin launched himself at my head, then I'd seen her sitting next to me on the bed and I'd opened my arms wide. She'd fallen into them and I'd held her little body really tightly against mine. For that moment, I'd felt happy and I hadn't missed D'Artagnan.

But Nina had. After a while she'd wriggled out of my embrace and glanced at the empty space next to me. 'Where is the *prince, Princesse* Nicole?'

D'Artagnan had given her the idea of princes and princesses and castles on the day we'd discovered her standing in the horses' paddock, a scrawny kid who was utterly besotted with horses. She'd seemed so tiny and so devoid of fear as she leaned against Espiritu's dark, muscular flank and stroked his forehead while she chattered away to him. I wasn't quite sure how I was going to dial down the *prince* and *princesse* nomenclature in the future; 'mama' and 'papa' seemed mundane in comparison, and I didn't want to dampen Nina's vibrant imagination just yet.

When I was Nina's age, my mama hadn't been a princess – not to me, anyway. And my father, who had definitely not been a prince, had been permanently absent, fighting endless Indian ocean waves on his surfboard and endless paternity suits on terra firma. Probably.

'Oh, he's very busy.' I stroked her satiny hair gently. 'He had something really important to do, so he's had to go away for a bit.' I fixed her with my eyes.

'Will he be back soon?'

I nodded confidently. 'Of course!'

She relaxed and smiled toothily. 'Good!' She slipped off the edge of the bed. 'Because he said that maybe we should go and look for a pony for me so that we can ride together.'

I smiled back at her and my heart swelled with just a tiny bit more love. She was so beautiful, so perfect, so innocent, so untouched by all the shit that the adult human world was so full of, all the ugliness, the duplicity, the abuse.

But I knew very little about horses and even less about ponies. That was D'Artagnan's provenance.

Apart from my having fallen insanely in love with Espiritu, that is.

Chapter Two

Ah, Espiritu. He of the long, thick, dark mane. He of the muscular, dark-chocolate body, the body that dances at the end of four perfectly formed hooves. He of the imperious, blue-black stare.

My spirit animal, the wild horse, the 'dangerous' horse that, a year after he'd arrived, somehow was no longer dangerous. I had dared to sit on him one mild winter evening in December. That night, I'd felt as if everything I'd ever been afraid of was suddenly unimportant because I'd just done the most incredible thing: I'd sat on the back of the most beautiful creature in the world. I'd felt his warmth under me, his raw, animal power, and it had empowered me in a way I'd never experienced before.

Other than cats, I had no experience of animals before I arrived at the Duchess. As a kid I lived on the fourteenth floor of a block of flats just behind the Durban beachfront in sunny, sub-tropical South Africa. In the gardens around our apartment block I had gradually encouraged the stray cats in the area with food, patience and supplication to come close enough so that I could touch them. Eventually they let me stroke them and then finally, the holy grail! I could pick them up and hold them tightly against me. I had a lot of very deep cat scratches as a child.

But horses? They were a whole other thing. I had never encountered an animal so frighteningly large until I met Emperador and Espiritu, and I was mesmerised. They were the most incredible creatures I had ever seen, particularly Espiritu.

D'Artagnan had stood behind me that day, his arms around me as I leaned back against him, and he'd murmured, 'Aren't they beautiful, *mon ange*? Aren't they the most beautiful animals ever created?'

I had nodded, entranced as I watched them, and he had kissed my cheek so softly. I'd never heard him speak with such reverence, and the realisation that D'Artagnan was humbled by these two magnificent creatures made me love him even more.

***

The morning after I'd spoken to Jules, I was awoken as usual by Mr Muffin patting my nose with his softly padded paw with only a hint of claw. I knew if I did not respond it would quickly become less of a hint and more of a command, so I staggered groggily into the bathroom and served their breakfast. These days, I prepared their breakfast tray at night and brought it up to the bathroom in order to serve breakfast with the minimum of fuss.

D'Artagnan had not approved of this arrangement. 'There is cat food all over the bathroom, Nicole. Why is the bathroom now a *buffet* for the cats?' We were drinking our morning coffee in bed. I turned to look at him. His dark-eyed gaze was disapproving.

'Well, sweetheart,' I said, 'you could always get up, go downstairs when they start shouting about breakfast at 6.30am and feed them in the kitchen. I'm really not stopping you. Feel free to do that. Personally, I prefer an easier solution – Mohammed to the mountain rather than the mountain to Mohammed.'

He frowned. 'Who is this Mohammed, Nicole? Another one of your imaginary friend?'

'No, D'Artagnan.' There was a little smirk at the edge of his mouth, despite his irritation. He put his empty coffee cup down on the bedside table as I continued. 'It's a saying that means "why do it the hard way if you don't have to"?'

'*Pfffff.*' He gave that well-known French response to things that are eminently dismissible. 'Well, there is now cat food on the floor in the bathroom, Nicole. I step on some this morning.'

I stared at him. 'Well, here's an idea, Guy. Why not pick it up? You do have opposable thumbs, you know.'

He'd rolled his eyes and shaken his head in exasperation, then he'd reached over and put his hand around my neck in mock strangulation. I'd tried to push him away, grinning a little, and he'd persisted before leaning over and kissing me. And then the kiss had become more intense; it became a kiss that had heat, that had intention, and I had slid down in the bed again as he'd taken my coffee cup and put it on the bedside table. And then his hand had slipped down between my legs and then...

I missed him so much. I *ached* for him.

***

I took a deep breath, banished that thought from my mind and reminded myself that it was Wednesday, the best day of the week because Nina finished school at midday and always came straight to the Duchess.

D'Artagnan had wanted to tell Nina before Christmas that we were going to adopt her but both Marion, our neighbour who was fostering Nina, and I had dissuaded him.

'What if they refuse us?' I demanded. 'We can't tell her we're going to adopt her then tell her that we can't after all! That would be terrible, it would crush her!' I'd frowned at him and Marion had frowned at him too as she nodded in agreement.

'They will not refuse us. Don't be stupid.' He sniffed dismissively.

'You don't know that for sure, Guy!'

'Why would they refuse? We are married, we have money, we are responsible people and we love Nina. We are perfect to adopt her!' The imperious gaze.

'It's too early! We've only just submitted the paperwork to start the process. We have to wait, at least until we've had the psychiatric interview!'

He blinked at me. 'That will not be for some months.'

'Well then, we have to wait for some months. But please don't tell her yet. I couldn't bear it if for some reason we were refused. She's only seven and she's already had such a difficult start. At least she's more or less happy living with Marion now.'

'She does not like going home in the evenings, Nicole. She wants to stay with us.' He had switched to English, knowing Marion wouldn't understand.

I scowled at him. 'Do you think I don't know that, Guy? Of course she doesn't want to! Of course she wants to stay with us, but I refuse to risk breaking her heart if for some reason we can't adopt her!'

His blinked his eyelashes at me rapidly, which is usually what he does when he's trying to absorb something that his innate arrogance is blocking. Finally, he shrugged. 'Okay, we will not tell her yet. We wait a bit.'

I refused to allow myself to dwell on the thought that our adopting Nina might now be in jeopardy. D'Artagnan was hurt and angry and had gone away to sulk, but he was hurt and angry at *me*, not at Nina. I held onto that thought tightly.

***

It was a blisteringly cold morning as I crossed the courtyard behind the château. The frost had been heavy overnight and Espiritu and Emperador's thick winter coats still glittered with moisture in the bright winter sunshine. Their breaths steamed as they munched on the hay that Camille had put out for them that morning.

Camille was sitting on the top paddock rail, her slight body wrapped in several layers, a woollen hat pulled down over her eyebrows and a thick scarf wrapped several times around her neck. She turned and smiled her enigmatic smile as I arrived at the paddock rails, her black eyes shiny like olives.

'Nicole, *ça va*?' she bent towards me and we exchanged kisses. She smelt of cinnamon and fresh hay. Her face was cold.

'*Ça va, merci,* Camille. *Et toi*?'

She shrugged and we both turned back to watch the horses eating their hay. After a while she turned to me again, her gaze very frank. There was the slightest smile around the corner of her mouth. 'So Nicole, do you think maybe some time you would like to do a bit more than just sit on Espiritu?'

My chest felt like I'd swallowed a balloon that was filling spontaneously. It was so weird to finally understand how Nina had felt when she first sat on Emperador, when D'Artagnan in full *conquistador* mode had leant down off Emperador's back and effortlessly lifted her off the mounting block to sit in front of him in the saddle as he trotted Emperador around the paddock, one hand around Nina's waist, the other holding the reins. Nina had positively *radiated* joy. Now I knew how she had felt.

I grinned hugely at Camille and nodded my head really fast.

By the time Nina finished school that Wednesday lunchtime and came hurtling down the drive as fast as her stick-like, jodhpur-clad little legs would carry her, I had already ridden Espiritu around the paddock *on my own*, bareback, using his simple string halter. I felt extraordinary, as if I could conquer the world.

I completely forgot about D'Artagnan while I was on Espiritu's back. There wasn't any room in my head for anything other than the feeling of wonder that I was riding a horse – and that horse was Espiritu.

***

Xavier rang me at 9am the following morning and I fumbled groggily for my phone. It had been a late night and I'd drunk more wine than I should have. I'd woken at 3am bathed in sweat, my heart hammering wildly in my chest after yet another dream in which Satan plunged a long gleaming dagger into D'Artagnan's chest and D'Artagnan died, right there in front of me. Nina had also been in the dream at the far end of the Marble Villa in Hell, screaming as Satan stabbed D'Artagnan.

I'd woken with my gasp of horror still echoing in my ears and automatically reached out for Guy, for his warm body against which he always held me when we slept. There were only cold bedsheets. I'd felt so desolate then, and my heart was hammering so hard, that I'd allowed myself to take 5mg of diazepam. Suffice to say it had not been a good night's sleep.

'Nicole, good morning. How are you?' Xavier's voice was bright and chirpy.

'Urrrrr,' I croaked. I cleared my throat. 'I'm ... here, Xavier. Why are you calling me so early?'

'It is *neuf heures,* Nicole, a normal time. I start work at eight. I call you because this morning I have a call from Francesca. She is quite ... *bah*, angry? *Furieuse*? She want to meet with you, with us. In Biarritz. On Monday.'

I sat up properly in bed. Fuck. I'd forgotten all about Francesca, Guy and Satan's other business partner. Francesca of the ancient, semi-aristocratic French-Spanish family, the family that owned *that* Spanish fashion label. Francesca, who glanced at me when Guy had introduced us and was instantly bored by what she saw because, as far as Francesca was concerned, she'd seen my type hundreds of times before: ex-model marries investment banker, spends lots of money on clothes and shoes and decorating the house, pops out some kids. The End.

Except for the popping out of the kids in my case, obvs.

'Fuck,' I said. 'Fucking Francesca, I'd forgotten about her. I'm so sorry, Xavier. I should've said that she would probably call.'

'It's okay, Nicole, I expect this. I am not surprised.' A pause. 'Well, I am a little bit surprised that she is so – *bah*, aggressive on the phone, but I am prepared for the questions. She have a lot of questions. She want us to go to Biarritz to answer her questions. Can you do this? On Monday?'

I frowned crossly. 'Why do we have to go to Biarritz? Why can't she bloody well come to Bordeaux if she wants to talk to us?'

Another pause. 'Well, Nicole, if you want me to tell her this I will call her back and tell her to come to Bordeaux. But I think she will be very annoyed. She is already very ... *bah, agacée*, annoyed.'

I reached for my water glass and took a sip. 'Do you want me to call her, Xavier? I have experience with these people. I'm not going to take any shit from Francesca. She doesn't have any right to order us about. It's not as if she's going to be financially impacted by the joint venture getting a bit messy when Sa— when Guillaume is prosecuted. It's just a hobby for her because she's obscenely wealthy. She's just pissed off because something has happened that she didn't know about, that she can't control. I'll call her and tell her to come to Bordeaux if she wants to talk to us.'

A sharp intake of breath. '*Non,* Nicole. I am your lawyer. If this is what you want, if you want Francesca to come to Bordeaux, then I phone her and I tell her this. You are my client and I do not let someone... *bah, donnez des ordres à mon client*!'

Which made me raise an eyebrow.

Xavier clearly had a pair and they hadn't shrivelled up, even after he'd been verbally abused and ordered about by Francesca. Because that's what happened to most men's balls after any sort of interaction with Francesca. The inbred sociopath that I used to work for would practically prostrate himself on the floor of his office in his grovelling attempts to please her when she called from New York to shout at him. The sick thing was that it was undoubtedly deeply orgasmic for him.

Anyway, I felt quite pleased to know that Xavier's balls were still intact and, when our call ended, I wasn't in such a bad mood anymore.

***

My mood lightened even more when I remembered that today I had a lesson with Bérengère.

I arrived at her house at 10.30am precisely and opened my car window to fling the dog treats I always carried as far as I could so that her dogs hared off after them and I could get out of my car without my clothes being customised with mud.

Bérengère was coming back into the yard as I headed towards her house. I noted with interest that today she was wearing a very fetching Russian fur hat, a long, fur-lined suede coat over her ankle-length green skirt, and the ubiquitous cowboy boots. They even had authentic spurs that clattered and clinked as she walked.

'Nicole,' she purred as she reached me, slipping her gloved hand around my shoulders as we exchanged kisses. She smelt of musky black roses, ones that had died slowly, wrapped in velvet and soaked in vampire blood.

'*Ça va, mon trésor*?' She leaned back and gazed at me, her soft grey eyes calm and serene.

I'd decided that Bérengère and D'Artagnan had been separated at birth. They are both innately sensual; they both exude nonchalant confidence that nothing in their world is – or ever will be – other than exactly as it should be.

'I like the hat,' I said. Despite the fact that the fur had almost certainly once belonged to an animal, even I had to admit that she looked gorgeous in it. Her long, steel-grey hair was complemented by the glossy black fur that covered her ears. 'Is it an heirloom?'

She smiled lazily and put a long finger against my lips. 'In French, Nicole, *s'il te plait, ma belle*.' There are very few rules for my French lessons with Bérengère but one of them is that I speak in French. Towards the end of my lessons she will sometimes let me lapse into English if she can see that my brain is getting fried.

The dogs had finished the treats and surrounded us again, gazing up at me expectedly. The biggest one tried to take my hand in his mouth playfully and I snatched it away, frowning.

'That's because they associate you with food.' Bérengère shrugged. 'You arrive, you throw them food, they think you are the waitress.'

They're not the only ones who think that, I thought as I followed her into her old, chalkstone, Hansel-and-Gretel farmhouse. It was marvellously warm inside thanks to the gnarled old vine-wood burning in the open fireplace.

She removed her hat and coat, which I noted was lined with the same fur, went into the low-doored pantry and returned with the bottle of *Pineau des Charentes*. This was how we started all of our lessons; as she'd confidently informed me when we first met, alcoholic aperitifs at 10.30am are the norm in south-west France.

I removed my thirteen outer layers of clothing and sat down, lifting her cat Agatha off the chair next to mine and placing her on my lap. She gave a little stretch, purred for a minute and then slumbered on. I love lazy Agatha.

'It belonged to my grandmother.' Bérengère reached for the fluted *Pineau* glasses.

I stared at her. 'What, the *Pineau*? I fuckin' hope not – it's going to be a bit past its sell-by date!'

She gave me a withering look as she filled my glass with the thick, amber liquid. 'My hat,' she said. She filled her own glass, pushed the cork firmly back into the bottle and sat down across the table from me.

She raised her glass and clinked it against mine, her head a little on one side. Bérengère has the most perfect skin, olive with pink undertones. A year after meeting her for the first time, I still had absolutely no idea how old she was – anything between forty and fifty-five, maybe sixty at a push, I reckoned.

She took a sip of her *Pineau* and regarded me coolly with her doe-shaped eyes.

'Is it real?' I asked.

She nodded. 'Yes. Real Russian muskrat.'

I raised an eyebrow. 'Your grandmother was Russian?'

'Yes. My grandmother's family escaped the Bolsheviks in 1918 and went to Nice.' She paused. 'A lot of the White Russians went to Nice.'

The *Pineau* was rich, sweet and woody. There was no label on the bottle because it was produced by one of Bérengère's many neighbours who kept her supplied with free firewood, or free meat in the form of a dead cockerel that had shouted too loudly about how virile he was, or a quarter of deer shot by *la chasse* in winter. In the spring and summer, she always had an abundance of fresh vegetables and fruit. It was clear that all of Bérengère's neighbours were a little in love with her, and it wasn't just the men.

'What's a White Russian?'

She told me the story of her *ushanka*-hatted grandmother who, at the age of sixteen, had escaped Russia in the winter of 1917 and arrived on the sunny, blue-skied French riviera (long before it was 'The French Riviera'). Her grandmother had fallen in love with and married a humble fisherman from St Paul de Vence and consequently been excommunicated by her aristocratic Russian family.

She paused when she'd finished and gazed at me frankly. 'So, Nicole. Have you heard from Guy yet?'

I sighed tiredly. I'd so enjoyed being caught up in the saga of Bérengère's exotic Russian roots that I'd forgotten all about D'Artagnan. I shook my head. 'No. He's totally AWOL. He's not talking to anyone and nobody seems to know where he is.' I paused. 'I miss him so much and I feel very bad. Everyone is telling me that I was wrong not to tell him.'

She snorted scornfully. '*Pffff*. Everyone is an idiot. It is your choice whether you tell him or not. This didn't happen to him, this happened to you. You decide who you want to tell.'

I gave a deep shrug; I even added some subdued hand motions. 'We are married, you know. And D'Artagnan is always banging on about the fact that I keep secrets. He hates that.'

She did the most perfect Gallic pout, all rolled eyes, raised shoulders, pursed mouth and another loud expulsion of air. '*Putain de merde,* Nicole, you are not controlled by your husband! You should have secrets, it is normal! It is healthy to have secrets! *Merde*, this is one of the many reasons why I never get married! This idea that a couple should know everything about each other, it is bullshit!'

'That, and the fact that you're bisexual,' I offered.

She smiled. 'Being bisexual is not an impediment to marriage, Nicole.'

'It is to being in a monogamous, heterosexual marriage. Unless you marry a hermaphrodite, but I've heard they're quite rare.'

She started laughing, which made me laugh too. Bérengère always abandons herself to laughter; sometimes her snorting makes me snort and then we end up hysterical and my stomach muscles still ache when I leave to drive home.

'*Très drôle*, Nicole,' she said when she finally stopped laughing. She blinked a few times, sighed and sipped the last of her *Pineau*. A frown gradually formed on her forehead again. 'I think you should be more positive about this. It is completely understandable why you didn't tell Guy about what happened, and he needs to accept that you have the right to make that decision. Even if it takes him some time to accept it.'

I nodded glumly. 'The problem is that I'm starting to wonder if he'll *ever* accept it.'

Big Gallic shrug, a very drawn-out one. 'Well then, Nicole, maybe you need to move on if he doesn't accept it.'

And that just made the rest of the day horrible. I didn't want to move on, I wanted D'Artagnan back. I loved him. Nina loved him.

Everything was all ... fucked up.

***

Francesca agreed to come to Bordeaux. Boy, was she pissed off about it.

'It's like I ask her to go to the moon, Nicole.' Xavier's voice was slightly amazed, shocked even, when he phoned me later that evening. 'This is a difficult woman. She have a very clear idea of her world, how it must be, she is not at all ... *bah*, *contente* when she have to change her plan.'

'Well, Xavier, that's because Francesca has never had anyone tell her "no". No is not a word that exists for Francesca. It doesn't exist for people like her, for ex-investment bankers. Don't you know that they are the self-proclaimed masters of the universe?'

He was quiet for a while then he asked curiously, 'You have a lot of experience with people like this, Nicole? I thought you work as a *mannequin* in fashion.'

I frowned. 'Well yes, from the age of seventeen. But then everything went tits-up after what happened in Milan, and I gradually realised that I needed to get off that crazy fucking carousel. But you know all about that – we went over it when we did my statement before we went to see the *procureur*.'

Long pause. 'What does "tits-up" mean, Nicole?' I could *hear* his frown and it made me smile.

It was after seven o'clock and I was lying on the couch in the library doing my yoga exercises while I talked to him, sipping wine and occasionally eating a mouthful of supper, which was yoghurt and roasted nuts and seeds (or *rodent-cocaine*, as D'Artagnan called it, with extra '*rrrrr*' in the *rrrrrodent* part. His fluent Spanish language skills are never under-utilised).

'It means everything started going wrong. And when I met Karl, that's about the time that the tits started going up.'

'Your ex-boyfriend. Yes, you mention him to me.'

'So, Karl was basically a high-functioning heroin addict. I'm pretty sure he isn't now, because last time I checked he was quite a successful film director. But I'm not really in touch with him anymore. Anyway, when I met Karl I was pretty messed-up after Milan, and it was only a little hop, skip and jump until I was also a fairly high-functioning heroin addict.'

I paused. 'I suppose it helped that Karl's daddy was obscenely wealthy, and it wasn't as if we had to go out and score on street corners or anything. Our dealer always came to the flat in Mayfair.'

Xavier was very quiet.

'Are you still there?' I asked, before spooning another mouthful of supper into my mouth.

'You were addicted to heroin?' I could hear him frowning.

'Yes, Xavier. I explained this to you.'

'You said you had some problems with drugs, Nicole.'

I shrugged. '*Voilà, le problème,* Xavier.'

I heard him take a deep breath. 'You know, Nicole, we need to have a big talk about your life. I did not imagine that it was so ... *bah*, diverse. I think – I thought—' He pronounced that '*taught'*, which was sweet. 'I thought you were a mannequin and then you meet Guy and then you marry him and come to live in France.'

'That *is* what happened. Only, between the bit where I was a model and meeting Guy, I was in rehab for heroin addiction.

Then I was a secretary and I worked for an investment banker. That was where I met lots of other investment bankers, almost all of whom were inbred sociopaths. Then Guy turned up.'

Another long pause. 'And Guy was not a sociopath?'

It was my turn to pause. 'No,' I said finally. 'He was just massively arrogant.'

And the sex we had made me feel as if I were somersaulting slowly backwards in thick, luscious liquid into a black vortex of ecstasy. But I decided that perhaps that might be too difficult to explain to Xavier. I took a sip of wine instead and said, 'No, he wasn't a sociopath.'

When Xavier spoke again, his voice was pensive. 'I remember meeting him when I work for Laurent. Guy have a very big personality like Laurent – they were very similar. I meet him one or two times when he come back to Bordeaux to see his sister and Laurent.' He paused. 'And then when Laurent die, I remember him at the funeral. He cry so much. He was devastated. It was very sad.'

My eyes had filled. 'He still misses him. They all still miss Laurent.' I stopped, annoyed at myself. 'I mean obviously they do, it's stupid to even say that.' I put my wine glass down on the floor. 'I can't imagine how I'd feel if I lost Jules, or how Françoise must have felt to lose her husband when he was only forty. Or how their girls felt to lose their father.' I wiped my eyes.

'I miss him too.' Xavier's voice was bleak. 'He was so good to me when I just start my career, he was such an inspiration, so clever. And so funny!' He paused. 'After he die, I think again about why I have chosen to be a lawyer and then I decide that I don't want to be a commercial lawyer. I want to help people, I want to make the world better. That is why I become a criminal lawyer.'

I nodded slowly, staring into the dying flames in the wood burner. 'I can understand that.'

He sighed deeply. 'Anyway, Nicole. After we meet with Francesca on Monday, you need to tell me about your life. I am worried by this problem with the drugs, the bad drugs. I need to understand all of this in case the *juge d'instruction* want to know about all of this.'

I frowned. 'Why would the *juge d'instruction* need to know about my life?'

'*Bah*, because you take a lot of drugs? Because you are addicted to heroin?'

'Why would that change anything?' I snapped. 'Does that somehow make what Satan did more ... acceptable?'

'*Non, non, non* – please Nicole, don't become angry about this! It is just that I need to know about you, I need to understand your life.' He paused. 'Nobody is going to say this make it more acceptable.'

I got up off the sofa to put more wood in the burner. 'I didn't expect to have to go over all that shit again, Xavier.'

A long pause, a very long pause, and then it was back, subdued but evident, the '*I told you so*' tone. 'I tell you this is going to be difficult in the beginning, Nicole. I tell you this is why you need your family, the people that love you, to support you while you do this.' I swear I heard a little self-righteous sniff. 'This is why I tell you to tell Guy.'

I counted to ten very slowly then I said, 'Well, Xavier, I didn't. So could we stop flogging that particular dead fucking horse, please?'

I swear I could hear his thick eyelashes sweeping over his eyes.

'Okay,' he said. He didn't dare to ask what horse I was talking about.

***

We met with Francesca in Xavier's offices in Bordeaux the following Monday.

Francesca came armed with not one but two lawyers. Well, she wasn't exactly armed with them, they just kind of trailed behind her and tried really hard not to annoy her. Every time they opened their mouths to speak unbidden, she either snapped at them or gave them such a glacial stare that they decided to swallow whatever pathetic morsel of nonsense they had stupidly thought might be relevant. The only exception was when she barked a question at them; then she listened to maybe seven or eight seconds of the answer before shutting them down with a dismissive wave of her hand.

I had arrived early as Xavier had suggested. When he came out of his office to greet me, I stared at him. He was wearing a crisp, new, grey shirt that matched his eyes. And he'd *definitely* brushed the curls that morning and thrown away the blunt old Bic razor because his stubble was only at 7am.

'Nicole, *ça va*?' He smiled as we exchanged kisses.

I raised an eyebrow and then put it down again. I was not going to comment on the new look. Anyway, it wasn't *all* new: the NHS glasses were still taped up though perhaps he had replenished the Sellotape. It didn't have a hair sticking to it any more.

'*Très bien*, thank you, Xavier. You?'

He held my upper arms very lightly. His aftershave was Bleu de Chanel. '*Très bien, merci.*' He seemed relaxed today – and the grey shirt *really* suited him.

We both turned as a very large, highly polished Mercedes Maybach edged its way into the office car park. Francesca had arrived.

Apparently I still had to do Kissies with Francesca, though I didn't have to do them with her two muzzled rottweilers. Xavier did not do Kissies with any of them; he did manly handshakes, even with Francesca. So, I learned a new thing about Kissies' etiquette – or at least I think I did.

We all sat down in the meeting room. I sat next to Xavier; Francesca and her mutts sat in a row on the other side of the table.

She was wearing a high-necked silk blouse (that season's Prada) and the recycled mohair Saint Laurent Playboy jumper that I'd seen online and coveted (but then reminded myself that I lived in the Land of Mud and had nowhere to wear it). She was also sporting black leather trousers and 'in-your-wildest-dreams-will-you-ever-fuck-me' patent-leather stiletto boots. Her short, spiky, blonde hair was as perfectly cut and styled as ever, her sharp, androgynous face tanned and only lightly made-up.

She got straight down to business. 'Where is Guy, Nicole? Why is he not here? Why is he not taking my calls?'

It was the perfect opportunity to unfurl my best-ever impression of a Gallic shrug. I raised my shoulders as high as I could, I opened my eyes wide, I raised both my eyebrows and my eyes to the ceiling, and I did a theatrical 'who knows' with my hands. 'That, I'm afraid, Francesca, I don't know.' Then I stared at her.

God, it was fun not having to answer to these people, these sociopathic self-appointed little gods. Not having to find a way to imply without actually saying, 'You don't impress me, you don't scare me and you don't intimidate me. But, if you like, I can help you back into your pram.'

Her pale-blue eyes narrowed and her carefully mascaraed eyelashes closed slightly. 'How can you "not know" where your husband is, Nicole?' She did the little finger-inverted commas that I find *phenomenally* irritating. It was hard to stop my eyes rolling of their own accord.

I leaned forward and put my elbows on the table, my fingertips pressed together in Xavier's trademark thinking-pyramid, and gazed at her. 'He left, Francesca. He left when he found out about the charges I brought against Guillaume. And since then he doesn't seem to want to be contacted by anyone.'

She frowned. 'So Guy did not know about these things you say – that you *allege* – that Guillaume has done to you? Is that what you are saying? How is that possible, Nicole? You are his wife!'

Then the pale-blue eyes narrowed viciously. 'Is this because he would not believe you, Nicole? Is it possible that you keep these allegations from Guy because you know he will not believe you? This is a very big, very serious thing that you have done. They are not accusations to make easily. If Guy does not believe you, then it is very difficult for me to believe you either!'

I nearly lost it then. I felt the fury rising up in me and I leaned back in my chair, my eyes equally narrowed, equally vicious. I hated her at that moment; I wanted to kill her, kill her words, kill her insinuation. How dare she imply that I was lying, the privileged, spoilt, entitled ... foot-stamping little madam! I was *furious*.

And then Xavier put his slender hand onto my forearm and leaned over, his breath warm on my ear as he whispered, 'Don't be angry, Nicole. She want you to be angry. Your case is very real, what happen is very real. Do not forget that, and do not forget Léa.'

That was exactly what I needed to hear. I swallowed the anger easily; it slipped back down smoothly and was asphyxiated.

I drew a deep breath. 'Francesca,' I said, not trying to keep the condescension from my voice. 'Your business partner – your *friend* – Guillaume raped me. He drugged me and he raped me in a villa outside Milan nearly twelve years ago. He watched me at Milan fashion week that year – where, by the way, I was walking for *your* family's label – and he selected me the way one might choose from a menu. A victim menu, if you like.'

I took a breath. Our eyes were locked together. 'He drugged me and then he and two of his vile, bastard friends raped me. He has raped or sexually abused other women, too. Young women, younger even than I was. We have the testimony of another women from Bordeaux, and as we proceed towards the trial and the charges become public, we're pretty sure that other women will come forward too.'

Francesca's cheekbones had become more pronounced as if she were sucking in her cheeks.

'So,' I continued, 'I don't actually give a flying *fuck* whether you believe me or not, because I am going to make sure that that bastard is put exactly where he belongs, in prison where he can't harm any other women.' I blinked at her several times when I'd finished talking and sat back in my chair.

Xavier was smiling at me, his grey eyes were wide, his gaze intense.

It was Francesca's turn to do the Gallic shrug, but hers was very muted. She sat back in her chair, raised an eyebrow, gave a small pout and blinked. 'You have some fire in you, Nicole,' she said finally. There was the tiniest note of admiration in her voice. Admiration! From Francesca!

One of the rottweilers dared to interrupt and started talking about 'alleged' and 'unconfirmed'. She turned and glared at him and he instantly melted, a pool of blood and gore forming on the floor beneath his chair where he had been sitting. On a slightly parallel plane, obviously.

'But what I still don't understand, Nicole, is why Guy is not here,' Francesca went on. 'Why is Guy not a part of this process? Why is he missing?'

I took a deep breath. I was getting very tired of having to explain why Guy had left. 'Well, Francesca, here's the thing. I didn't tell Guy about Guillaume because I really didn't fancy visiting him in prison. And that is more than likely where he'd have ended up after trying to kill – or succeeding in killing – the man who raped me.'

I paused. 'So I decided not to tell him until Guillaume was in custody. Unfortunately that seems to have annoyed him, so he's gone. I don't know where he is at the moment.' I tried to blink away the annoying tears that were starting to form.

She gazed at me, clear-eyed. 'I am sure that he is very angry with you about that, Nicole.'

I nodded. 'Yup, he is. He is very angry.' I was furious at the tears that were making Francesca wobble in my vision.

She shrugged. 'Well, I am not surprised, Nicole.' Her eyes flicked thoughtfully onto the ceiling before she turned them back on me. 'But yes, I can imagine this is what he would do. I know he is very, *bah*, alpha. So I think I understand why you didn't tell him.'

I frowned deeply because I didn't want to have to be grateful to her for saying she understood why I had done what I did. Then I had to wipe the tears from my cheeks, and that *really* annoyed me because I didn't want to show any sign of weakness in front of her.

She turned to one of the muzzled rottweilers and they had a whispered conference. When she directed her Medusa gaze back across the table, it was trained on Xavier. Her voice was hard, interrogative. 'Explain to me again, *Maître*, how this trial is not going to cost me money? How this is not going to affect my share of the joint venture with Guy and Guillaume? Because this is what you tell me on the phone, and I am not clear about this. I want my lawyers to listen to your explanation.'

It was my turn to rally behind Xavier. I put my hand on his surprisingly muscular forearm and leaned towards him. He leaned towards me and my lips touched one of his soft dark curls as I whispered in his ear, 'Don't forget, Xavier, she's fucking loaded and she doesn't care about the money. She just wants to dominate you. I think it turns her on.'

I could see that he had to try *abundantly* hard not to start laughing. His mouth was slightly contorted as he explained why my case against Guillaume would not impact on her financially. She already knew that, anyway; she just wanted to see if she could shrivel Xavier's balls. I already knew that she couldn't.

That pleased me.

***

The goodbyes were very formal. Francesca and I did Kissies again, but this time she actually looked into my eyes for a second as if she'd clocked that I possessed a personality she hadn't noticed before.

She shook Xavier's hand firmly, her head slightly tilted to the side as if she were contemplating something, her jaw imperiously raised as it always was. Francesca is not tall; she's probably ten or twelve centimetres shorter than I am. But the way she carries herself makes her *seem* tall, particularly that defiantly lifted chin that projects confidence. Actually, it is more than confidence: it projects power, wealth and entitlement.

But for the first time I thought that maybe Francesca was also smart, that she was capable of learning. She had learned something that day about me and my resolve, and about Xavier and his resolve. I sensed that the meeting had gone differently to the way she'd imagined it would.

***

'*Mon dieu, quelle femme*!' His eyes wide, Xavier turned to me as we stood in the foyer watching Francesca's chauffeur negotiate the stately Mercedes out of the parking lot. He looked a bit shell-shocked.

I nodded. 'Yep. I did warn you.'

'You work for someone like this?' He stared at me.

I started laughing 'God, *no*! The wannabee-sociopath I worked for was kindergarten level compared to her. Even in his wildest dreams, he'd only have dared to imagine that he might, y'know, one day be allowed to lick the mud off her boots.' I shuddered. 'Eeeuurgh. I really shouldn't have summoned that image. I feel a bit sick now.'

Xavier laughed at that, a low, warm laugh, then he glanced at his watch. 'Nicole, it is lunchtime. Shall we take a lunch together? I find a very good vegetarian restaurant for you that I think you will like. It is not far, maybe twenty minutes' walk.'

I smiled at him. 'Thank you, Xavier. That would be lovely.'

His soft grey eyes smiled back at me. 'I go get our coats.'

Chapter Three

It rained the following Wednesday. It had started raining on Tuesday morning, a dense, relentless, freezing rain that had not stopped. I stood at the back window, wrapped in the usual seventeen layers, looking out towards the paddock where I could just make out Espiritu and Emperador in their shelter.

I was feeling very dejected and very alone standing there in D'Artagnan's vast, cold ancestral home in the depths of my new, unfamiliar homeland. Camille had come, filled the horses' hay trough and left before I'd come downstairs. There would be no spending time with the horses today, and for that reason Nina would almost certainly not come.

I turned away from the window and my footsteps echoed as I walked slowly back across the flagstone floor of the dining hall to the kitchen. I contemplated making myself another coffee from D'Artagnan's unnecessarily complicated coffee machine. A wave of melancholy washed over me as I remembered the many times we'd bickered about my coffee consumption.

***

'*Deux cafés par jour,* Nicole, *pas plus*. It's not healthy to drink more than two coffee a day.' D'Artagnan would frown as he glanced at me from across the kitchen, usually in the midst of conjuring up some complicated culinary masterpiece on his beloved range-cooker. It was a vast, navy-blue-and-silver creature that had breathed it's blackened, fiery breath up the ancient black-and-white tiled wall behind it for many years. It was a creature that I could occasionally coax into not cremating my home-made muesli, my '*rrrrrrodent cocaine*' – but only very occasionally. Normally I just asked D'Artagnan to do it.

I don't cook. I don't really get all the fuss about food, despite being married to the world's most exacting amateur chef. But it was over three weeks since D'Artagnan had left, and it was starting to dawn on me that perhaps I was going to have to learn a bit more about food because there might come a time when Nina would want to eat something other than cheese on toast.

Cheese on toast was the beginning and end of my cooking repertoire.

D'Artagnan did all the cooking. The kitchen was his *domaine* and he its master.

'Nina thinks she's vegetarian,' I'd told him. 'But she eats chicken and fish. So just, y'know, roll with it.'

He'd blinked at me a few times. 'Maybe, Nicole, you can take some lessons from Nina about being *végétarienne.*'

'I'm not seven years old, Guy. I know chicken and fish aren't vegetables.'

'Maybe you just need to try, Nicole. You know, I am a very good *chef...*' He'd winked at me, sauntered across the kitchen and slid his hands around my waist. 'Then we can all eat the same lunch and I don't have to make you something different.'

I gave him a withering look. 'You don't make me something different. I eat the same things that you and Nina eat for lunch, just without the chicken. Or the fish.'

'Or the rice. Or the *pommes de terre*. Or the bread.'

'That's nothing to do with being vegetarian.'

'*Ouais, je sais.*' A pause, then a small inclination of the head. 'You are not a model anymore, you know, Nicole. You don't have to always be a size 34. You can eat some proper food now.'

I frowned at him. 'I'm not a size 34, I'm a size 36.' I paused. 'Also, I'm perfectly healthy so I don't think you need to concern yourself with what I am or am not eating.'

'*Bah* ... but you are always cold, Nicole, and this is because you don't eat proper food!' He stroked a strand of hair behind my ear, fixed me with eyes that were caramel coloured in the morning light. 'You need to eat more food, *mon ange*. Maybe you need to accept to have a little bit of extra weight.' And then the lazy smile just curving at the edge of his mouth and the slow, sensuous blink. 'I think you will be even more beautiful than you already are with some extra weight, *mon amour.*'

I raised my index finger in front of his face and pointed upwards. 'Have you forgotten about Heaven, D'Artagnan? Heaven is crammed full of my beautiful clothes and they are all size 36. So no, I'm not going to "accept to have a little bit of extra weight", if that's okay with you.'

He'd rolled his eyes and turned away from me crossly. He went back to chopping whatever was going to be the *menu du jour* that day. '*Bah,* Nicole, maybe you need to accept that heaven can also be other things.'

Frowning, I wrinkled my nose at him. 'What on earth is that supposed to mean, Guy?'

He gave a slightly irritated shrug and threw a glance at me. 'A dressing room is not heaven, Nicole. Heaven is when our life is filled with—' And then he'd paused again and his brow had furrowed.

'I'm listening, Guy.'

'*Bah, pffff.* Never mind. It is not important.' Grumpy, now. 'I just think sometime you should eat more.'

It had been a slightly strange conversation, but I'd chalked it up to a combination of bad-weather boredom and his voracious desire to control everything, including me and my eating habits.

***

I stood in the silent kitchen and stared at the range cooker, wondering how difficult it would be to force it to obey me. And then, out of the corner of my eye, I noticed a movement at the front of the Duchess through the kitchen window. I went over to the window and stared out. The bare trees that lined the drive leading out of the château grounds were almost obscured by the heavy rain but my eyes gradually adjusted and that was when I saw her.

My heart gave a lurch and I gasped, my hands inadvertently flying up to cover my mouth. I crossed the kitchen, wrenched open the back door and ran out into the freezing rain around the side of the château towards the poplar tree under which she was standing.

Nina was completely drenched and rigid with cold as I lifted her into my arms and ran back inside the château, her body clasped as tightly as possible to mine.

I took her straight upstairs to our room, turned the tap on full blast to fill the bathtub as quickly as possible then carefully started to remove her sodden clothes. The freezing rainwater formed a puddle around her feet, and within minutes my fingers were numb with cold.

She was shivering violently, her teeth chattering – more than that, they were *clattering* against one another. She was so, so cold. I willed the hot water to fill the bath more quickly – *quicker*, dammit!!

'Why didn't you come to the door, Nina darling? Why didn't you knock on the door? I was only in the kitchen, sweetheart,' I asked quietly as she held onto my shoulder with her icy hand as I removed the last of her soaked clothes. I wrapped her in my bath towel and held her close.

She shrugged her skinny little shoulders and didn't say anything. She was crying silently, tears running down her cheeks. I struggled to control my own tears.

I helped her into the bath when it was half full. She looked so tiny in there on her own and she was still shivering, so I thought, *Fuck it, I'm getting in too*. I climbed in wearing my underwear, put my arms and legs around her and embraced her as the hot water continued to pour into the bath and she gradually – very gradually – stopped shivering.

When she had finally warmed up and we'd got out of the bath, I wrapped her several times in D'Artagnan's towel. I crouched down in front of her and gazed into her big green eyes. 'Is that better? Are you warmer now?' She gave a little nod, tried a timid smile.

'Come, then. Let's go into my dressing room and find you some warm clothes to wear. And then we'll go downstairs and I'll make you something to eat. Are you hungry?'

A little shrug. 'Maybe,' she whispered.

She sat on the chaise longue as I dressed her. I put one of my long cashmere vests over her – it went down to her knees – then I put one of my thin cashmere sweaters on top and rolled up the sleeves. I put another, slightly thicker cashmere sweater on top of that and rolled up the sleeves of that, too. I cut a pair of my thick cashmere-blend tights into leggings and put the fleece-lined slippers I'd bought for her that winter on her feet.

When I'd finished, I sat her down on the stool in front of my dressing-table and dried her silky hair with my hairdryer. She looked up at me as she carefully stroked the sweater. 'It's very soft,' she said and smiled another timid little smile.

'Yes, it's cashmere. It's the softest wool in the world.'

She tried the word out, mouthing 'cashmere' several times, then said softly, 'I like the sound it makes. It sounds like it feels.'

And I thought, with only a hint of irony, this is *my* daughter – she's definitely my daughter. I had to wipe the tears from my eyes again.

I took off my bathrobe and wet underwear and dressed in cashmere too. My last layer was one of D'Artagnan's sweaters and it smelled of Dior, of him. I sat next to Nina on the chaise longue and slipped my arm around her shoulders.

'You smell like the *prince,*' she said quietly because she knew his smell too. My heart felt like it would shatter when she asked, '*Princesse* Nicole, where is the *prince*?'

I wiped my eyes with the back of my hand. We gazed into each other's green eyes, and I had to bite my bottom lip hard before I spoke. 'Nina, I don't know where the *prince* is. He's very unhappy about something I did, and he has gone away to think about whether he can forgive me.'

She nodded slowly. Her eyes were sombre as she asked, 'Is he unhappy with me, too?'

I couldn't stop the sob that escaped me. I gathered her up in my arms and held her against me as I made a majestic effort to get a grip. 'No, Nina, he is not at all unhappy with you. He loves you very, very much. And I love you very, very much. We both love you so much,' I whispered, my mouth against her silky hair.

Her little arms were tight around my neck. 'But what will happen if he doesn't come back? Will you go away too?'

So I said it. I knew I wasn't supposed to but I didn't care anymore. I needed to say it and she needed to know it. I sat back a little so that we were eye to eye again and I took a deep breath.

'Nina, I am never going to leave you. And I need to ask you a question.' I gazed into her wide, clear eyes. 'Would you like it if we adopted you? If you became our daughter? Do you know what that means, to adopt?'

She narrowed her eyes and gave the slightest shrug. 'Yes,' she murmured. 'I know what that means.' She paused but she didn't look away from me. 'I would like that.'

I gathered her up in my arms again and I said, 'I would like that so much too, Nina. I never, ever, ever want you to go away again. I want you always to be here, with me.'

She nodded her little head, her hair soft against my cheek and her arms clasped around my neck.

***

'Yes, I *know* I shouldn't have told her,' I said crossly. 'But it was just— I *had* to tell her. For fuck's sake, she's so worried about where Guy is. *I'm* so bloody worried about where Guy is, but I *have* to reassure her, I have to tell her how much we love her, how much *I* love her!'

Xavier didn't say anything.

I shook my head angrily. 'Please try to understand my position, Xavier. I've always wanted children and now Nina has been – well, gifted to me. I can't imagine her not being in my life. I know that she needs me – and I know that I need her!'

I did not say that Nina and I were perfectly suited because I also knew what it was like to feel abandoned, to have no confidence in the adults who are supposedly in control. I knew what it was like not to know unconditional love. I didn't want to tell him all that in case he wanted to wade into it when we met with the *juge d'instruction* the following week because that would take ... like, *years* of therapy and we really didn't have time for that.

I heard him breathe in then breathe out. 'Yes, I understand Nicole,' he said finally.

I took a deep breath, too. 'Look, Xavier, could you help me with this? I know you're a criminal lawyer, but you're French and you understand how the legal system works. I – well, I don't really.'

I gazed out the window at the naked poplar trees at the end of the lawn in front of the Duchess. The rain had finally stopped on Wednesday evening. I'd woken up really early on Thursday morning and rung Xavier just after eight o'clock as I sipped my coffee in bed.

'What do you want me to help you with, Nicole?'

'With Nina. I need to know what will happen if Guy doesn't come back. How will that affect our application to adopt Nina?'

Another long pause. 'You really think Guy will not come back? Why do you think this?'

'It's been more than three weeks. He doesn't want to speak to me. He's not speaking to anyone.' I sighed tiredly. 'And even if he never comes back, I still want to adopt Nina. I'm starting to think maybe I need to consider other options.'

'What options?'

I took a sip of my coffee. 'Do you lawyers always just ask questions? You're a bit like analysts, aren't you? I tell you something and you answer me with another question.'

'I need to understand what you are asking me, Nicole.' His voice was very measured.

I took another deep breath. 'Would it be possible for you to do a little research into whether I could adopt Nina on my own? I'd be really grateful because, quite frankly, I've Googled it a thousand fucking ways in French and I still don't know what the bastard answer is.'

'Of course I can do this, Nicole.' The warmth in his voice made my eyes mist over. I was starting to wonder where all these tears were coming from. There seemed to be a limitless supply. Was it something I was eating or drinking?

'Thank you, Xavier.' I wiped my eyes with the back of my hand.

Another long pause and then he said with a smile in his voice, '*Bah*, but you know, Nicole, you are maybe going to need to learn not to say all these bad words when you are Nina's mama. You cannot be saying "fucking this" and "fuck's sake" all the time.' He pronounced it '*furcking zis'* and '*furck's* sake', like D'Artagnan did.

I couldn't help but smile. 'Thank you for the parental advice, Xavier.'

'It is my pleasure, Nicole.' I could imagine his softly crinkled grey eyes.

***

Bérengère stood in the Duchess's kitchen, surveying it loftily from the point of view of a conqueror, her hands on her narrow hips which were clad today in a grey corduroy skirt to her ankles, split to just above the knee. The spurs on the cowboy boots flashed as she crossed the creamy flagstones in the dining hall; her loose, dusty-pink silk shirt was open at the throat, and a faded, chartreuse-coloured scarf trailed behind her.

I caught a glimpse of the Duchess in her usual observation position on top of the stone fireplace. She was looking Bérengère up and down approvingly. Bérengère was definitely the Duchess's kind of woman.

'So Nicole, *apéro* first, before we start! Where is the *Pineau*?'

I had asked her if she'd come to the château for my French class instead of me going to her because I wanted to introduce a new theme to our lessons: 'Learning to Cook, Age Thirty-eight-and-three-quarters.'

'Really?' she'd asked, astonished. 'Your mother, your father, your grandparents – no one in your family ever taught you to cook? Not even an omelette?'

I shook my head and wondered if I should describe the kitchen situation in the apartment where I grew up with Tiffany, my abusive, alcoholic mother. Perhaps the fact that pretty much the only ingredient in the kitchen was vodka would go some way to explaining my lack of cooking skills. But I was tired of sharing misery with other people; I had already done a lot of misery sharing that year and it was only the end of January.

Instead I said, 'Yeah, they were all rubbish at cooking. So no, I didn't learn how to cook, and when I was a model we weren't really encouraged to indulge in food.' On the other hand, Champagne, nicotine, cocaine – heroin, for those on a particularly self-destructive path – were fine.

Bérengère had raised an eyebrow and made a pouty, disapproving face. Clearly cooking lessons were going to be more rigorously taught than French verb *conjugaisons*.

I took the bottle of *Pineau des Charentes*, the fifteen-year-aged one made by D'Artagnan's cousin Benoît, out of the fridge and put it on the counter top while I reached for the special fluted *Pineau* glasses. Bérengère picked up the bottle and studied the label. 'This is a good *Pineau,* Nicole, this one that Benoît makes.'

I nodded. 'Yes, I agree.' I was becoming quite the expert in *Pineau des Charentes*. I filled our glasses and passed over hers. We clinked them and exchanged a '*santé.'*

She leaned back against the granite countertop. 'Still no D'Artagnan?'

I looked away and shook my head.

Bérengère made a face, the one with both eyebrows raised, then she shrugged. '*Bah*, he is a stupid man, Nicole.'

'Unfortunately, I'm a stupid woman too, because I love him. And I miss him,' I said despondently.

She blinked a few times. 'You know, Nicole, I had a long conversation with someone about you and Guy recently.'

I frowned. 'Who with?'

She reached into her pocket and pulled out her solid-silver cigarette case. I only knew it was solid silver because it had fallen on my bare foot the previous summer and it had bloody well hurt. 'Who do you think?'

I frowned. 'Xavier?'

She shook her head and smiled. She opened the cigarette case and took out a pre-rolled cigarette, or maybe it was a joint. 'Can I?' She made a smoking motion.

I shrugged. 'Knock yourself out.'

She lit it, inhaled, blew out a cloud of blue smoke. It was not a joint. 'No,' she said, and deftly removed a flake of tobacco from her tongue. 'I did not speak to Xavier. Since Guillaume was taken into custody, Xavier talks to you directly.'

In order to avoid arousing D'Artagnan's highly inquisitive antennae, all communications with Xavier had gone through Bérengère in the months leading up to Satan's arrest.

She lowered her eyelids and a hint of smile appeared on her mouth. 'Why did you think it was Xavier I spoke to?'

'I dunno.' I took a sip of my *Pineau*.

She gazed at me serenely for a while before her eyes narrowed. Finally she said, 'Do you think about Xavier a lot, Nicole?'

I made a face. '*No*, Bérengère. I just know that you know him.'

She took another sip of her *Pineau* and carried on regarding me with a very frank gaze. 'But you talk about Xavier often, Nicole.'

'Fuck's sake, Bérengère, he's my lawyer! This case is a big thing in my life at the moment, so it's only natural that I mention him. Anyway, you're deflecting. Tell me who it was that you were talking to!'

She grinned, crossed the kitchen to the sink and flicked the ash into the drain. 'Stephane called me.'

I started laughing. 'Oh my God, you spoke to Darth Vader? That's hilarious! Is he back from his inspection of South-East Asian cathedrals?'

Her grin widened. 'No, not yet. He's in Vietnam. We talked on WhatsApp.'

I stared at her. 'You do know that he's slightly obsessed with you, don't you? Even though he's like ... rabidly Catholic? And rabidly disapproving of women who are not dutiful wives and mothers, women who do not *obey* their husbands!'

She carried on grinning as she shook her head slowly. '*Bah*, Nicole, you have a very clear script in your head about everyone you meet, don't you?'

'Of course I do,' I laughed.

She was still smiling but she tilted her head appraisingly. 'But your script is quite rigid, you know. People change all the time. They are not rigid, they are more nuanced than you imagine, Nicole.'

Then I really started laughing; I might even have slapped my thigh. 'Oh my God, Bérengère, you're falling for Darth Vader!'

She rolled her eyes. 'No, Nicole, I am not "falling for" Stephane! I am just saying that he is not what you imagine him to be.'

I made a pouty face at her. 'So, Bérengère, how are *you* "imagining" Stephane? I mean, he's very fertile – we know that because he has six children. And until very recently, he was really – I mean *seriously* – uptight and disapproving of *everything*.'

She shrugged. 'Stephane has been very depressed for a very long time. Now he is starting not to be so depressed.'

I stared at her. 'Is that what he told you?'

Final drag then she turned on the tap and put her roll-up under it. She threw the butt in the bin. 'No. Yes. A little. We talked about his life. He is a complicated man, Nicole.'

The arch in my eyebrow was completely uncontrived. 'Wow. Just wow, Bérengère. I'm kind of blown away by that. You and Stephane – you're like at waaaaay opposite ends of the life spectrum. He's super-religious and goes to church four times a week or something, and you're a libertarian, bisexual, dope-smoking, disrespectful, sexy hippy chick. You must see that the idea of you two as an item is kind of bizarre. Though admittedly fascinating.'

'We are not an item, Nicole. We just talk on the phone sometimes. And like I've told you many times before, *ma bichette*, life is complicated and people are complicated. Stephane is complicated. He is not a simple character.'

She drained the last of her *Pineau* and set her glass down on the countertop before she turned to me, her grey-eyed gaze very direct.

'You, Nicole, you tell yourself a story about the people in your life and then you are confused when people don't behave in the way that you have constructed the story. But life is not like that. People change paths and they react in ways that we don't predict. They do things we don't think they would do because they are more complex, more nuanced, than the stories we make up about them.'

I held her steady gaze. 'Is that your way of telling me that I shouldn't be surprised that Guy left?'

Her eyes remained fixed on mine. 'Nicole, I think it is good that you were surprised that Guy left you, because in your story about Guy he didn't leave you. He stayed. You need to learn that he is more complex, more complicated, than the story you tell yourself about your husband.'

As tears misted my eyes, she crossed the kitchen and gave me a big, smoky-rose smelling hug and said, 'But enough, Nicole! Enough philosophy! Now it is time for you to learn how to make the most important thing every French person knows how to make. I am going to teach you how to make an *omelette*!'

***

The fifth omelette I made was actually passable. I was finally allowed to put the buttery chopped mushrooms and onions, which had been gently simmering on the back plate while I fucked up *omelettes* one to three, in the fifth one. (The fourth one had looked okay to me but not to Bérengère.)

We stood at the granite countertop and shared it. I was pretty surprised because it tasted delicious and the texture was light, fluffy, almost as good as the omelettes D'Artagnan made so effortlessly. I could cook an *omelette*! Nina was not going to starve to death or become stunted and deformed because she was malnourished as a result of her mother's woefully inadequate cooking skills.

I was very proud of my first-ever omelette.

***

The following week, Xavier and I met with the *juge d'instruction*, the magistrate responsible for conducting the investigation into Satan. Xavier had explained the French criminal justice system to me in detail during our initial meeting. It was very different to the highly adversarial criminal trials depicted in US and UK courtroom dramas, those melodramatic verbal battles of intrigue performed by strutting, preening lawyers in front of a jury.

In France, the adversarial element is largely absent. If it is a serious crime, the *procureur* refers the case to the *juge d'instruction*, who then investigates the case before it comes to court. And Satan's crime was serious; it was a felony, punishable by more than ten years in prison. It meant that the *juge d'instruction* had ordered that Satan be arrested and taken into custody on his return to France in late December the previous year.

Perhaps it was because Xavier had prepared me for it that I'd resolved not to be intimidated – or not *too* intimidated – and the meeting with the *juge d'instruction* was not as scary as I'd expected. She was a short, plump, well-dressed black woman who wore gold earrings shaped like shells and a matching necklace. Her reading glasses dangled on a gold chain around her neck when she took them off to question me after she'd perused my dossier.

Her questions were very direct, and Xavier had been right: she wasn't very *gentille*. She didn't smile and there was no emotion in her voice as she fired questions at me. I was actually okay with that, and I answered factually and didn't let emotion into my voice either. She made me tell her everything that I could remember about the night in the Marble Villa in Hell and what had happened afterwards.

She asked why I had not reported the crime immediately. When I explained that I had no memory of anything that had happened, that the flashbacks only started a couple of weeks later, her eyes narrowed and she pursed her lips.

'But you knew that something had happened, it says so here in your dossier.' She put her reading glasses back on and looked at the documents again. She read out the part of my statement where I'd woken up in my hotel room with a swollen eye, with blood smeared across my face from my split lip, with bruises in the shape of fingerprints on the inside of my thighs. She paused and looked up at me. She didn't continue to read the statement aloud, the bit about semen, the blood, the pain and where the pain was. I was grateful to her for that.

'So, Madame du Beauchamp, you knew that you had been raped. You should have known you had been drugged because this is something we all know about, that these drugs are used. Why didn't you go to the police the next day?'

I took a deep breath and explained that I'd been afraid of going to the Italian police to report a rape of which I had no memory when I'd been at a party and had been drunk and doing cocaine. I said that at the time I'd felt it was partly my fault for being drunk, for being careless. Coupled with the fact that I was due to check out of the hotel and fly back to the UK that afternoon, it was easier to try to push all thoughts of what had happened away.

I was already quite good at doing that; that was what diazepam was for. And when diazepam no longer worked, well, hello there heroin! That worked.

She nodded slowly, made some notes on the dossier and then started questioning me about my drug habits, about the drugs I had been taking at the time, both legal and illegal. I briefly explained that the fashion world was heavily dusted with white powder and that diazepam was distributed like sweeties to de-string us when we were strung-out from too much champagne, too much cocaine, too much partying. I explained how I had met Karl a month or so after the night in the Marble Villa in Hell and that by then I was starting to have terrifying flashbacks. Karl suggested that heroin would dull all of that. Heroin could soothe away everything.

I took a deep breath and I forced myself to meet her frank, impassive eyes. I said that at that time in my life I didn't take a lot of convincing to try heroin because I was very self-destructive. I had quickly become addicted, but two years later I decided to get clean and go through a drug rehab programme. And although I had relapsed the first time because Karl was determined to reclaim me, the second time I had succeeded and I had been clean ever since.

Next she asked me about my current drug habits. I told her that my doctor prescribed diazepam for the panic attacks but I was very careful not to take it often, that I was very aware that it was addictive and I only took it occasionally now, when I really needed it.

'And apart from the diazepam that you are prescribed? Do you take any other drugs?'

'No,' I said firmly. 'I don't do drugs at all now. I haven't done drugs since I came out of rehab. I haven't touched any other drugs for more than seven years.'

I'd decided that she didn't need to know about my brief flirtation with oxycodone the previous summer. No-one apart from Jules knew about that – well, Jules and Annabelle the wedding planner. It wasn't relevant to our discussion.

She nodded slowly and continued staring at me as if she were trying to gauge if I was telling the truth. Finally, it seemed that she accepted I was and she continued with questions about what had happened when I'd found out that Guillaume was Satan.

We went over the events of the previous year, how Bérengère and I had got video evidence of him admitting to what he'd done to me in the Marble Villa in Hell. We went through that in a lot of detail. She said that she would need to interview Bérengère and I said that was fine; Bérengère knew she would be required to testify.

The *juge d'instruction* said the video evidence would go before the next court. Finally, she explained the difficulties in identifying Satan's vile little friends. Unless Satan could be persuaded to divulge their names, it would be difficult for the Italian police to make much progress, although they were making enquiries.

She asked how I felt about not being able to bring them to justice. I shrugged and said that of course I wanted them to be tried, but if it was impossible to find them I would still feel relieved if Guillaume was convicted and imprisoned. At least that would stop him abusing other women.

She nodded, looked down at the dossier again, made some more notes.

Xavier turned to me and gave me a warm smile, as if he were proud of the way I'd handled the interview. He mouthed, '*Bien joué*, Nicole.' Well done. I really wanted to hug him at that moment but I just smiled back at him.

We turned back to the *juge*, who had looked up again. She actually gave me a small smile as she said, 'Good. I have everything I need. Thank you for coming to see me.'

***

After we left her offices, Xavier and I went to a nearby bar. We sat on stools at the zinc counter and he ordered us both a double Cognac. 'You too?' I raised a querying eyebrow.

He nodded. '*Mais oui*, for me that was also a bit ... scary? She is a very strict *juge*. The dossier must always be perfect to go in front of her.'

The barman put our drinks in front of us and Xavier raised his. 'Well done today, Nicole. *Félicitations*.'

I touched my glass to his. 'Thank you, Xavier. I couldn't have done it without you.' I smiled at him. He really did have very long black eyelashes. 'Down in one?' I asked.

He frowned. '*Quoi*?'

'Y'know, like shots. Like the cowboys used to do.' I raised my glass.

He looked slightly offended. '*Mais non*, Nicole. It is a very good Cognac. You drink it slowly.'

I knew he didn't understand why I rolled my eyes as I took a sip.

'I think the meeting go very well.' He nodded approvingly.

I didn't want to think about it anymore; I was tired of having to spend time in the Marble Villa in Hell so I changed the subject. 'I like the new shirt.' It was a subtle pale blue, crisp and undecorated with food and drink and ink.

He inclined his head graciously. '*Merci, Nicole.*'

I took another sip of my Cognac, which was actually very good. 'New suit, too?'

He made a face that involved some pouting. '*Bah, ouais*.' He looked slightly embarrassed.

'It looks good. *Très élégant*.'

'*Merci encore*. You are also very ... *bah*, very elegantly dressed.'

I was wearing charcoal-grey Chanel, 2003 autumn/winter, with a cream silk Lanvin blouse. And black Louboutins, though not the very high ones, not the ones that made D'Artagnan's eyes melt with lust.

'Thank you, Xavier.' I smiled at him. 'So, have you got a new girlfriend? Is that what the wardrobe update is about?'

His brow furrowed lightly and his grey eyes narrowed as he contemplated me for a while. Finally he gave a little shake of his head. '*Non*,' he said. But his dark curls had been brushed again, his full lips were the loveliest shade of dusty pink and the dark stubble was only at two o'clock.

I had to look away as it dawned on me, not for the first time, that Xavier was actually ... kinda quite attractive.

Chapter Four

'*Non*!' shouted Camille. '*Non, non, non,* Nicole! Don't go all tense like that. If you make your body tense then Espiritu will also be tense and then it will be a disaster!'

I managed to throw her a bewildered glance as I clutched a fistful of Espiritu's abundant mane in one hand and scrabbled for the reins I'd dropped with the other. I was bouncing around on Espiritu's back while he trotted at high speed around the paddock, his head in the air.

'*Relaxe toi*!' she shouted again.

It occurred to me briefly that being shouted at to relax was counter-intuitive.

Espiritu heard the sharpness in her voice, gave a little snort, arched his neck and broke into a canter. It was both terrifying and at the same time absolutely wonderful; suddenly his movement was a whole lot less straddle-a-jack-hammer and a whole lot more rocking-horse. Suddenly I could feel the one-two-three-four of his hooves on the ground, could feel the hypnotic rhythm. I leaned back slightly in the saddle, my legs firm against his sides. It felt *incredible.*

'Not canter yet!' Camille barked crossly. '*Putain*, you don't even know how to trot on him and you're asking for canter?'

I threw another glance at the small, fey, angry creature in the centre of the round paddock. I wasn't aware that I'd been asking for anything, but canter felt so good. I didn't ever want to stop cantering on Espiritu.

I banged my nose rather badly on his neck when Camille finally stepped in front of us and I learned that horses can go from 30kmh to zero in less than a second when they have to.

Nina giggled a lot as she helped me mop up the blood when we were sitting at the table in the medieval dining room. Camille had not been interested in my nose bleed. She'd taken advantage of the beautiful, sunny February day and ridden out on Emperador, her flaxen locks shimmering in perfect harmony with his flaxen tail as they'd strolled out of the courtyard.

‘I told you, *Princesse* Nicole! I told you that you would ride Espiritu properly one day!’ Nina leaned towards me, her eyes shining as she shoved another tissue under my nose. ‘You looked very good together!’

I grinned at her as I held the tissue firmly under my nostrils, my eyes still watering. ‘Nina, I was terrible! I’m a terrible rider!’

She did a child-sized Gallic shrug that made me want to gather her up in my arms and cover her with kisses. ‘But it is only the third time that you ride a horse, and you cantered! I’ve never cantered! Camille let me trot on Emperador, but she said it’s too soon for me to learn to canter.’ She paused. ‘And also that he is too big for me.’

I knew what was coming next.

‘Has the *prince* forgiven you, *Princesse* Nicole?’ Her brow furrowed slightly.

I took a deep breath. ‘No, not yet.’

She put her head slightly on one side. Her coffee-coloured skin was so perfect, her pale-green eyes so devoid of subterfuge. ‘Did you do a very bad thing?’ she asked finally.

I removed the tissue from under my nose and looked at it. The nose bleed was finally slowing. I shrugged. ‘He thinks it was very bad. But I did it because I wanted to protect him.’

‘From the dragons?’ she asked, wide-eyed.

I nodded. ‘Yes. One particular dragon.’

Her gaze was intense. ‘Was it very big?’

I nodded again. ‘It was very big. Enormous.’

She blinked at me. ‘But the *prince* is very strong. He could have fought the dragon and won.’

I took a deep breath. ‘Yes, he is very strong. But I was worried that he would be hurt if he fought it. So I didn’t tell him where to find the dragon because I didn’t want him to get hurt.’

She leaned back in her chair and regarded me coolly, swinging her little legs slowly as she did so. Finally she took a deep breath and nodded. ‘Yes,’ she said. ‘I would not want him to become hurt fighting the dragon either.’

I found that tears, snot and blood are really disgusting combined in a tissue, and also, it really *hurts*!

***

I made her an omelette. I thought she would be impressed but she wasn't. 'The *prince* puts some of the orange dust on it and that makes it taste really good.' Her legs were swinging rhythmically back and forth under the table as she ate.

'Do you want me to try and find it?' Thinking, *Wtf is orange dust*?

She smiled. 'No, it's okay. It's okay just with cheese.'

I thought it was pretty bloody marvellous considering that two weeks earlier I would only have been capable of welding mashed egg to the saucepan.

She took a sip of her orange juice and put it carefully back down on the table. 'What about Annie? What's she going to have for her lunch?'

I stared at her, confused. 'Who?'

'Annie,' she said again. She turned to the empty chair on her left and made a little movement with her hand as if to say 'here'.

'Who's Annie, Nina?' I asked.

She frowned. 'She's my friend.'

'Oh, okay.' I nodded slowly. My invisible friend when I was about Nina's age was Julian the rabbit. I remembered Julian, how I would return to the apartment with my pockets stuffed full of leaves and grass for him to eat for his dinner. 'What do you think Annie would like to eat?'

She turned to her left again for a minute then back to me. 'Honey,' she said confidently. 'She likes honey.'

'Just honey?'

She nodded. 'Yes, Annie likes honey. With bread.'

I narrowed my eyes. Nina was very fond of *pain au chocolat*, so I knew she had a sweet tooth. 'Maybe you and Annie can have some honey and bread after you've finished your omelette?'

She blinked at me a few times then turned back to her left. 'Okay,' she said, looking back to me. 'She can wait until then.'

We continued to eat our lunch. When we'd finished, I reached for her plate.

'Annie wants to know, are you a *princesse* because your mama was a queen?' Nina asked suddenly, frowning up at me.

I made a thoughtful face and wrinkled my nose, which made it throb. 'Not really.' The image of a drunken Tiffany in a tiara floated unpleasantly across my mind.

It was becoming increasingly clear that we needed to change the fairy-tale terminology sometime soon. I dreaded to think of her referring to me as a *princesse* at school; even in French I was pretty sure the connotation would be the same.

'Nina,' I said carefully. 'You know, you don't have to call me *princesse* anymore now that we're going to adopt you.'

She looked confused. 'What should I call you then?'

I took a deep breath; I had not fully thought this through. Finally I suggested, 'Uh, just Nicole?'

She was still frowning and she'd stopped swinging her legs. 'But if you are going to become my mama, shouldn't I call you mama? Chloe in my class is adopted and that's what she calls her mama. She told me.'

As I gazed at her, I thought my chest would cave in with love for her. At the same time, I howled inside at the thought that something might prevent her becoming a permanent part of my life.

***

Xavier had done the research. He called me when I was at the supermarket, standing in the aisle staring at the hundreds of ways in which French parents could destroy their children's teeth and health with chocolate spread.

'*Mais* Nicole,' he said, 'if Guy and you are no longer living together, this is going to be a problem. The *demande d'agrément* that you send to the *autorités d'adoption*, this will have all of the information about both of you. It will say that you are married, that you live together. It will give details of your finance, where you live. And they will do all the checks with the police and the local *mairie*. Then, after they have done all the checks, they make you come for the interview with the *puhseek*.'

'The what?' I asked weakly.

'The *puhseek*,' he repeated.

I sighed tiredly. 'What's a *puhseek,* Xavier?'

Slight pause. 'The *puh-syciatriste,'* he said.

The French language is wonderfully arbitrary; words are filled with lots of consonants and vowels that one doesn't pronounce, but then suddenly consonants that would otherwise slip by unobtrusively are categorically required to be pronounced.

‘Thanks for the translation,’ I said glumly. ‘And what if we aren’t living together? What if we’re no longer a couple?’

There was a long pause. ‘You really believe this, Nicole? You really think Guy will not ever come back to you because you don’t tell him what happen?’

I sighed. ‘It’s been over six weeks and he’s still AWOL. I feel like I no longer understand anything about him. I didn’t expect him to do this. If I had, perhaps I might have done things a bit differently.’ I held my breath and waited for the ‘I told you so’ refrain. It didn’t come.

‘*Bah,* Nicole, you do what you believe is right at the time.’

I raised an eyebrow as I stared at the breakfast cereal bars coated in chocolate.

‘I find this difficult to believe, that he will not come back.’ Xavier’s voice was soothing.

I shrugged. ‘Whatever you believe and I believe, what happens if he doesn’t? I have to prepare for the worst, Xavier.’

Long pause. ‘It will be difficult for you to adopt Nina on your own.’

‘How difficult?’

‘*Bah* ... difficult.’

‘Impossible difficult or just difficult difficult?’

There was a smile in his voice when he spoke again. ‘Just difficult difficult, not impossible difficult. And—' A long pause, his voice almost tender. ‘And I will help you. I will help you to go to *les autorités.* I will help you to prepare a dossier for this, so that you can adopt Nina even if Guy is no longer living with you.’

I realised I was smiling too. ‘That would be wonderful, Xavier. I would appreciate that *so* much.’ Relief flooded through me and it felt luxuriously warm.

‘It is not a problem. I will be happy to do this for you, Nicole.’ I could tell that he was still smiling.

And after we’d hung up, I was in such a good mood that I bought a very, very small jar of Nutella for Nina (and Annie, of course, who seemed to be joining us for all her meals now) because – well, Rome, Romans, etc. And all of the French kids I’d seen were delightful and seemed to have the requisite number of teeth. Who was I to argue with local customs?

***

The next time I spoke to Xavier, he was slightly overexcited. 'Can you come to Paris with me, Nicole?'

I ran through the immediate range of smart responses that sprang to mind, starting with 'Business or pleasure?' and then opted for a neutral one. 'Why?'

'I take a call from a colleague in Paris. She have a client that say she is raped by Guillaume three years ago. But she is nervous and she want to speak to you before she bring a charge against Guillaume.' Pause. 'So, can you come to Paris with me, please, Nicole? It is very important. This week?'

I took a deep, triumphant breath, thinking, *Yesssss*! We were *definitely* going to get bastard Satan!

'Of course I can – but only after Wednesday. Nina comes on Wednesday afternoons and we have supper together.'

'*Bah* ... then maybe early on Thursday?'

'How early? Like, stupid o'clock or just normal early?'

He laughed. 'Just normal early. There is a TGV from Bordeaux at 7.15 that gets to Paris around 9.30.'

I frowned. 'That's stupid o'clock. I'd have to leave here at, like, 5.30am because the traffic around Bordeaux is so bloody capricious.'

'*Bah* ... but you can join the train at Angouleme at eight o'clock?'

I paused, calculating that I'd only have to leave the Duchess at 7am. 'That's marginally less stupid o'clock, I suppose.'

'I book the TGV for us. And I speak to my colleague to make the meeting with her client on Thursday morning, okay?'

'Okay, great. Thank you, Xavier, that would be brilliant.'

I gazed out of the bedroom window at the bare poplar trees at the end of the lawn and the naked forest beyond them. I was sure that I could see the faintest peppermint-green hue on the otherwise dull branches because, even though it was only late February, winter was finally starting to recede and spring was waiting in the wings, poised to tiptoe onto the stage.

It had been fifteen degrees Celsius that morning, more in the afternoon sunshine. As I sat on the front step of the Duchess, I pulled up the sleeves of my long-sleeved top to expose my forearms and closed my eyes as I basked in the sun's warmth.

It was nearly two years since I'd sat on that same step for the first time, a time when everything about my new life with D'Artagnan in France was so much more innocent, so much less complicated.

I had leaned back against his legs as he stood behind me and he'd asked, 'Happy, *mon amour*?'

I had squinted up at him, nodded and said, 'Yes, I really am.'

And his smile was so soft as he'd reached down and stroked my cheek gently with his thumb. 'Me too, *mon ange.*'

***

Xavier and I were standing in the foyer of the hotel in Paris. When the lift arrived and the doors opened, he motioned to me to enter ahead of him. Neither of us spoke as it ascended. I studied the surprisingly ornate ceiling and he studied the floor. When I sneaked a glance at him as the doors opened, I saw a slight frown creasing his forehead.

I gave him a quick smile as he caught my eye. 'I'm in 301,' I said.

He shrugged almost apologetically. 'I'm in 302.'

We walked down the corridor together. Was the tension palpable? Yes, it was. I always imagine the world 'palpable' to be like sitting on a hot-air balloon when it's laying on the ground filling with hot air, while simultaneously trying to stop it filling with hot air.

I was trying to push away all of that palpable tension as I reached the door of my room. I stopped and raised my eyes to his. They were soft and grey and long-lashed in that sculpted, Michelangelo face that was now darkened with stubble around his pale-rose mouth.

'Goodnight, Xavier. Thanks so much for a lovely dinner.' I leaned forward and placed my fingers very lightly on his shoulders. They felt muscular beneath my hesitant touch. Bleu de Chanel enveloped my senses as I brushed my lips against his cheeks.

His lips on my cheeks felt incredibly warm, almost hot. His hands were firm but gentle on my upper arms. '*Bonne nuit,* Nicole.' His voice was very low.

Even though I knew I shouldn't, I raised my head and looked into his eyes. He returned my gaze with the same intensity.

Neither of us could mistake it. I looked down again quickly and turned away. 'Tomorrow at nine, then?'

He paused for a minute and then said, 'Okay. We have a breakfast together?'

I nodded. 'Sure. I'll meet you in the foyer.' I opened the door to my room and went inside. '*Bonne nuit*, Xavier.'

'*Bonne nuit*, Nicole.'

We exchanged another fleeting glance loaded with tension before I shut the door behind me. I leaned against it for a long time afterwards, focussing all my thoughts on D'Artagnan. I summoned all of the images of D'Artagnan and his beautiful brown eyes, his strong, muscular body, his inquisitive fingers, his insistent mouth. How robust he had looked as he'd crossed the courtyard with Nina on his shoulders the previous autumn, how she'd giggled uncontrollably as she'd placed her little hands over his eyes and he'd pretended to be blind. How soft his gaze had been when he told me that he'd already started the procedure to adopt Nina even though I hadn't yet dared to ask if it was possible.

I thought about how liquid with desire his eyes were when, after an exquisite eternity, he was finally deep inside me. I thought about the waves of ecstasy that radiated through my body when he thrust again and again, wrenching a primeval cry from my very core, and I focussed on remembering that euphoric sensation.

I kept my eyes closed as I leaned against that hotel door and I replayed all of those images in my mind in order to banish the thought of Xavier, alone in the room next door to mine.

***

We had not planned to stay overnight in Paris but the meeting with Elodie on Thursday morning had been postponed at the last minute. We were already at her lawyer's office when she took the call from her client. After she hung up, she explained apologetically that Elodie's daughter had fallen ill and she had to stay at home to look after her. Elodie could meet with us the following morning instead, when she'd been able to arrange childcare.

Xavier turned to me. 'What do you want to do, Nicole? Do you want to wait until tomorrow?'

I bit my lip. 'Yes – if you can. I think it's really important that we meet with her, don't you? Can you stay until tomorrow?'

He nodded. 'Yes. I can do some work while I am here. It is not a problem.' Pause. 'We will have to book a hotel.'

Paris at the end of February is busy, but it's not heaving with tourists like it is in spring and summer. We found a hotel near to the lawyer's offices in the sixteenth *arrondissement*.

We stood together in the foyer after we'd reserved rooms for that night. 'Will you like to get some lunch, maybe?' Xavier asked hesitantly.

I smiled at him. 'I'd love to.'

'Do you want to walk a bit? There is a very good vegetarian restaurant that I know in Montmartre – or we can take the metro if you don't want to walk.'

I tucked my hair behind my ears. 'Xavier, it's such a lovely day and we're in the most beautiful city in the world. I'd love to walk.'

And so we did.

We walked in the surprisingly warm February sunshine all the way from the *seizième* to the *dix-huitième.* Along the way, we talked about the eight years he'd spent working in Paris as a criminal lawyer. We talked about the spectacular Monets in the Musée d'Orsay, and we talked about the drug problems and the social problems in the city's outer suburbs. Then we talked about his childhood in Agen in south-west France and he told me about his family.

It was one of the best lunches I'd ever had, and I think Xavier was pleasantly surprised at how much he enjoyed the food too. We shared a bottle of wine and afterwards we stopped on the pavement outside Pigalle metro.

'I have to go and buy some knickers,' I said, feeling pleasantly warm and surprisingly happy to have found myself in my other favourite French city on a sunny February day. 'I thought I'd take the metro to Opéra, go to my favourite shop in the whole world and do some shopping.'

I could see him processing 'knickers' then figuring it out. He grinned. 'Okay. I buy some knicker too. But maybe I just buy some near to the hotel.' He gazed at me very steadily, his head slightly on one side.

I had not yet said anything about his new glasses. They were frameless and they really suited him. The lenses were reactive so they darkened in the sunshine. It was impossible not to acknowledge that Xavier had undergone a full dull, country librarian to sexy metropolitan lawyer transformation since the beginning of the year. I didn't want to remark on it because I didn't want him to think that I cared only about physical appearance.

'Will you like to have dinner tonight with me?' he asked.

I pursed my mouth tightly as I held in a smile, thinking, *Why is this happening? Why, God, why are you tempting me*? Even so, I nodded. 'That would be lovely. Will you choose the restaurant? Because lunch was brilliant. I loved it.'

He nodded. 'Of course. I will think about this.' And then he leaned in and we exchanged kisses, and I touched his shoulder and he touched mine. 'I meet you downstairs in the hotel at 7.30?'

I nodded. 'Bye, Xavier.'

'*A plus*, Nicole.'

I sat on the metro as it rattled and clattered along beneath Paris and I thought, *D'Artagnan would not be comfortable with this.* But then I thought, *Well, if he hadn't buggered off in a massive tantrum, he'd be here with me in Paris and I wouldn't have to be wondering whether having dinner with my tall, gorgeous lawyer in the most romantic city in the world was appropriate.*

I went to Printemps Haussmann – my favourite shop in the whole world – and spent the rest of the afternoon trying on twenty-five different outfits because the shop assistant kept suggesting new ones. She had a great sense of humour and we bonded immediately, but I was very good and only bought one new dress. One new dress and a divine silk scarf to go with it. And I bought Nina a dress too, and I bought emergency knickers, tights and cosmetics.

I stood in front of the mirror before going down to meet Xavier and wondered whether the dress was too much. It was a figure-hugging, off-the-shoulder Missoni in shades of blue with metallic highlights, and it showed rather a lot of *décolleté.* I had hesitated before buying it, wondering if it was an extravagant purchase that I would regret should I find myself divorced in the near future, but then I thought fuck it. It was ages since I'd bought anything lovely and it went well with my boots. I smiled at myself in the mirror. The dress was gorgeous and I looked great in it.

I took a deep breath, wrapped the soft, creamy scarf around my throat several times and put on my coat.

'You left,' I said out loud to D'Artagnan, who was lurking behind me disapprovingly in the shadows. 'You left, and you're not speaking to me, so I don't see why I shouldn't enjoy dinner in Paris with my friend and lawyer. Suck it up, sunshine!'

I held my head high as I walked down the corridor towards the lift and allowed myself to feel happy and light-hearted and not at all guilty.

***

Elodie was one of those exquisitely beautiful black women with high cheekbones, doe-shaped eyes and silky, dark-caramel skin. Everything about her was precise, elegant, perfect. And she was a research scientist who spoke three languages fluently. It was hard not to feel intimidated by her.

It was also hard not to cry when she cried – though she did it delicately without smudging her mascara – as she told us what Satan had done to her. I wanted to kill him by the time she'd finished. She explained that initially she had gone to the police but the reception had been hostile. The implication was that since she'd been in a bar and agreed to have a drink with someone, she'd automatically waived her right to consent to sex. Their scorn was so obvious that she'd decided not to pursue any action.

'But my daughter is five now. When I look at her, I think that I don't want what happened to me to happen to her. When I read that Guillaume has been charged with rape, I knew I had to come forward.' She gave a sad little smile. 'So thank you, Nicole, for being so brave and for giving me the courage to do this.'

I held her hand tightly. 'You don't have to thank me, Elodie. We all have different ways of dealing with the bastards we come across in life. I'm just so grateful that you've decided to join the court case.'

She paused. 'There is one more thing, though.' She looked away from me. 'He told me afterwards that he took a video of this and that he will sell the video to the—' her voice was very quiet, almost a whisper '—to the pornography sites if I ever say anything.'

I rubbed my forehead with my fingers and closed my eyes, thinking, *Oh you fucking bastard. I'm going to get you. We're going to get you.*

'Yes,' said Xavier softly. 'This is what he do with Léa, too. But worse.' He told Elodie what Satan had forced Léa to do and tears started running down her face again.

Her hand covered her mouth. 'Oh! he is such a bastard!' she finally exclaimed. 'In that case I don't care about the threat. I am not going to let him carry on doing this. Nicole, Xavier, we have to stop him doing this.'

I nodded. 'We are going to stop him, Elodie,' I said firmly. 'He's already in custody, and the more of us that come forward, the longer he'll be locked up for.'

'And I will add blackmail to the charges you are bringing against him,' said Elodie's lawyer. 'Sometimes that can be enough to make someone think carefully about releasing the video because blackmail is also a serious crime.'

Elodie looked glum. 'I know this shaming of women has happened to others, that it often happens now on social media. But I'm not going to keep quiet any longer.' Her eyes were shining with tears but narrowed, resolute. 'We are going to get him, Nicole. We are going to get this man locked up for a very, very long time.'

I couldn't stop a wide smile spreading across my face. When we parted company later that morning, we hugged tightly. I felt so happy and so proud that there were women like Elodie and Léa in the world, women who were prepared to fight back even when there was so much at stake.

All that was at stake for me was that D'Artagnan might never forgive me. But although the thought of that hurt, I knew it could ultimately become bearable.

***

Because D'Artagnan still refused to be contacted. 'I'm worried about him,' Françoise said when we spoke on the phone in early March. 'No one has heard anything at all, Nicole. What if something has happened to him?'

I was watching Espiritu and Emperador playing tag in the paddock. 'Nothing has happened to him, Françoise.'

I heard the frown in her voice. 'How do you know, Nicole?'

I told her about the conference call Xavier and I had had with Francesca and her muzzled rottweilers a week earlier. Francesca had set the rottweilers onto the lawyers for the property development joint venture, the first phase of which was finished and was shortly being put up for sale.

D'Artagnan had already reserved one of the apartments for us. During our call Francesca had let something slip. '...Guy assures me that he still wants the apartment.' She had quickly corrected herself. 'The lawyers assure me that Guy has reserved the apartment.' So I knew that Francesca had been in touch with D'Artagnan recently.

Françoise sounded relieved. 'So he is just behaving like a child, Nicole.'

I didn't say anything. The late evening sun caught the end of Emperador's flaxen tail and made it shine like gold. His neck snaked out as I watched and he took a big bite of Espiritu's butt. Even through the double-glazed windows I heard Espiritu's squeal of outrage before he gave a huge buck and one of his hooves narrowly missed Emperador's golden head. Despite my mood, it made me smile.

'He'll get over it soon, you'll see,' Françoise said comfortingly. 'I'm sure he'll realise he's behaving stupidly and he'll come back, Nicole. Don't worry about that.'

I wasn't sure that I believed that anymore.

***

I stared at the letter and tried desperately to comprehend what it said. I knew it was from the adoption agency, but my heart was beating so fast and I was so nervous that I couldn't focus. I could see that they wanted me to do something but I couldn't understand what. There was also a date in early-June in bold print when something was going to happen but I couldn't work out what that was all about, either.

My phone rang while I was staring at it. I was relieved to see it was Xavier; I could send him a photo of the letter and he'd tell me what it said. 'Hi Xavier.' Even I was aware of the smile in my voice.

'Nicole.' His voice was terse.

I frowned. 'What's wrong?'

'We have a problem.'

'What do you mean?'

Pause. 'Is it possible, Nicole, that you forget to tell the *juge d'instruction* something when we meet with her in February?'

'Forget what, Xavier? I told her everything that happened. You were there, you heard me. It was everything we'd discussed, everything in my statement. Why do you think I forgot something?'

A deep intake of breath. 'When the *juge* ask you about the drugs you take, you tell her you don't take any more drugs. But now Guillaume have a witness who say you take a very strong drug, an opiate drug, last year. That you beg her to give you this drug, that you are addicted to this drug and that you make everything up about Guillaume because you are—' he hesitated '—because you are a drug addict.' His voice was very subdued.

I think I stopped breathing. I was standing in the salon, looking towards the trees at the end of the lawn. Today their tips were gilded with sunlight because it was a beautiful morning on one of the best days of the week, Wednesday.

'Nicole?' His voice was solemn. 'Can you answer me, please?'

'Xavier,' I said finally. 'I'm not a drug addict – and I know who the witness is. It's Annabelle.' Now that I thought about it, I should have known that Annabelle was one of Satan's minions. She'd had his bastard cloven hoofprints all over her.

A long pause. 'But you took these drugs last year, Nicole? When you say you confront Guillaume?'

I carried on staring out of the window. 'Yes, Xavier. I did take oxycodone for a while last summer, but I can explain why. And I stopped taking it in July last year and I haven't taken any drugs since then.'

There was a very long pause. When he finally spoke, Xavier's voice was low and sombre. 'Nicole, we need to speak urgently. I need to understand this because I must respond to the *juge* very quickly. Please can you come to Bordeaux? You must come to my office now, today. I need to make a new statement for you.'

I frowned. Wednesday was *our* day; Nina was coming and the sun was shining and we were spending the afternoon with Camille and the horses. We had both been looking forward to it because it had rained all weekend, and it had rained the previous Wednesday. So I thought: *No, I'm not going to do that.*

'No, Xavier, I can't come to Bordeaux today. Nina is coming here and I'm not going to let her down. Why can't we do it now, over the phone? I can tell you everything and you can prepare the new statement and submit it.'

Another very long pause. I could hear him breathing down the phone. 'Nicole, this is very serious. Now I worry that the case is in danger.' His voice was hesitant. 'I need you to explain to me very ... *bah* ... clearly about this other drug problem that you have because I did not know about this. And then we need to prepare a statement that will ... *merde*, what is the word? *Mitige...*?'

'Mitigate?'

'*Oui, c'est ça.* The statement need to mitigate the problem, Nicole.' A short pause. 'The *juge* does not trust you now because you have lied to her. And Guillaume's witness is saying many bad things about you.'

I sighed deeply. Suddenly I felt so tired, so tired of myself and my phenomenal success at fucking up so much of my life so easily and with such gay abandon. 'What about you, Xavier? Do you still trust me?' I already felt detached, already assumed he no longer trusted me and that our professional relationship was probably over.

I was surprised at his quick response. He didn't even hesitate. 'Yes, Nicole, I still trust you.'

Tears pricked my eyes. 'Really? But you said the *juge* doesn't believe me now, so why do you?'

His voice was gentler when he spoke. 'You make a mistake, Nicole. You should have told me about this and you should have told the *juge* also.' I heard him take a deep breath. 'But you are not the first person who make a mistake. Although it is very bad to lie to the *juge*, we can explain carefully why you lie to her and why this is not affecting the case against Guillaume.'

I wiped away a tear.

'It's okay, do not worry about this. I trust you Nicole. I am ... *bah*, committed to you.' His voice was tender but then, as if he had recognised that tenderness, he suddenly became business-like again. 'But we need to prepare a very good statement together. We need to work hard to prepare this statement because we need to send it to the *juge* tomorrow morning.'

'I can come down to Bordeaux after about seven o'clock this evening, after I've made Nina dinner and taken her home. I can be at your office at 8.15, 8.30 maybe?'

I heard him turning pages. 'No, it's okay. I come to you. I will drive to you. I can leave my office at 3.30 so I will be there by 4.30 – maybe five o'clock. Then we can work to prepare the statement and it will not be very late. Otherwise you will be driving back very late and I don't—' He hesitated. 'I will worry if you drive back from Bordeaux all the way to Cognac by yourself in the night. It is not safe to be driving so late, so I come to you. Okay, Nicole?'

I tried not to think about the fact that he was worrying about my safety. 'Thank you. I really, really appreciate it, Xavier.'

A slight pause. 'It is no problem, Nicole. I am your lawyer.' I knew he was smiling. 'You can make me dinner, too, Nicole. And I can meet Nina. We have dinner together, the three of us.'

That made *me* smile but it was a weird smile, kind of pleased, kind of horrified. The three of us having dinner together like a family? In the château? While D'Artagnan was missing? What would the Duchess think?

I suddenly remembered. 'Oh, speaking of Nina reminds me – I got a letter today. I mean, there was a letter addressed to us from the adoption agency and I don't understand it. I need you to read it and tell me what it says, if that's okay?'

'Of course I can do this. I will explain it to you when I am there. *Donc, à plus tard*, Nicole. I will be there at about five o'clock.'

'Great. See you then.' And I *just* managed to stop myself saying '*bisous*' because that's how all calls end in French: with kisses. Bérengère and I said, '*Grosses bises*'; Françoise said, '*Je t'embrasse, bisous*'; and D'Artagnan breathed, '*bises pleines d'amour, mon ange*'.

But it probably wasn't appropriate to say '*bisous*' to Xavier even though it now seemed perfectly natural.

***

The sun was low in the sky but it was still bright when Xavier arrived. It was one of those perfect, early spring days: azure sky, Van Gogh yellow sun, no wind. I heard his car pull up and I went around the side of the château to meet him with Nina skipping along beside me, her small hand in mine.

That day I had done a shaky, wobbly, rising trot on Espiritu's back, and then Camille had told me how to ask for a canter. I'd cantered around the paddock and felt like I was flying, like I was in a fairy tale. Afterwards Camille had ridden him with Nina sitting between her arms in front of her. Nina grinned when Espiritu changed gait into a canter, and it was as if a thousand candles had been lit inside her. Watching them both, I had decided: I was going to buy my daughter a pony, one that was the perfect size for her, so that she could canter on her own.

Xavier had just rapped the Duchess's heavy front-door knocker and was standing back on the terrace gazing up at her. At first, he didn't see us.

As I walked towards him with Nina's hand in mine, I allowed myself a moment to appraise him, his tall, athletic frame, his dark curly hair that was just a little long. I loved the way that disobedient lock slipped over his forehead and hung into his eyes, and I often felt an urge to lean forward and brush it back.

As he became aware of us, he turned and gave the loveliest smile, his grey eyes bright with light from the evening sun.

'Xavier! *Bonjour*, *bienvenue*!' We exchanged kisses, and I inhaled his scent and felt the gentle pressure from his hands on my shoulders. I was aware that I couldn't stop smiling at him, that he was smiling back at me.

I glanced away quickly and turned to Nina. 'And this is my little girl, Nina. Nina this is Xavier.'

Nina reached out her hand solemnly and he bent down, took it and shook it very gently. '*Enchanté,* Nina,' he said courteously.

She regarded him solemnly before giving him a little smile. 'Bonjour, Monsieur Xavier,' she replied. She turned to me. 'Did the *prince* send him?' she asked.

I started laughing, then stopped abruptly because it would be waaaaaay too complicated to explain that no, the *prince* had definitely *not* sent Xavier. It would also be complicated to explain to Xavier that Guy had yet another nickname, that he was the *prince* to Nina. I knew that by now the *prince* would probably be quite uncomfortable about Xavier and, more importantly, about the way the *princesse* was feeling about Xavier.

But the *prince* wasn't in his castle. He had left the *princesse* all alone to fight the dragon, aided only by loyal, devoted and very attractive Sir Galahad.

Was it possible I was becoming a bit … *bah*, angry about that?

***

We had mushroom omelette (passable) and bread and cheese for dinner, and fruit yoghurt for dessert. Afterwards, Xavier and I walked Nina back to Marion and Thierry's house. When we returned, we sat side by side at the table in the dining hall sipping a very good 2010 Margaux that I'd fetched up from the cellar. I was careful as I walked down the slightly green, slightly slippery steps into the cellar, the stairs down which the Duchess had once contrived to make me fall, because I had a feeling that this particular evening she would very much like me to fall again.

Xavier read the letter addressed to Guy and me from the adoption agency and explained that it wanted us to confirm that our *situation familiale* hadn't changed since we'd submitted the formal adoption demand in December. The date in bold in mid-June was the date of the interview with the *puh-sychiatriste* to decide whether we would be suitable parents.

I stared at him, my heart beating fast. I was both thrilled and terrified to think that Guy and I now had an actual date. Xavier was watching me closely. 'How long do I have to reply to the letter?' I asked.

'Fourteen days.'

I nodded slowly. I knew what I had to do. 'Thank you for explaining it to me.'

He handed the letter back to me with a slightly quizzical look on his face.

I put it to one side, took a sip of my wine and turned back to him. 'Right, let's get to work on the statement, Xavier. Let's do what you came all this way to do.'

He sat back in his chair and watched me, his head slightly tilted, as I explained why I'd started taking oxycodone the previous summer. I told him how horrified I'd been when I found out it was Guillaume, whom I'd disliked from the very moment

I'd set eyes on him, who had raped me all those years ago. How, having realised that I couldn't say anything about it without causing D'Artagnan to do something potentially life-changingly stupid, I had decided to keep the knowledge to myself. But keeping that secret was very difficult, and the only way I knew how to keep it was to numb myself with drugs.

When Annabelle offered me oxycodone, ostensibly to dull the – psychosomatic – back pain I was suffering, I grabbed it with both hands. I explained that at first it did what I needed it to do. At first the knowledge was dulled adequately, but then so was everything else. I was permanently stoned. I started forgetting things, I stopped eating, stopped being interested in sex or in anything really, and gradually that became unbearable. So, I womanned up. I decided that I wasn't going to let Satan get away with it, that I was going to protect other women from him, to protect the child who would become my daughter from men like him. And once I'd figured out how to bring Satan down without Guy's knowledge, I stopped taking oxycodone. I knew that I would never take drugs again; I was going to be a mother and drugs were no longer a part of my life.

When he'd written and rewritten the statement so many times that the paper looked like a blur of blue ballpoint, Xavier typed it laboriously into his laptop. I watched him, the lock of hair brushing against his glasses as he typed, frowning with concentration. Stubble was now at midnight o'clock but it suited him; it added that necessary dose of masculinity around his full-lipped mouth.

He stood up when he'd finished and gave a big yawn as he stretched. His shirt was now unbuttoned far enough for me to see that the dark curls on his head started again below his throat. It was completely untucked at the waist and there was dark hair there too, just above his belt. I caught a glimpse of it as he stretched.

He looked at his watch and I looked at mine. It was just after 10pm. 'Coffee?' I asked.

He smiled at me tiredly and nodded. '*S'il te plaît*, Nicole.'

We sipped our coffee while he read the statement to me slowly, making some adjustments along the way. Then Xavier read it to me a second time and translated the text whenever he thought I might not fully understand it. He made a few corrections on the screen and then finally he was happy with it.

He let out a deep breath. 'I need to print this now, Nicole, and you need to sign it.'

'The printer's in the library. This way.' I led him through the salon.

There was a full moon, and bright silver light was streaming in through the windows and bouncing off the silky oak floorboards. I led him into the library at the far end of the château and turned on the small lamp on the ancient, green-leather-topped desk. I turned on the printer and he spent some time fiddling with his laptop to connect it. The printer started whirring and gradually spat out the statement.

Xavier read it through one final time then placed the two pages side by side on the desk under the lamplight and held out his pen. 'Now you need to initial and sign it, Nicole.'

I leaned over to initial the first page where he indicated, then the second page. When I stood up again and turned, I was suddenly aware that we were very close, suddenly aware that his body was radiating warmth next to mine. I was aware of the heat, his *presence,* only a hand's breadth away.

The room was in shadow; the light from the lamp on the desk was angled down and the moonlight was behind us, streaming in through the window.

When I examined it later, it seemed as if I spent ages gazing into his grey eyes before he reached out and touched my face so, so gently. Before I put my hand on his waist and felt his firm body beneath his shirt. Before his lips touched mine and we were kissing, a long, deeply sensuous kiss. His arms slid around my body, gradually tightening around me, holding me firmly against him. It was a kiss that made me feel as if I were dissolving.

And his supple, athletic body? I wanted to dive into his body and drown in it.

Chapter Five

I clung to him in the lift on the way up to his apartment. I wanted him so much that I climbed him, into him, onto him, and he anchored me, his hands under me, my legs locked around his hips, our mouths sealed together.

And when the lift stopped and we finally made it through the door of his apartment, by then we were both deranged, insane with desire. I slid off him and he pushed me back against the wall, peeled down his wetsuit and pulled me against him. He was hard, fully erect. I fumbled with the zip on my jeans, desperate to feel him inside me, craving him like I craved oxygen.

He pulled my jeans down roughly, urgently, as we locked eyes and then he blinked that slow, sensuous blink. I knew there wasn't time to take off my boots, my jeans, so I just turned around, every cell in my body aching for him. He swept all the objects off the console table – a vase, a jar of pens, a book, something metal. They clattered onto the floor as he pushed me over the table, his strong hands on my hips positioning me exactly as he wanted me, as he needed me, as I needed him.

And then ... *ecstasy*. He was still cool from the Atlantic Ocean as he slid into me like hard marble. He fucked me so slowly that I lost the use of my voice. I gasped, but it was a silent gasp because I was nothing except the feeling of him inside me, so hard, so deep that I flinched. He had never felt this deep before.

He stopped and withdrew a little, his voice hoarse. 'Am I hurting you, *mon amour*? Do you want me to stop?'

I managed to gasp, 'No, don't stop. Never stop, my angel. I need you ... like that, so deep.'

And then he groaned an intense, savage groan. His voice was raw, hoarse. '*Fuck*, Nicole, *je t'aime, je t'aime,* ' and then he thrust again, so full, so hard, harder again, and as I started to come, he lifted my pelvis. One of his palms was on the small of my back, the other directly underneath me, the heel of his hand hard against my pubis as he served my body up into his. He held me still in his hands as I orgasmed and, as he pulsed inside me he roared, like a lion.

D'Artagnan roared like a lion.

***

Because I did not dive into Xavier; I did not drown in Xavier's body, even though the temptation was strong. I disengaged my mouth from his and I put my fingers firmly against his lips. The stubble on his chin was rough on my palm as I made space between us, between our mouths. I placed my hand flat against his warm, hard chest and I pushed my body away from his. The effort of doing so made my eyes heavy because I really, really didn't want to but I knew I had to.

'No, Xavier. We have to stop. I can't do this.' But my heart was beating fast and the warmth inside me betrayed me. But I knew that if I did this, D'Artagnan and I really would be no more. It would end everything between us and, as much as I really, *really* wanted Xavier in that moment, I wasn't ready to do that.

So I pushed myself away from Xavier, who was leaning against the ancient desk in the moonlit library, and I gazed into his eyes that were limpid with desire under his long, thick eyelashes. With his dark, curly hair framing his classical features, he looked like a young Roman emperor.

I shook my head very gently. 'I can't... Xavier, I can't do this, not now. I want to, but if I do it will change everything. I still love Guy. I love my husband. I love him very much.'

Xavier didn't say anything, just gazed at me, his hands gently on my waist. I was conscious of the slight pressure of his long fingers as he held me, conscious that I wanted that pressure to increase, and conscious that it must not be encouraged to increase.

We exchanged a full, frank gaze during which I tried very hard not to imagine what sex with Xavier would be like. I collected all of the images of sex with Xavier that had been flashing through my mind over the last couple of weeks and I bundled them in a tight ball. I shoved them into a velvet bag with a silk drawstring, drew the string tight and tied a knot in it. Then I pushed the bag into the back of a deep drawer in a dark recess of my mind.

Xavier is smart and sensitive; he knew that I meant what I said. He gave a little nod and a small shrug. 'It's okay. I understand.' He held my gaze 'But Nicole, you must know this.

If he cannot – if Guy will not come back to you, you know that I am here for you. I am in love with you, Nicole, and I think you are a bit in love with me, too. I think we would be happy together. We could adopt Nina together, and maybe we could also have our own children. We could have the future we both want.'

He slipped his long, elegant hands around my face, leaned forward and kissed my forehead lingeringly. 'I am always here for you, Nicole. Do not forget this, okay?' he whispered.

'I will never forget it, Xavier.' As we held each other tightly and I felt the solid but sleek shape of his body, a body somewhere between Karl's and Guy's, I realised that Xavier was the physical embodiment of the two great loves of my life: Karl, slender, feline, androgynous; Guy, robust, solid, masculine.

But while Karl no longer occupied my thoughts, D'Artagnan was very much in them. I still loved him.

***

Xavier drove off as I stood at the front door, shivering slightly. Although it wasn't warm out, the clear sky was so high, so full of the universe that it felt as if winter were finally ending and spring was beginning.

***

After Xavier left I phoned Francesca. She knew where D'Artagnan was. It was 11.35pm and her phone went to voicemail. I hung up and pressed dial again. It went to voicemail. On the third attempt, she answered. 'Nicole?'

'Francesca.'

'Why are you calling me?'

I paused even though I knew I didn't have very much time; Francesca's attention span is very short, especially when talking to the estranged wives of her business partners. 'Francesca. I know that you know where Guy is. Please tell me, because I need to speak to him.'

Can one *hear* an eyebrow being raised over the phone? I swear I heard hers.

'He did not say he wanted to speak to you, Nicole.'

'Did you ask him if he wanted to speak to me?'

A pause. 'No, I didn't ask him that.'

'Did *he* call *you*, Francesca?'

Another pause, longer this time. 'No. He didn't call me.'

'So how did you find him? How did you speak to him?' This time I distinctly heard the ice cubes as she swirled them around the glass of whatever she was drinking. Freshly-squeezed cobra blood, probably.

A sigh. 'I have people who find people that I need to find. So I found Guy. I don't like to not have contact with my business partner. It annoys me.'

'Well, I'd be really grateful if you could tell me where he is, Francesca, because I need to speak to him urgently.' I made sure my voice was polite: firm, but polite.

The ball landing squarely in her court made a soft, chalky sound.

'Why do you need to know, Nicole? If Guy wants you to know where he is, I am sure he will contact you.' A sip. Those perfect white teeth stained by cobra blood in an evil, bloody smirk. I could see it in my mind's eye.

I took a deep breath. 'Well, here's the thing, Francesca. Guy and I have begun a formal process to adopt Nina. I'm not going to go into any detail about Nina because I'm sure you'll be profoundly bored by the idea that adopting a seven-year-old child is something desirable, but it's all I've ever wanted. I love Nina very much, so much that even if Guy never wants to speak to me or to see me again, I still want to adopt her.'

I paused, aware that the Duchess was gradually materialising on the sofa opposite mine, the one I'd recently had upholstered in pale-gold silk randomly scattered with tiny rose-gold flowers. Her body wasn't quite solid so I could see the pattern through her as she lay on the sofa, but she seemed more real, more tangible than she'd ever been.

She was leaning on her hand, her bent elbow on one of the dusky-pink scatter cushions, watching me. There seemed to be two bees buzzing lazily around her, big, fat-bottomed, furry black-and-yellow bees that I'd never seen before. Then again, I'd never seen the Duchess so vividly before in the two years since I'd arrived at the château.

I observed her with a detached interest.

'But I must know if I need to amend the adoption papers to exclude Guy from the procedure because I now have a date for the formal interview. And if Guy no longer wants to adopt Nina

– if Guy doesn't want to be married to me – I need to know that now so that I can be completely honest with the adoption agency. Because I have to sign a declaration saying that nothing has changed since we began the procedure, and I don't know the answer to that. The only person who can tell me is Guy, so that's why I need to speak to him.'

I paused again and gazed at the Duchess. She wasn't wearing the preposterous wig I'd always assumed she wore; her hair was swept up in a slightly untidy arrangement on top of her head. She was wearing a pale dress that was quite modest, and her cheeks weren't overly rouged. I realised that she was actually quite beautiful. Her eyes were narrowed as she watched me. I couldn't quite fathom her mood but I knew it wasn't hostile.

I turned away from her and looked out of the tall window closest to me. The night sky was lit by the full moon and sparkling with stars, stars in other galaxies where other Nicoles pleaded with other Francescas to take pity on them, to empathise.

Francesca took a deep breath then she said, 'Guy is in San Sebastian, Nicole. He has rented an apartment near the beach. According to my sources, he is spending a lot of time surfing. That is all that I can tell you.'

I exhaled an enormous, exhausted breath. It was more than a breath, it was an accumulation of all of the breaths I'd been holding onto for so long: the breath when Guy left; the breaths when Nina asked where he was; the breaths when I saw the confusion in her eyes; the breath when I stopped myself from diving into Xavier and his firm body and the unconditional, uncomplicated love that he offered. All of that was in the breath I exhaled.

'Thank you, Francesca. Thank you for telling me that.'

'I wish you luck, Nicole.' She paused and her voice sounded almost kind. 'Guy is very – *bah*, depressed. I have never known him to be like this and I have known him for more than thirty years. I don't know whether you can fix this – but I hope you can.'

Although my heart shrivelled a little when she said that, I also felt elated. I knew where he was now. I knew where to find D'Artagnan.

***

I walked along the promenade in San Sebastian. It was very early, around seven o'clock in the morning and, although it was still dark, dawn was breathing light into the dark horizon. It was the twenty-first of March, the first day of spring. The season of new life.

Before I'd left the car, I'd drunk the last of the coffee in the flask I'd brought with me. My hands were shoved deep in the pockets of my fake-Patagonia coat, my scarf was wrapped so thickly around my neck that it was almost mummifying me, and I was wearing my fleece-lined woolly hat.

I walked along the curve of the bay, gazing out to sea, looking for surfers. I couldn't see any. At the very end of the bay I turned and walked back along the sweeping promenade. There was a smaller bay on the other side of the bridge that bisected the city. The waves were bigger there, and I could see two or three surfers far out in the water.

The sky was leaden and heavy as dawn broke. There was a cold wind and the air was damp, either with a light drizzle or spray from the sea, I couldn't tell. I stood and watched the surfers as the sky gradually lightened. The sullen grey clouds remained and the waves crashed relentlessly on the shore; further out they were quite big, their white foam brilliant against the dark water.

I leaned against the parapet overlooking the bay and tried to stop myself shivering. I knew I wasn't shivering because I was cold, I was shivering with the knowledge that D'Artagnan was here in San Sebastian. And while I watched the three wet-suited surfers, I gradually realised that he was the one on the right.

I don't know how I recognised him because I'd never watched him surfing closely before, but that surfer had an elegance about him. It was the same easy elegance that D'Artagnan had when he walked across a square towards me, the same subtle elegance when he leaned down and slipped a hand gently around my jaw, tilted my face and kissed me. He had that elegance on a surfboard a hundred metres out to sea. I knew it was him.

I leaned against the sea wall, watching him balance and re-balance his body as he piloted his surfboard expertly into the froth then lay down on it and paddled out again, waiting for the next wave.

Eventually he decided to come in. He lay on his board, paddled into the shallows and lifted himself off it. He walked out of the water with his board under his arm and, as he walked up the beach towards me, he unzipped his wet suit to the waist. He was leaner, more muscular. His body wasn't covered by that layer of good-living that he normally wore, and his beard and hair were long, longer than I'd ever seen, and unkempt. He ran his hand through his wet hair as he walked up the beach and blew sea-water snot out violently through the right and then through the left nostril.

He hadn't seen me. He stopped at the bottom of the stairs leading up from the beach, bent down and unstrapped his board from his ankle. He stood up again, and that was when he saw me. He looked up, straight into my eyes. He didn't move. He didn't smile. He just stared at me.

I stared back at him. His face was gaunt – tanned but gaunt. It wasn't the same shape I remembered, but there was no mistaking that it was the face of the man I loved.

That moment as we stared at each other seemed to go on forever. I was shaking from head to toe with fear that he would turn away, that he would reject me.

Finally, the moment ended when he blinked that slow, sensuous blink over those incredible brown eyes. It was an intensely carnal blink, a long, luxurious lick of his eyes.

And then he took the stairs up from the beach two, three, at a time and I threw myself into him and he wrapped his arms around me, absorbed me into his body. I felt as if my heart were going to explode. The feel of his arms around me, his body against mine; it was so right.

***

After we'd been consumed, poleaxed by that orgasm, we collapsed in the hallway next to the console table. Guy's wetsuit was still around his knees, my jeans around mine. He held me in his lap, and I leaned into his luscious mouth. His beard still wet with the sea as I kissed him. 'I missed you so, so much my darling,' I whispered softly.

'I miss you too, Nicole.' He brushed back my hair from my face and his thumb caressed my cheek.

I gazed into his eyes. 'I'm so sorry, my darling, that I didn't tell you but you have to understand—' I began.

His brow creased. He closed his eyes and turned his head away. 'Nicole, please. I don't want to talk about this now.'

I frowned too. 'But Guy—'

He sighed loudly and started to get up, lifting me by the elbow so that we were both standing in the hallway. I was suddenly aware of my jeans around my knees and reached down to pull them up. As I did, he removed his wetsuit by standing on it and lifting his legs out of it one by one, then he reached down and picked it up before walking naked down the corridor into the bedroom.

I watched him go feeling very confused. This had never happened before; after sex, D'Artagnan still radiated passion. He always held me, continued to kiss me, caress me, murmur his love for me. He never just got up and walked away.

After a minute, he stuck his head around the door again. 'We go and get some breakfast, okay, Nicole?'

I shrugged nervously and nodded.

***

We held hands as we walked in the old town of San Sebastian. Guy always referred to it by its Basque name, Donostia. This was where we had come on our first-ever weekend away and, because he's so passionate about food and Donostia is Mecca for food lovers, we had visited several times the previous year. Whenever we were there, we'd wander lazily through the ancient labyrinth of pedestrianised streets in the old quarter, his arm loosely around my neck, my thumb hooked through the belt loops of his jeans as I savoured the heat of his body under his shirt.

This time he held my hand and kept me at arm's length. He didn't look at me as we walked purposefully through the busy streets; it was as if he had a specific destination in mind. There was nothing romantic about our walk. I tried to believe it was because he had low blood sugar and was very hungry, that it wasn't because there was no romance. We'd just had sublimely good sex; how could there be no romance?

We went to one of the few *pintxo* bars that was open that early. He clearly went there often because he greeted the restaurant staff behind the bar where all the *pintxos* were displayed, and they greeted him in return. We took a table at the back of the restaurant and he motioned to one of the staff; he raised two fingers and an eyebrow, pointed, nodded.

Two coffees with milk appeared at our table, together with a basket of bread and a plate of small, elaborate pastries, as well as a plate of the local speciality: thinly sliced, wet-with-fat ham made from the very happy, extremely well-fed local pigs. Guy had always made a big thing of telling me how happy the pigs were, that they roamed free in the Basque hills while they foraged for food, gorging on acorns, grubs and mushrooms. It did not make me want to eat them any more than I wanted to eat unhappy, badly fed, dead animals.

At the beginning of our relationship, D'Artagnan had found my vegetarian diet puzzling. He tried to get me to eat fishy *pintxos* on the grounds that fish weren't really meat (I pointed out that they weren't actually vegetables, either), or to 'just try a little, a tiny piece of the ham, Nicole, *mon amour*. It is like silk in the mouth, I promise' as if the reason that I was vegetarian was simply because I'd never eaten *tasty* dead animals. He pronounced mouth '*mouse*', and in the early days I found his French accent inexplicably sexy. Actually, that hadn't changed much. But it was still not sexy enough to make me want to eat ham. This enervated him; it was almost as if he took it personally – but then D'Artagnan is very passionate about his food. He's passionate about everything he cares about.

But that day in San Sebastian there were no references to my picky eating habits. He ate the ham hungrily, layered it thickly on chunks of bread and ate it while his eyes flickered to mine occasionally then away again. I realised that although he was indeed hungry, there was definitely no romance. All of the words of intense, consummate pleasure we'd exchanged that morning were gone, forgotten.

He wasn't the same man. He wasn't the suave, charming, arrogant D'Artagnan with whom, against all of my instincts, I had fallen in love. That D'Artagnan was missing and in his place was a wary man, a man without charisma, without confidence; he was a bit wild, almost feral.

I reached over and put my hand on top of his. He stopped eating and raised his hooded eyes to mine. 'Guy,' I said gently,

'I'm so sorry. I'm so sorry I didn't tell you what happened but I couldn't bear the idea of you being in danger. Please try to understand how much I love you, how much I couldn't bear the idea of you going to prison because of something that happened to me *long* before I met you. Or worse, you being hurt or killed in self-defence. I couldn't contemplate that happening, my darling.'

I gazed into the eyes of the man I had never thought it was possible to love as much as I did, but they were shielded, mistrustful. When he finally spoke, his voice was very quiet. 'Why did you think I would not be able to understand that, Nicole?'

I took a deep breath. 'Guy,' I said, 'you *told* me. We sat there together in the hotel in Bordeaux and you said, quite clearly – I remember you were smiling and you were completely confident, serene even – you said to me, "Nicole, if he ever touches you, if Guillaume ever touches you, I will kill him."'

I fixed him with my eyes across the white Formica table top, willing him to understand. 'And I *believed* you Guy. I believed you because you nearly died when Karl came to the château. You just sat there, bleeding all over the place, basically bleeding to death, and you nearly *died*. How the fuck do you think that made me feel, the guilt that I would have felt if you had died?'

And how empty my life would have been without you. But I didn't say that because I was suddenly angry. He was being so bloody *obtuse*! 'So I thought if he can do something like that once, there's absolutely no reason to assume he isn't capable of doing something equally dangerous in this case!'

Guy picked up several slices of ham and spread them across another piece of bread, bit it in half and chewed it, continuing all the while to watch me through narrowed eyes.

I took a sip of my coffee and ate one of the small, elaborate pastries even though I wasn't hungry.

Finally, he spoke again. His mouth was hard and his voice was hard. 'It is not the same thing, Nicole. What I tell you then, that is different. This thing – this thing that Guillaume do to you all these years ago – this is different. It is fucking *different*, Nicole!'

He slammed his fist down on the table so hard that both of the plates with the pastries and what remained of the ham jumped. I jumped too. The couple at the next table turned to look at us. We ignored them.

I stared at him. He was furious, I could see, but I was too, because I *knew* what he was like! 'So tell me, Guy, tell me honestly. How would you have reacted if I had told you what Guillaume did?'

He looked away from me, his expressive mouth pursed in a hard pout. I was treated to the aquiline nose in profile as he gazed across the restaurant and stared straight through the now-anxious couple next to us.

When he finally turned back to me, his voice was softer. 'Nicole, I don't know how I would have reacted. But yes, it is true – I want to kill Guillaume.' He paused and blinked. 'There is not one day, one moment in any day, when I do not want to kill Guillaume, that I don't imagine how I would kill Guillaume.'

I made big I-told-you-so eyes at him.

'But I would not have done it,' he continued quietly. 'Because I will have thought that you need me, that you will need me while you bring this case against Guillaume, that you will need me to stand beside you. But *apparemment*, I was wrong.' There were tears in his eyes.

'Because this is always what you do, Nicole. You do not trust me. Even after all this time we are together, when we make a life together. I watch you and I see how much pain you have in your life and I try, I do everything to make this pain better. I see you fall in love with Nina. I fall in love with Nina because I see you, my beautiful wife, the woman I love so much, fall in love with Nina. And I think now it is time to make a new family. I want to make a new family with this woman I love so much, and then – '

His voice broke and he started crying. It was horrible, utterly horrible to see him so destroyed. I started crying too.

'But then you push me away. You keep this terrible thing from me, you do not trust me to be at your side while you do this terrible, difficult thing without me. Nicole, when you do this you tell me—' he raised his anguished eyes to mine '—you tell me that you do not need me. That you do not want me by your side because you do not trust me. And this is why I leave, Nicole. *This* is why I leave.'

My heart was shattering in slow motion as I gazed at him through my tears. His beard was more salt than pepper now and he looked gaunt, lonely and unkempt. He was no longer the suave, robust, charismatic French musketeer I had married. I ached with a terrible pain as I realised what I had done to him. I had made him this feral, mistrustful hermit-surfer, hiding away from everyone, from the people who loved him.

I leaned forward and put my hand on his forearm. 'Please, my darling, please forgive me. I didn't understand that. I didn't think about it properly. I told myself a story about you and it was wrong, *I* was wrong. Please, please, forgive me, Guy.'

He focused his eyes on me again and they were so full of sadness. 'I want so much to forgive you, Nicole, and I am trying so hard – but I don't know how to do it. I have so much pain and so much anger, and I don't know how to make it stop.'

I put my hands over my nose and mouth. Tears were streaming down my face and I thought, *Well, I don't know how to make it stop either. Maybe neither of us can make it stop. Maybe this is it. I've broken D'Artagnan. I haven't tamed him, I've broken him.*

But that left Nina and I could not break Nina, too. If I broke Nina, that would be the end for me. There really would be no point in living any more.

My voice was barely above a whisper. 'What about Nina, Guy? What are we going to do about Nina?' And I told him about the letter, about the date for the adoption hearing, and then I asked him because I had to get a straight answer, 'Do you want a divorce? Because we have to explain if our circumstances have changed.'

We had both stopped crying. We sat opposite one other eviscerated, exhausted, drained.

He frowned deeply. 'Do *you* want a divorce, Nicole?'

I frowned back at him and my frown was deeper. 'No, Guy, I do *not* want a divorce. I love you. I love you so much and I want you in my life. Nina wants you in her life.'

And I ache for you; I ache for your touch. I ache to have you hold me against you as we fall asleep. I ache to gaze into your beautiful brown eyes first thing in the morning, to see that sleepy, lazy smile lift the corner of your mouth when you gaze at me, to feel your mouth on mine in greeting.

'But…' I breathed in. 'We have to sign the paperwork to say that our situation hasn't changed since we made the application and it seems that it *has* changed. I don't know whether we're still a couple and I don't know whether we both still want to adopt Nina. I know that I still want to adopt Nina – that hasn't changed – but I don't know whether you still want to.'

My hands were folded untidily together in front of my face and I felt utterly exhausted. It wasn't just about Nina, and it was all so much more difficult than I'd ever imagined it would be. So much more difficult and so much more painful, pain on a scale that felt as if it would crack glaciers hundreds of metres thick, pain that would cut through continents, through planets, pain that would split stars and destroy galaxies.

He raised his agonised eyes to mine. 'Nicole, I know how much Nina mean to you, and she mean so much to me too. We will go ahead with the adoption process without changing anything. I will be there for the rendezvous with the agency and we will still be married. And afterward—' he blinked at me '—afterward we see. We see how it all is, how our life is, how we feel about our life together. If we have a life together.'

My broken heart ached to hear him say that but I also felt the faintest sense of relief. At least I had an answer about Nina.

***

I could not bear to stay in San Sebastian after we left the *pintxo* bar. Guy tried to insist that I needed to sleep because I hadn't slept the night before, but I was too hurt, too sad to sleep in the same bed as the man I loved so much, to wake up in his bed and to know that I had broken him. To know that perhaps he no longer loved me in the same way. That was too painful.

We agreed that he would prepare and sign the letter to say our situation hadn't changed and send it to me by courier so that I could sign and submit it. I didn't mention that Xavier had offered to help me draft the letter; Xavier was absolutely unmentionable in the current circumstances.

I drove home from Donostia to Cognac. It only took four hours because the distance that separated D'Artagnan and I was not far geographically. But emotionally? Emotionally, we were thousands, millions, billions of fucking light years apart.

I hadn't realised how far apart we were.

Chapter Six

Xavier frowned at me across his desk, his slender hands pressed together in a pyramid shape, his fingertips against his mouth. Finally he pointed them at me, double-barrelled. 'But that is ... *bah*, concealing the truth, Nicole.'

I glared at him. 'Xavier, given that I don't know what the truth is because I don't know whether we can stay married or not, it is not *concealing* the truth. I don't know what the truth is.'

Once again I was left in no doubt that Xavier was definitely French. He gave an arrogant jerk of his head and his nostrils flared in a contemptuous sniff. 'Well, he is a stupid man to say he does not know whether he want to stay married to you. He should tell you! He should be clear about this now – this is an important time. He know about the case and he know that it is difficult for you, and that you also worry about how the procedure for the adoption of Nina will happen. Why does he not come back? He should be here with you if he loves you, Nicole!'

I was aware that Xavier might not be totally objective about D'Artagnan. That day he was wearing the smart, pale-blue shirt, open at the neck, the sleeves folded back to expose his lightly suntanned forearms. Stubble was only at ten o'clock and the soft curls had been brushed.

I was the first to break the gaze we seemed to have found ourselves locked into. 'Nothing is going to change as far as adopting Nina is concerned. We'll make the declaration that the situation is the same and we'll go to the interview together.'

Xavier's expression was stern. 'That is the deception you are making, Nicole. If you do this and you are not living as a family with your husband and the agency find out, there will be a risk that they will take Nina from you. You remember, I explain to you that the decision that you can adopt Nina is revocable. They are very careful, the agency – they will find out if you are not living together.'

He leaned forward across his desk and spoke more softly. 'If Guy cannot forgive you now, you must take back the previous application and make a new one. I will help you to do this, Nicole.'

I sighed, feeling very tired. 'Xavier, please try to understand my position. Guy and I are going through a difficult time. I know that you and I have feelings for each other and that might complicate your viewpoint, but you need to accept that things are *not* over between Guy and me.' I was holding on to that really tightly; it was my current mantra.

Disdainful sweep of the thick eyelashes, slight Gallic pout. 'Okay, Nicole. I say no more on this subject.' A last shake of the head to make it clear that he was doing so under duress.

He picked up the dossier in front of him. 'Now we talk about the interview with the *juge d'instruction*. This time she is going to be very, very hard with you. You know this, I think, Nicole? Are you ready for this?'

I swallowed; I was very nervous about the second interview with the *juge*. I took a deep breath. 'Yes, Xavier, I'm ready.'

***

But I wasn't ready. Afterwards, outside the *juge's* chambers, Xavier wrapped his arms tightly around me and I sobbed and slobbered snot into the shoulder of his smart new suit jacket as he rubbed my back soothingly. 'It's okay, Nicole. It's okay, you did it very well. You were very good – she believe you again,' he whispered into my ear as he stroked my hair.

And then we went to a wine bar nearby and got really pissed, so pissed that we started snogging in the corner. So pissed that I really, really wanted him again. But Xavier is a gentleman, and he took me to a hotel nearby and booked me a room. He handed me the card key as I stood red-eyed and blotchy-faced, swaying in the hotel foyer, then he kissed my forehead as the lift doors opened and put me in the lift on my own.

I had an appalling hangover when I woke up, and I was gutted that I'd kissed him so wantonly the night before, but I forgave myself; it had been a horrible, stressful day. When my phone rang and I saw it was him, I answered immediately. We commiserated about our hangovers and giggled about how pissed we'd both been.

And then I drove home.

***

I sent the letter to the adoption agency the same day that I received it from Guy. There was nothing else in the envelope, just the letter. It was very factual. It said that nothing about our situation had changed in the three months since we'd made the initial application and confirmed that we would be at the formal adoption interview in early June.

I signed my name next to D'Artagnan's, noting that his signature was less ostentatious than usual. That made me feel desperately sad again.

Every time I thought of him, of that day in Donostia, I felt achingly sad. Sometimes I thought about the sex that morning, when we'd been so utterly consumed by each other. I replayed that and it was wonderful, except that it made me miss him and want him so much. But it also confused me. How could we have had that yet not been able to sort out the other shit? How could he be so passionate and then so removed afterwards? That was new.

D'Artagnan had always had a very high sex drive (we have *very* compatible pheromones) but his innate sensuality was a fundamental part of his character. There had never been the separation there was that day: earth-shattering sex followed by a cold withdrawal.

That made me doubt myself, and I spent a lot of time thinking about what he'd said that day. Eventually I came to the conclusion that he was right; I should have trusted him to put aside his desire for revenge in order to support me, even though part of me still believed he might have done something stupid. It was hard to realise that I'd been wrong – and even harder to accept that my error had been so catastrophic for our relationship.

***

I took a very deep breath on the Nina days and put D'Artagnan out of my mind, especially on the sunny days when we were outside with the horses and Camille.

Nina's school holiday started at the beginning of April. Gabriela joined us for lunch on the first day and we sat at the table in the dining hall. The tall windows at the front of the Duchess were wide open as the warm spring breeze wafted the smell of jasmine and the sound of birdsong through the room.

We spoke about nothing except horses. I finally plucked up the courage to say it out loud. 'I think we should find a pony for Nina. Don't you think so, Camille?'

Nina turned to look at me, her eyes huge, her face brimming with joy.

Camille gave a smug little laugh. 'It takes you *so* long to say things out loud, doesn't it?' She turned and grinned at Gabriela, a high-five grin as if to say '*finally*'!

Then she turned back to me and said, 'Yes, Nicole, I think this is a good idea. I will speak to a friend of mine who breeds ponies. But it must be the right pony because Nina is a sensitive rider. And it must be a pony that can live with Emperador and Espiritu, so he must have a good personality. And it must not be a mare.' She fixed me with her black eyes. 'You must let me help you to find the right pony.'

The temptation to go full Homer was strong, but I wasn't sure how well 'Duh' translated, so I just said, 'Of course, Camille. I could never imagine *not* asking for your help.'

'Will the *prince* come back to help us choose a pony for me?' Nina beamed toothily at me.

I had to draw on every reserve of willpower I had to smile brightly back at her. 'I'll ask him the next time I speak to him, Nina. Okay?'

She nodded vigorously. 'Yes, you must ask him. I know he will want to help me choose one.'

Oh my God, I thought, *I need him back in my life. We need him in our lives, Nina and me.*

***

On one of the days when Nina wasn't with us, I explained the Satan saga to Camille and Gabriela. Gabriela blinked her dark Portuguese eyes at me, reached over the table and took my hand, squeezing it tightly.

'*Quel connard*!' She spat the words venomously and I knew immediately that she meant Satan.

She went on to tell me that she'd clocked Satan at our wedding in August the year before. Despite not wanting him to come, I knew I couldn't un-invite him without D'Artagnan wanting to know why. Guillaume's plus-one had been a pretty blonde girl, as always too young. Gabriela had seen them arguing and then she'd seen him slip his hand around her neck.

'And his face, Nicole, this horrible look on his face. It was so evil! I wanted to go straight over and hit him, but Camille said no, don't create a scene. So instead, Camille walked towards them with her head turned the other way and spilled her glass of red wine all over him, so that he let go of his girlfriend! He was very angry about that but Camille just smiled and said sorry. She pretended that she was a bit drunk and walked away.'

Gabriela took a deep breath. 'I remember this man, Nicole. He is a very bad man, very bad to women. I am so sorry to hear what he did to you but I am so proud that you are going to put him in prison. *Chapeau*, Nicole! *Félicitations*!' She clinked her espresso cup against mine and I grinned at her and felt very proud.

Once that burst of euphoria subsided, I asked, 'But do you think I was wrong not to tell Guy? Because he's very angry that I didn't tell him and he doesn't seem to be able to forgive me. And I miss him so much, and so does Nina.' I pressed my lips together hard and tried to keep the tears from my eyes.

Gabriela did her Portuguese version of the Gallic shrug, which is even more disdainful if it's possible to imagine such a thing. '*Bah*, French men and their egos,' she said dismissively. She rolled her eyes. '*Pffff*, they need to know that women are strong too, that we are just as strong as them and that we can do things on our own. Guy will eventually realise this, Nicole.'

She paused. 'But he has a penis, so it will take him much longer to realise because the connection between his brain and his penis is ... *bah*, not so good. The connections are always very slow in men, Nicole, like before we have Wifi and everything take forever to load. Men still have a dial-up connection between the brain and the penis. Not even 3G.'

And then I started laughing and she started laughing. I laughed so much that I sprawled across the dining table and afterwards my stomach muscles ached, which felt really good.

***

Françoise had rung me the weekend after I'd got back from Donostia and invited me to the impromptu lunch she was giving the following weekend for Stephane's sixtieth birthday. He had recently arrived back in France. The whole family would be there – except for D'Artagnan, who was still not returning anyone's calls, and Antoine, who had made some excuse.

I told Françoise about my trip to Donostia without going into any detail. I said that Guy was still struggling with what I'd done and didn't seem able to forgive me just yet. Or maybe at all.

She was quiet for a while then she said, 'He will forgive you, Nicole. It will just take some time.'

I took a deep breath. 'I hope so, Françoise.'

We both let the 'I told you so' percolate, then she asked if I would bring Bérengère to the lunch because Stephane had asked her to come. I hid my smile and said that of course I would.

Then she asked if it would be okay for her to invite Xavier.

I hesitated. Would that be weird, Xavier coming to lunch with D'Artagnan's family? 'Sure,' I said cautiously. 'He's a really good lawyer.'

She gave a little laugh. 'I'm not asking him to lunch for his legal skills, Nicole! I'm asking him because he's been so supportive of you and I knew him well when he was Laurent's protégé. I've always been fond of him. But I also think it would be a good idea for everyone to understand what's happening with your case against Guillaume. Xavier can help you to answer any questions about the court procedure.'

She hesitated. 'Only if you don't mind – if you wouldn't find it too formal to have your lawyer present at a family lunch.'

And I thought, *Françoise, it's not the formality that's the problem. Xavier and I are waaaaay past formalities.* But I smiled and said, 'Of course I don't mind, Françoise. Xavier is lovely and I have absolutely no problem with you inviting him to lunch.'

***

By far the most shocking thing at the lunch in April was Stephane.

Bérengère and I had driven down to Françoise's house on the outskirts of Bordeaux, a beautiful old *longère* perched on a gentle hill from which the endless rows of estate vines flowed uniformly away into the valley. With its white-shuttered windows and creamy stone walls covered in glossy green ivy, it was like a wet dream for *la vie à la française*.

On the way down we'd argued about feminism. Specifically, twenty-first century feminism and the fact that I'd been part of undermining it because I'd been a model.

Bérengère was wearing a blue-and-white striped shirt over loose linen pants. The shirt was also linen and had been washed many, many times because it was faded and looked marvellously soft. It was buttoned between buttons six and eight only. I was sure that Bérengère had never been a bra-burner simply because she'd never had a bra. Button five and its unmarried buttonhole reaffirmed this particular non-secret.

'But the fashion world is an entirely male construct!' She shook her head in exasperation. 'Everything about it is designed by men to control women, to make them aspire to an unnatural body shape in order for them to feel bad about themselves. And that subdues them.'

'Bérengère,' I said. 'The human race has been following fashion since the dawn of time. In Elizabethan times women plucked their hairline because it was fashionable to have a very high forehead. They rubbed lead into their skin because white skin was considered beautiful. It was completely unnatural but it was the fashion – and to the best of my knowledge there wasn't a fashionista literati forcing them to do it. Look at that tribe in Thailand that consider an abnormally long neck desirable, or the tribes in Africa that scar their bodies.'

'That is to signify their social standing in their tribe. It's nothing to do with fashion,' she replied scornfully.

'Okay, perhaps. But the modern-day equivalent in western society is having fat injected into your lips or your bum or your thighs to make them bigger! Is that a social construct or is it fashion?'

She pouted a little. 'It's an image driven by men, by male standards of what makes a woman desirable.'

I shrugged. 'Yes, there's almost certainly an element of that, but it's also women competing with one another to "be fashionable". And it's highly unnatural.'

'Ah, but there is the flaw. Why are women competing with one another? In order to attract men, that's why!'

'Well, if you think the inherent heterosexual desire to attract the opposite sex is fundamentally flawed, it may disappoint you to know that it's probably not going to change in your lifetime.'

She reached over and poked me lightly on the arm, shook her head and grinned. 'You are very opinionated, aren't you, *ma petite biche*?'

I snorted. 'Oh my God, Bérengère, that's quite rich coming from the most opinionated woman I've ever met!'

She smiled slyly. 'I still think the world of fashion is exploitative and unnatural. I don't understand how clothes can be so important.'

'Because they're beautiful,' I said.

She snorted again. 'No, Nicole. Nature is beautiful, art is beautiful, music is beautiful. Clothes are just a way of disguising our bodies because we've been taught to be ashamed of them.'

I shook my head. 'I disagree. Clothes that are well-made are works of art. To start with the most clichéd example, how can you not look at Dior in the 1940s and see that the New Look was art?'

'It was a male idealisation of the female body – an unnaturally tiny waist and voluminous hips,' she replied grumpily.

'Wearing them made women feel beautiful. That's why the New Look was so popular.'

'In order for their beauty to appeal to men.'

'Again, you're probably not going to eradicate heterosexual attraction rituals in your lifetime, dearest Bérengère.' I gave her a quick smile.

'*Pfffff,*' she exhaled dismissively. That made me miss D'Artagnan, the world expert in dismissive verbal expressions, so much.

***

Stephane was a revelation. For a start, Darth Vader had hair! Admittedly he was the forerunner in the future of how male-pattern baldness was going to pan-out for D'Artagnan, but it seemed the future wasn't going to be so bad. Stephane had clearly not had his hair cut in many months because it was longer and shot through with silver now that it wasn't so monastically cut. He was suntanned after his cathedral-visiting tour of South East Asia and he'd grown a salt-and-pepper beard like D'Artagnan's.

He now looked like a laid-back, rather attractive Parisian intellectual. Perhaps it was the open-necked, cream-linen shirt. It suited him. He walked across the vast kitchen and he seemed really happy to see us, which was weird because I'd never seen Darth Vader happy. The last time we'd met, in November of the previous year, he'd beamed himself disapprovingly into the Duchess to try to make our lives miserable for a while.

'Nicole! It's so lovely to see you again.' He placed his hands gently on my shoulders as we did Kissies. His brown eyes sparkled with warmth. He looked at me intently. 'I'm so sorry to hear about what happened to you in Italy, Nicole.' He paused and blinked. 'But I'm so proud of your decision to bring that man to justice. I think it is very brave what you are doing. Well done!'

That shocked me. Stephane approving of something I was doing? WTF had happened to Darth Vader? How had this phenomenal metamorphosis happened without my knowledge?

'Thank you for saying that, Stephane. It really means a lot to me.' I meant every word. 'And happy birthday!' I thrust a bottle of very expensive 1996 Margaux at him that I'd selected from D'Artagnan's meticulously catalogued stash in the Duchess's cellar.

He took it and smiled. 'Thank you, Nicole.' He paused again, his gaze very direct. 'I imagine it is very difficult to do what you are doing, to bring this case against Guillaume on your own while my brother is away fighting his demons.'

I frowned at him, not quite sure I'd understood his French. 'His demons?'

He raised an eyebrow and gave a little shrug 'Yes, his demons. We can talk about this later, okay?'

When he let me go and turned to Bérengère, his eyes really lit up. He wrapped his arms around her and she wrapped her arms around him, and I thought, *OMG there's so much more going on than she's telling me, the sneaky bitch!*

Xavier was coming towards me. I couldn't stop my heart giving a lurch and a delighted smile spreading across my face because he looked bloody gorgeous, all dark curls, soft grey eyes and those insanely long black eyelashes. He wasn't wearing glasses and the collarless, open-necked white shirt and slim dark jeans made him look ... *very*. Just very. I didn't add an adjective because I was too busy doing a full mental reset about how I needed to act around him.

I modified my face to a polite smile. He raised an eyebrow slightly as he registered the modification.

'*Bonjour,* Xavier, *ça va*?'

'*Bonjour,* Nicole. *Oui, ça va. Et toi*?' When he gave me a big grin, I was powerless not to grin back. We exchanged Kissies and his shoulders were warm beneath his shirt. I really wanted him to put his arms around me and hug me like Stephane had hugged Bérengère. I wanted to feel the whole length of his body against me ... but obviously that would *not* have been a good way to start lunch with D'Artagnan's family. There would probably be raised eyebrows and possibly even questions if we did that.

So I touched his shoulders lightly, and he touched my shoulders lightly, and I breathed in Bleu de Chanel and smiled at him.

Françoise was busy in the kitchen and Pascal was helping her. I could see them as I chatted to her youngest daughter, Amandine, and her new boyfriend, Thomas. I rather missed Matthieu, Amandine's previous boyfriend, he of the wide smile, funky dreads and excellent taste in music, but I didn't say anything. Amandine was only twenty-four; she had all of her life ahead of her to find someone she was happy with.

I could see Françoise and Pascal in the kitchen and the way he sometimes touched her or she touched him, just gentle touches to say 'yes that goes there', or 'no, it's over there'. There was so much love between them. It made me happy to know that without me they might not have found each other.

Françoise's eldest daughter Emma, five months pregnant with her second child, was there with her husband, Conor. I held their baby, Rose, now nearly a year old, on my lap at lunch and I caught Xavier's eye across the table. His gaze was so wistful that tears pricked the back of my eyes.

I focused on Rose and her blue eyes instead. She giggled at me with delight and I giggled back then blew a big raspberry on her stomach, which made her shriek. She grabbed a sticky handful of my hair and yanked it so hard that Conor had to untangle it before he lifted her into his arms.

I felt bereft without the weight of her, and Xavier's gaze was very intense when our eyes met for a moment.

I'd last seen all of Françoise's daughters at Emma's wedding the previous year. Emma had her mother's dark hair and brown eyes, but her younger sisters were both blonde and blue-eyed like their father in the photo on the old oak dresser. It was the photo of Laurent and Guy that I loved so much, taken when they were young, both covered in sand and laughing, Guy's arm locked around Laurent's neck and his other hand pressed down on his best friend's curly blond head.

It was that photo at which Stephane pointed after lunch. I had stood up to help as the plates and dishes were cleared away but Stephane put his hand on my arm. I turned to him. 'You wanted to know about Guy's demons, Nicole?' he asked.

He immediately had my full attention. 'Yes. What did you mean by that?' I sat down again.

There was laughter and chatting and the clattering of dishes in the kitchen. Bérengère had gone outside for a smoke with Xavier – apparently Xavier was also an occasional smoker like D'Artagnan. Stephane and I were alone at the table.

Stephane pointed at the photo of Laurent and Guy. 'There, Nicole, that is one of Guy's demons. Laurent. Well, not Laurent but Laurent's death. Guy was so angry when Laurent died,' he said softly. 'They were always so close, like brothers – because Guy and I were never close. I was already eight years old when he was born, and Guy and Antoine… *Pfffff*, Antoine...'

We both rolled our eyes and exchanged a knowing grin.

'Laurent was like Guy's brother,' Stephane repeated. 'They were the same age, they went to school together and they spent all their time together. Laurent always came on holiday with us, and Guy went with Laurent's family to the Côte d'Azur every year.'

He paused and sighed deeply. 'And, of course, Laurent and Françoise fell in love and got married. They had their family and Guy was their godfather.' He reached for his wine glass and took a long, contemplative sip before he continued, his voice very sombre.

'At first, Laurent did not tell Guy about the cancer. Nobody told Guy about the cancer. Guy was living in London with

Isabelle and he was always very busy, always travelling all over the world. When it was too late, when it was clear that Laurent was not going to live, only then did Françoise tell him.' He shook his head slowly. 'He was so angry when he found out. Angry and devastated.'

He leaned forward and put his long-fingered hand on my forearm. He was gazing at me intently. 'Because, Nicole, this is what you need to understand about Guy. He is the youngest child. My mother adored him, my father adored him, my grandparents adored him – he was the special child, the gifted child, the favourite child. Everyone loved him and he was spoilt, more than any of us were spoilt. That created resentment.' He paused again. 'It's true that I have resented Guy and his easy life for a long time.'

He swirled the wine gently around in his glass. 'Because Guy was the special child, he was brought up to think he can do *anything* he wants to do. He has so much confidence, so much charisma, and he is so naturally charming that everything is easy for him.'

He took another sip of his wine, leaned forward and put his glass on the table. 'But actually, this is a problem when he becomes an adult. When he is a child, he is a little god. He just smiles charmingly at people and they do what he wants, or he wants something to happen and it just happens. So Guy really believes that he is a bit like a god.'

I stared at him as he spoke, mesmerised. It was fascinating listening to D'Artagnan being deconstructed by his older brother.

'And then Laurent died and Guy could do nothing about it. It is the second time that Guy must accept that he is not a god, and this is incredibly difficult for him to do. He has been beaten by another demon because when Laurent dies, Guy has already fought his first demon and lost.'

His gaze was very pensive. 'The first time Guy must accept that he is not in control of everything is when my father died. He was only sixty-two and he had a heart attack and died very suddenly. Guy was twenty-six, and at first he refused to believe it, he refused to accept it. He was devastated by the death of my father and furious with the world.' He leaned back in his chair, his eyes still fixed on mine.

'He has *never* talked to me about his father. I just assumed they weren't close,' I said quietly.

Françoise came into the dining room carrying a beautifully sculpted bowl full of chocolate mousse, which she set down in the centre of the table. She paused as Stephane continued.

'No, you must understand that my father and Guy were very close, Nicole, but he finds it very painful to talk about this. He loved my father so much, and my father adored him. But for Guy, who was always told he can do anything, that he is capable of changing the way the planets move around the sun, when my father died he was forced to accept that he does not control the world. He encounters his first demon and the demon won. And when Laurent dies, he encounters his second demon. Both times he cannot beat the demons. He has to accept that he is not a god and he cannot control the bad things that happen to the people he loves.'

'It's true,' said Françoise softly. 'He was inconsolable. He didn't know how to deal with the sorrow other than to rage against it, which was so futile.'

I glanced at her then back at Stephane. 'He *never* talks about any of this.'

He frowned and snorted. 'He doesn't know any of this, Nicole. He is incapable of self-analysis because there is nothing wrong with him – he is a god! He is sitting there in Donostia, brooding about how he cannot control his world, brooding because another demon has won. He is angry all over again.'

'Because I didn't tell him about Guillaume?'

He narrowed his eyes thoughtfully. 'I think maybe that is what he is telling himself. But really, he is angry at what Guillaume did. He is angry that another demon has appeared in his life and he can't beat this demon either.'

'I agree,' said Françoise. 'And this time he's even more furious because Guillaume was a demon he knew his whole life, a demon we warned him about that he ignored. A *mortal* demon – but still, Guy has no power against this demon either. All he has is anger, anger that once more there are bad things that happen that he cannot control.'

She shook her head and sighed. 'Aiee, my little brother. Always out there fighting the elusive dragons!' She squeezed my shoulder gently. 'Don't worry, Nicole. He will soon realise that it's futile and he'll come home. Trust me.' She gave me a quick smile before returning to the kitchen. I really wanted to believe her.

Stephane and I sipped our wine and then I said in English, because my brain was aching with the effort of translating into French, 'What you've been saying is absolutely fascinating. And it's fascinating how perceptive you are because, to be honest, Stephane, you've always seemed so – disapproving of your brother's life.'

And then he did the most perfect Gallic shrug, so reminiscent of D'Artagnan that I wanted both to burst into tears and throw myself into his arms because it made me miss Guy so much. But I did neither of those things.

Stephane sighed deeply and gave a sad smile. 'My life has been very cold for a long time now, Nicole. But I am seeing a very good therapist, and also ... I have some warmth in my life now.'

And his brown eyes twinkled because Bérengère had just come back inside. He transferred his gaze to her. Even though I had tears in my eyes, I still thought, *Man, that sly bitch. How dare she not tell me about this!*

***

'Today,' said Camille, 'we are going to ride out together.'

I glanced up at her. 'What? Not in the paddock?'

She smiled her enigmatic smile. Her flaxen hair was bound tightly in a ponytail on top of her head as she brushed Emperador's gleaming gold body. 'Yes, not in the paddock. Today we will ride out in the countryside.'

I frowned as I carried on picking out bits of gravel and mud from Espiritu's hoof, holding it in my hand as he nuzzled my butt. When I'd finished, I put it down gently on the ground and moved to his back feet. He obligingly lifted his hoof as I bent down. I had learned that he was a very polite horse who seemed to enjoy a pedicure.

'Do you think I'm ready to do that?' I'd finally done a rising trot on Espiritu the previous week that Camille seemed happy enough with because she'd stopped making sarcastic eyes and sarcastic comments at me. She had actually barked, 'Good! That's good – you understand the rhythm.'

I had been utterly exhausted afterwards, every muscle in my body aching as I got ready for bed, but I'd also felt extraordinarily happy. I – the *princesse* who'd spent most of her life doing nothing more challenging than walking down the catwalk in six-inch heels and pouting – I had ridden the most beautiful horse in the world around the paddock. I'd matched my rhythm to his rhythm as I rose and descended in the saddle, and for maybe two or three seconds we had been in perfect harmony, in perfect balance, and it had been *amazing*.

I had no dreams that night, no nightmares. I just slept, a deep, exhausted, happy sleep.

But the idea of leaving the safety of the round paddock where Espiritu could not gallop off and buck and kick his heels like I'd seen him doing in the big paddock with Emperador… That was a *very* scary thought.

***

'Oh my God, Jules, it was absolutely incredible! I mean, she didn't give me any warning at all! One minute we're riding along at the bottom of this valley and everything is lovely and calm and the sun is shining, and the next minute she turns to me and she just grins—'

I started laughing despite myself. 'And then she says, "So now, Nicole, you are going to learn to use those muscles inside your thighs!"' I breathed in, swallowed a bit of saliva and started coughing uncontrollably down the phone.

'You okay, babe?' Jules sounded concerned.

I nodded, finally caught my breath and continued croakily, 'And then, the bitch, she turns Emperador towards this enormous hill and gallops up it, flat out. And Espiritu's like, "*wait for me!*" and suddenly I'm galloping up this hill, clinging to him with every muscle and bone in my body! It was bloody terrifying!'

I could hear her laughing. 'It was absolutely in-*fucking*-sane!' I finally managed to gasp, my heart beating almost as hard as it had been that morning.

'Oh my God, Nicky.' Jules finally stopped laughing. 'I can just imagine it! You must have been scared shitless!'

'Totally! But at the same time I absolutely loved it. It was the most incredible feeling – the power, Jules, the incredible power of galloping on a horse! It was like nothing I'd ever imagined! It was insanely dangerous but afterwards, when we got to the top of the hill and finally stopped, Camille was like, "*Bah* Nicole, you need to learn how to stay on a horse and that is the best way." That was the end of the conversation as far as she was concerned.'

I shook my head, thinking about Camille's calm gaze and quiet smile and the way my heart had been hammering, my knees weak and my hands shaking. I sighed happily. 'You know, Jules, I would never, ever in a gazillion years have imagined that I could do that.'

I heard the grin in her voice. 'Ah, Nicky sweetheart, I can honestly say that in a gazillion years I would never have thought you would ever do that either.' She paused. 'But I'm so happy that you did. You sound so – exhilarated! Well done you!'

I was still smiling at the memory. 'My thigh muscles are in agony but it was worth it. It was almost as good as sex with D'Artagnan.'

She gave a long, low laugh, but when she stopped there was a slightly empty silence. 'Still nothing? He still hasn't been in touch?'

'Nothing since San Sebastian, and that was more than two weeks ago. I'm starting to wonder whether it wasn't just a vivid, erotic dream.'

That made her laugh again. 'Your D'Artagnan is a bit more complicated than you imagined, isn't he, Nicky?'

I rolled my eyes. 'And then some. Y'know, after I spoke to Stephane last weekend it all started fitting together. It's D'Artagnan and his Zeus complex. Zeus is furious that I dared to keep something secret from him, or that something terrible happened that he couldn't control. Because it's exactly like Stephane says – Guy really does think he is a bit of a god, that he's in control of everything. And now he's furious that not just one, but two of his subjects have hidden something from him.' I shook my head glumly.

I heard Jules take a deep breath then she said quietly, 'Don't do that again, Nicky. Don't make up stories about Guy. He's not

Zeus, he's not D'Artagnan, he's your husband and he's hurt that you didn't trust him to help you.'

That made my vision wobble with tears, but it made me angry too. 'No, Jules, don't *you* do that. I made a decision based on information that I had at the time about how I believed he would react – and I'm still not entirely sure that I made the wrong decision.'

I paused, sipped my wine. 'He's been gone for three months. He's had plenty of time to think all this through, to think about what I did – what I'm doing – to think about how it's affecting Nina who's done *nothing* wrong. Yet he still chooses to stay away! So no, actually, Jules, fuck all that "he's hurt" bullshit. I'm hurt too! Every day I wake up and I hurt and I worry and I'm anxious that Nina's adoption is in jeopardy! And Nina misses him too. There's not a day that she doesn't ask when he's coming back and I absolutely *hate* having to lie to her.'

Jules gave a big sigh. 'I'm so sorry, Nicky. I can imagine it's very hard, but he did say he'd come to the adoption meeting. He said he still wants to adopt Nina.'

I laughed bitterly. 'And then what? We adopt Nina but Zeus is still sulking and Nina and I have to live with someone who can't forgive me? I don't want that, Jules.'

I took a deep breath, then I dared to say it aloud because it was becoming a constant echo in the back of my mind and I was tired of having to push it away. 'And all the while, Jules, there's gorgeous, kind Xavier, who's my age and single and who says he's in love with me and wants to have a family. Can you see where I'm at with this? Can you see what it looks like from my point of view?'

There was a sharp intake of breath. 'Nicky, don't do this,' Jules said abruptly. 'Don't let Xavier get in the middle of what you and Guy are going through. You're angry and Guy's angry, but you'll get past this. You need to take a big step back and think – really think – about why you married him and why you love him. And I'll tell you this, Nicky, just in case you try to tell yourself it was because of the sex. It wasn't. I'm sure Xavier is gorgeous and he's your age and all that but, trust me, you are *so* not done with D'Artagnan yet. If you do anything with Xavier before you and Guy have sorted out this current shit, you'll end up just as messed up as you were with Karl. In fact, I'm willing to bet that what you went through with Karl will be a wander in the park in comparison with the emotional trauma you'll have to deal with if you get involved with Xavier!'

I spent a lot of time blinking after she stopped speaking. Jules knows everything about me and she was in her second year of psychology (or *puh-sychologie* in French) so I had to pay some attention.

And I knew she was right: D'Artagnan and I were not done.

Chapter Seven

The following Sunday was Easter Sunday and Mother Nature was in a spiteful mood. At 6.30am, I was holding a torch between my teeth and a bag of Easter eggs in one hand. With the other, I was pushing away branches heavy with rainfall, all the while searching for an obvious – but not too obvious – place to hide those eggs.

How fortunate that I'd bought enough for Nina's whole class, I thought wryly, as I wedged five into a fork of one of the walnut trees. I snatched my hand away as a large, radioactive-green caterpillar careened over the branch nearest to me, clearly peeved that his home was being decorated with multi-coloured tinfoil. The branch that I recoiled into promptly dumped fifteen litres of cold water down the back of my waterproof jacket. I swore loudly, then thought fuck it and threw the rest of the Easter eggs into the undergrowth beneath the forest that started at the edge of the front lawn.

By the time I returned inside, completely drenched, Nina was in the kitchen. Marion and I had reached a tacit agreement that Nina would spend Saturday nights with me, which made both Nina and I very happy. We'd found an old stool in the laundry room; when we were together in the kitchen, she always sat on it, half-sprawled across the cool granite countertop, her arms crossed under her head while she watched me prepare our meals.

That morning, she was sitting on her stool and pouring rodent cocaine from its Tupperware container into two bowls. She glanced up as I came in, having towel-dried my wet hair but with my wet jeans still sticking to my legs.

'I came to wake you up, but you weren't there! Where did you go?' she asked accusingly, unaware that her hand had moved and that she was now pouring the contents of the Tupperware over the countertop.

I crossed the kitchen quickly and gently took the container from her. 'Oh – er– I thought I heard something outside so I went to have a look.' I went to the sink to get a cloth and started scooping up the spilled nuts and seeds.

She stared at me, her eyes enormous. 'Do you think it was the bells that you heard?' In France and Italy it is *les cloches*, the church bells, that bring the Easter eggs to dispense their brightly-wrapped, sugary tidings of joy and hyper-glycaemia after having broken free of their housings in the holy city of Rome. Yes, France is a sectarian country. Yes, almost all the public holidays are Catholic. Go figure.

I made a face as if that hadn't occurred to me. 'Well, it's possible that was what I heard.'

Her eyes lit up. She glanced to her side. 'Do you think they know that Annie's here, too?'

I nodded firmly. 'Of course they know that Annie's here!'

She started to get down from the stool but I put a hand on her arm. 'But first, Nina, you have to eat your breakfast.'

Nina and I had recently had our first battle of wills and, unsurprisingly, it had been about food. I'd taken her to the supermarket and, while my back was turned, she'd dumped two enormous boxes of congealed industrial sawdust, heavily flavoured with corn-syrup, into the shopping trolley.

'No,' I'd said firmly. I smiled at her as I removed the two boxes of breakfast cereal. 'You don't normally eat this, Nina. Put it back.'

Although I am not a breakfast person, I made an effort to eat a bowl of my rodent cocaine with her in the mornings when we were together. At first she hadn't wanted to eat my muesli, but when I'd mixed hers with strawberry yoghurt she'd devoured it without comment.

She glared at me. 'Yes, I do,' she said crossly. 'I eat it at Madame Marion's.'

I took a deep breath and carried on smiling. 'Well, you're not at Madame Marion's when you're with me, so you don't have to eat this.'

'I like it,' she said sullenly. 'That's what I want to eat for breakfast.'

'But Nina – it's ... rubbish. It's terrible food.'

No change in expression. 'I like it,' she repeated.

We locked eyes while I quickly rifled through my very slim parenting manual. 'I bet you Espiritu wouldn't eat it,' I said finally. It was the best I could come up with.

'I bet he would.' She tilted her head to one side, her gaze defiant.

I nodded slowly. 'Okay, how about this? How about we do an experiment? We'll offer Espiritu a choice – a bowl of this breakfast cereal or a bowl of the muesli I make. And whichever he chooses, you agree that you'll eat that for breakfast from now on. Okay?'

She narrowed her eyes and gazed at me contemplatively, then nodded slowly. 'Okay. I agree.'

If I had learned anything in the six months I'd spent as Katie and Josh's nanny when Jules went back to work, it was that deception is an invaluable tool in child raising.

Just before Nina and I ceremoniously carried the two bowls out to Espiritu for his delectation, I crushed up a hard peppermint and sprinkled it over the bowl of crap without Nina seeing. Most horses absolutely adore peppermints, but to Espiritu they are the devil's bonbons.

He recoiled from the bowl Nina held under his nose as if she were trying to poison him. He was still reluctant to approach her when she held out the bowl with muesli, but once he'd ascertained there was no peppermint involved he ate it with such enthusiasm that he forced the bowl out of her hands. His attempts to lick out every last trace of it made her giggle in the way that makes me want to squeeze her to death.

Of course, since Annie joined us Nina's muesli has been drowned in honey so I'm not sure I've achieved much in the healthy breakfast stakes, but at least honey is a natural sugar and not industrial corn syrup.

Nina finished her breakfast and ran outside into the now gloriously sunny Sunday morning in search of the hidden Easter eggs. I was just scraping Annie's uneaten bowl of congealed honey and rodent cocaine into the compost when my phone rang. I crossed the kitchen and picked it up.

'Hi, Françoise! Happy Easter!' I smiled.

'Hi, Nicole. Thanks – happy Easter to you, too.' Her voice sounded tense.

'Is anything the matter? You sound a bit – down?'

I heard her intake of breath. 'It's my brother, Nicole. Your husband.'

My chest instantly constricted. 'What's happened? What's happened to him?' I sat down abruptly on Nina's stool, aware that I could hear the blood pulsing in my temples.

'Nothing's happened, Nicole. I'm sorry to frighten you – it's just that he's done a very stupid thing.' Her voice was grave.

'Oh my God, please tell me he's okay! Please tell me—'

She interrupted me. 'He's fine, Nicole. There's nothing wrong with him, there's nothing to worry about.' I managed to breathe out, albeit with difficulty. 'Although there might be something to worry about,' she added, sounding cross again.

Even I could hear the hysteria in my voice. 'I don't understand, Françoise. Please explain! Is he okay or isn't he okay? What's he done? Please tell me what's happened!' All the while thinking, *Have they let Satan out of jail without my knowledge? Or has D'Artagnan somehow managed to get inside the jail*?

'He's fine, Nicole,' she said firmly. 'There's nothing wrong with him. He's not hurt, he's not in danger.' She paused. 'It's just that he's done a really stupid thing and I need to talk to you about it. Are you at home this morning? Can I come and see you?'

I put my fingers against my forehead, aware that they were trembling, that my whole body was trembling. 'Yes, I'm here. Of course you can – but why can't you just tell me what he's done over the phone? Are you sure he's okay, that he's not injured, or in prison or ... I dunno, holding the prison staff hostage until he's allowed to fight Guillaume in a duel to the death?'

Françoise started laughing. 'No, Nicole, he's fine. There's nothing wrong with him and he's not in danger.' Her tone of voice changed and she sounded annoyed again 'Well, he's in danger of getting a massive slap from me for what he's done. But apart from that, he's fine.'

I was really confused. 'Look, Françoise, do I need to worry about this? Because you know what I'm like. I'll worry like mad until you tell me what he's done.'

'No, Nicole,' she said firmly. 'You don't need to worry.' She paused. 'Look, Pascal and I have been invited for lunch with friends not far from Cognac. Could we stop off on the way? I really want to speak to you face to face about this, it's not something I want to do over the telephone.'

'Of course! I'm here with Nina – she's hunting Easter eggs in the garden. Come whenever you're ready.'

'Great.' I heard a little smile in her voice. 'It'll probably be about 11.30.' She paused again 'And please don't worry in the meantime, Nicole – it's incredibly stupid what he's done, but it's not life-threatening.' She paused again. 'In fact, it might be the opposite, but let's talk about that when I get there, okay?'

After we hung up, I spent ages staring out of the kitchen window while my stomach churned and my brain whirred. I tried to think of all the many stupid things D'Artagnan was capable of doing that would piss off his sister so much but couldn't be explained over the telephone. And as for her last comment 'the opposite of life-threatening' – what the hell did that mean?

I left Camille and Nina with the horses when I heard Françoise's car come down the drive later that morning and ran back inside the house. There were enough butterflies in my stomach to fascinate a team of lepidopterists for several years as I hurried to the front door. When I opened it, Françoise was standing on the doorstep. Pascal waved as he walked around the side of the chateau towards the paddocks.

'He's got an Easter egg for Nina,' Françoise explained as we exchanged kisses. 'And I want to talk to you alone.'

'Coffee?' I asked, trying to keep the edge of hysteria out of my voice.

She shook her head. 'No, thanks. Just a glass of water.' She paused at the entrance to the salon. 'I'll wait here for you, okay?'

I nodded and walked briskly into the kitchen, returning with two glasses, one of which I spilled as I set them down on the coffee table between us. I sat on the sofa opposite her, and tried to take some comfort from the fact that she looked very pretty and cheerful in her red-and-white polka-dot dress.

'Please tell me what he's done,' I begged. 'I'm going crazy trying not to imagine something terrible.'

She gave a slightly wan smile. 'It's not terrible, Nicole, but it is going to make you very angry.'

I stared at her as I sipped my water, my heart tight in my chest. 'Is he cheating on me?' I managed to whisper. Of all the things I had considered, I'd never imagined D'Artagnan might cheat on me.

She grinned and shook her head firmly. 'No, Nicole, he definitely isn't cheating on you! You don't need to worry about that.'

I gave a sigh of relief. 'Please just tell me,' I said quietly. 'I can't bear the suspense.'

She took a deep breath. 'Okay, but first I have to ask you a question. It's a bit personal.'

I shrugged. 'Fire away.'

'Since you went to Donostia to see Guy, have you had a period?'

I frowned at her, confused.

'I'm sorry,' she said. 'But I really need to know.'

I made a face and thought for a minute. My periods are never particularly reliable, but after I'd thought about it for a minute, I answered, 'Yes, I did. The week after.'

'Oh, thank God!' She gave a huge, relieved sigh.

I stared at her. 'Why on earth is my period relevant, Françoise?'

She pressed her lips together. 'It's relevant because Guy has done something you don't know about.'

'Yes, I *know* that! You keep telling me this, Françoise, but you won't tell me what it is he's done!' I had to make a concerted effort not to shout.

She took a deep breath. 'Nicole,' she said, her voice hesitant, 'do you remember when my brother went to Argentina with Emmanuel last September to ride across Patagonia?'

I frowned. 'Well, yes, of course I do.'

'Well, the thing is, he didn't go to Patagonia. He went to Paris. He went to Paris, and he reversed his vasectomy.'

I sat on the sofa immobile, staring at her. She held my gaze.

I'd asked to see the photos from Patagonia but the photos had never actually materialized, because apparently Emmanuel had taken all of them. D'Artagnan hadn't taken any photos and then, when they'd got back to France, Emmanuel had lost his phone and so, even though there were Clouds and ephemeral storage now, somehow all of the photos were lost…

I'd been too busy focusing on that bastard Satan to think about that at the time; I'd just accepted it. I was just so happy that Guy was back from his two-week riding holiday with his son. As I recalled, when he returned he was slightly sore from two weeks on horseback but still capable of an afternoon of pretty mind-blowing sex.

I closed my eyes for what seemed like several minutes. Finally, I opened them and said, 'What?' My voice sounded faint, even to me.

She pressed her lips together again. 'He had a reverse vasectomy in Paris last September.'

We did some synchronised blinking. Finally, she said softly, 'Are you very angry?'

I had absolutely no idea how I felt. I was, however, aware that I was now frowning. 'He never mentioned that.' My voice was slightly tremulous.

'I know. He told me he never discussed it with you.'

I took a deep breath and picked up my glass, went to take a sip and put it down again. 'Sorry – when did he tell you this? When did you see him?'

'Last night. He came to our house. He's staying with us.'

'So he's left San Sebastian?'

She gave what I thought was an apologetic shrug on her brother's behalf. 'He misses you terribly, Nicole. He wants to come home.'

I picked up my glass again and this time I did take a sip. I put it down again and looked at her. 'So does that mean he's got over the whole me keeping the Guillaume thing a secret, then?' I asked, slightly surprised at the sharpness in my voice.

'Yes, he's over that. He said that after you came to San Sebastian he realised he was being an idiot. He's very angry with himself for leaving in the first place.'

I held her eyes. 'I don't know if you'd agree with me, Françoise, but perhaps he's also realised that on the secret-keeping front he's trumped my secret with the secret he's been keeping?'

A carousel of conflicting emotions was slowly beginning to twirl in my brain. One of them was a vivid orange-red colour that I knew did not represent calm.

She reached forward and picked up her glass of water. 'I warned you that you'd be angry,' she said quietly, before she took a sip.

I sat back against the sofa cushions. Mrs Muffin was on her way through the salon from the kitchen. She stopped and meowed at me accusingly. 'I don't care if you don't like it! You liked it yesterday! Eat it or starve!' I growled at her. She glared at me and continued walking out of the salon, flicking her tail at me in annoyance.

Françoise was still watching me closely. I made Xavier's praying-hands pyramid in front of my face and stared beyond her, into the hallway. The carousel in my head was speeding up and everything was becoming very jangly.

'So,' I said finally, making an effort to keep my voice low. 'I could have got pregnant any time since he returned from—' I paused '—*Patagonia*. Is that right?' I was powerless to stop my fingers making inverted commas around 'Patagonia'.

She shook her head firmly. 'No, you couldn't. The operation takes at least three months to work, if it's going to work at all. And there is no guarantee that it will work. Guy had a vasectomy ten years ago. The chances are relatively good that it can be successfully reversed, but by no means guaranteed. And there's no way you could have got pregnant until January this year, at the very earliest.'

'By which time he'd walked out. How do you know all this, Françoise?'

'Because I spent all of last night quizzing him about it, the stupid man!' she said exasperatedly.

I smiled a little, despite myself.

She sighed deeply. 'I just... I can't believe he made a decision like that without discussing it with you! But he said he wanted it to be a surprise. Oh, hang on—' She opened her handbag, searched inside and pulled out a thick white envelope bound with a scarlet ribbon. It was sealed on the back with a red wax seal – no doubt made by the solid-silver du Beauchamp family seal that I knew each sibling owned. D'Artagnan could never resist a bit of theatre, I thought sourly.

She held it out to me. 'He wanted me to give you this.'

I raised an eyebrow. 'That looks like a rather elaborate attempt at an apology.'

'It's not. It's the letter he was going to give you on New Year's Eve, the night you told him about Guillaume.'

I narrowed my eyes. I remembered that night so well. Françoise's annual New Year's Eve party had been cancelled because she, Pascal and most of the rest of the family were ill with bronchitis.

D'Artagnan and I had stayed in and celebrated the new year on our own. In the afternoon, we'd gone for a long walk in the countryside around the Duchess and in the evening he'd made my favourite meal: grilled *cèpes* with a garlicky, buttery sauce, and spinach with a poached egg on top. We'd shared a bottle of Dom Perignon and after dinner, we'd taken the cheese and a bottle of Château Margaux into the salon, where he'd lit a fire in the vast stone fireplace.

We'd shared a lingering kiss in front of that fire. I remembered feeling, not for the first time since D'Artagnan had sashayed into my life, that I was living in a fairy tale; a fairy tale where I really was a princess and he really was my prince.

It was when we were sitting on the sofa together that he'd said, 'Nicole, I have something to tell you.' I was feeling so chilled and so full of love for him, so happy because Satan had been taken into custody two days earlier, and I'd said, 'So do I, my darling.'

He'd insisted I go first. And then all hell had broken loose.

Come to think of it, I vaguely recalled seeing the thick white envelope bound in its scarlet satin ribbon on the sideboard that New Year's Eve when we'd walked into the salon.

Françoise was still holding the letter out to me. When I didn't take it, she put it on the coffee table.

'But I could have fallen pregnant in San Sebastian,' I said.

'Yes, he knows that. That's why he came to see me. That's why he didn't come straight back to you.' She paused. 'He was very worried that you might be pregnant and that you wouldn't know.'

I raised an eyebrow. 'Oh, *that's* what's worrying him, is it?' I suddenly wanted a very large Cognac, so I drained my glass, stood up and went over to the baroque drinks' cabinet.

I glanced back at her. 'Would you like something a little stronger to drink, Françoise? I'm afraid water just isn't cutting it for me after this revelation.'

She shook her head. 'No, it's okay. But you should definitely have something.'

I had already poured myself a generous measure of Benoît's finest '*fine de champagne*' Cognac. I took up my position on the sofa again before I took a large sip of the amber liquid. It was wonderfully smooth and soothing when it hit my stomach. 'Do you know about what happened to me in my early thirties?' I asked after a while. 'Has Guy ever mentioned what I went through when I was trying to have children?'

Her expression was grim. 'He's told me. He said that you had IVF and that you had multiple miscarriages.'

I nodded slowly, aware that anger was now my dominant emotion. 'Yes, I did. It was an extremely painful time.' I paused. 'So why the *fuck* does your brother think I want to go through all that again?'

Françoise flinched, then closed her eyes and massaged her forehead with her fingertips. 'I told him all this, Nicole,' she said helplessly. 'But you know what he's like. He said it wouldn't be the same. He said that you're healthier now, happier, much less stressed.' She stared at me beseechingly. 'Nicole, please. I know my brother is an idiot sometimes, but he only did it because he loves you so much and he wants to make you happy.'

I placed my palms against my eye sockets; it felt soothing.

'I know it was wrong. And he knows it was wrong now, too.' Françoise paused. 'So, I've come to offer you a solution.'

I removed my hands and blinked at her. 'There's a solution to this?'

'Yes. Guy and I agreed it, late last night.'

I picked up my glass of Cognac. 'Go on.'

'This is what he's proposing. He loves you, Nicole. He loves you so, so much, and he loves Nina so much too. He just wants to come home. Nothing else matters more to him than to be with you.'

I felt slightly sick then. Nothing else mattered to me either except – *how could he do that without my consent?*

'So, what's the solution, Françoise?' I kept my voice level.

She took a deep breath. 'It's entirely up to you. You can say no to what he's done, and he will have another vasectomy.

Straight away, before he comes home. And what he did will never be mentioned again.'

I stared at her. 'That's the solution?'

She nodded. 'Yes. He's absolutely adamant about it. You just have to say one word; yes, or no. It's entirely up to you.'

I blinked at her several times. 'But it isn't that easy, is it, Françoise? There will always be residual anger on either side, won't there?'

'We talked about that, the idea of residual anger. I suggested to him that perhaps he should just go and get the vasectomy done again so that you never had to know about it – assuming that you hadn't fallen pregnant in San Sebastian which, thank God, you haven't.'

I took a sip of my Cognac but I no longer felt the need to gulp it down.

Françoise gazed out of the window for a long time before she looked at me again. 'We talked about this a lot, Nicole. I said perhaps that's what he should do, because that way you would never know, but he refused. He said he wanted you to know because, despite how angry I told him you would be, he really believes that you want to be a natural mother. It's nothing to do with Nina – he knows how much you love Nina – but he insists that you should have the choice. But if you say no, he'll immediately have another vasectomy and he will never mention it again.'

She leaned across the coffee table and held out her hand to me. I took it, partly because it would have been rude not to, but also because I suddenly felt very emotional.

'Nicole.' Her voice was very low. 'I know how arrogant my brother is, and I know he behaves like he's a god. But he did this because he loves you and he wants you to be happy. It was just his stupid, misguided way of trying to make your dreams come true.'

***

My hand on Nina's shoulder as she leaned against me, I waved at Françoise and Pascal when they drove away. After we went inside, I made her an omelette with cheese and spinach for lunch. Even though I sprinkled it with smoked paprika (the elusive 'orange dust') she still wasn't very interested in eating it, mostly because she'd already eaten several of her Easter eggs. The sugar rush had clearly peaked because she got angry at me when I snatched the honey jar away from her when she reached for it saying, 'Annie says she'll have my omelette – but only with honey.' Then she sat at the table with her bottom lip sticking out. In a rather futile lesson about wasting food, I tried to eat her omelette even though I wasn't in the least bit hungry.

By now, the carousel was careening around my brain at full speed. How dare he do that? How could he ever think it was a unilateral decision for him to make? And all the while, I was aware of a tiny creature sitting at the very back of the carousel, an indistinct little creature with D'Artagnan's eyes. And each time the carousel twirled, there it was staring at me with his liquid eyes and asking, 'But what if?'

It was so exhausting to have all that going round in my head that for once I was almost relieved to hug and kiss Nina goodnight when I took her back to Marion's house.

***

She was back early on Easter Monday morning. Even though I was exhausted because I'd hardly slept, it was a beautiful sunny day and we rode out on the horses. Nina sat in front of Camille on Emperador, and I was on Espiritu. We had prepared some sandwiches and filled our water bottles, and we stopped in a sunny spot next to a stream after we'd been riding for about two hours. We took off the horses' saddles, removed the reins from their halters and let them wander off to drink from the stream and to graze, while we spread our jackets on the grass and had our picnic.

And once again I was amazed that I'd completely forgotten about D'Artagnan and his machinations while I'd been riding Espiritu.

I slept much better that night, partly because I'd slept so badly the night before but also because it had been the most perfect day. I felt so fortunate to have spent it with the people and animals I loved so much in the country that I had gradually come to realise I could never leave.

***

The following day didn't start so well. Xavier called me at 8.15. 'Hi, Xavier.' My voice was still raspy as I sat up in bed. I cleared my throat and tried again. 'Hi, Xavier. What's up?'

'Hello, Nicole.' He sounded cross. 'Nicole, I take a call from Guy this morning. He want to meet with me today. Why does Guy want to meet with me?'

I let out a deep sigh. D'Artagnan had clearly come galloping back into town, intent on meddling in the lives of his subjects – as if he hadn't meddled enough already.

'I have no idea why, Xavier,' I said tiredly. 'Tell him to fuck off. The case is nothing to do with him.'

Pause. Some breathing. 'I cannot tell him to fuck off, Nicole. Only you can tell him to fuck off.'

I reached for my water glass and took a sip. Mr Muffin gave a big stretch and glanced at his metaphorical watch. He stared at me, his big yellow eyes very round. 'Why have you not rung the breakfast gong?' he asked, his goldfish attention span having failed to register that breakfast had been served at 6.30am in the bathroom as usual.

'Did you speak with Guy again, Nicole?' Xavier was clearly making an effort to sound neutral.

'No, I didn't. But I spoke with his sister and apparently he's back in town.' I took a deep breath. 'So the chances are that he's going to be making a nuisance of himself for a while.'

Silence. Then, his voice curious, 'He is not back at the château with you?'

'No, he's not,' I snapped.

More silence. 'But he is not in San Sebastian anymore?'

'Nope. Last I heard, he's at his sister's house.'

'But you are not speaking to him?'

'For the moment, no, I'm not. He's done something completely unacceptable.'

'*Ah bon*?' There is no other French phrase that embodies a question mark so succinctly.

'Yes.' I paused. 'I'm very angry about what he's done. So for the moment, we're not speaking.'

A long silence. Finally, 'Okay, I understand. But I need to know, Nicole, must I meet with him? He seem very determine that we need to meet. Very ... *bah*, insistent about this.'

'A bit like Francesca, was he?'

'*Exactement*! The same voice,' Xavier agreed.

I took a deep breath 'Okay, Xavier, leave this one with me. I'll get to the bottom of it and get back to you, okay?'

I went downstairs and padded through the salon in my slippers, trying not to trip over Mrs Muffin as she wove back and forth in front of me, occasionally stopping so that I was forced to step around her. She was really becoming quite adept at her kill-them-if-they-don't-feed-you-the-right-food strategy.

After I'd made myself a double espresso, I went into the salon and flopped onto the sofa. I pulled my kimono more tightly around me; it was cooler downstairs than it was in our bedroom.

I dialled Guy's number. He answered after two rings. 'Nicole, *mon amour*. How are you, *mon ange*?'

D'Artagnan, aka Zeus, was back; the purr was rich, seductive, imperious. He'd clearly drowned the feral surfer and sauntered out of the ocean smiling benevolently at his kneeling subjects, their heads bowed so as not to presume to gaze directly on his magnificence.

'Why did you ring Xavier?' I snapped. 'Why do you want to meet with Xavier?'

Pause. '*Bah*, Nicole, *mon ange*, I want to meet with him so that I can help you to bring this case against—' his voice hardened; there was no breeziness when he said '—my business partner.' He took a deep breath. 'I think I can be helpful, Nicole. I know this man very well.' The menace was unmistakable.

I took a sip of my coffee. 'Well, I don't want you to meet with my lawyer unless I'm there.'

'I agree, Nicole.' All charm; in my mind's eye I could see the smile. 'I make the rendezvous for two this afternoon. Why don't we have a lunch first? There is a very good—'

'No!' I was conscious that I was almost shouting 'I'm very, very, *very* angry with you, Guy! We are not going to "have a lunch first", for fuck's sake!'

'Okay.' Really mild. 'We just meet at Xavier's office at two o'clock then, okay?'

'Again, *no*, Guy!' I was furious. I gazed out of the window at the pale-blue, early-morning sky, my eyes wide as I mouthed, 'For fuck's sake, the arrogance!'

'Okay, I just go on my own then.' Pause. 'So, how is everything at the château, *mon ange*? How is Nina? Please tell her I love her very, very much, okay?'

I facepalmed into my free hand. 'Guy,' I said, making an effort to control my voice. 'I don't want you meeting Xavier unless I'm there, and at the moment I don't want to see you. Do you think you could possibly understand that?'

Long pause. 'You don't want me to meet with Xavier?'

'Exactly.'

'Why, Nicole?' The tone was edgier now.

'Because he's *my* lawyer, it's my case and, as I've repeatedly explained to you, I don't want you to meet with him unless I'm there. And I'm not ready to be there!'

Slightly more jaunty tone. 'When do you think you will be ready, *mon amour*?'

'Possibly never,' I snapped.

Longer pause. 'I am sorry for what I do without telling you, Nicole.'

I didn't say anything.

'But I do it because I love you. Because I want to make you happy.' I noted that he was aiming for abject contrition but not quite reaching it.

I took a deep breath 'Yes, well, I'm still working through that, Guy. And that wasn't why I called you.'

Thoughtful pause. I could almost hear him nodding. 'You know, Nicole, I take the TGV to Paris today if you want me to. Snip snip, it's all done, everything is like before. You just tell me.' Pause. 'I do anything for you, *mon ange*, you know this. Just tell me, okay?'

I pressed my lips together very firmly, then I said, 'Don't pressure me on this one, Guy.'

There was a very long silence. When he spoke, his voice was so low it was almost gruff 'Okay Nicole. *Mais tu sais je t'aime*. Don't ever forget this, okay? And I miss you so much. I just want to come home and hold you, *mon ange*.' Another deep breath before he finally accessed it; he did sound genuinely contrite. 'I am very, very sorry that I do this without talking to you first, Nicole. Please forgive me.'

I didn't know what to say, so in the end I just said, 'Guy ... I'm trying to.'

I hung up and I held my phone against my chest, against my heart. I closed my eyes, which were full of tears and I thought, *I love you so much too, but why does everything have to be so unbelievably fucking complicated with you?*

Chapter Eight

I told Bérengère what he'd done during my lesson the following Thursday. She continued to pour *Pineau* into our fluted glasses while I told her, then re-corked the bottle. She put it back down on the table and raised her glass. I touched mine to hers. '*Santé,*' she smiled at me, taking a sip.

Frowning slightly, I sipped mine. 'Don't you think what he's done is outrageous?'

She fixed me with her sensual grey eyes. 'But you always wanted to have children, Nicole. Why is it so terrible?'

I stared at her. 'Bérengère, it's my fucking body! He can't just decide to impregnate me because he's decided that's what I want! Surely you, a first-wave feminist on the original board of directors, can understand that?'

She shrugged. 'Yes, I see that. He should have talked to you about it first.' She took another sip of her Pineau. 'But this is what you want, Nicole. Even I can see this, and I have never wanted to have children.' Her gaze was very frank, very clear.

She reached across the table, picked up her cigarette case and selected a roll-up. She paused before lighting it and pointed it at me. 'I saw you at the lunch for Stephane's birthday. I saw you with the baby, and I saw that look that you had when you were holding her. And—' she gave a little pout then put the roll-up between her lips '—and I could see how much you wanted that. Everyone saw what you want, so I am not very surprised that your D'Artagnan has also seen it and that he decided to try to make it happen.'

I suddenly felt very vulnerable. 'Is it really that obvious?'

She took a deep drag, shrugging as she exhaled 'It's not *very* obvious, Nicole – but for all us women who have had to consider this one big, important question at some point in their lives, yes. For us, it is very clear.'

I looked away.

'And Stephane, he saw it too. And he also saw the way you looked at Xavier and the way Xavier looked at you.'

I started. 'What?'

She smiled slowly. 'Yes, Nicole. It's very easy for those of us who know about desire to see it when it manifests itself.'

I started laughing and, annoyingly, blushing. 'Let's face it, I'm not sure Stephane has seen much desire in his life, Bérengère.'

She gave me a big smile and pointed her roll-up. 'Very good deflection, Nicole. I'm impressed.'

I thought it was too. I opened the notebook in which I kept a note of my lessons and she took the hint because after that we focused on my French lesson.

***

Jules was horrified. 'He did *what*?' she squeaked. 'Without telling you? Oh my God, Nicky, your fucking musketeer— He really is medieval, isn't he?! Has he never heard about consent, for fuck's sake?!'

I blinked rapidly at her. 'To be fair, Jules, he only did it because he thought it was what I wanted.'

'For God's sake, Nicky, that's what every woman in denial says about her abusive partner!'

'Guy isn't abusive, Jules,' I said crossly.

'No, I know that, Nicky. But he clearly has a very warped idea about where and when consent is necessary!'

We blinked at each other on our video call. Her eyes were very blue and her mouth was tightly set. 'Did you ever explain to him what you went through with Karl?' she asked finally.

I nodded. 'Yes. I told him about the IVF and about the miscarriages.'

'Did you tell him how devastated you were, how incredibly painful it was for you?'

'I think so. I think he understood how difficult it was.'

Her eyes flashed angrily. 'And yet he goes and does this, reverses his vasectomy knowing full well that you might have to go through all that again. And he does it without discussing it with you! How dare he?'

'Well, I think the thing is that D'Artagnan doesn't focus on the negatives. I think he saw something I wanted, thought for a minute about how he could make it happen, and then went and did it.' I frowned as I thought: *I wonder if the procedure was painful*. I raised my finger to Google 'reverse vasectomy pain' then realised I was already on the phone.

Jules took a deep breath and raised her glass of wine. I did the same. When she'd put it down again, she said more quietly, 'Nicky, how can he not understand that you were raped, for fuck's sake? That he's effectively violating your body, violating *you*, by not telling you that you could fall pregnant?'

I took a deep breath. 'He was going to tell me. He was ready to tell me what he'd done but then I told him about Satan, all hell broke loose and he buggered off to sulk in San Sebastian.'

Her eyes narrowed. 'But he should have told you when you went to find him in San Sebastian – he should have told you before you had sex. Him not telling you was unacceptable.'

I laid my head back against the sofa and took a deep breath. I held it a minute before I exhaled again. 'Jules, that day – that morning – it was just insane. Neither of us was capable of doing anything other than what we did. There wasn't time to talk – it was *primal*. That's the word. It was primal – it was caveman sex, cavewoman sex.'

She stared at me so long that I thought the screen had frozen so I tapped it.

'I'm still here, Nicky,' she said sharply. 'I just... I guess I don't really understand your relationship with Guy. I get that he's super-arrogant and super-controlling, even though I know you don't let him control you. But I don't get that you're okay with him reversing his vasectomy without discussing it with you first.' She shook her head. 'I just don't get that.'

'He did it because he thinks I want to have children.'

There was a long silence. Finally, she said, '*Is* that what you want? Even after the shit you went through with Karl? Even though you're thirty-eight and it could be even more difficult?'

I pressed my lips together to counteract the tears that were filling my eyes, then I gave a very, very small nod. 'I think it is,' I managed to whisper.

'Well then,' she said softly, 'you should take him back, if that's what you want.' She paused. 'Even though the next time I see him I am going to sit him down and give him a *very* thorough explanation about women and the necessity for *expressed* consent!!'

And after we ended our call, I went into the salon and picked up the thick, white envelope bound in crimson ribbon that I hadn't touched since Françoise had left it the previous Sunday. I sat down on the sofa, opened it and I read what D'Artagnan had written to me:

Nicole, tu es l'amour de ma vie. I love you so much, and I see you with Nina. I see how Nina make you so happy, and I know that you want to have a family. So, I make a change. I have the vasectomy I have ten year ago, reverse. I do this three month ago, in Paris. Because, mon amour, I think we must try to have a family. You want this so much, and I feel pain to see how much you want this – and even if it might be difficult, I believe we can do this, Nicole.

Tu es l'amour de ma vie, Nicole.

And attached to the thick sheet of writing paper covered in his looping, extravagantly cursive script were several pages of a medical report with his name at the top, followed by the words '*Vasectomie Inversée*' and then a lot of other words and figures that mentioned '*spermatozoïdes*' quite a lot.

It was that same night, that Thursday night, that I dreamed of him. It wasn't him, and yet it was. He had dark-blond hair and a little tuft of it stuck up from his forehead, and when he smiled and held his little arms out to me, his eyes were the same colour as mine but his smile was all D'Artagnan. His gaze was pure D'Artagnan.

I lay there in the dark, listening to Mrs Muffin snoring gently and then I picked up my phone, opened it and sent him a WhatsApp.

It was only one word. The word was 'Oui'.

***

I must have fallen asleep again because I woke to the scent of his cologne. His hands slid around my body, his mouth like liquid velvet on the curve of my neck, and I turned over and slipped my hands around his firm, familiar body, and opened my eyes sleepily to gaze into his. We kissed, a slow, deeply sensuous kiss. When we broke off, I whispered, 'You're such an unbelievable arsehole,' and he whispered, 'Yes, but I just want you to be happy.'

I traced the long, familiar muscles in his smooth back. 'Was the operation painful?'

He gave a little smile 'A bit. But it was worth it.'

I closed my eyes. His hand slipped over my hips and he pulled me against him so that our bodies moulded together. It felt wonderful to be embraced so closely again, to inhale his scent, to feel him hard against my stomach. He gave the slightest groan as I wrapped my legs around him.

'Thank you, my darling.' I kissed his mouth softly. 'But you know it's possible that it won't work, that I won't be able to—'

He put a finger against my lips and took a deep breath. His shining eyes were fixed on mine. 'I don't care if it doesn't, *mon amour*, but I think we should try,' he replied softly.

***

So, we tried, and the trying was almost unbearably wonderful. Where the sex had been primal in San Sebastian, now it was tender. After what felt like eternity, when every cell in my body was aching for him, aching for orgasm, he held my arched body firmly in his hands as I closed on him and then closed again, tighter still, as one of those rare, mythical, orgasms gradually unfurled from my core. The groan that forced its way out of my mouth felt as if it had been mined from the very depths of my soul, and then he cried out, and his entire body shuddered, his hands around my hips as I felt him pulse repeatedly inside me. And it felt ... absolutely *exquisite*.

We slept for a while then, I think.

When we woke around dawn, it was raining and our bedroom was in semi-darkness but there was just enough dull light through the gaps in the thick curtains for him to gaze into my eyes and caress my body, for me to caress his as I rode him deep, deep inside me. His hand was splayed on my pubic bone, his thumb insistently massaging me as he watched the orgasm shudder through my trembling body, brushing my hair back from my face, murmuring, '*Fuck*, Nicole, *tu es si belle,* so beautiful. *Je t'aime, mon ange, je t'aime.*' He arched up into me and I gasped at the intensity of my body pulsating around him pulsating inside me.

Sometime in the late morning we went downstairs and he made us coffee. As I leaned back on the table in the dining hall, my kimono loose and my ankles crossed behind him, he sliced a ripe pear and alternately fed me and himself slices off the end of a knife. He opened the jar of honey that was now always on the table, sliced an apple and dipped the slices in honey before feeding them to me. His eyes were fixed on mine as he started smearing the honeyed slices on my lips, then he dipped his fingers into the honey and slipped them into my mouth, followed by his mouth on mine, luxuriously soft and sweet.

And as we kissed, he dipped his fingers deeply into the jar again and smeared my nipples with honey and then slid his fingers thick with honey into me before he licked it very slowly off me as I lay back, my body taut with pleasure on the dining table, in a state of pure ecstasy for the third time that day.

***

Later, he phoned Marion and asked her if it would be okay if we fetched Nina from school. We stood at the school gates with the other parents and I felt choked with emotion to think that one day very soon, I would – *we* would – be Nina's parents.

When the kids started streaming through the school gates and were being gradually reclaimed, I spotted Nina. She saw us and she started running, a huge, delighted grin on her face as she ran straight into D'Artagnan's arms. He lifted her up and she wrapped her little body tightly around him.

I laid my forehead against her and slipped my arm around D'Artagnan's waist, overwhelmed with the love I felt for both of them.

Eventually she leaned back, her green eyes sparkling as she gazed at Guy and then at me, then back at him. She grinned her wide, gap-toothed grin as she said, 'Can we go and find a pony for me now?'

***

D'Artagnan had gone downstairs to make us coffee when Xavier called the following Monday morning. He sounded excited. '*Bah* Nicole, they really find him! The Italian detective find your waiter, the one from the Milan villa! And he remember you! Well, he think he remember you. This is very good news, Nicole, so good for us just before the case go before the *chambre d'accusation*.'

'That's brilliant, Xavier – and amazing after all these years. But how does he know it's me?'

Xavier had gone over everything I could remember from that night at the Marble Villa in Hell in fine detail. Although I hadn't remembered it at first, I later recalled a waiter who'd been circulating with a tray of Champagne. I had deposited my empty glass on his tray and reached to take another full one, smiled at him and said thank you. He'd looked me straight in the eye and said in Italian-accented English, 'Be careful, there are bad men here.' Then he'd glided away, tray held aloft. Since there were bad men *everywhere* as far as I was concerned, I had shrugged, taken a sip of Champagne and continued partying.

'The Italian police have a photo of you from back then. I find it and I give it to them.' He paused and his voice softened. 'You were very beautiful, Nicole. Then he realised he'd made a terrible faux pas. 'You are *still* very beautiful, Nicole. I did not mean that...'

I did not have time to listen to the splatter of displaced earth from the hole he was digging himself out of, so I stopped him. 'Thank you, Xavier, I get all that. But how do *I* know it's the same waiter? What if it's someone Sa— Guillaume has set up, someone he's paid to say he remembers me? And then at the last minute the waiter will fuck everything up and say I was – I don't know – compliant? How do we know it isn't a set-up like it was with Annabelle?' Annabelle's statement had made me sound like a compulsive liar, a hopeless drug-addict and a sex-starved nymphomaniac.

'*Bah*, Nicole, of course I already think of this!' Xavier said dismissively. 'We are going to make a video call with him. Can you come to my office on Thursday, please? We can maybe have a lunch after. I find a new vegan restaurant last week that I think you will like.' I could hear the smile in his voice.

D'Artagnan was just coming into the room with our coffee. I glanced at him. He was frowning a little. 'Who are you talking to, Nicole?' he asked.

I moved my phone to mute the speaker against my shoulder. 'Xavier,' I whispered.

'Yes? Why are you whispering?' Xavier's voice was faint.

D'Artagnan's frown deepened. 'What does he want?' He sounded cross.

I frowned back at him, still holding my phone against me. 'He's my lawyer, Guy.'

Xavier squawked something indistinct.

'I know that, Nicole. Why is he calling you?' Guy got back into bed and held out his hand.

I stared at him and then at his hand. 'What? What do you want?'

'Your phone,' he said. 'It's too early for him to call you. I tell him to call later.'

'Fuck off!' I said crossly and pushed his hand away. I put my phone back against my ear. 'Sorry, Xavier, what were you saying?'

'Is Guy there, Nicole?' he asked.

'Yes, he is.'

D'Artagnan reached out his hand again to take the phone from me. I smacked it away and glared at him. Xavier didn't say anything.

'What were you saying, Xavier?' I asked. 'About the video call?'

'Thursday. I arrange the call for Thursday at 11.30. Can you come to my office at eleven o'clock, so that we can have a talk before the call?' His tone had become very business-like.

'Sure,' I said firmly. 'Thursday at eleven. I'll be there.' I would have to cancel my weekly French lesson with Bérengère.

D'Artagnan started shaking his head vigorously. '*Non,* Nicole. Thursday is not good – I have a meeting with the architect on Thursday.'

I turned to look at him and moved the phone away from my mouth again. 'Well, you go to your meeting with the architect and I'll go to my meeting with Xavier.'

'*Non*!' D'Artagnan said vehemently. 'From now on, I come to all the meetings with you – any meeting with Xavier, with the *juge,* I come to all the meetings now, Nicole!'

I carried on staring at him, thinking: *Ah, here we are already. About to have our first row of the new* époque.

I put the phone back to my mouth. 'I'll be there on Thursday at eleven o'clock. Thank you so much for organising that, Xavier.'

'Is Guy going to come with you?' he asked.

I sucked in some air thoughtfully and gazed at the ceiling for a while before I answered. 'I don't know yet, Xavier. It depends. Anyway, I have to go now so I'll see you Thursday, okay?'

'Okay. Goodbye Nicole,' he said gruffly.

'Bye, Xavier. *Bisous,'* I said, and hung up.

'*Bisous*?' barked D'Artagnan 'Why the fuck are you saying *bisous* to Xavier, Nicole?'

I turned to him and smiled sweetly. It had been very enjoyable, the three-day hiatus during which we'd had a lot of spectacular sex and he had not annoyed me but, like so many good things, it had come to an end. Not the sex, I was sure, but the lack of irritation – that had clearly ended.

It took until Tuesday evening for us to reach a negotiated settlement in which I agreed that he could come to the meetings, and he agreed he would keep quiet and not interfere in any of the proceedings unless *expressly* asked to contribute. And he would definitely not interfere in my professional relationship with Xavier.

Because I could tell he was on edge about Xavier and it wasn't because of my *bisous* comment, which I'd made deliberately to wind him up. I suspected Francesca had said something to him. Our meeting with her and her rottweilers had been very professional – apart from my hand on Xavier's arm and the whispering in each other's ears. But surely that was normal in lawyer–client relationships? In fact, one of the rottweilers had whispered in Francesca's ear during the same meeting. Admittedly, she had turned and snarled at him, but that was her way of petting him…

***

The mood in Xavier's office on Thursday was predictable. An atmospheric change took place as the receptionist showed us into his office – the days of informal, easy Kissies in the foyer when Xavier greeted me personally and took my coat were clearly over. Now, we were all very formal.

Xavier wore the pale-grey shirt that matched his eyes and the dark-blue, fine-wool suit that I'd sobbed into the shoulder of. His dark curls were firmly brushed off his face, and he wore an expression of professional reserve behind his new, frameless glasses. He was remarkably attractive. I knew D'Artagnan would see this too and I mentally shrugged; there wasn't a whole lot I could do about it.

'Nicole, how are you?' He reached over his desk and shook my hand.

'I'm fine, thanks, Xavier. You?'

'Very well, thank you.'

He turned to Guy and held out his hand. 'Guy. It's good to meet you again.' He reached over his desk and D'Artagnan grasped his hand in a way that made me wince inwardly. They nodded curtly at each other.

Xavier motioned to the two chairs on the other side of his desk and we sat down. Even his office looked more organised. Testosterone swirled around the room. I decided It smelled a bit like wet earth after a thunderstorm.

Xavier explained, very formally, what the Italian police had communicated to him. He started reading through the statement that the waiter, whose name was Andrea, had made. First it stated his name, age and profession; it seemed that he was no longer a waiter, he was now a writer.

'Really? What does he write?' I asked.

Xavier stopped reading aloud and looked over his glasses at me. He frowned, his grey eyes fixed on mine. 'He write books, Nicole. He write … *bah, des romans policières*. Crime books. I read one translated from Italian once.'

'Was it any good?'

His frown deepened and a quizzical smile curled onto his face.

D'Artagnan turned to me. His frown was much deeper. 'Why is this relevant, Nicole?'

I shrugged. 'Well, it's just that if he's a struggling writer then maybe he's making all this up and it's not him at all. But if he's successful, then he's less likely to be making up stuff. *N'est-ce pas*?'

Xavier nodded slowly, one eyebrow slightly raised. '*Bah* – that is interesting, Nicole, this idea.' He started to smile at me again, then realised that D'Artagnan was glaring at him, so he frowned again as if he were thinking seriously about what I'd said. 'But yes, he is a successful writer, I think.'

He cleared his throat, looked down and carried on reading Andrea's statement aloud in English. I silently willed – really willed – D'Artagnan not to correct Xavier's French-accented English with his own French-accented English. My will was strong: he did not try.

When the call finally started on the flat-screen monitor opposite Xavier's desk, I immediately recognized Andrea. He was definitely the waiter who had looked hard into my eyes that night and warned me about the 'bad men'. There was something instantly recognisable about his eyes and the shape of his face. He recognised me straight away and smiled at me, although his smile was a bit sad. He spoke only a little French and some English, but he had a translator with him.

In the course of the video call, he confirmed that he had seen Satan and his little friends – one of his little friends, he didn't recognise the other one – at a party at the same villa for spring/summer fashion week the previous October, six months before I'd had the misfortune to become Satan's victim. Andrea had been waitering then, too, and he'd seen Satan slip something into a woman's drink. He'd tried to warn her but, like me, she was already pretty wired and had ignored him. Fortunately, one of her colleagues had seen her starting to behave oddly and had insisted on taking her home.

He'd seen Satan watching me at the party after the autumn/winter show in late February. He'd tried to alert me but I'd ignored him because I was already a bit pissed and had been to the loo three times to do lines with the make-up artist. I was invincible; I knew all about 'bad men' and how to avoid them. I'd been avoiding them for five years by then, ever since I'd got rid of the last 'boyfriend' who had attached himself to me and my naivety. I was a world-weary expert on 'bad men' by the time I celebrated my twenty-first birthday.

I only glanced at D'Artagnan once while we were on the call. His jaw was set hard and his eyes were narrow, furious. He oozed rage – but he didn't say anything. That mouth that I knew so well was set in a rigid pout of unadulterated fury. Once again the thought crossed my mind that perhaps I had not been wrong to deceive him.

After the call ended, we discussed Andrea's testimony and whether he was a reliable witness. Xavier thought he was, and explained that Andrea had agreed to give evidence *in camera* at the pre-trial hearing. This hearing was crucial in deciding whether the case would be heard in front of the *Cour d'Assises* and it would take place in three weeks' time in the rather aptly named '*chambre d'accusation*' of the *Cour d'Appel*. If the *Cour d'Appel* agreed with the *juge,* the case would be referred to the *Cour d'Assises* and heard before three judges and six jurors.

It was the crucial next stage in getting Satan locked away for a long time, and it was not yet in the bag. Xavier warned us that Guillaume had appointed a notoriously successful criminal lawyer with a strong track record of getting his clients acquitted.

'And already in Italy the detective in charge of the case are having some problem with witnesses. On Wednesday, I speak to the detective and he say that he think he find this woman that take you to the party, the woman that you think is paid by Guillaume to bring you there. But when he issue a subpoena to her to be questioned, she disappear. He cannot find her now.'

I felt a little despondent hearing that. D'Artagnan glanced at me and squeezed my hand. I shrugged. 'Well, we still have Léa and Elodie and the video evidence I made, and now we have Andrea as a witness, so surely we have a strong case?'

Xavier nodded slowly. 'Yes, it is a strong case. And if we are successful and the case is referred to the *Cour d'Assises*, we will have more publicity and some other women might also contact me.'

'Like the woman who works in *La Defense*?' I asked.

Xavier nodded. '*Exactement.*'

'What video evidence you make, Nicole?' D'Artagnan was frowning.

I took a deep breath and turned to him. 'Bérengère helped me to make a video where Guillaume more or less confessed to what he'd done.'

'I want to see it,' he seethed.

'No.' I said. 'I don't think it's a good idea for you to see it.'

His eyes narrowed viciously. 'I want to see it, Nicole.'

'No,' I said again, very firmly. 'It will serve absolutely no purpose other than to make you furious, and I don't have the energy to waste trying to calm you down afterwards. So, no – you can see it in court when everyone else sees it.'

Xavier's gaze flickered from me to D'Artagnan and back again.

'Nicole—' said D'Artagnan warningly.

'I'm fucking serious, Guy! The answer is *no*!'

He blinked at me a few times, surprised at my vehemence. To be honest, I was also surprised at my vehemence. We stared into each other's narrowed eyes for a while before he turned away with an annoyed '*pffff*', which I ignored.

One of Xavier's eyebrows was raised very high on his forehead. Although he didn't say anything, I could see he was kind of impressed.

***

We left Xavier's office at around 12.30. When we were on the street, D'Artagnan stopped and turned to me. He gently brushed my hair away from my forehead, his eyes the colour of deep, polished mahogany.

'I am so, so sorry, *mon ange*, that I was not here with you while you make this case against Guillaume. I am hating myself for being so stupid, so *égoïste*.' He said it quietly, his voice full of regret.

I touched his cheek and he took my hand in his and kissed it, his mouth soft against my palm. 'I'm sorry too, my darling, for not trusting you,' I said.

He closed his eyes for a moment, then he slipped his hands along my jaw, cradled my face in his hands and kissed me as we stood on the pavement. It was a kiss so full of love that I felt as if I were melting, slipping through his fingers, becoming ethereal with the intensity of that kiss, the intensity of him.

***

But D'Artagnan is mercurial. We went to one of his favourite restaurants and after we'd had the *entrées* – poached egg on a thick white-asparagus gazpacho for me, animal-terrine with toast for him – I sat back against the velvet banquette and took a sip of the excellent 2015 Saint Émilion he'd ordered.

He fixed me with a very direct gaze. 'So, Nicole, tell me. How long have Xavier been in love with you?'

To subterfuge ... or not to subterfuge: that was the question.

I shrugged. 'Dunno. Not that long, I think.'

He pursed his mouth and raised an eyebrow, took a sip of his wine and put his glass down again. 'What happen between you and Xavier, Nicole?'

I took a deep breath. 'Well, we've been working on the case together since last September, and I suppose we've become quite close. It happens, I guess.' I fixed him with a firm stare. 'He's a very good lawyer, Guy, and I trust him. Remember, you expressly agreed not to interfere in our professional relationship.'

His nostrils flared slightly. He took a deep breath, blinked the slow blink at me but edgily this time. He breathed out again. Then he asked, his voice low, 'Did you fuck Xavier, Nicole?'

I gazed steadily at him. 'No, Guy. I did not.'

He nodded slowly, carried on watching me from across the table. Finally he gave a little shrug. 'Okay. I believe you. But he is in love with you. *Why* is he in love with you? Has he been … *bah, encouragé* by you, Nicole? This is not a man that is just hopeful, this is a man with feelings, with strong feeling for you. What happen between you and Xavier, Nicole?'

I took a deep breath; after all, I had been anticipating this conversation. 'We kissed, twice. The first time because, well – just because. We were working together, it was late and it had been a very emotional day and I was – well, we both were, I suppose, very susceptible. It was something that was coming from a distance.'

I paused and continued to hold his eyes. 'And I stopped it. I said no, and I stopped it going any further.' I leaned forward and returned his very direct gaze with bells on. 'Because I love *you,* Guy, and I knew things were *not* over between you and me.'

He blinked and nodded slowly. 'When did this happen, Nicole?'

'The night before I came to you. I drove down to San Sebastian that night, after I persuaded Francesca to tell me where you were.'

He pouted again, still nodding thoughtfully. 'Okay. But then why was there another time? You say you stop him the first time. When was the second time you kiss him? Why was there a second time?'

'The second time I was really upset and drunk. We both were. It was after the second meeting with the *juge d'instruction* at the end of last month.'

'Why were you drunk with Xavier, Nicole?' His voice was soft, almost menacing.

'Because I'd been grilled horribly by the *juge d'instruction* about the lies that Annabelle – Do you remember Annabelle, the wedding planner that you found? By the way, how *did* you find poisonous Annabelle?'

He frowned. 'Who is Annabelle?'

'The wedding planner. Don't you remember? Last year you insisted that we hire a wedding planner for our wedding celebration because I really wasn't up to it. I was a bit fucked up, even though you didn't know why. Anyway, I'm curious – how did you find her?'

The frown deepened. 'I ask Guillaume—' And then the fury was back in his jaw, in his eyes, in his body – it was everywhere.

'*Voilà.*' I leaned back against the banquette. 'So Satan got a little cloven hoof through the door through that vile woman.'

He stared at me. 'I don't understand, Nicole. Who is Satan?'

I took a deep breath and started explaining everything that had happened since the day when Satan had let slip who he really was: Annabelle; the oxycodone; how I realised that Guillaume was Satan; that Annabelle had kept Satan apprised of how his victim, now addicted to opioids again, was faring.

Guy put his elbows on the table and rested his chin on his folded hands as I talked. He closed his eyes and shook his head slightly every now and then as I explained what Annabelle had said about me, how I'd had to persuade the *juge d'instruction* in my bad French that no, I wasn't a drug addict, I wasn't a nymphomaniac, I wasn't a liar and I hadn't made anything up about Guillaume. I explained how that had been very difficult and afterwards, Xavier and I had got pretty drunk and snogged each other in the corner of a wine bar. But it hadn't gone any further – Xavier booked me a room in a hotel and had *not* come up to the room with me.

I stared hard at D'Artagnan. 'He did not come up to the room with me, Guy. Xavier might think that he's in love with me but he has *never* taken advantage of me.'

He gazed back at me, then his eyelashes swept over his eyes again. 'Nicole,' he said quietly, 'Xavier does not think he is in love with you, he *is* in love with you. I can see this. Stephane already tell me that Xavier is in love with you.'

'Oh?' I raised both eyebrows. 'When did Stephane appear in this story?'

The waiter had brought our main courses by then; pasta with parmesan, sun-dried tomatoes and walnuts for me, steak *bleu* (of course) and *frites* for him.

Guy made a face and did a little evasive wiggle of his shoulders, the one I call the 'evasive cockatoo' wiggle. He took a sip of wine. 'I speak to Stephane.'

I nodded. 'That's interesting. I spoke to Stephane too. I had a really fascinating chat with him when we were at Françoise's house for his birthday. When did you speak to him?'

He speared several *frites* with his fork, put them in his mouth and chewed as he gazed at me across the table. 'So Nicole, you kiss Xavier twice. Is that all that happen?'

I nodded. 'Yes. That's all that happened. When did you speak to Stephane?'

And did he explain your god complex to you? Did he explain your demons to you? I really wanted to ask him that, but I knew I had to be a bit more subtle. D'Artagnan is very good at avoiding questions he doesn't want to answer.

'And you don't have feelings for Xavier?'

I rolled my eyes. 'Yes, Guy, I do have feelings for Xavier. I have to admit that I was attracted to him – but I'm not in love with him. I feel bad that I kissed him, that I perhaps made him think there was the possibility of things going further between us. That was wrong of me.'

He was still pouting. I gave him a hard stare. 'I'm sorry that I kissed Xavier. In my defence, I was going through a bit of a tough time. I didn't know where you were or when – or even if – you were coming back, and that was hard. And then, after I came to San Sebastian, I still didn't know whether or not we had a future together.'

I paused. 'But I never stopped being in love with you. I love you, Guy. That hasn't changed. It never changed.'

He reached forward and took my hand. 'I love you too, Nicole. That has never changed for me, either. I am very, very sorry that I leave you. It was *incroyablement stupide* that I leave you like that. Please, *mon amour*, forgive me for this.'

'Of course I forgive you, Guy.' I smiled softly at him and we continued gazing at each other for what seemed like a long while. Then I said, 'So when did you speak to Stephane?'

He glanced down at my plate 'Nicole, you are eating pasta! You never eat pasta!'

'I'm hungry, Guy. Sometimes I eat pasta.' I paused and stared into his evasive brown eyes. 'And which specific part of your body would you like me to torture so that you finally answer my question about Stephane, my darling?'

He started to list his preferred body parts – they weren't very original. When he saw me roll my eyes, he reluctantly told me about Stephane's visit. Apparently, his brother had decided that he was going to explain D'Artagnan's god complex to him and he'd driven down to San Sebastian the day after his birthday lunch. Stephane had strolled on the promenade and waited until angry, feral D'Artagnan emerged from the cold Atlantic Ocean with his surfboard and then they'd gone for breakfast together.

We'd finished our main course and were waiting for the plates to be cleared. D'Artagnan was holding my hand and stroking my wedding rings. 'And of course, then I am starting to worry that we have sex and that maybe there is a possibility that you are pregnant, and you will not know. And then Stephane tell me that I am being an idiot, and that Xavier is falling in love with you and you are falling in love with Xavier.' He paused. 'And, Nicole, I suddenly realise how stupid I am being and that I must come home to you.'

'But you didn't think to call me and tell me about what you'd done – about reversing the vasectomy?'

He made a *mea culpa* gesture with his shoulders. '*Bah*, Nicole, I pick up my phone many time to call you to tell you this, but every time I think no, I want to tell her when I see her.' He hesitated. 'And then I start to think maybe you are going to be a little bit ... *bah*, annoyed by this? So I decide to talk to Françoise first.'

He was still stroking the wedding rings on my finger. He lifted my hand to his mouth and kissed it, smiling his most charming smile.

'A little bit annoyed, huh?' I repeated.

Another shrug and that fake-contrite smile. 'Just a little bit, maybe. But I know this is what you want, and I want this too.'

He took a deep breath, sat back in his chair and smiled at me benevolently 'And it will happen, Nicole. You must not worry. I know you will have our children.'

'Children?' I asked incredulously 'Plural? Let's not get ahead of ourselves, Zeus!'

Slightly puzzled frown. '*Quoi*?'

'Never mind,' I said, shaking my head, unable to hide my smile.

Chapter Nine

D'Artagnan's return seemed to release the tension in both my body and my mind. As the month of May started, I started to feel increasingly tired. I struggled to wake in the mornings, and I felt sleepy after lunch. It was the most marvellously luxurious thing to do, to finish my tea in the morning and then snuggle back down under the duvet with Mrs Muffin and dive back into the velvet blackness.

'You are tired, *mon ange.* You must sleep some more.' D'Artagnan was sitting next to me on the bed, stroking my hair off my face. 'I take care of the animals and my *projet.*'

I frowned sleepily. 'What project?'

He smiled sweetly. 'Just a little *projet.* I take care of it, don't worry.'

But my eyes were already closing again and I was sinking into the welcoming darkness. I didn't really care what his '*leetle projet*' was; if it kept him busy then it was a good thing, given that I'd rather torpedoed his joint venture with Satan and the Queen of the Rottweilers.

The luxurious sleep interlude ended abruptly when the *leetle projet* kicked off. It was not at all *leetle*; it was a bloody massive project that involved a lot of heavy machinery that arrived at 7am on Monday of the following week.

I stood at the bedroom window staring out at the huge digger ripping up the lawn in front of the kitchen window. I could feel the Duchess vibrating with anger under my bare feet. Shaking my head, I turned to D'Artagnan. 'When exactly did you decide to press "go" on the swimming pool?'

He was pulling on his T-shirt. '*Bah,* we talk about *la piscine* last year, Nicole. We need to have it ready for the summer.'

'But we haven't discussed it *properly.* We haven't discussed any of the detail!' I protested.

Little shrug, pout. '*Bah, ouais,* of course we discuss it. You say if I change the shape and make the pool at the side of the chateau you will be happy. So I do that. I tell the architect and she draw up the plan.' He smiled brightly, fluttered the charming eyelashes.

I stared back at him tiredly, shook my head again and headed towards the bed. I propped up some pillows behind me and sat back as I reached for my coffee. It didn't taste very nice so I put it down again and took a sip of water instead. 'When were you doing all this?'

'In Donostia.' He went into the bathroom and I heard him unzip his shorts and start peeing.

'Sulking, surfing and swimming-pool design. You were a busy little bunny, weren't you?'

'*Quoi*?' he shouted.

'Nothing,' I shouted back. 'It's just that it would have been nice to discuss it a bit more before you made a unilateral decision to turn the front garden into Agincourt.'

He came back into the bedroom, zipping up his shorts and frowning. 'Do you not want a *piscine*, Nicole? Last year, you said "this would be nice, Guy, to have a swimming pool". Now, you don't want a *piscine*?'

I took another sip of water. 'No, it's not that I don't want a swimming pool. It would be great to have a swimming pool. I just wasn't expecting to have one this week.'

He frowned and made a face as if I were stupid. 'Of course it will not be this week, Nicole. It will take at least three weeks.'

I felt very tired again. Arguments were never a straight line with D'Artagnan. 'Weren't we supposed to get, like, planning permission or something?'

A classic pout, imperial sniff. '*Pffff*. We get it afterwards. It will not be a problem.'

I rolled my eyes. His ego didn't seem to have diminished while he was sulking in Donostia. 'I hope you've explained to the Duchess that this was your idea.'

He frowned. 'What do you mean?'

'The Duchess – y'know, the château. She'll be bloody livid about all the noise and disruption.'

He shook his head slowly, a slight smile curving the edge of his mouth. 'You and *ze furcking Duchesse,* Nicole...' He rolled his eyes.

***

We stood on the edge of the field behind the electric fencing looking at the ponies. Nina was peering intently at them. She turned around to look up at us, her green eyes luminous in the bright sunshine. 'That one,' she said, pointing.

D'Artagnan frowned. 'The brown one?'

She nodded very firmly.

'But Nina – the golden one, he is much more handsome. Why do you not like the little gold pony?'

The golden pony was standing on the only part of the paddock that was slightly raised where the hay feeder was. He was perfectly proportioned and very good looking. He had a small, well-bred head, a compact, muscular body and a flowing chestnut mane and tail. Occasionally he took a mouthful of hay and chewed it slowly while he surveyed the other two ponies from his elevated position.

They were all Welsh Section-D ponies, a breed I had learned from Camille all pony-desiring little girls dreamed of. Get a good one and you would never, ever part with it; get an opinionated one and your child might spend a lot of time scribbling on the plaster-of-Paris that was attached to whatever limb was the latest casualty.

Every time one of the other two ponies tried to approach the hay feeder, the handsome gold pony flattened his ears and bared his teeth and they retreated. Then he took another mouthful of hay and carried on calmly chewing while he surveyed the world of which he was master.

It wasn't entirely surprising that D'Artagnan favoured the gold pony.

'No,' said Nina dismissively. 'I don't like him. He is not nice to the other ponies. Emperador and Espiritu will not like to be friends with him. I like that pony, the brown one.'

Camille put her hand on Nina's shoulder and smiled at her. 'I think you are right, Nina. I like the brown one too.'

The brown pony was also beautifully proportioned and, although it was clear he would also like a snack from the hay feeder, he seemed reasonably content to stand quietly until the gold pony decided he had finished eating.

The brown pony was led into the paddock, tacked up with his saddle and bridle. The brown pony's name was ... Hermès.

My eyes widened when his owner, Florence, told us his name and I couldn't stop the grin spreading across my face. *Yep*, I thought, *that makes perfect sense. My daughter is going to have a pony called Hermès*. Admittedly, Hermès after the Greek deity and not the shop, but still…

Nina was fizzing with excitement. This time it was D'Artagnan who put his hand on her shoulder and said, '*Calme toi,* Nina. If you are too excited, Hermès will get excited.'

She turned, looked up at him and smiled toothily. He smiled back at her and stroked her head gently.

The third time Nina trotted Hermès around the paddock, Florence turned to us and smiled. 'She's quite a good rider, your daughter,' she said.

That overwhelmed me; it was as if a tap had been turned on. Tears filled my eyes and spilled down my cheeks as I tried desperately to wipe them away. I leaned back against D'Artagnan's strong body and he tightened his arms around me. He kissed the side of my forehead and murmured, 'She is a *very* good little rider, our daughter.' His breath was warm on my ear and my hands tightened on his forearms. I held on to him so tightly because I felt in that moment as if I might float away with happiness.

***

But life throws curve balls. Or rather, Satan seemed to be capable of throwing curve balls even from behind the bars of the prison he was being held in.

Xavier called again a few days after we'd agreed to buy Hermès for Nina. It was the day before the hearing at the *chambre d'accusation* where he'd be presenting the evidence against Satan. This time my phone was on speaker and D'Artagnan was sitting next to me.

There was a problem with the case. 'Andrea, he has – he take back … *bah*, what is this word, Nicole? He un-make his testimony.'

'Withdraw,' I said, my voice as dull as I felt.

'*Oui,* withdraw. *C'est ça*. He withdraw his testimony. I think this is something Guillaume do.'

'But Guillaume is in custody! How could he have done this?' There was a childish whine in my voice.

Guy made a face and turned away, his expression both resigned and furious at the same time.

Xavier didn't answer at first then he said softly, 'I warn you about this, Nicole. I tell you in the beginning that Guillaume is very good at – *bah*, evading justice. He is very good at avoiding legal action. I see this when I make enquiries, when I do research on him.' He paused. 'I am very sorry, Nicole, but Andrea does not want to give testimony. Something has happen to make him afraid.'

And then *I* felt afraid. I put my hand over my mouth and stared, unseeing, out of the window. Guy slipped his arm around my shoulders and pulled me carefully against him. 'What do you mean "afraid"?' I asked finally.

Another pause; I swear I could hear the Gallic shrug. Xavier's voice was low. 'I speak to the Italian detective and he tell me that he think someone has told Andrea that something bad will happen to him, or maybe to his family, if he testify.'

I rubbed my forehead. My neck and shoulders felt tense. 'Is this because of his mother? Is this something his family has done?'

'The mother of who Nicole?' Xavier sounded confused.

'Satan's mother.'

Pause. 'I don't know what you mean, Nicole.'

D'Artagnan spoke then. He explained in French what I was trying to say. He explained about Guillaume's background and his Italian mother, who would do anything, say anything, pay anything, pull any strings in order to help her precious son Satan avoid ever having to answer for the things he had done. Including, probably, giving his younger sister the drugs on which she had overdosed and died. Her death had caused the premature death of his father, according to Françoise.

My family was fucked up, that was indisputable, but Satan's family? That was both fucked up and *evil*.

'You know his family very well, Guy?' Xavier finally asked.

'Of course I know him well, Xavier! I went to school with him. Laurent and I were at school with him – I've known him all my life! I knew his sister and I knew his mother and father I know ... *bah*.' He shook his head. His voice was bleak. 'I thought I knew Guillaume very well. But I was wrong.'

‘Do you think that his family could have organised this so that Andrea withdraw his testimony?’

D’Artagnan looked out of the dining-hall window. When he turned back to the phone his voice was subdued. ‘Xavier, after I found out what Guillaume did to Nicole there is nothing – nothing – that I think he would not or could not do. His family has many connections in Italy.’ He shook his head. ‘Even though I never think this can happen, now that it happen I am not very surprised.’

I frowned at him and made a ‘how?’ movement with my hand. He gave a sad little shrug and shook his head.

‘Well, there is not very much we can do now,’ said Xavier. ‘We have to strike Andrea’s testimony from the submission to the *chambre d’accusation* tomorrow. I need to do this now.’

Another pause and then he went on in English. ‘I am very sorry about this, Nicole, Guy. But please don’t worry. We still have a very strong case against him. And they will see the video that you make Nicole because this has been accepted as evidence and it is very, *bah ... compromettantes*.’

I frowned.

‘Compromising,’ said D’Artagnan, seeing my confusion.

‘*Oui, exactement*,’ said Xavier.

I felt cold and very tired. If Satan was capable of getting at witnesses from prison, what was to stop him getting someone to threaten Léa or Elodie? Or me? Would he threaten me?

D’Artagnan’s face was sombre too. ‘Okay, Xavier, we wait to hear the result tomorrow after you present the case to the *chambre d’accusation,*’ he said. He took my hand in his and kissed the back of it gently. ‘We are both supporting you strongly tomorrow for the submission to the court.’

Xavier’s voice was resolute. ‘Do not worry, I am confident. It will be fine. I call you tomorrow after the submission. *Bonne soirée a vous deux*.’

And thus did D’Artagnan forgive Xavier for kissing his wife because he finally accepted that Xavier really was a good lawyer, that he had my back – and that he was not going to let Satan win.

***

I slept badly that night and woke at 3.30am with a terrible, breathless gasp. The image of Satan smiling horribly at me while he slid a long, gleaming knife into D'Artagnan's heart as I watched helplessly was crystal clear in my mind's eye.

D'Artagnan, sleeping soundly beside me, stirred a little and pulled me closer in his sleep. His arms tightened momentarily and his body felt so reassuring curved around mine, his breath warm in my hair, one of his legs between mine that, after a while, my heart calmed and I fell asleep again.

***

It happened the following day. It was Wednesday, just after midday when I'd gone upstairs to change into my riding clothes before Nina arrived.

D'Artagnan, in his new role as my gynaecologist, wasn't very happy about that. 'But when, Nicole? When was your period?'

I shrugged. 'I don't know, Guy. My periods are never very regular. I can't remember!'

He stared at me. 'But you do not have a period since I come back.'

'Well no, I haven't. But I don't think I would normally have had one,' I said crossly.

'Maybe we should do a test.' Unsurprisingly, we now had a large stock of pregnancy tests.

I frowned. 'Can we do one later? It's already after twelve and Nina's going to be here at quarter past. I don't really have time to do one now.'

'*Bah*... Okay, but you cannot ride Espiritu until you do a test,' he said.

I stopped in the entrance to the kitchen and took a deep breath. 'Yes, Guy, I can.'

'But what if you are pregnant?' He glared at me. He was making a spinach and asparagus risotto for our lunch.

I glared back. 'Guy, sweetheart, you need to get over this idea that it's going to happen quickly – if it happens at all.' I took a deep breath. 'And also, women can ride until the sixth or seventh month of pregnancy. So you don't need to worry about that, okay?'

Some blinking. 'Who tell you this, Nicole?'

'The internet,' I said. Then I added quickly, 'Anyway, I'm not pregnant and we're just going for a short ride, so please don't fret, my darling.'

‘Hrrrummpph,’ said my gynaecologist.

I was lacing up my riding boots and musing about the fact that the lunchtime ceasefire at Agincourt had begun a bit earlier than normal. It was quiet outside; the grumbling, guttural, earth-digging machines had fallen completely silent so that the sound of birdsong through our bedroom windows was once again the predominant sound.

And then I heard her, very faintly. I stopped lacing my boot as I listened, and then I heard it again. Her voice was high, panicked. ‘Mama! Mama! Where are you, where are you?’

I stood up and walked to the window. Nina was running across what remained of the lawn at the front, her face crumpled with distress, her pale pink T-shirt stained with what looked like blood. I could hear the sobs in her voice and my heart shrivelled. Without pausing, I ran out of the bedroom.

I was at the top of the stairs when it happened. I’d forgotten that my right boot was still unlaced. I stood on one of the trailing laces with my left foot, went to lift my right foot to take the next step down but couldn’t. My right foot was trapped and the banister was just out of my reach. My hand grasped wildly at nothing as I felt myself starting to fall forwards – and I got that sensation in my nose, that presentiment of what smashed sinuses and cartilage were going to feel like in the immediate future.

I started to fall through the space between the top stair and the ground floor seventeen steps below. Gravity was now my master and I was its experiment in how bodies fall and how they might break.

***

It had been a very wet weekend in March; for once, the weather forecast had not been wrong. It had said a hundred percent chance of rain and rain was what we got. All weekend.

Nina and I had decided to make a cake. When I’d Googled the recipe for sponge cake, Mary Berry had loftily assured me that it was the easiest thing in the world to make.

Nina was sitting on her stool and I was standing behind her, my arms around her as she tried to read out loud the recipe on my phone in English; her pronunciation was making me press my lips together very hard. We’d been to the supermarket on Saturday morning to buy the ingredients. Returning home, we’d carefully measured the flour, caster sugar and baking powder into the mixing bowl and I'd shown her how to break open the egg shells with a butter knife into a separate bowl. We fished the bits of eggshell out before adding the eggs to the other ingredients and I whizzed the mixture together with the electric whisk. It was satisfying to note that its consistency was exactly as required by the recipe. Now it only remained to persuade D'Artagnan's beast of a range-cooker to cook the mixture we had prepared so carefully.

Nina was bored by the time the 'oven-ready' light came on and she went to sit in the library with the cats. I'd lit a fire in the wood-burner late that morning and it was cosy in there. I slipped the two cake tins onto the oven shelf, set an alarm for twenty minutes on my phone and started washing up the bowls and utensils.

Did the Duchess intervene? Did she have a quiet little word with the *piano de cuisson*? Because even though I opened the oven door as soon as the twenty minutes were up, the two cakes were significantly browner than the picture in the recipe.

I turned the tins upside down on a wire rack and, after a while, managed to free what looked like two large biscuits from the tins. I stared at them glumly, and then I glared at the range-cooker for a while. I was sure I'd set the temperature right.

I cut a small piece off the edge of one of the biscuits. It was still very warm but it actually tasted quite nice, so it wasn't a total disaster after all, given that it was my first ever attempt at baking. I smeared honey over the top of one of the large biscuits and glued the other biscuit onto it before getting the squirty cream out of the fridge. Annie had apparently insisted that the only correct sandwich filling for cakes was honey, and Nina had insisted that squirty cream was also non-negotiable. I put the can of squirty cream on the tray, together with the large honey-biscuit and a pot of mint-tea, and headed towards the library.

Nina didn't look up when I entered. I glanced at her then frowned. 'What's that you're looking at?'

She was turning the pages of a thick, leather-bound photo album. The photos were sepia-tinted. She looked up at me, her eyes shining. 'I found it in the secret place,' she said. 'It was hidden right at the back of the shelf at the top.'

'What secret place?'

'The secret cupboard.' She smiled her gap-toothed smile and returned her attention to the album.

I was aware that I was still frowning as I sat beside her. The pages of the album were the colour of ivory and stained with pale yellow spots.

'What secret cupboard?' I gazed at a photograph of a very glum-looking family staring at the photographer as if he'd just told them the end of the world was nigh. The woman whom I assumed was the matriarch was wearing a long, dark dress with a high collar, and her husband a formal three-piece suit. He had some pretty spectacular sideburns., His hand was resting on the shoulder of a gangly teenage boy, the tallest of the three boys and two girls who were ranged in order of descending height in front of their parents. The château was slightly blurred in the background.

Nina frowned at me. 'You know, the secret cupboard.'

As I wondered how to rephrase the question to get slightly more information, I turned to the next page in the album. The texture of the paper was very thick and the photographs had elaborately scalloped edges. There were two on each page, separated by a thin sheet of transparent paper.

I was staring at a picture of a young girl. She was quite small, perhaps only seven or eight years old, and was dressed in a long white dress, white gloves and shoes. She was wearing a wide-brimmed hat from which a long veil hung almost to her waist, covering her upper body and obscuring her features. She was standing between what looked like two large wooden beehives.

In the second photograph, she had turned and laid her hand on top of one of the hives. There was a woman, similarly attired, standing directly behind her. Even though she was also shrouded from head to toe in a long white dress, hat and veil, she was clearly quite old because she was stooping slightly as she leaned her hand on the little girl's shoulder.

And as I stared at the photo, I was suddenly aware that the hairs on the back of my neck were standing up. The sensation was very faint; faint but unmistakeable. Someone had just breathed on the back of my neck.

Chapter Ten

That photograph flashed through my mind as I started to fall down the stairs, because that was when the weirdest thing that has ever happened to me in in my whole life took place.

To this day, I still get goose-pimples thinking about it. It *still* makes me shiver because there is absolutely no logical explanation for what happened. Obviously, now I know *why* it happened – but that doesn't make the *how* any more explicable.

As I fell, I became aware of a loud humming sound, as if a wall of sound had suddenly swept up the staircase towards me. I felt a force against my body, like the force you feel when you try to walk against a strong wind. Except there was no wind, only this intense, deep, buzzing as something incredibly strong and insistent pushed back against me.

I was pushed backwards effortlessly until suddenly I felt my bum land on the third step and my right hand, which previously had been frantically grasping at thin air, on the banister. The loud buzzing stopped immediately.

I sat there on the third step, thinking: *What the actual fuck just happened*? My nose was still stinging in anticipation of the forthcoming sensation of smashed cartilage and bone and my eyes were already watering.

Then Nina ran up the stairs, her face wet with tears. There was definitely blood on her T-shirt. 'It's Espiritu, Mama! Come quickly, it's Espiritu – he's been hurt!' She was crying hysterically. I reached for her hand and stood up, still in shock.

There was a trail of blood in the sand around the edge of the round paddock and even more on the concrete outside the stable into which Camille had taken Espiritu. She was crouched down beside his back legs and Guy was standing at Espiritu's head, holding the rope from his head collar. He raised his palm towards me when he saw me and said, '*Non*, Nicole, *non*, don't come in, please don't—'

I ignored him and walked quietly over to Espiritu. His head was low and he looked confused. He tried to raise his head and stand on his four legs when I placed my hand gently on his neck but then he flinched and his head drooped again. I was surprised at how cool he felt; I couldn't feel the warmth that normally radiated from him.

Nina was standing at the stable door, her eyes stricken, her little hand covering her mouth. Guy handed the halter rope to me and lifted her up. She slipped her arms around him, buried her face in the crook of his neck and started crying again. As he carried her into the courtyard, I heard him talking to her, his voice low and soothing.

Camille was still crouched down trying to hold Espiritu's left fetlock, wiping angrily at the tears that were pouring down her face. There was blood all over the pale gold straw around her.

'What happened?' I asked, aware that my voice was trembling.

She shook her head slowly. 'He got a fright. He got out of the paddock and jumped over something and landed badly.' Her eyes filled again. 'I think he has severed the tendon in his fetlock.' She bit her lips together hard as the tears continued to run down her cheeks.

'Yes, but it'll heal, won't it?' I asked, aware that my voice was higher than it should have been. 'It's only an injury, isn't it?'

She put her hand over her face and gave a terrible sob.

'But it'll heal, won't it?' I insisted desperately.

She drew a deep breath. 'No, Nicole.' She shook her head, her eyes full of grief. 'It's a terrible injury. I've already called the vet.' She stood up slowly and took a step towards me. 'I'm so sorry, Nicole, but Espiritu will have to be euthanised. He cannot survive this.'

My heart felt as if it had dropped through my body and exploded on the hard, blood-splattered floor of the stable. 'No,' I whispered. 'No, not that. Please, not that, Camille.'

She raised her black eyes to mine and the sorrow that I saw in them was as deep as the most fathomless lake in the deepest bowels of the earth. 'The vet will decide,' she said, 'But I know what he will say already. I have seen this injury in a horse before.'

The vet arrived about twenty minutes later and, after quickly examining Espiritu, gave him an injection of pain-killer. By that time, Gabriela had arrived as well; she'd taken Nina from Guy and together they went to groom Emperador. Nina had stopped crying because Guy had reassured her Espiritu would get better.

When he came back to the stable, I leaned against him. He crossed his arms over my body as we watched the vet examine Espiritu's fetlock. Camille was standing next to Espiritu's head and I was chewing the edge of my thumbnail so hard that it was bleeding.

Finally, the vet gave a deep sigh. 'I'm very sorry,' he said, 'but he needs to be euthanised.'

Camille put her hand over her face and made a terrible, anguished noise. I felt a wave of nausea rise from my stomach. I took a deep breath. 'No,' I said loudly.

The vet frowned as Camille turned to me, her face ravaged. 'Nicole, you don't understand – this is a terrible injury that he has.'

I blinked at her, aware that my eyes had misted over, and shook my head. 'No, you can't do that. *We* can't do that.' I wiped my eyes angrily and turned back to the vet. 'Is there even the slightest chance that he can recover from the injury?'

As he stood up, he continued to frown at me. He was quite young, perhaps in his late twenties, and he had sad brown eyes. 'It is very unlikely that he will recover from this.'

'But there is a chance that he will?'

The slightest Gallic shrug. 'I don't know exactly how bad the injury is, but the ligament has been damaged quite severely. He will need to have a scan to see how serious it is but, in any event, it will be very difficult for him to recover from this. It will be very expensive. And even if he does recover, he can never be ridden again.'

I touched Camille's shoulder and she turned her anguished eyes on me. 'Camille,' I said quietly. 'Please, please, *please* don't do this. Please don't have him euthanised, I beg you. I will buy him from you and I will do whatever it takes to nurse him, to help him recover. I will do everything I can to help him get over this. Please, I'm begging you, Camille, don't put him to sleep.'

She gave another terrible sob. 'Nicole, I don't want to do this, but he is in so much pain – and he might always be in pain. It's so difficult for a horse to recover from an injury like this.'

I glanced at the vet. 'Can't we manage the pain?'

He scowled at me. 'I have already given him a pain-killer injection. He is still in some pain, but he is sedated. The pain will come back when the injection wears off.'

So give him another injection! I thought angrily.

I turned to look at Guy; his eyes were glassy, too, but he was also frowning. 'Camille,' he said quietly. 'At least get a second opinion. You should not just rely on one vet's opinion to make a big decision like this.'

Another tear rolled down her cheek as she looked at him. 'Guy, Nicole – I have seen how difficult it is for a horse to survive this. We tried with my father's favourite horse and he went mad. He went crazy to be kept in his stable, and he was in constant pain. He would not stop moving and in the end... It was terrible. After all that extra pain we had to make the decision to euthanise him anyway. I don't want Espiritu to suffer like that.'

'Just a second opinion,' Guy said quietly.

Finally, she shrugged resignedly. She shook her head slowly without looking at either of us, then she closed her eyes for a long moment. 'Okay, we get a second opinion.'

The young vet did not look happy.

I breathed out an enormous sigh of relief; I wasn't aware that I'd been holding my breath for so long.

Guy nodded, 'Thank you, Camille. I will call Benoît and ask him to recommend another vet. His daughter has a horse. I'm sure he can recommend someone.'

It was 6pm by the time the second vet arrived. She was an older woman, friendly and cheerful. She examined Espiritu, listened to his heart rate and his breathing, took his injured leg very gently in her hand and examined it carefully. Then she stood up, her eyebrows raised high as she pouted thoughtfully.

We were all standing in the doorway of the stable on tenterhooks.

'I think…' Her voice was slow, deliberate.

I wanted to scream, 'Get the fuck on with it!!' There were times when my frustration at this nation that likes a bit of drama in their discourse made me want to explode. But I bit my lip and kept quiet.

She breathed in and finally she spoke. 'I think it is possible that he might recover from this injury.'

I suddenly felt exhausted, as if all of the energy had been vacuumed out of me. I sagged back against D'Artagnan and his hands tightened around my shoulders. He rested his forehead against the back of my head and I felt his warm breath in my hair.

Camille didn't say anything.

'He is a young horse and he is in good health. If he was an older horse, I would probably not have much hope – but he is young. And I don't think he has completely severed the ligament, so he might be able to heal. But he will need an ultrasound scan to see how bad the injury is. He will need medication twice a day, and he will need the bandages changed every day.'

She paused and looked at us each in turn. 'And he will need to stay in his stable for at least a month, maybe longer. After that, another ultrasound scan.'

She paused again, her face very serious, before continuing. 'And then he will need very gentle, very small amounts of exercise. Every day for another three months or more, and then another scan. And after that, maybe another six, nine months of very light recovery work before he might possibly be ridden.'

She turned her gaze on me then on Camille. 'It will not be easy to treat him and it is possible that the ligament will not heal if he moves around too much, or if he does some damage to it when he is finally allowed out of his stable. There is a strong possibility that it will not heal. You must be prepared for that.'

I nodded. 'I can do all of that. I will take care of him.' I turned to Camille. 'Camille,' I said, my voice low, 'I beg you, please let me do this. I will pay for all of his treatment and I will do everything necessary to make sure he recovers. Please let me do this.'

She sighed tiredly, tried to smile but the smile died on her face. Finally she gave a little shrug. 'Okay, Nicole. I know how much he means to you, and he means so much to me too. But I am very worried that the same thing that happened to my father's horse will happen to Espiritu.' She stared at me intently, as if she were mining my soul. 'But I know that you will understand if he is in too much pain and we have to euthanise him.'

Our eyes were locked. I nodded solemnly.

'But okay,' she said. 'We will start the treatment.'

I let out a huge sigh of relief. 'Thank you, Camille. Thank you so, so much.'

She finally managed a sad smile. 'Nicole, you are going to quickly become an expert in how difficult it is to take care of a horse with a severe ligament injury. It is going to become your *life*.'

I smiled back at her. 'Y'know, Camille, since I came to live in France I've done things I never dreamed I was capable of. And helping Espiritu to recover is something I would happily dedicate the rest of my life to.'

I had a strong feeling that I could do this. I had confronted Satan, I had protected Guy from himself, and I was going to become Nina's mother. It was inconceivable that I could not help Espiritu recover.

***

It was almost 8pm by the time we went inside. We had watched closely as the vet cleaned and bandaged the wound on Espiritu's leg. She would return the following morning to give us a more detailed briefing on the routine we would need to follow.

Having reassured her that Espiritu was going to recover, D'Artagnan drove Nina home. She gave me the tightest hug before she left. 'I knew you would be able to make him better, Mama,' she whispered in my ear. At that moment I hadn't ever wanted to stop hugging her; D'Artagnan was forced to prise her out of my arms in order to take her home.

When he returned, he toasted the *baguettes* he'd bought for lunch and we ate them with the roasted garlic and tomatoes I'd made under his supervision earlier that week. As we ate, Camille explained what had happened to Espiritu. One of the men working on the swimming pool had driven a digger into the courtyard at the back of the château in order to turn it around. He was not an experienced driver and as he turned, he miscalculated where the long, heavy arm of the digger was and knocked over part of the paddock fencing near to where Emperador and Espiritu were grazing.

Espiritu had been terrified, jumped over the fallen paddock rails and galloped around the side of the château – where he was confronted by a trailer blocking his path. He jumped that and landed on the grid of metal reinforcement that was going to be used for the terracing next to the swimming pool. His back leg landed in the wrong place, the metal sprang up behind him and partially severed the ligament just above his left fetlock – the equivalent of the ankle in human anatomy. Short of an actual broken bone, it was the worst possible place for a horse to be injured.

***

It was only after Gabriela and Camille had left that I suddenly remembered Xavier and the fact that the court hearing had been that day. I went to find my phone. There were several missed calls from him. It was now 9.30pm, and he sounded pretty pissed off when I called him back.

D'Artagnan's long fingers were massaging the back of my neck beneath my hair. He brushed it gently aside so that my neck was exposed and leaned in and kissed it softly. I was utterly exhausted, drained, but his mouth on the nape of my neck made me feel liquid inside.

'Xavier,' I said, 'I'm really, really sorry, but my horse – well, technically he's not mine, but anyway – he had a terrible accident and he nearly had to be put to sleep. So that's why I haven't called you back. I'm so sorry, but it's been a traumatic afternoon. Please forgive me.'

A long pause, then Xavier said, 'I am sorry, Nicole.' The pissed-offedness was toned down.

'Please tell me everything went okay today at court.' My voice was almost a whisper.

Another pause. His tone quietly triumphant, he said, 'Everything went okay today, Nicole. The case will go to the *Cour d'Assises*. On the twenty-seventh of September, Guillaume will be tried in front of the *Cour d'Assises* in Bordeaux. And he is going to stay in prison until then. It was a successful day for me. For us.'

I laid my forehead down on the ancient, pock-marked surface of the medieval dining table as I gave thanks to the universe for not making the court hearing go wrong. 'Thank you, Xavier. Thank you so much. I can't tell you how brilliant it is to hear that.'

'*Bien fait.*' D'Artagnan's voice was gruff. '*Merci*, Xavier.'

'It was my pleasure. I am pleased with the *resultat,*' said Xavier.

'Listen, Xavier,' I said. 'I'm absolutely knackered and I'm not sure I'm capable of absorbing anything more now. Can I call you tomorrow and get the full download then?'

'Of course, Nicole.' Slight pause. 'It is late. I am very sorry about your horse. I hope he recover quickly. I will wait to talk to you tomorrow. *Bonne soirée,* Nicole, Guy.' And then he hung up.

I laid my face down on the table again. It felt marvellously comfortable and I closed my eyes and dived into the welcoming embrace of sleep.

Guy carried me upstairs to bed; he must have done because I have no memory of going upstairs, of taking off my clothes and climbing beneath the covers.

***

I was so exhausted that I slept like a whole forest of logs that night; nothing disturbed me. I woke groggily when D'Artagnan put my coffee cup down on my bedside table and leaned over to kiss me. '*Reveille-toi, mon amour*. The vet will be here in half an hour.'

I tried to clamber out of the thick fog of sleep, then remembered Espiritu. My eyes flew open and I sat up quickly. 'What time is it?'

D'Artagnan got back into bed. 'It's seven-thirty. Don't worry, *mon amour*, I already go to check on Espiritu. He's okay. Camille just arrive.' He paused. 'Drink your coffee before you go.'

I smiled at him wanly. 'Thank you, my darling.' He smiled back softly.

I reached for my coffee cup and took a sip. 'Eeurrrgghhh!' I spat the mouthful back into the cup. 'Guy, it's disgusting! This coffee's got vinegar in it! Did you forget to rinse the machine?'

He stared at me. 'What do you mean?'

I put my cup on the bedside table. 'You've cleaned the machine and left vinegar in it again. The coffee tastes disgusting – it even smells disgusting. How can you not tell?'

His eyes narrowed and he continued to stare at me without saying anything. When he finally spoke, his voice was very soft. 'Nicole, I have not cleaned the coffee machine. There is no vinegar in the coffee machine.'

I stared at him. 'Well, it tastes and smells disgusting. I'm not drinking it.' I threw back the bedclothes and marched crossly into the bathroom, splashed cold water on my face then went into the dressing room to put on my scruffy jodhpurs and trainers.

D'Artagnan followed me downstairs a few minutes later. He seemed particularly pensive that morning, leaning his chin on his folded arms on the stable door as the vet explained the daily routine to Camille and me. For once he had little to say, and every time I glanced at him he was gazing at me thoughtfully.

Camille left shortly after the vet. She'd refused a coffee, saying she was already late for work with Gabriela. We exchanged kisses and wan smiles, and she squeezed my hand tightly when I said, 'It will work, Camille. I know he'll recover. I just know it.'

D'Artagnan and I walked back to the château, our arms around one another. 'Do you want me to make you some more coffee, Nicole?' he asked when we were back inside.

I frowned. 'Have you cleaned the machine yet?'

He tilted his head to one side. 'I already tell you, Nicole, I have not cleaned the machine. There is no vinegar in the machine.'

I shrugged. 'Okay. Then yes, please.' I sat on Nina's stool while he made it. Before he was halfway across the kitchen with the cup, I put my hand up and made a 'Stop! Disgusting!' face. The smell of it was making me feel very nauseous.

D'Artagnan stopped, his eyes narrowed, then he turned and dumped the coffee into the sink. He leaned back against the countertop, his arms folded. I was still trying to quell the wave of nausea that the coffee smell had kicked off.

Finally, he took a deep breath and spoke. His voice was very measured as he asked, 'One last time I need to ask you this, Nicole.' He paused. 'Did you fuck Xavier?'

I rolled my eyes. 'Oh my *God*, Guy, please tell me you're going to get over this one day. I'm getting really tired of telling you that no, I did not fuck Xavier.'

A smile spread across his face. He crossed the kitchen to me, reached out and brushed my hair behind my ear. His thumb gently caressed the back of my neck. His eyes were that wonderful mahogany colour and his scent was suddenly strong in my nostrils. 'Nicole,' he said, 'you are pregnant.'

I took a very deep, very annoyed breath.

He smiled benevolently at me.

'Have you been secretly testing my pee?' I asked.

'We don't need the test. This tell me enough, this coffee addiction that you have and now it stop so suddenly.' He kissed me. 'Nicole, *mon ange*, this means that you are pregnant.'

I frowned. 'What coffee addiction?'

He rolled his eyes. '*Mon Dieu*, Nicole! You are always drinking coffee, we argue about how much coffee you drink! And now, suddenly you cannot drink coffee! This is because you are pregnant, *mon amour*!'

We gazed at each other for a while. Finally I said, 'I think it's possible that they've invented more scientific ways of diagnosing pregnancy than liking or disliking coffee, D'Artagnan.'

The eye-roll was accompanied by Gallic hands, flung out in a theatrical gesture. '*Bah...* Nicole! Okay, come with me now. We go upstairs and we do some test.' He was looking quite affronted, as if his gynaecological qualifications based on coffee consumption were being heinously dismissed.

'Do I have to pee?' I asked.

Big pout. 'Of course. That is how the test work. You pee on the stick.'

'But I don't want to pee.'

'*Merde...*' he muttered, shaking his head. 'Okay, so I make you some tea – you like the mint tea, *n'est çe pas*? I make you some mint tea.' He glared at me. 'I make you a big pot of mint tea, okay? And then we go do some test, okay?'

I sighed and said, 'Okay.' I didn't want to argue anymore; I didn't want to argue because I'd suddenly made the connection. I'd suddenly remembered what had happened the day before when I was falling down the stairs. More than that, I'd suddenly realised *why* what had happened the day before when I'd been falling down the stairs, had happened. It made me feel really weird; it made me think, *Oh my God, I* am *pregnant. And oh my God, the Duchess knows that I'm pregnant.*

When I'd drunk the entire pot of tea, we went upstairs. Guy insisted on coming with me into the bathroom. He was carrying three pregnancy test kits. 'Three?' I asked, one eyebrow raised.

'Nicole,' he said snootily. 'I know what you are like. One test, you will never believe this. Two test, you will say it is an accident. Three test ... *bah*, maybe you believe it then.'

He tore open the boxes and handed me the tests one by one. He held up his hand as I peed on the plastic test-strips like he was the pee-police, telling me when to stop and handing me another test. Then he lined up each of the peed-on test sticks on the edge of the basin.

I sat on the loo, my elbows on my knees and my chin on my hands. D'Artagnan was sitting cross-legged on the floor in front of me. We stared at each other across the short distance that separated us. After a while I said, 'You know, it doesn't necessarily mean anything if I *am* pregnant. Staying pregnant was always the biggest problem.'

He gave a nonchalant shrug 'So, we see. This time I think it will be different.'

'Why do you think it will be different this time?'

He did that slow blink and smiled the smug smile. 'Because Nicole, my babies they are very ... *tenaces*. They hold on. They don't let go.'

I gave a little snort and shook my head. 'My God, Zeus! You really don't have any concept of failure, do you?'

Big smug smile. '*Non*, I don't.' Pause. 'Also, Nicole, why am I Zeus now?'

I couldn't help smiling. 'It was something Stephane said.'

'I prefer D'Artagnan,' said Zeus. He knelt in front of me, slipped his fingers beneath my chin and kissed me softly.

'I prefer D'Artagnan, too,' I whispered. He kissed me again, a sensuous kiss that made my eyes close involuntarily.

When we stopped, he glanced at his watch then at me again. 'It's time,' he said. Without looking at it, he handed me the first test. 'One line is negative; two line is positive.'

I looked at the stick. There were two lines; it was positive.

I raised my eyes to his. He smiled, handed me the second test.

Two lines; it was positive. I stared at it, looked up at him again. He smiled, raised a self-satisfied eyebrow and handed me the third test.

Two lines: positive.

I suddenly felt horribly nauseous. 'Gonna be sick,' I muttered, pushing him out of the way as I clambered off the loo and then, very elegantly, threw up in it. Except it wasn't at all elegant.

He stroked my back and made soothing noises while I retched. When I'd finished, he handed me a damp flannel and I wiped my mouth. I sat down on the cool marble tiles with the toilet bowl against my back.

Guy was counting on his fingers, starting with April. '*Décembre!* A baby for Christmas, Nicole! This is the best Christmas present, *n'est çe pas*?'

I stared at him and wondered if I was going to be sick again. 'Need some water. Mouth horrible,' I said faintly.

He smiled at me again like a particularly self-satisfied Santa Claus, half-filled a toothpaste mug with water and passed it to me. After I'd rinsed out my mouth, he reached for my hand and pulled me up. He wrapped his arms around me tightly and held me for a very long time. It felt wonderful to be held like that and I never wanted it to stop. I didn't want to have to consider that my notoriously unreliable body once again contained the possibility of new life. That was too bewildering to think about.

When he finally released me, he leaned back a little and gazed at me, his eyes soft as we kissed. It was a kiss that started full of tenderness and love but gradually changed into something else, into a kiss with ... heat, desire. I gradually became aware that my arms were tightening around him and I was pressing my body, moulding my body into his, and that I was very aware of his erection hardening against my stomach.

We broke off, both breathing heavily. His eyes were liquid chocolate. '*Mon Dieu* Nicole, I love you so much,' he whispered. 'I need to fuck you now, *mon ange.*'

My breath caught in my throat as a surge of desire pulsed through me. 'But what about...?' I whispered back. 'Is it safe? Is it okay for the—'

He smiled softly '*Ouais*, *mon amour*, it's fine for the baby. It's good for her. She need to know how much her parents love her.'

He picked me up and I wrapped my legs around him. He carried me into our bedroom and laid me gently down on the bed, and when the orgasm finally pulsed through me, it made me groan as if I were dying. His strong hands held my hips firmly as he gasped, '*Oh mon dieu je t'aime tellement.*'

Afterwards, trailing my fingers in his chest hair as I lay against him, I asked, 'Why do you think it's a girl?' I hadn't forgotten the child with the tuft of hair, the child reaching his arms out to me, the child with my eyes and Guy's smile.

He gave a nonchalant shrug. 'I don't know, I just think this.'

And I wondered what the Duchess knew. Did she know if it was a boy or a girl she was saving when she stopped me falling down the stairs? Did that matter to her? And I also thought, *If she's that powerful, does that mean it will happen this time? Is that why she saved me?*

Wondering that felt really strange.

Chapter Eleven

The weeks that followed were occupied with three major tasks: Espiritu's daily care; counting down the days to our interview with the *puh-syciatriste* for Nina's adoption, and my egregiously unjustified desire to murder D'Artagnan's culinary sensibilities as horrifically as possible. Specifically, those sensibilities concerned with acceptable food combinations.

For a pretty committed carnivore, D'Artagnan is surprisingly good at vegetables. In the spring and summer months he drizzles them with olive oil and a generous sprinkle of sea-salt, pepper and herbs, then roasts them in the *piano* until they are lightly blackened on the edges. For a vegetarian, they are divine; just the right amount of texture and flavour and ... scrumptiousness.

Except ... the broccoli just lacked a little something.

I was still picking bits of vegetables out of the roasting tray when we'd finished dinner that evening. Guy was stacking the dishwasher. 'It just needs something else,' I mused, putting a sprig of slightly blackened broccoli in my mouth. 'Something sweet, perhaps,' I mused.

He gave me a little frown. 'It is a vegetable, Nicole. It is not meant to be sweet.'

'Yes but...' I wandered into the dining hall to collect the rest of the dishes from the table. 'It just needs a little—'

And there it was, staring at me. 'Well, hello!' said the jar of organic honey. 'I've been waiting all of my life to be married to a bit of blackened broccoli. What's taken so fucking long?'

D'Artagnan's face fell when I brought the jar into the kitchen. 'You cannot eat honey with vegetables, Nicole!'

'Wanna bet?' I dipped the sprig into the honey and left tiny broccoli spores floating in it. I popped it into my mouth and chewed. 'Heavenly!' I smiled. 'It's perfect! Quick, ring the French culinary police and trademark a new thing – oven-roasted broccoli and honey!'

His gaze was disdainful. 'Vegetables roasted with honey is not a new thing, Nicole.'

'Yes, but it's all in the presentation, my darling. Oven-roasted vegetables *dipped* in honey – that's a whole new thing, isn't it?'

He stared at me as I selected another broccoli sprig from the oven tray and dipped it in honey. A slow grin spread across his face as he watched me pop it into my mouth and crunch it up. '*Ça alors,* Nicole...' He shook his head, grinned, then came over and slipped his arms around me. His mouth was warm on my forehead. 'My crazy wife – is this what you are going to do now? Eat everything with honey?'

D'Artagnan can be oddly perceptive at times.

***

The rest of the time was filled with caring for Espiritu. Each morning, my alarm went off at 7am and I dragged myself from D'Artagnan's warm embrace, staggered into the bathroom to wash my face in cold water and brushed my teeth. Then I rummaged around in the only drawers I ever seemed to open in Heaven these days, the drawers filled with clothes that were compatible with dust and sweat – or mud and sweat, depending on the level of moisture outdoors. I pulled on a pair of shorts and a T-shirt, sat down on my cream-leather chaise longue and tied the laces on my grubby trainers then twisted my hair into an untidy bun on top of my head and fastened it with a hair grip. I never seemed to have time to brush it anymore.

Espiritu's head always lifted a little when I arrived at his stable door. I'd stand quietly at his side while I rested the palm of my hand against his forehead and I'd imagine we were exchanging energy; I was giving him as much of my healthy energy as I could summon and he was absorbing it. In exchange I took some of his dull pain, his boredom and frustration.

I was becoming aware of what it felt like to be an animal full of suppressed energy and despair at the inability to express that energy. I tried to think soothing thoughts while we stood there; I closed my eyes and remembered how he used to canter around the paddock, his tail out behind him, his thick neck arched and his noble head held proudly. I focused on those images and imagined that I was sending them to him through my hand against his forehead. I was trying to say, 'This will be you again. You will do this again.'

I don't know whether he received the images or not; maybe he did because he always seemed to take a deeper breath. But we project, we humans, and we constantly anthropomorphise. Our view is human-centric; we don't really try to understand what it is to be an animal in the human world.

D'Artagnan always followed with the wheelbarrow and the manure scoop and he would start mucking out Espiritu's bedding while I went to the kitchen to get the warm water, the antiseptic wipes, clean bandages and antiseptic spray to start the daily routine of nursing my beloved Espiritu back to his beautiful, proud, four-legged self.

And then, when we'd finished, Guy and I went back inside to have another incredulous (on his part) discussion about what I wanted to eat for breakfast.

***

I am ashamed to say I was now a lapsed vegetarian; I had become a pescetarian.

It happened the week after I found out I was pregnant. It was a Wednesday, and D'Artagnan had gone to Bordeaux for a meeting with Francesca and the property development lawyers. I had asked Nina what she wanted in her omelette for lunch and she'd frowned and shaken her head.

'I don't want omelette,' she said.

'Well, what would you rather have?'

'Sardines,' she said, firmly. 'Papa made me sardines with rice at the weekend and I liked it a lot.'

I made a face. 'Well, I don't have any sardines. I'm really sorry.'

'But you haven't looked.' She was gazing up at me from under her fringe.

I frowned at her. 'What do you mean?'

'You haven't looked in the cupboard to see if there are any sardines.'

'I'm quite sure I would have smelled sardines in the cupboard by now,' I said, blinking at her.

'How?' She looked confused.

'With my nose?' I suggested, wondering if my French language skills were really so poor that we were talking at cross purposes.

She started to giggle, the tip of her tongue between her teeth. 'I know you smell with your nose, but I don't think you can smell sardines in tins, can you?' The giggles took over, which made me giggle too, so that by the time I opened the cupboard and found the tins of sardines in olive oil we were both doubled over with laughter.

When we finally managed to stop, I opened one of the tins. She turned her head and blinked up at me. She was lying across the cool granite worktop, her head on her arms as usual while she watched me. 'Now you have to make rice,' she said patiently, as if I were a bit thick.

Which I was when it came to rice. I rummaged around in the same cupboard and found a bag of rice. I studied the cooking instructions while she continued to watch me.

'I'm starving,' she said weakly.

I glanced at her. 'Have some bread then.' I motioned to one of the fresh *baguettes* D'Artagnan and I had fetched from the boulangerie that morning.

She shook her head, still not moving from her prone position. 'I'm starving for rice and sardines,' she murmured.

I rolled my eyes at her. 'So not *that* starving then.' I read the rice instructions again.

She blinked at me a few times. 'Papa puts some in a pan with water and boils it. It doesn't look complicated.' Her tone was rather condescending.

I returned her snooty look. 'Okay, *Mademoiselle Masterchef*.' I read the instructions a third time. That was pretty much what it said: put rice in water, boil, add salt, if desired.

I followed the instructions and jumped onto the countertop to sit next to Nina while we shared some of the baguette and waited for the rice to boil. When it was cooked to her satisfaction, I drained the remaining water carefully into the sink and turned to her. 'Now what?'

She sat up properly. 'Now you put the sardines in the pan and mix it all up.'

I tipped in the tin of sardines, mixed it all up and put the pan on the countertop. I handed her the spoon I'd used, and she dipped it in and put a big mouthful of the mixture in her mouth. She grinned at me as she chewed, bits of rice and sardine all over her teeth and gums.

'It's really good, Mama,' she said enthusiastically. She filled the spoon again and held it right in front of my face. I leaned back away from it. She frowned. 'You can eat it, it's vegetarian,' she said encouragingly, her green eyes wide.

It was strange, because it did smell rather wonderful. She smiled her fishy smile at me again. 'Go on, eat it!' she insisted.

So I opened my mouth and she put the spoonful in and ... that was the end of my vegetarianism. I was hooked. Sardines and rice were the *best* thing that I'd ever eaten.

***

I had admitted my lapse to Guy a couple of days later. He'd done eyelid Morse-code at me while his brain tried to process what I'd just told him. 'But *les sardines* are not vegetables, Nicole. They are a little fish that swim in the sea, *mon amour.*' He gave me the intensely annoying smile that meant, 'Aw, bless! Talking to an imbecile here.'

'Really?' I said, making very big, very sarcastic eyes back at him. 'I thought they grew on sardine trees. Silly me.'

Withering look. 'So you decide to eat sardines with rice because this is what Nina like to eat?'

I nodded and resisted giving him round of applause. 'Yes.' I paused. 'Is that okay?'

His eyes were brimming with superiority. 'That is food for children, Nicole, *mon ange.* That is not food for adults.'

I glared at him. 'Well, I like it.' I paused. 'If you think about it, it's really just deconstructed sushi.' That caused much culinary hilarity.

I blinked at him crossly. 'Well, that's what sushi is, isn't it? Fish and rice?' His mirth was so condescending that I wanted to kick him. 'Fine. Whatever. I'll make my own fucking breakfast then...'

I rummaged around in my brain for the name of a famous chef but could not find one because the only one the British know is

Jamie Oliver, and when you say that to French people they look at you blankly.

I got off the stool and went towards the cupboard where the sardines and rice were kept. Still laughing, D'Artagnan moved in front of me quickly, slid his arms around me and held me tightly. '*Non, non, non*! I make this for you, Nicole, *mon ange*. I make you *sushi déconstruit* if this is what you want to eat for breakfast!'

***

The following week we went to see our doctor, Doctor Malin. He was in a very enthusiastic mood having recently returned from a year's sabbatical in Outer Mongolia where he'd been eating sheep's eyes, goat entrails and sleeping in bug-infested yurts. He delighted in telling us the gory details and I started to feel nauseous again.

Eventually, he asked why we had come to see him. 'Nicole is pregnant,' said D'Artagnan proudly.

Doctor Malin looked puzzled. 'But you had a vasectomy.'

'I reversed it.' Smug smile.

'And it worked?' Doctor Malin's eyes were wide. 'I've never had a patient who reversed a vasectomy!'

'Well, I am Zeus, after all,' said D'Artagnan, or something similar.

After Doctor Malin had finished being fascinated that it was possible to successfully reverse a vasectomy, which was significantly more interesting than the mundanity of pregnancy, he got around to examining me. He asked me when my last period had been and when I told him he confirmed what we already knew: I was about eight weeks pregnant.

He listened to my heart, took my blood pressure and asked me how I was feeling, nodding sagely when I told him I was actually feeling pretty good apart from the tiredness and occasional nausea. He told me dismissively that they would pass and I seemed perfectly healthy. Then he put his stethoscope on my belly and concentrated while he listened. I tried not to hold my breath.

After a while he shrugged, sat back and gave a little smile. 'I think everything is okay, but it's best if you see your *sage-femme*.

I am only here if there is a problem. Your *sage-femme* will conduct all the obligatory examinations from now on.'

I turned to D'Artagnan. 'What's a wise woman? That sounds a bit woo-woo to me.'

D'Artagnan frowned back at me. 'What wise woman, Nicole?'

'Doctor Malin said I need to see a *sage-femme* and that translates as a wise woman. What kind of wise woman? Wise about what exactly?'

He smiled the condescending smile he gives me when I've yet again mangled some aspect of the French language. 'A *sage-femme* is a... I don't know this word in English, but it is a professional woman who takes care of the mother, who help with the birth of the baby. It is not someone at all – what do you say?'

'Woo-woo.'

The smile widened. 'No, she is not at all woo-woo, *mon ange*. She is very well qualified. This is normal in France, Nicole. While you are pregnant, you will consult often with the *sage-femme* and she will tell you everything you need to do to have a healthy baby.'

'So why did we come to see Doctor Malin if I should be seeing a *sage-femme*? And how does one find a *sage-femme*?'

'We come to see Doctor Malin just to record that you are pregnant and he can give us a list of *sage-femmes* that he recommends.'

I nodded slowly, 'Right then, D'Artagnan. Let's go find me a *sage-femme*.'

I was kind of relieved that Doctor Malin would not be the primary medical person for my pregnancy. I was fond of him and his very laid-back attitude to treating his patients. He had always prescribed whatever I asked for without batting an eyelid, and that was great when it was diazepam that I wanted, but I wasn't sure I really fancied having someone who was quite so medically passive as my primary pregnancy adviser.

The first *sage-femme* we met with at the end of that week was very disapproving. She didn't seem a particularly happy soul by nature, but what made her thoroughly unhappy was the fact that I was almost thirty-nine. That displeased her enormously; she told me that I ought to have been much, *much* younger if I wanted to be a mother.

I started to explain that I had considered this but D'Artagnan intervened. He stood up and pulled me up gently but firmly by the hand. He turned to the *sage-femme* and said, very abruptly, '*Merci madame*, for your time. We will find someone who is more suited to helping my wife.' And then we walked out.

As we returned to the car, he held my hand against his chest and ranted about '*putain de merde* women with opinions we don't want to hear'.

On the Saturday morning, we went for a rendezvous with another *sage-femme*, who was quite a lot younger than the previous battle-axe. This *sage-femme* was lovely. She insisted that I call her by her first name which was Sylvie, which instantly relaxed me, and I told her to call me by mine. She was kind, gentle and very professional. She made me do a pregnancy test and checked my blood pressure and heart rate like Doctor Malin had done. When she asked whether I'd been pregnant before, I explained haltingly what I'd gone through in my early thirties.

She put her hand on my forearm and pursed her lips as I told her. D'Artagnan stood to the side of me and stroked my nape comfortingly. When I'd finished, he said quietly, 'But at that time Nicole was much more stressed. Her life wasn't happy like it is now.'

I turned to look at him, half-frowning, half-smiling. It was true – but he had no real way of knowing that, apart from being Zeus the All-Seeing, obviously.

Sylvie smiled. 'Well, this time you are already eight or nine weeks. Your health is good and your weight is good. But if you see anything odd, if you see any blood, if you have any pain, you must immediately lie down and call me, okay? I'll come to examine you straight away.'

I swallowed, nervous again. 'Do you think there's more of a risk now because I'm older?'

'*Pfffff, non*, it's nothing to do with your age,' she said dismissively. 'Just last week, I helped one of my patients who is forty-three give birth to her first child. And last year a forty-year-old friend of mine gave birth to twins! So no, Nicole, you are not old to be a mother for the first time.'

A wave of relief washed through me.

She paused. 'But I want to see you in ... *bah*, three weeks' time for a scan, okay?'

I took a deep breath. 'Is that the scan that will tell us whether it's a boy or a girl?'

She smiled. 'Yes, normally.'

I glanced at D'Artagnan then at Sylvie again 'He thinks it's a girl.'

She grinned. 'And you?'

I gave a big shrug. 'Sylvie, I really don't care. I just want to have a healthy baby.'

She touched my arm again. 'There is no reason why you won't, Nicole.'

I loved Sylvie very, very much.

***

And then all the dates had been crossed out on the calendar and it arrived: *the* day. The day of Nina's adoption meeting.

At first, I was too anxious to eat anything for breakfast.

'You need to eat something, Nicole.'

'I feel nauseous,' I said. I really did.

D'Artagnan shrugged. 'So, you eat something and then, if you need to be sick you will be sick.' He paused. 'But you must eat something, Nicole. The meeting is at eleven o'clock and you need to eat something now, *mon amour.*'

'I still don't feel hungry.'

'I make you sushi *déconstruit*, okay?'

I thought for a minute. 'Can I have an omelette instead?'

'Of course.' He started preparing it. 'What do you want in it?' he asked.

'Nothing. Just plain, thanks.'

He slid the plate with the perfectly cooked omelette in front of me. I reached for the jar of honey. He removed the plate from in front of me. I glared up at him. 'What are you doing?'

'You are not going to put honey with it!' His eyes were wide with horror.

I grabbed the plate back and put it down again. I was now actually quite hungry and omelette with honey was exactly what I wanted to eat. 'Yes, I am. I know you think it's disgusting but I really don't care.' I stared at him.

He let go of the plate. 'It is an *omelette*, Nicole! How the fuck can you have honey with it?' His expression was pained, as if I'd demanded steak '*bien cuit*' or something equally blasphemous.

I smiled sweetly. 'So it is, my darling. And it's excellent with honey. Trust me.'

He turned away and went back into the kitchen, muttering words like '*merde'* and '*putain'* and '*I probably wouldn't have had a reverse vasectomy if I'd known my wife was going to massacre my culinary sensibilities so brutally.*'

Only kidding. He never said '*putain'*.

When he brought his rather boring breakfast of toast and boiled eggs to the table, I took his hand and kissed the back of it. '*Your* baby, D'Artagnan, don't forget.' And I blinked very sweetly at him.

He shook his head at me and grinned. '*Ouais, mais* Nicole, I never have this when Isabelle is pregnant with Manu and Charlotte. This baby only want to eat crazy food because you are always so ... *bah, bizarre* with what you will eat!'

I shook my head. 'No, it's not. Before, I was vegetarian, and it's only since I've been pregnant that my tastes have got a bit bizarre. I reckon it's the baby's revenge for your obsession with food.'

He shook his head and blinked at me slowly. '*Mon Dieu*, if this baby want to eat crazy food after she is born you will have to cook for her. I am not going to make this disgusting food forever...'

I frowned at him. 'Why are you so convinced it's a girl?'

Pouty shrug. '*Bah* ... I don't know Nicole. I just feel this.' Pause. 'Also, a boy is not going to eat crazy food like this, only a girl will do this.'

I rolled my eyes, then started eating my omelette with honey because I was suddenly quite hungry and I needed strength to engage in Battle 29.3 of the War of the Sexes.

Food Discrimination? Really?

***

Somewhat surprisingly, the omelette stayed down that morning.

We parked in one of the narrow streets in the centre of Angoulême. Even though it was only June, and despite it having rained that morning, it was another swelteringly hot day.

I had spent a lot of time in Heaven that morning agonizing about what to wear. I had tried on and discarded so many different outfits that there was a huge mound of clothes on the chaise longue. It was too hot to wear anything fitted and everything smart had felt uncomfortable.

D'Artagnan had eventually come to get me because I was taking so long. 'Just wear the pretty summer dress you wear on the weekend, Nicole.' He picked it up off the chaise longue and held it out to me.

'Are you sure?' I hesitated. It seemed a bit frivolous, a sundress with tiny red roses all over it, but it was loose and very comfortable.

'Yes, I am sure!'

So I had worn it, but now that we were in Angoulême I was convinced that it was the wrong thing and I should have dressed more formally. Also, it had taken more than fifteen minutes to find parking and I had become increasingly agitated as we drove around and around looking for a space. I kept glancing at my watch and biting the edge of my thumbnail. When we finally parked, I got out of the car practically hopping with agitation.

As usual, D'Artagnan was completely unperturbed. He took his time getting out of the car, stopped on the pavement to polish his sunglasses, smiled the lazy smile at me.

'Come on, come on, we're going to be late!' I started marching off down the road.

'Nicole, stop!'

I turned around crossly 'Why?'

'Because you are going the wrong way. It is the other direction for the *rendezvous*.'

I turned around and marched back towards him. He stood on the narrow pavement directly in my path, blocking my way, and reached for my hands. When I reluctantly put them in his, he gazed at me from behind his sunglasses. 'Nicole, *calme toi.*' His voice was soft. 'You need to take some breaths, you need to try to be calm.'

I frowned at him. 'Guy, stop standing in my way. We're going to be late if we don't hurry up!'

'*Non*, we will not be late. The *rendezvous* is in ten minutes. We have time. And you need to be more calm, *mon amour*. It is not good for you to be so *bah ... agitée*.'

'I can't help it, Guy! It's kind of a really, *really* important thing that's about to happen.' I was so on edge, so anxious.

He shook his head. 'Nicole, take some deep breath and look at me, *mon amour*.' He took off his sunglasses and gazed into my eyes very deeply. '*Relaxe, mon amour. Ça va aller*, it will be fine. You will be Nina's mama, she will be our daughter. You don't need to worry about this.'

I stared back at him. 'You don't *know* that, Guy. They could easily say no.'

A pout, just a little one, and a shake of his head. 'No, Nicole, they will not say no. Nina will be our daughter. This time you need to believe me. You need to trust me, Nicole.'

His eyes were hypnotic. I took a very deep breath and, for once, I allowed myself to dive into them, to orbit Planet Zeus, that planet of supreme calm, supreme self-assurance, where everything that Zeus wished came to pass because ... well, he was Zeus.

It was a very smooth ride on that orbit. I became conscious that my heart was slowing, that my breathing was becoming deeper as I gazed into his tranquil eyes and let myself believe, actually believe, that he was right. It would happen; everything would work out the way we wanted it to.

It worked. I felt calm again.

He smiled the lazy smile, leaned in, kissed me gently. Then we walked calmly – well, fast but calmly because there are limits to his hypnotic powers – to the most important rendezvous of my entire life to date.

***

We'd decided not to say anything about my pregnancy. We hadn't told anyone because, after all, it was very early. But it gave me a weird confidence to know that the Duchess was on my side. She might not be strictly on *my* side, but she needed to protect D'Artagnan's progeny and that meant protecting me.

Sometimes I wondered what would have happened if I'd had sex with Xavier that night when he came to the château and I had fallen pregnant. Would she have saved me? It was an interesting question, and not one to which I could fathom the answer.

And I'd still not told D'Artagnan about what had happened on the staircase.

***

We were interviewed by two people: the *puh-sychiatriste,* who was a severe and disapproving woman, and the social worker responsible for Nina's case, a man with sad eyes and some facial growth that wanted to be a beard but hadn't quite persuaded his hair follicles to do as he wanted.

Nearly-Beard-Bloke deferred to his colleague, who did all the talking. She had clearly had a lot of experience in the world of irresponsible adults and damaged children, and she did not trust us.

She explained Nina's history factually and unemotionally. Her mother was of Tunisian origin from Marseille and had been a drug addict and a sex-worker in Paris. She had died of an overdose when Nina was six months old and Nina had been taken into care by social services. Her father was unknown.

Nina had been placed for adoption with a couple from Nantes, but after two years the wife had unexpectedly died of cancer and the husband had felt unable to continue with the adoption without his wife. Once again Nina was abandoned and unloved, adrift on the cold, vast ocean of human misery.

She gradually became more and more withdrawn, and stopped engaging with those who were trying to care for her. The social worker had recorded her as being 'psychologically troubled'. She was sent to a series of foster families, the first in the suburbs of Paris; when that hadn't worked out and she'd become even more withdrawn, she was sent to a different family in the suburbs of Lyon. Again, it didn't work out and she became very difficult: she wouldn't speak to anyone, wouldn't engage with anyone, wouldn't eat properly, threw violent tantrums. She was a difficult, damaged child. When she was five, she'd been sent to Marion and Thierry in the countryside where she'd seemed marginally happier, although she was still withdrawn and difficult.

The psychiatrist frowned at us over the top of her glasses, glanced at the file in front of her and said, 'But I have read the latest report from my colleague in November last year.' She glanced at Nearly-Beard-Bloke and then glared at us. 'It says that she is less withdrawn. She is still very wary, but she seems happier. She talked a lot about—' another frown '—horses and a château, and a *prince* and a *princesse*. Is this you that she is talking about?'

Guy and I both nodded and smiled. That didn't seem to please her. She glared at us some more, this woman who held our fates in her hands. 'Why this child?' she asked bluntly, her tone hostile.

And then D'Artagnan turned on all the charm. He turned the full-beamed, million-watt charisma on her as he held my hand on his thigh. He stroked my hand as he spoke, and when he turned and gazed at me his eyes were full of love.

He spoke lyrically of our life together, about how much we loved each other and how much I wanted children but hadn't been able to have them. He spoke about how Nina had come into our lives and how much we loved her, how we would do anything to make sure she was happy. He told her that we were fully aware that Nina had had a difficult start in life, but we were prepared for, and sensitive to, the issues that would probably arise as a result. He told her that we would never, ever abandon Nina, and that we might adopt other children, too.

He winked at me when I glanced at him, and I thought – why not? I loved that idea.

D'Artagnan seduced this hard-bitten, extraordinarily cynical (with good reason) woman; he completely seduced her. By the end of our interview, she was fully locked into the Planet Zeus orbit. When the interview was finally over and she'd explained how the rest of the procedure would happen, we all did Kissies. *She* actually kissed us both and her eyes were slightly moist; Nearly-Beard-Bloke gave us a lovely, happy smile as he shook our hands.

Afterwards, in the gardens around the magnificent cathedral in the centre of Angoulême, we stopped and Guy wrapped his arms around me. I cried then; I cried with relief and I cried because of the things he had said. I cried because I loved him so much and he held me tightly and stroked my hair. When I finally stopped crying, his eyes were also wet.

'So, Nicole, we will hear in about three weeks, maybe less. But I think it is okay to accept that you will be Nina's mama.'

I gazed at him and said, 'Thank you, my angel. Thank you so, so much for everything. For all of this, for just being so amazing. I don't know how I came to be so lucky to have you in my life.'

He shrugged, as if he might once have had a passing acquaintance with the notion of modesty, then leaned forward and kissed me softly. 'For you, Nicole, I will do anything. You make me so happy, *mon ange. Je t'aime tellement.*' Then another one of those swooning, wonderful kisses there in the beautiful gardens around the magnificent cathedral under the endless azure sky.

Chapter Twelve

Xavier was on the phone the next morning sounding very pleased with himself. 'Nicole, yesterday I am contacted by a *journaliste* from *Le Monde*. She want to write an article about Guillaume, about the case, and she want to interview you and Léa and Elodie too, maybe. But she really want to speak to you. Do you think you can do this? It can be very helpful to our case. It can make any other women who have experience of Guillaume to come forward as well.'

We both spoke at once.

'Yes, of course I can,' I said.

'No, she cannot,' said D'Artagnan.

I glared at him. 'Yes, Xavier, I can do it. Where and when does she want to do the interview?'

'Do you know this *journaliste,* Xavier?' D'Artagnan demanded. 'How do you know she will not write lies about Nicole? I don't want my wife to be under stress, she have enough stress in her life already.' His eyebrows were fierce.

'*Bah...* Guy, Nicole, I meet this *journaliste* once before when I work in Paris but I don't know her very well. But I know she is a serious *journaliste.* She is on the side of Nicole. she write an article earlier this year about this "metoo", *en France. Tu sais, le mouvement* "*balance ton porc*"?'

'*Balance ton quoi*?' D'Artagnan demanded crossly.

'Xavier, can you give us a minute, please?' Clearly, my thunderous glares were having no effect.

'Sure, Nicole.' Xavier sounded a bit irritated, a bit 'oh FFS'.

I muted the phone, turned to D'Artagnan. 'I don't believe for one minute that you don't understand what "metoo" is, or what "*balance ton porc*" is, either. If you really don't know, then I'll be pretty shocked. But in case you need a little summary, I am not the first woman who has had enough of being sexually assaulted and abused by men. There are lots of us and we're *not* prepared to keep quiet about it anymore. So I am going to meet with the journalist, and I am going to give her an interview, and with any luck other women who have had the misfortune to be targeted by that *bastard* Guillaume – or indeed by any other *bastard* men – might say, "Hell, yeah, I'm also going to do something about it. I'm not going to keep quiet!" Please *don't* interfere with this and *don't* try to make decisions for me. I have waited twelve years to resolve this, to get justice, and I'm *not* stopping now just because you're worried that it might be a bit stressful. *Capiche*?'

He stared back at me, eyes slightly narrowed, mouth in full pout. 'Why can the journalist not interview Léa and Elodie? Why does she need to speak to you?' He paused, and his voice became more supplicatory. 'Nicole, *mon amour*, you are *un peu fragile* with the pregnancy and the worry about Espiritu. I don't want you to have extra stress in your life. If you speak to this journalist, this can mean that other journalist will want to speak to you, and that is more stress.'

I shook my head angrily. 'Guy, I am not at all *fragile,* I feel perfectly fine and I'm not stressed!' I took his hand and stared forcefully into his eyes. 'I *need* to do this and I'm *going* to do this. I'm sorry if you don't agree, but that's just the way it is. Please don't let's fight about it – and please don't try to stand in my way. This is absolutely non-negotiable.'

He took a deep breath then finally shook his head and exhaled through pouty lips. 'Okay, Nicole, I am not going to fight any more on this. But I come with you to the interview. I want to be there with you for the interview.'

I shrugged. 'Fine. Whatever. Just remember, she's interviewing *me* and it's my decision how I respond. I don't want you butting in unless you're expressly asked to do so. Okay?'

Sullen, pouty blink, that 'dis' around the mouth, the 'dis' that means 'whatever'.

I unmuted Xavier and we fixed a time for the interview the following week in his office in Bordeaux while D'Artagnan went into the kitchen and prepared sardines and rice for my breakfast. Sulkily.

***

That same week after the adoption meeting, we walked Nina back home on the Wednesday evening. D'Artagnan explained to Marion how well the meeting had gone, and Marion smiled very softly and embraced me warmly.

As a result, we now picked up Nina on Friday afternoons after school and she stayed with us until Monday morning when we took her back to school.

On the Saturday morning, we had breakfast together. 'What would you like for breakfast, Nina?' asked Mr MasterChef kindly.

Nina thought for a minute. 'Omelette,' she said firmly.

'What would you like in the omelette, *ma petite* Nina?'

She grinned up at him gummily. 'Smoked salmon,' she replied.

'Excellent choice!' smiled D'Artagnan benevolently, his gaze turning to me. 'And what would you like, love of my life?' Maybe he didn't say those exact words, but it was equally smarmy.

'Also omelette, my love.' I smiled at him. 'With spinach and honey.'

Deep frown. '*Bah*, Nicole, this is shit! You cannot—'

I turned to Nina. 'What's Annie having? I'm sure she'll want honey with it, whatever it is.'

She frowned at me. 'Annie's gone away.'

'Really? Where did she go?' I realised that I hadn't noticed D'Artagnan wasn't having to prepare two of everything like I had done before he'd returned.

She shrugged. 'She said she had to go away for a while.' She didn't seem bothered by the fact that her imaginary friend had disappeared.

I nodded slowly. 'Okay. Is she coming back, do you think?'

She turned and gave me her gap-toothed smile 'Yes – she said she's coming back for Christmas!'

'Oh, lovely!' I smiled back at her. I tried to recall at what point Julian my imaginary pet rabbit had disappeared from my life, but I really couldn't.

D'Artagnan was frowning at us both. 'Who is Annie?' he asked.

Nina turned to look at him. 'Annie is my friend. She likes honey.' But of course, she was talking to him in French, so she didn't say, 'Uhnee is my friend. She likes uhnee.' Which is what she would have done if she was speaking to him in French-accented English.

Instead she said, '*Annie est mon amie; elle aime le miel.*'

So nobody got freaked out – nobody being me, of course.

***

On the thirtieth day after Espiritu had been injured, the vet came and did yet another ultrasound scan with the portable scanner. This time she smiled as she looked at the screen then turned to Camille and me, nodding slowly. 'It's good. The healing is going well. Today I think he can take a little walk. Just once, around the courtyard.'

I was thrilled. Camille turned to me and she was clearly thrilled too. She squeezed my arm. 'You will take him for the walk, Nicole. It's because of you that he is healing!'

A huge grin spread across my face. 'It's because of us both, Camille. But it isn't over yet – he could still do something stupid.'

D'Artagnan was leaning on the half-open stable door. 'Yes, this is true. Is it safe for Nicole to walk him around the courtyard?'

Puzzled, Camille turned to look at him. 'Guy, Nicole has ridden Espiritu many times. Of course it is safe for her to walk him around the courtyard.'

More frowning. I frowned at him, he frowned at me. In his role as my secret gynaecologist, he was clearly starting to re-develop latent control issues similar to those he'd suffered when he stopped mastering the universe and no longer had minions to boss around. It was becoming rather tiresome.

Finally a full-on Gallic pout, a shrug and a gruff 'okay', as if it were in his gift to approve or disapprove it. As-fucking-if.

I looked at my watch just before Camille opened the lower half of Espiritu's stable door wide; it was Wednesday, 12.15. I wondered if the school bus had dropped Nina off already. Normally she arrived at the end of the road just after noon, and I so wanted her to see Espiritu walk around the courtyard. I wanted her to see that he would recover, because she had been so distressed to see him confined to his stable.

She came every day after school and she and I spent time with Espiritu before she went to groom Hermès and tack him up. She would put her face against Espiritu's velvety muzzle and blow kisses at him. Sometimes he blew kisses back at her, big, floppy-lipped horse kisses that made her giggle delightedly. She would stroke the area above his eyes gently and he would blink his big blue-black eyes slowly.

I brushed him all over until he gleamed, then I brushed his long, thick mane and tail with his hairbrush until they both shimmered like finely-spun silk. Every day I knelt beside him and massaged his legs with chamomile oil, lifted each leg and pulled gently but firmly backwards until it was almost straight. The vet and Camille had shown me how to do this; it allowed him to stretch all the muscles and the tendons in his good legs – effectively, it was horse yoga.

The *pièce de resistance* of our daily care routine was tummy scratchies. I would bend down and scratch all along the underside of his tummy with my nails and he would stretch out his neck and stick his nose in the air and ... *gurn* with pleasure. It was hilarious, but Espiritu didn't care that we laughed at him. He absolutely *loved* his tummy scratchies.

D'Artagnan had taken several videos of Nina and me giving him tummy scratchies, of Espiritu's lips moving in opposite directions over his mouth like some sort of camel in the throes of ecstasy. In the videos, Nina's childish laughter was the most wonderful thing to hear as she watched him abandon himself to pleasure.

D'Artagnan showed me one of the videos one night when we were in bed. By the end of it I was hysterical with laughter too, watching Espiritu and his gurning face. But I was also blown away by Nina, our daughter, bent double with laughter. The sound of her laughter made me want to cry tears of pure love.

***

I fastened the halter around Espiritu's head and held the halter rope loosely as we both gazed out at the sunshine in the courtyard. His head was still low, as if he had given up hope of ever going outside again, but Camille had anticipated this and she'd gone to get Hermès. Espiritu was absolutely fascinated with Hermès.

Hermès had arrived after Espiritu's accident, when he was already stable-bound. He'd been introduced to Emperador, who had arched his beautiful, golden neck over the paddock rail. Hermès had raised his small, perfectly formed head to Emperador and nostril to nostril they had breathed each other in. They'd decided pretty quickly that they liked each other.

Camille had breathed out and nodded. 'It's okay. They can go in the paddock together.' Hermès and Emperador had been in the paddock ever since, grazing quietly together side by side.

Espiritu, on the other hand, was so fascinated by Hermès that every time we brought the pony into the courtyard he became quite agitated. His head came up, his nostrils flared and he stood up straight and barged forward to lean over his door, trying to straighten his injured leg and, more worryingly, put weight on it.

At that point we'd decided that perhaps it wasn't such a good idea to introduce Espiritu's little brother to him just yet. But now we needed him to be interested in going outside, so Camille fetched Hermès. I put my mouth close to Espiritu's ear and explained to him that it was not a good idea to get excited. I put my hand on his forehead, underneath his mane while I talked to him and scratched his forehead. When I looked up again, Nina was standing at the stable door holding Hermès' halter rope and grinning at me. D'Artagnan was just behind her.

Espiritu perked up, raised his proud head and gazed at Hermès. I turned to him and asked, 'Would you finally like to meet your little brother?'

'Ooh, yes please,' he said. No, of course he didn't, but he did want to meet his little brother very much, so we walked him into the courtyard very slowly, very haltingly. He was really lame on his back leg and was compensating with his other legs. Despite my daily massages and yoga stretches, all his muscles were atrophied from lack of exercise. It was heart-breaking to watch.

And yet, he was walking. He wasn't running around like an idiot; he had realised that he was injured and that he needed to heal, and that was so important.

As I cautiously walked him into the courtyard, I realised that he understood what he needed to do to get better; more than that, I knew that he knew he would recover. He would be Espiritu again, my spirit horse, my spirit animal.

Espiritu, Nina and I, we were all survivors. D'Artagnan, having been brought up thinking he was Zeus, did not understand what it meant to be a survivor. It is difficult when you walk on water to comprehend how life feels for those of us who resurface, gasping for breath having been sucked under, pummelled, pounded and half-drowned by the treacherous currents and violent tides of life.

That day Espiritu arched his strong neck and lowered his head so that he could breathe in the scent of his new brother, and Hermès did the same. They flared their nostrils as they breathed each other in, Nina holding Hermès' halter rope loosely, me holding Espiritu's halter rope loosely. We were so focused on what was going on between the horses that we weren't aware of D'Artagnan taking the photograph that now hangs over the fireplace in the dining hall, the photograph that he had enlarged and framed of me and our daughter Nina with our wonderful horses.

I am wearing scruffy denim shorts that are slightly stained, Wellington boots, and a grubby T-shirt that is hanging slightly off my shoulder. Nina is wearing beige jodhpurs that have a long muddy streak down the side. The sun-bleached ends of my hair in the usual messy hair-grip bun on top of my head are catching the midday sun; Nina's straight, dark hair has a halo of sunlight around it. We are gazing directly at each other and we are both laughing.

It is one of the photographs I treasure most; my eyes mist over every time I look at it.

***

The meeting with the journalist, Virginie, was the following Monday in Xavier's office. I liked her immediately. I guessed that she was probably in her mid-thirties. Her dark blonde hair was tied back in a ponytail and wisps framed her pretty face. She had the loveliest eyes, big and round and hazel-coloured, and she was smart, kind and funny.

She shook my hand firmly. 'Nicole, I'm so pleased to meet you. Thank you so much for agreeing to do this interview.' Her French-accented English was light, and her gaze was direct and frank.

Even D'Artagnan was pleasantly surprised. I could tell because he decided to be charming rather than hostile and he hardly interrupted her questions. Once – shock, horror – he actually nodded and agreed with something that Xavier said.

I had to admit that it was really useful that Guy was there because he knew Satan's background so well. He filled Virginie in on stuff that Xavier and I didn't know, and she asked us both lots of questions while she made notes.

Afterwards we went to the bistro that Xavier had taken me to the first time we'd had lunch together, the bistro with the cracked, red-leather banquettes. Virginie sat next to me, Xavier opposite her and Guy opposite me.

I glanced at Xavier occasionally when I dared, noting the way he was looking at Virginie. I could see that there was a spark there. She was kind of flirting with him too, and that made me feel a bit wistful. I felt sad knowing that I was going to lose Xavier, that the gorgeous, sincere Roman emperor with the dark curly hair and the perfect, full-lipped mouth was going to fall out of love with me. The realisation that perhaps he already had done was bittersweet.

Then I shifted my gaze onto D'Artagnan opposite me. He lifted his eyes from the slab of dead animal he was carving up and he did that lick with his eyelids; he licked me, bathed me with that soft blink. And I licked him back with my eyes and Xavier was suddenly very far from my mind.

***

'Shall we keep the apartment?' D'Artagnan asked later that day. We were standing in the street in front of their development, which was now finished, his arm loosely around my neck.

It was a street down which I had run away from Satan on two different occasions. Both times I had survived and both times I had become stronger as a result. It was off the main pedestrianised street in Chartrons, a street with vegetarian restaurants, yoga studios, organic *boulangeries*, shops with cool, sustainable clothing for children, and my favourite stall in the antique market, the one with the vintage designer clothing where I could spend ages browsing happily and chatting with the charming owner.

'Yes,' I said decisively. I turned to him. 'Yes, we should keep the apartment. Fuck that bastard. He will be in prison for the next forever, I hope. I love Chartrons and I love Bordeaux, so screw him. He's not going to spoil it for us, my darling.'

D'Artagnan smiled a big, proud smile, wrapped his arms around me and held me tightly. 'Okay, *mon amour*, we keep it.'

I felt good about that, about being instrumental in making a decision I knew he had been uncertain about.

***

Life felt good. Espiritu's leg was healing well. I walked him around the courtyard several times in each direction every day while Nina rode Hermès around the paddock under Camille's expert eye, her voice low and measured as she asked Nina to change gait, to slow down, to speed up. Nina responded smoothly. Sometimes Espiritu and I stood watching the two of them. I had never understood what the term 'a natural' meant until I saw Nina riding Hermès.

Xavier had been contacted by a German woman who'd been a model in Milan and was now living in Geneva; he was going to Geneva to take a formal statement from her. The detective in Italy had found a dresser who said she'd heard Satan talking to the make-up artist backstage that week in Milan, and he was going to take a witness statement from her. The case against Satan continued to strengthen.

And I was still pregnant. I allowed myself five minutes in bed every morning while I sipped my mint tea to examine the idea that perhaps this time I really would give birth to a healthy child. But no more than five minutes. If fate thought I was gloating, it would intervene. The happiness that I felt in those five minutes set the tone for the day and, coupled with the fact that D'Artagnan and I seemed to be spending rather a lot of time making up for the first three months of the year when he'd been sulking, meant it was turning into a pretty idyllic summer.

And the cursed swimming pool was finally finished. I wanted to hate it; after all, had it not been for the swimming pool project, Espiritu would not have been injured. But even though it was only mid-June, summer already felt like one endlessly long, sweltering day.

The pool looked good; my idea for its position had been right. It was perpendicular to the château on the west side so that the kitchen window looked directly over it and, although it was a clean, modern L-shape, it didn't look out of place. In the shallow end were the wide steps where I planned to spend the oppressive summer afternoons semi-submerged in the water, reading my book.

It did not deface the Duchess; it did not make her look as if an ill-thought-out, naff-shaped pool had been plonked down in front of her like D'Artagnan had wanted. If anything, the stone wall and the pretty, wrought-iron gate in the archway leading into the pool enclosure made her look more gracious. I thought so, anyway.

***

Virginie's article was published later that week. She'd emailed us the final copy that would appear in the newspaper but it was still a shock to see it online, to see our names, to see the full extent of Satan's evilness laid bare for all of the world to read.

D'Artagnan decided to cycle into Cognac to buy copies of the newspaper; when he returned, sweaty and red-faced, he was holding a letter. He smiled a huge, wide smile as I took it from him.

I saw it was from the adoption agency.

I saw that it started '*J'ai le plaisir de vous informez que...*'

I saw that it had Nina's full name in it, her date of birth.

I stared at him. 'Is this it?' I hardly dared to breathe.

He raised his eyebrows, opened his eyes wide and beamed delightedly as he nodded. '*Oui, mon ange, c'est ça*. Nina is our daughter.'

I don't know how many times he spun me around. There are no words to describe the joy I felt to know that I was now Nina's mother, that D'Artagnan was her father. When we went outside to tell her, she wrapped her skinny arms around his neck so tightly and I wrapped my arms around both her and D'Artagnan. I laid my head against her body and thought, *I have never, ever been as happy as I am in this moment.*

We called Marion and told her, even though the formal bureaucratic adoption handover wasn't due to take place until the following week. She sounded happy and quite emotional to hear the news, perhaps because I was crying with happiness as I told her.

After the formal adoption meeting in Angoulême the following week, we went to an Italian restaurant for pizza and ice-cream. I had had wild mushroom risotto. With honey. That had caused much confusion with the waiter and much mirth for D'Artagnan and Nina, but I insisted and I got what I wanted. I was aware that I was putting on weight, that I was almost certainly no longer a size thirty-six. It didn't matter. When I thought about my clothing collection in Heaven, I thought about what Nina would one day choose to wear from it, and what her sister (assuming Zeus was right) would also choose to wear, and that made me feel so happy.

***

During our second appointment with Sylvie when I was thirteen weeks pregnant, she did the ultrasound scan and we saw for the first time the shape of our daughter in grainy black and white. Because it *was* a girl.

Sylvie paused as she moved the cool, gelatinous probe over my belly and asked if we were sure that we wanted to know. I nodded, then I laughed through the tears and the snot when she said it was a girl. I shook my head in disbelief at D'Artagnan and he grinned back with wet eyes and did a little pout, a little shrug, as if to say, 'Of course, I didn't *necessarily* know for sure.'

It was a snotty, tearful consultation, but very happy snot, very happy tears.

Sylvie took a blood sample and we had a brief discussion about tests for disorders. I gazed at the black-and-white print-out of our baby, and asked, 'What will happen if any of the tests are – not good?'

She gave a small shrug. 'Well, Nicole, then you have to decide whether you want to continue with the pregnancy or not.'

'I'm not terminating,' I said, surprised at the vehemence in my voice. D'Artagnan squeezed my hand.

'I'm sure everything is fine,' said Sylvie soothingly. 'I don't see any anomalies in the scan, so I don't think you need to worry. I'll have the results back early next week and I'll let you know then. But please don't worry, Nicole. It's very rare.'

As we left, I realised how pleased I was that Sylvie was my *sage-femme*, that she would be at my side as my pregnancy progressed. And I finally figured out what *sage-femme* means: in English it's a midwife, but I much prefer the literal French translation, a wise woman. Because women who help other women to become mothers are exactly that: wise. Kind, knowledgeable and wise.

***

We didn't discuss when to tell Nina; it just happened on the weekend after our appointment with Sylvie.

It was early evening and Nina and I were lying together in the shallow water on the wide top step of the pool. D'Artagnan had made it his mission to teach her to swim that summer because, although she wasn't afraid of water, she didn't really know how to swim. That day's lesson had finished and he was now snoring gently in the evening sun on one of the sun loungers behind us.

I was on my back, leaning on my elbows, Nina on her front. I turned to look at her. 'Nina, I want to ask you something important,' I said gently.

'Okay.' She looked very serious, sat up and squatted on her haunches, fixing me intently with her green eyes.

I took a deep breath and reached for her hand. 'Nina, how would you feel about – how would you like to have a little sister?' I smiled, holding her eyes with mine.

She frowned thoughtfully. 'How little would she be?'

'Very little. A baby.'

She smiled that gorgeous, gapped-tooth smile. 'I would love to have a little baby sister. When will they bring her?'

I was puzzled. 'What do you mean?'

She paused and narrowed her eyes. 'The adoption people,' she said.

I raised my eyebrows and made big eyes at her, partly to stop the tears that had formed instantly. 'Your baby sister isn't going to come from the adoption people, Nina.' I bit my lip very hard after I'd spoken, determined not to cry.

She frowned really hard then. 'So where is she going to come from?'

I placed her hand on my belly. 'She's going to come from here. Papa and I are growing you a baby sister. We are growing one for you because we love you so much and we think you should have a baby sister.'

Her eyes widened. 'You're growing one?'

I nodded sagely.

She stared at my stomach for a while then she asked, 'When will she be ready?'

'Around Christmas time.' I brushed some strands of hair from her face, which was now set in another frown.

'But Christmas is ... in December.'

I nodded. 'Yes, it is. In about six months' time.'

'That's a very long time.' She put her head on one side and gazed at me thoughtfully. 'Where did you order her from? Did you talk to Papa before you ordered her?'

I started to laugh and then I had to sit up because I started coughing, too. I was spluttering and coughing so much that I woke D'Artagnan from his poolside slumber. He made concerned noises, and I waved my hand at him to say I was okay. I finally stopped spluttering.

Nina wrinkled her nose. '*Bah,* mama! You ordered from the wrong website! It is normally much quicker – Papa says it should only be three days, four days maximum! My new riding boots came in three days.' She paused. 'Maybe you should have asked Papa where to buy the new baby. He is very good at ordering things.' She glanced at D'Artagnan.

I made a herculean effort not to laugh again. I could hear D'Artagnan sniggering.

She shook her head in exasperation. 'Why are you laughing, Papa? It's too long to wait, six months.'

Then his voice, very serious but also slightly exasperated. 'I know, Nina, it *is* very long. But mama already ordered the baby and now we can't cancel the order, so we just have to wait. Next time I will be sure to be there when she makes the order so that she uses the correct website.'

I reached out a hand behind me, the hand that Nina couldn't see, the hand with my middle finger raised very high from my otherwise clenched fist. *Next time*?

She nodded in agreement. 'Yes, I think you need to help mama next time.' Another frown. 'But I don't understand why you have to grow her inside of you. Why can't they just deliver one that's ready now?'

I took a deep breath and thought about how to answer that. 'Well, Nina, babies are a bit more complicated than it was when we adopted you. I need to take some time to explain to her about us, about you, about the château, the Muffins and the horses. I have to tell the baby how everything happens here because she needs to know what a wonderful big sister you're going to be. She needs to know all about the animals so that when she's ready to come out she won't be frightened by anything.'

'Okay.' She nodded sagely. 'That's a good idea, Mama. Because, you know, some children in my class are frightened of horses! I tell them about Hermès and Espiritu and Emperador, and they are frightened! It wouldn't be good if the new baby is frightened of the horses.'

'That's exactly what I mean, Nina,' I said and then squeezed her hand tightly. 'I'm so pleased you are going to be such a wonderful big sister! I'm so proud of you!' I wrapped my arms around her, kissed her forehead, her eyes, her cheeks.

She squirmed away from me, giggling, then suddenly she was serious again. 'When will we buy a pony for her? We will need to start looking soon for a very small pony.'

I heard D'Artagnan snigger again. 'Yes, Nina, we will need to think about this. But in the meantime, let's just wait until she's ready to come out.'

She nodded sagely and put her hand on my belly. 'Can she hear me if I talk to her?'

'Of course she can,' I replied.

And I stroked her wet head as we lay in the pool in the early evening sunshine, her head on my belly while she explained to her new baby sister what kind of pony would be best suited to her. And I felt as if I would dissolve with happiness, lying there in the cool water listening to my daughter explain the many intricacies involved in buying the perfect pony to her unborn sister.

Chapter Thirteen

On the first Thursday in July after Nina's school holidays started, she came with me to Bérengère's house for my weekly French lesson. Bérengère was already under the pergola, lounging on the cushions that lined the benches underneath the wisteria, her bare legs on the table. She rose languidly and her aqua-blue skirt tumbled around her ankles. The dogs were absent.

'Nicole, *ça va, ma biche*?' Her voice was soft as we exchanged kisses.

'*Oui, ça va. Merci, Bérengère.*' I kissed her back; her signature scent was faint but omnipresent.

Then she saw Nina holding my hand and trying to hide behind me. She smiled and looked curiously at her. '*Bonjour, Nina. Ça va, ma petite*?' She smiled warmly.

'*Bonjour, Madame Bérengère,*' Nina mumbled, looking down.

I stroked her head gently and exchanged a glance with Bérengère. She continued to smile. 'Do you like dogs, Nina?'

Nina raised her big green eyes and nodded seriously.

'Can you guess how many dogs I have?'

'Two?' ventured Nina.

'More,' said Bérengère.

'Three?' Nina's eyes widened.

'More.'

'More?' Nina started to smile too.

Bérengère gave her a big grin. 'Yes. More.' She paused. 'Would you like to meet them?'

Nina nodded fervently. Bérengère put two fingers in her mouth, gave an ear-piercing whistle, and within a minute all of her dogs came charging into the courtyard from the direction of the big field behind her house.

Nina's face was a picture. Her eyes lit up and a delighted grin spread across her face. Even though I was anxious at first that she was so slight and the two biggest dogs were almost as tall as her, I could see that she wasn't in the least afraid.

As the dogs gathered around us, Bérengère raised her hand slightly and regarded them serenely down her proud, aquiline nose. They immediately calmed down. The larger two and the smallest fluffy one sat in front of her; the other two remained standing, wagging their tails and gazing up at her. Their tongues were lolling out of their mouths.

'Go over there and get their ball,' Bérengère said to Nina, indicating the battered ball in the corner of the courtyard, the one soaked in several petri-dishes of saliva. Nina ran over and picked it up.

The dogs carried on gazing up at Bérengère. Nina handed the ball to her and she smiled slyly. 'Ready to run?' she said and gave her a little wink.

Nina nodded enthusiastically.

Bérengère threw the ball with a surprising amount of force into the field alongside her house and the dogs immediately shot off in pursuit – closely followed by Nina. It was then that a tall, lithe, suntanned man wearing a sarong came out of the house and crossed the courtyard.

I blinked as I watched him walk towards us. Then I blinked a lot more, and then I just stared as I realised that...

It was Stephane.

A lazy smile spread across his face as he reached us. 'Nicole! *Ça va*?' He stopped in front of me, placed his hands on my shoulders and leaned in to exchange kisses.

I kissed him back, unable to speak. I just stared. How the fuck had Darth Vader metamorphosised into this rather attractive silver fox/cool hippy dude, all muscular torso, trendy beard and man-bun?

'Shut your mouth, Nicole.' Bérengère grinned at me. 'You look like an idiot.'

I did so abruptly. 'Hi, Stephane. You look ... very different,' I said finally.

His smile was incredibly like D'Artagnan's. 'Good different, I hope?'

I nodded. '*Very* good different.'

'You too, Nicole. You look very good different.'

I frowned. 'Do I?'

He nodded. 'Yes. You look very ... *bah*, happy, relaxed. Not so anxious.'

I was puzzled. Had I always looked anxious to him? Had I always looked anxious to everyone?

Nina charged back into the courtyard with the dogs behind her, holding the ball up high, giggling hysterically. As she stopped in front of me, the smaller dog tried to jump up to take it from her and was immediately attacked by one of the larger dogs. There was snarling and some irritated yapping.

I looked at Bérengère. 'Is it safe for her to be around the dogs on her own?'

Bérengère frowned. '*Bah ... ouais*. My dogs will never harm her.'

Stephane leaned over her chair, slipped his hand under her chin and gently tilted her face up to his. He said something I didn't catch, and she shrugged and replied, '*Ouais, si tu veux.*' He bent down and kissed her mouth as I watched, open mouthed again. It was exactly the same gesture that D'Artagnan sometimes made when he kissed me.

He turned to Nina. 'Would you like to come and see the chickens that wear pyjamas, Nina?'

Nina stared at him. 'Chickens wearing pyjamas?' she asked, wide eyed.

'Chickens wearing pyjamas?' I also asked, wide eyed.

Bérengère started laughing. '*Mon dieu*, you two...'

We all went into the field behind the house to meet the latest addition to Bérengère's menagerie: Brahma chickens which were enormous, vibrantly coloured – and had feathered legs that looked as if they had just got out of bed and forgotten to take off their pyjamas.

After a while Bérengère decided that there'd been enough procrastination; it was time for my lesson. Stephane gave me a soft wink and said he'd keep an eye on Nina, and Bérengère and I headed back towards the pergola.

It wasn't a productive day French language skills-wise because we were interrupted ten minutes later by the nasal Glaswegian whine of incoming Randy Uncle Harry.

Bérengère's bare brown feet were on the armrest of my chair and my bare feet were braced against the table. I was concentrating hard, trying to form a sentence in French to describe how the meeting with the *puh-sychiatriste* for Nina's adoption had gone. I had leaned back in my chair and twisted up my hair into a knot on top of my head so that I could feel a bit of a breeze on the back of my neck. My loose dress was stuck to my body under my heavy, sweaty breasts.

I stopped and opened my eyes when I heard Harry's unmistakeable voice. Sure enough, there he was, bowling across the lawn carrying a large cardboard box.

'Eeeeeeee, hellooo there, ma looovely gerrrrrreeellls.' He put the cardboard box on the table and leaned in for Kissies with Bérengère, making sure to get a good gawp in at her breasts under her thin, coffee-coloured top.

When he turned to me he hesitated, as well he might. The last time Harry and I had met, he had not been feeling very well – mostly because I'd just kneed him very hard in the balls and left him lying in the foetal position in the car park of the local supermarket. Randy Uncle Harry and I were now on a footing I felt significantly happier about; he would think twice before getting familiar with my underwear again.

'Nicole, hoo arr ye? Yer looking verrrry well.' He blinked his watery blue eyes at me and held out his hand.

I shook it carefully. 'I'm well, thank you, Harry. How are you?' I resisted asking how his balls were.

'Eeeeeh, I'm well thank ye. How's my nephew, young Guy?'

'He's well too.' I smiled sweetly.

The big cardboard box on the table moved and a snuffling noise emanated from it. We all looked at it. Bérengère groaned. 'No, Harry, I can't! I already have five, I can't have any more!'

'Eeeeehhh, but these ones are really lovely. They're just ten weeks old and the mother is a retriever!' There were a significant number of 'r's' in retriever.

At that point, Nina ran around the corner again, breathless, flushed and followed by the dogs. She was grinning hugely as she flung herself across my lap.

'Now who's this lovely wee lass? Is this your daughter that I've heard so much about?' Uncle Harry then proceeded to massacre the French language as he introduced himself to Nina, yet Nina seemed to understand him and answered him politely.

The large cardboard box on the table moved again and made more snuffly, whiny noises. 'What's in the box?' she asked.

Uncle Harry waggled his eyebrows. 'Do you want to see?' She nodded enthusiastically.

So that was the day we adopted Fish and Chips. Or in French, *Feeeesh et Sheeeeps*. It seemed that Randy Uncle Harry did have a redeeming feature after all: he ran the local charity that rescued animals.

'All of my dogs came from Harry's charity,' Bérengère said when he'd left.

'Is it because he's trying to shag the women who work there, d'you think?' I asked, giggling as Fish (or maybe it was Chips) tried to lick the earring out of my left ear. When I tried to move him away from my ear he went to snog me, which made me laugh even more.

Nina was sitting in the swing chair in the shade across the courtyard from us holding Chips (or maybe it was Fish) in her arms and whispering to him as she stroked his golden head. He seemed to have decided that her arms were the best place to fall asleep and had done so within seconds.

Stephane had returned and was sitting beside Bérengère, rolling a cigarette. Or maybe it was a joint. I watched him, thinking, *Wow – Darth Vader has truly embraced his new alternative lifestyle.*

'What do you mean, Nicole?'

I gazed at her steadily. 'Uncle Harry is a lech. I'm sure I told you about the time he grabbed my arse in the supermarket car park.'

Bérengère shrugged. 'Yes, you told me. And now you and Harry understand each other.'

'Sorry? Hello? You're the world's original feminist – how the hell are you coping with Harry molesting women at every opportunity?!'

She took a deep breath then took the joint from Stephane and inhaled. She turned her calm grey eyes on mine again. 'Harry has some problems with women,' she said slowly.

I raised an eyebrow. 'Ya think?' My words were coated in sarcasm.

She offered me the joint but I frowned and shook my head. 'But he is very good to animals. He loves animals.' She took another drag. 'And once he understands that he must not touch you, he respects that.'

And that was the end of that conversation. Apparently rampant sexual harassment is cancelled out by being an animal lover. Who knew?

***

D'Artagnan thoroughly approved of our bilateral decision to adopt two puppies but the Muffins were considerably less approving. Both of them jumped on top of the enormous fireplace in the medieval dining hall and selected the 'fur afro' hairdo. I went over to try to soothe them, but they were having none of it.

'In the *house*?' demanded Mr Muffin, glaring at me.

'Apparently. Sorry,' I said meekly.

'But the house is *ours*,' objected Mrs Muffin, her eyes enormous.

'Well, I'm afraid you might have to share it. Tell you what, we won't let them come upstairs, okay?'

'Why are you talking to the cats, Nicole? They don't understand you.' D'Artagnan glanced up from the floor where he was sitting as Fish – or maybe Chips – tried to climb onto his shoulder. He laughed delightedly as he disengaged the puppy's claws from his T-shirt. '*Mais non, mon petit chou, tu ne peux pas y aller*!'

I blinked at him. 'You were saying?'

Nina was lying flat on the floor with the other puppy licking her face enthusiastically, giggling hysterically.

'We do NOT approve,' said the Muffins in unison.

***

D'Artagnan decided to organise a big family lunch on Bastille Day, the fourteenth of July, the most sacred day in the French calendar. He decided to share this decision with me two days beforehand, when he informed me that we would be sixteen for lunch:

- his son Emmanuel and his Italian girlfriend, Christina
- Françoise and Pascal
- Emma and Conor
- his daughter Charlotte

- our daughter Nina, of course
- his ex-wife Isabelle and her partner Julien—

I stared at him. 'Isabelle? Why have you invited Isabelle?'

Muted Gallic shrug. '*Bah*, Isabelle and Julien will stay with us on the way to the Côte d'Azur to Julien's family home. They are bringing Charlotte with them from Paris. She is also going to stay some days with us.'

I blinked at him. 'Did I know this, Guy? Did you tell me this and I just forgot, somehow?'

'*Pffff,* Nicole, don't make a fuss. I tell you before that some friends, some family, will stop with us in the summer. It will be fine.'

I glared at him. 'Who is staying overnight with us, Guy? I need to know this because I need to prepare bedrooms. They don't just prepare themselves, you know!'

'*Bah* – ask Angelique to prepare them.'

'Guy, I don't know if Angelique is going to come tomorrow. I never know if she's coming or not. I can't rely on her.'

Angelique, 'the blind cleaner' as she is known to D'Artagnan, was our unreliable, not terribly conscientious cleaning lady whom we had inherited with the château. However, she was fun and we had a laugh together even though we only ever understood about half of what the other was saying.

He stopped chopping whatever he was chopping and waved the knife at me. 'Nicole, *mon amour*, you need to relax. It's the summer, *c'est les vacances*. Everybody is very relaxed. We have a big lunch outside in the garden and then we all swim in the swimming pool and everyone will drink too much and they don't care where they sleep. It will be fine. Don't worry, *mon ange*. You worry too much!'

I looked around for the nearest object with which to brain him, then took a deep breath instead. 'Exactly *how* many people are staying over with us that night – or before that night, or after that night, Guy? How many and for how long?'

Having established that Emmanuel and Christina would be staying for 'two, maybe three nights', that Charlotte would be staying for 'some nights, Nicole, no, I don't know how many, just some nights, *merde*!', that Isabelle and Julien would be staying two nights, that Françoise and Pascal would be staying only on Bastille Day night, he added, 'And Emma and Conor, they will be staying too that night.'

I counted the names off on my fingers. 'That's five rooms, Guy. We only have four guest rooms.'

Another shrug. 'So, Charlotte can share with her new little sister for that night.'

'What, share the bed?'

Shrug. '*Bah, ouais. Pourquoi pas*?'

I stared at him. 'Do you think Charlotte will be okay with this? That Nina will be okay with this?'

'Of course, *mon amour*. They are sisters now.' He put the knife down, came over and gave me a hug and a smoochy kiss. 'It will be fine, *ma belle*. You worry too much!'

The thought that I'd had to fight him every step of the way to make the necessary renovations to the Duchess so that we actually had four guest rooms and an acceptable number of bathrooms still caused me quite a lot of residual irritation.

He paused thoughtfully. 'Oh, and Stephane and Bérengère.' He glanced at me. 'But they will not stay with us. They are now living together, you know.' Big gossipy eyes, a scandalised eyebrow.

I opened my mouth to tell him that it was me who had told him that, then shut it again. It wasn't worth bickering about.

***

We were sixteen for lunch on the fourteenth of July because Gabriela and Camille also came; we'd become so close that it was inconceivable that they shouldn't join us.

Nina wore the pale-green dress we'd gone shopping for together, the dress that set off her green eyes, the dress with the wide neckline edged in ecru-crocheted cotton with sleeves that fluted out from her shoulders.

All three of us had gone to Bordeaux and stayed in our new apartment for the first time. In the morning, Nina and I had sent D'Artagnan off to shop for boring men's things, and we'd gone shopping together as mother and daughter – and not just shopping for jodhpurs and boots and riding shirts. We went to the children's shop in Chartrons where all the clothes were either recycled or ecologically-sourced, and I bought her five dresses. I wanted to buy her more because she looked so pretty in all of them, but she made a face at me and said, '*Mais non, Mama.* I don't need any more dresses,' when I held up the sixth one with the delicate bluebells on it.

So I bought her some shorts and some pretty T-shirts instead and then we met D'Artagnan for lunch in the vegetarian restaurant I'd chosen. He made a lot of pouty faces while he read the menu, which made me smile.

***

Isabelle, Julien and Charlotte didn't arrive until about 6pm on the eve of Bastille Day, despite having set off from Paris at 7am. Paris is normally a four-hour drive (except if you're Zeus and speed limits don't apply to you) from where we live, except on every Saturday in July and the first half of August when it is never less than an eight-hour drive. This is because one sixth of the total population of the Île de France region, twelve million people, take part in the Great Annual Migration, which reaches its nadir on the fifteenth of August when Paris and the Petite Couronne (the departments surrounding it) are completely deserted. Then it all happens in reverse every day thereafter until the end of August.

The French ranks are swelled by the Belgians, the Dutch, the Germans and the Brits who are also big fans of 'sunshine', a mythical experience for most northern Europeans. Extra excitement is to be had by competing to see who can drive the most fuck-wittedly (the Belgians compete keenly with the Parisians in this), resulting in fun for everyone in the form of 30km long tailbacks while the wreckages are cleared.

These Saturdays are classed as 'red' days by the traffic authorities, which means you should try to avoid travelling south if you want to keep a grip on your sanity. But there are a couple of Saturdays classed as 'black', which means no, just no. Don't go there, don't do it; that way lies only misery and torment. So, of course, that's when everyone does it.

The Saturday immediately before Bastille Day is a black day. This is when the holiday season officially starts; from that date until the end of August, nothing – absolutely nothing – will get done anywhere in France because everyone is *sur la plage*.

This was the day Isabelle, Julien and Charlotte had chosen to travel. And here's another French contradiction. You may have an inkling by now that the French are quite hot-blooded, quick to anger, to become passionate. They are easily aroused and not very patient. And yet the Great Annual Migration is such an integral part of cultural tradition that, even if you have three children under the age of six, the large, stinky-breathed family dog in the back drooling over the seats, non-existent air-conditioning because you forgot to get it fixed before you left, and the outdoor temperature on the autoroute is thirty-six degrees Celsius (at least, it is on that part of the autoroute where you are currently sitting in the fourth 30km traffic jam that day since you left the Val d'Oise at 5.30am), despite all this, you are not bothered. You are calm, resigned.

Every year the television crews descend on this captive metal morass shimmering in the midday heat to interview the helplessly trapped captives. They rub their hands in gleeful anticipation of graphic human meltdown – and every year it is the same: the Gallic shrug, a little smile. '*Bah ouais*, it's a bummer, but hey, it's July. This is what happens on Saturdays in July. Whadayagonnado?'

When the three of them finally unfurled themselves from the car over ten hours later, they stretched, yawned, blinked.

'Welcome, finally! How was the journey?' I asked.

'Oh, you know.' Isabelle gave a little shrug, smiled vaguely 'It was long. But we are here now.'

I found it fascinating.

***

We ate outside on the eve of Bastille Day. We were eight around the big wooden table under the walnut trees at the front of the château. Beforehand, Isabelle had taken me aside in the salon. She who had arrived looking like she'd just stepped off a private yacht in clean, uncrumpled white Capri pants, high, strappy sandals (Vuitton, I guessed) and a dark-blue sleeveless silk blouse. I felt very frumpy in my loose cotton sundress.

'Nicole,' she said in her low, rich voice, 'you have done such *fabuleux* things to the château! Guy told me that it is all changed and that you have made it beautiful. But only now, when I see it, do I understand what he means!'

D'Artagnan happened to be walking through the salon from the front garden and overheard her. I raised an eyebrow at him and he smirked back.

'Thank you so much for saying that, Isabelle. Guy was – well, let's just say he was fairly obstructive about everything I wanted to do at first. I'm so pleased to hear he was happy with the renovations after all.' I smiled sarcastically at him.

He made a face at me. 'Don't listen to her, Isabelle. I always tell her she do wonderful things to the château. She exaggerate.'

After he'd disappeared, taking my highly sceptical eyebrow with him, she lowered her voice. 'Because, Nicole, my God! It was terrible before when I came here – the terrible furniture and that wallpaper...' She gave a little shudder and I could not help grinning, wondering if the Duchess was clocking this. 'But now it is beautiful! You have done a wonderful job. *Felicitations*!'

I liked Isabelle a lot more after that. Not that I'd ever disliked her, I'd just been a bit in awe of her.

***

Nina was very shy at first with all these new people in the house. She stayed close to my side, holding my hand tightly, looking down and away from everyone she was introduced to. She muttered her greetings but I didn't force her to do Kissies with anyone, I just held her hand and smiled. 'She's a bit shy. She'll be okay when she gets to know you better,' I said.

And that worked fine; everyone was fine with that, including Nina.

Later, while we were eating dinner, she giggled at the faces Emmanuel was pulling at her from across the table, and she chatted animatedly about the horses to Charlotte who was sitting next to her.

After the main course of fresh salmon stuffed with herbs, accompanied by a big bowl of new potatoes lightly seasoned with mint, and a deep dish filled with roasted vegetables (D'Artagnan placed a small pot of honey with a teaspoon next to me and gave me a sly grin), Nina took Charlotte's hand and they skipped off around the side of the Duchess to see the horses. My daughter's childish voice was clear in the cooling evening air as they disappeared from our view.

***

Bastille Day lunch the next day was epic. There was a barbecue involving lots of meat and seafood, but there were also lots of salads – I made a couple, including my favourite of mixed raw spinach and salad leaves, sliced fresh asparagus, walnuts and blue cheese. D'Artagnan grilled fresh sardines on the barbecue, mashed them up with olive oil and then mixed them with rice for Nina and me. I caught Isabelle watching him with a look of pure horror on her face and I had to look away and muffle my laugh by coughing into my napkin.

When Nina turned to me and asked, 'Do you want me to get some honey for you from the kitchen, Mama?' I smiled at her sweetly and said, 'Yes please, Nina darling. That would be lovely.'

I was very aware of Isabelle's gaze, and I knew that Françoise was watching me too, but I decided to ignore them both and not be embarrassed, to pretend that it was perfectly normal to eat mashed-up sardines and rice with honey.

In any event, D'Artagnan had decided that we were going to make The Announcement that day. 'Oh God,' I'd groaned. 'Do we *have* to? Does it have to be a big hoo-ha, all champagne and fireworks?'

He blinked at me for a while. 'I did not think to have fireworks. Should we have fireworks?'

'*No*!' I glared at him 'Apart from anything else, fireworks are absolutely fucking *terrible* for the animals. Do you even know how distressing it is for them? The horses will get completely freaked out, the dogs will be terrified and the cats will leave home, probably forever! Not to mention what the fireworks do to the wild animals! I mean, do you know that they cause the bats to eat their young, and it makes—'

'*Merde*! Okay, Nicole!' He held up his hands and rolled his eyes. 'I am not going to get fireworks, okay?!' He stared at me crossly for a while. 'We have to tell my family, Nicole. We have to tell my children. And Françoise, she will be so happy to know this.'

'Can't you just take them aside quietly and tell them?'

He rolled his eyes again. '*Mon dieu*, Nicole, you cannot always creep around and not let anyone make a fuss.'

'Well, *Sylvie* said I should stay calm and not make a fuss.'

'Sylvie say try not to do anything stupid, Nicole, like fall down the stairs.'

He gave me a hard stare.

***

I had finally admitted what had happened. We'd been in the library one evening, and I'd remembered the photo album that Nina had found. I went to the shelf, levered out the heavy tome and held it out to him. As I wiped off the dust on the leather cover, I saw that it was embossed with a coat of arms: the four quadrants contained a horse, a bee or a wasp, a sword and a *fleur de lys*. 'Do you know about this photo album? Nina said she found it in the secret cupboard.'

He held out his hands to take it from me. '*Non*,' he said slowly. 'I don't know this book. I have not seen it before.'

I came back around the chesterfield and sat down next to him as he opened it. 'Where *is* the secret cupboard, by the way?' I asked.

He waved a hand in the direction of the library shelves behind him. 'Over there,' he said. I sighed.

When he got to the page with the picture of the young girl in her nineteenth-century beekeeper's outfit, I shuddered involuntarily. Guy glanced at me. 'Are you cold, *mon amour*?'

I shook my head. 'No. I just get this really ... weird feeling, this weird sensation, whenever I look at that photo. And the one below it. Who are these people? Are they your ancestors?'

He nodded. 'Yes. I recognize this one.' He flipped back two pages to the photograph of a family that had just been informed they were about to undergo an extremely unpleasant experience. 'This one Françoise has. It is my great-great – uh, maybe even one more great – grandfather and his family. It is taken in front of the château, in ... *bah*, I think 1855. That's what Françoise say.' He paused. 'But I have never seen these other photographs and I have never seen this book. Where did you find it?'

I stared at him. 'Like I just said, I didn't find it. Nina found it in the secret cupboard. Where is the secret cupboard, for fuck's sake?'

He smiled at me and brushed my cheek gently with his thumb. 'So impatient, *mon amour*.' He stood up and went to the library shelves. He waited until he was sure I was watching closely then put a finger on one of the ancient books at the end of the third shelf and pulled it towards him. There was a 'click'. The shelf that ran the full length of the wall split in half and swung open to reveal a cupboard large enough for a small child to crouch in. It was empty.

I stared at it and then at him. It was the most wonderful thing I'd ever seen, as if all the Famous Five and Secret Seven books I'd devoured as a child had been true after all.

'*Voilà,*' said D'Artagnan with a flourish, clearly enjoying his new role as magician. 'The secret cupboard. I am sure I show this to you when we first visit the château, *mon amour.*'

'No, you've never shown me it.' Fascinated, I stood beside him and peered inside. There was a narrow shelf at the top that seemed to go back a long way; unless I crouched down, I couldn't see onto it. I realised that Nina, standing on the library stool, could have peered straight onto it.

'Wow.' I turned to look at him but he was already sitting down again. I shut the secret cupboard, which made a very satisfying 'click', and then it just looked like two rows of books on two shelves. 'Cool,' I remarked to myself.

I leaned over the sofa next to him as he continued to turn the pages of the album. The photographs, mostly posed, were of family groups with their progeny, one or two of them in the Duchess's front garden. She somehow looked even more like a fairy-tale château; there were climbing roses along her façade, and the east tower – the library tower that we were in – was covered in some sort of creeper.

I climbed over the sofa and sank down next to D'Artagnan. He'd started going through the album again from the beginning. When he got to the photo of the young girl in the beekeeper's outfit, I put my hand gently against the page and turned to him. 'Who is the child? And the old woman standing behind her?'

He shrugged. 'I don't know, Nicole. For this, we need to ask Stephane, or maybe Françoise. But Stephane have all my family papers – I think he will be able to tell us.' He paused and looked at me. 'Why are you so interested in these photographs?'

And then I'd told him haltingly about what had happened that day on the stairs. I told him about the incredibly loud buzzing sound, and about falling and then not falling.

He stared at me. 'Why were you not more careful, Nicole?'

I stared back at him. 'I wasn't being deliberately careless, Guy. I just forgot that I hadn't laced my boots up and I got a shock when I saw Nina with blood on her T-shirt.'

'Yes, but, you should have been more careful.' He paused. 'You could have been very badly hurt, *mon amour*. And you would definitely have lost the baby.'

'That's what I'm trying to tell you, D'Artagnan! The Duchess – she already knew I was pregnant! She stopped me falling down the stairs!'

Pouty dismissal. 'Don't be silly, Nicole. You imagine all this, that the château is a *duchesse.* It is just a château, it does not have feelings, it does not think or know things, *mon amour.*' He frowned. 'You must be careful not to say these things in front of Nina, otherwise she will begin to imagine these things too.' He took my hand. 'You nearly fall down the stairs Nicole, but you are lucky. You succeed not to fall somehow and you imagine that something happen to stop you. That is all.'

I took a deep breath. 'Guy, in all my thirty-nine years of existence, I swear I have *never* had an experience close to what happened when I started to fall down the stairs. What I've just told you is *exactly* what happened. And frankly, I don't really care whether you believe me or not because I know that it did, and that's all that matters.'

Condescending smile and accompanying condescending pat on the back of my hand. 'Okay, *mon amour*, if this is what you want to believe. But don't tell Nina these stories – I don't want her to start to think there are ghosts in the house.' A pause and another frown 'And, Nicole, you need to be more careful when you are going down the stairs, okay?'

I opened my mouth to respond and shut it again. There wasn't any point. D'Artagnan could be surprisingly sensitive on occasion, but when it came to anything illogical or unscientific it was like talking to a brick wall.

***

Late in the afternoon of our sumptuous Bastille Day lunch, D'Artagnan reappeared with a *jéroboam* of Champagne in one hand and a wide-brimmed sunhat in the other.

We'd just started the dessert course which, it being France, was copiously over-catered. Françoise had made a vast strawberry-and-cream tart, Bérengère had made cherry clafoutis, Gabriela had madc a thick, rich chocolate mousse, and D'Artagnan and Charlotte had made a lemon-meringue tart. Nina was working her way through a generous sampling of all four desserts and occasionally distributing bits from her plate to Fish and Chips, who were sitting patiently beside her chair and gazing up at her beseechingly.

D'Artagnan placed the sun-hat gently on my head, put the *jéroboam* down on the table, then pulled the sunhat down more firmly over my forehead. I immediately reached up and took it off, frowning at him.

He smiled sweetly. 'I bring you the hat so that you won't be embarrassed, *mon amour*, while I tell everybody our news.' He wedged it back onto my head again. I went to remove it. He put his hand on top of mine to stop me. 'But Nicole, it's perfect. Like this, you can hide from everyone!'

'Why does Mama want to hide from everyone?' Nina asked, her mouth smeared with chocolate.

'Because she doesn't want to tell everyone she's pregnant!'

I decided to keep the hat on.

'Oh, *félicitations*! That's wonderful news, Nicole!' I heard Françoise say, so I lifted up the brim up a bit and smiled at her shyly.

'Thank you, Françoise.'

'When are you due?'

'In December,' said D'Artagnan proudly, crouching down and giving me a big smoochy kiss on the cheek. Then he stood up again and reached for the *jéroboam*.

'But—' Isabelle sounded confused, just as the Champagne cork popped so loudly that I jumped. 'But—'

'Yes, Isabelle, it is my baby,' Guy said. 'I reverse the vasectomy.'

'*Ah, bon*?' I heard her say, then suddenly everyone was saying *félicitations* and getting up from the table, and I had to take off the hat and do Kissies and say 'thank you' a lot and try desperately to stop blushing, which I failed to do. D'Artagnan just looked very happy and proud as he did Kissies, then he refilled everybody's glasses and they toasted us with Champagne – and I had sparkling water instead, which was a bit boring.

Nina had filled her mouth with a spoonful of each of the desserts. 'I already knew,' she opined to anyone who would listen, while waving her fork nonchalantly in the air. Yellow lemon-meringue oozed out between her teeth when she caught my eye and grinned at me.

***

It was much later that evening after everyone had helped us clear away and we'd gone back inside. Isabelle and Julien had gone to bed because they had an early start and a long drive the following day, and Emmanuel, Christina and Charlotte were in the library streaming a concert onto the television. Gabriela and Camille had left earlier, followed soon after by Stephane and Bérengère.

I left Françoise and Pascal in the salon with D'Artagnan with their Cognac digestifs while I took Nina up to bed. After she'd brushed her teeth and put on her pyjamas, I lay next to her and read to her from the English language book we'd bought together in Bordeaux. Unsurprisingly, it was a book about a little girl getting her first pony.

Nina was asleep after less than a page. I smoothed her silky hair away from her soft forehead and leaned over to kiss her goodnight, feeling the same surge of intense love I felt for her every night when I did so.

On the way back down the stairs (very carefully), I remembered the photograph album and went to get it. Françoise had never seen it before and she was fascinated by it. She put her glass of Cognac on the table and started turning the pages slowly as she leaned against Pascal, who was smoking a cigar. D'Artagnan had lit one too.

He opened his arms wide to me and I snuggled against him feeling suddenly exhausted. He motioned to the cigar and asked quietly. 'It bother you, *mon ange*?'

I shook my head. I quite liked the smell of the cigar smoke.

After a while I asked Françoise sleepily, 'Do you know who the child is in the beekeeper's outfit? And the woman behind her in the photograph on the same page?'

She narrowed her eyes and pursed her mouth 'No. I've never seen these photographs before – well, apart from the one on the front page. But I know that there is a story about our great-great-great-great grandmother who kept bees.' She paused and frowned. 'But it was a very long time ago. I don't think photographs had been invented then.'

I stared at her. 'She kept bees?'

She nodded. 'Yes. Someone – I can't remember who, maybe it was my grandmother – said she was quite famous for her honey, that she even supplied honey to Napoleon!' She paused for a moment and laughed. 'Apparently, she was a duchess. But then the Revolution happened and she lost her title, of course.'

The world slowed down; it slowed down so much that even the gentle night breeze flowing through the open windows seemed to pause. Finally, I managed to say, very faintly, 'She was a duchess?'

'Yes, in theory. I think she was born a few years before the Revolution, and her mother died when she was young so she took the title. But then the family fled to England during the Revolution and when they came back, no-one talked about titles for a while. But really, you must speak to Stephane about this. He knows much more about the history of our family. He has all the family papers, and I think he even researched our ancestry.'

I turned to give D'Artagnan an 'I told you so' look. He was smiling at me and one of his eyebrows was slightly raised. '*Bah*, Nicole, you see – you find your *duchesse* after all.'

Chapter Fourteen

Obviously I wanted to go and talk to Stephane the very next day. I woke at dawn as I always did nowadays, invariably with D'Artagnan's arm lying heavily across my hips, the rhythmic, softly exhaled puffs of his breath warm against my neck, his nose tucked just behind my ear.

After I'd gently moved his arm and gone to pee, I stopped and looked through the bathroom window towards the east, towards where the earth was gradually turning to welcome the sun back to our part of the planet for another day. I watched it, the turn of the earth, the rise of the sun, as I stroked my belly. I whispered to my daughter inside my womb that it wasn't just me that was looking out for her, her ancestors were looking out for her too, and my heart swelled with love at the thought of that. And so, another day started, soaked in warmth and love.

I also made sure not to swear while I whispered to her about her sister Nina and how much I loved her, and about her father and how much I loved him, even though he had a god-complex and was often fucking irritating.

I didn't say that last bit.

***

But I was thwarted. 'No,' said Bérengère when I rang her later that morning. 'He's not here. He left early this morning. He decided after that conversation we had yesterday with Gabriela and Camille that he's going to Berlin to talk to his son.' She paused. 'I'm sorry, Nicole, but he's already gone.'

I had overheard some of their conversation towards the end of the meal the day before. Stephane and Bérengère had been having a fairly heated discussion with Gabriela and Camille about gender politics. I had glanced at them a couple of times, trying not to seem as if I were deliberately listening in. At one point I heard Stephane mention his gay son who no longer spoke to him, and his voice caught when he said his name. He'd looked down, looked away, and my heart had gone out to him in that moment. And I'd thought, *Life can be so incredibly complicated, so unbearably painful at times*.

I had to let the ethereal Duchess slip away from my grasp for a while, but after a couple of days I didn't give it too much thought because the countdown to something I'd been looking forward to for a long time was getting shorter and shorter.

Jules, Mark, Josh and Katie were coming to stay with us for the last week of July, and they arrived on my birthday. This time, when their car stopped on the gravelled drive, it wasn't the kids who were first out of the car it was Jules. She flung the door open just as I opened the heavy front door of the château and ran towards me. I ran towards her and, even though she's shorter than me, she lifted me off the ground.

We were both already in tears, but these were not the same tears that had flowed from that deep, deep well of sorrow after the first miscarriage and the second, the third, the fourth, after all of the miscarriages until I'd finally stopped trying all those years ago. These were tears of joy.

When we finally finished hugging, and after we'd wiped the tears off our faces, she placed her hand on the bulge, because it was an unmistakable bulge now, and lifted her sapphire-blue eyes to mine. We made utterly delighted grinning faces at each other, and then we hugged again very, very tightly.

Then I hugged gorgeous Katie, the spitting image of Jules when I'd first met her aged seven, and I kissed her over and over until she squirmed away from me. I hugged Josh and managed to get one-and-a-half kisses in before he wriggled away from me looking embarrassed, exactly like his father always did. And then I hugged Mark – lovely, shy, grey-eyed Mark – and he actually hugged me this time, this Englishman who was normally so wary of physical contact. This time he hugged me tightly, slightly awkwardly but tightly, and he whispered, 'I'm so happy for you, Nicky' and that made my eyes fill with tears again. Because I knew it took a lot for Mark to break the physical seal.

Nina came running out of the Duchess and accepted Kissies from Jules and from Mark (sort of), ignored Josh and grabbed Katie's hand. 'Do you want to see my pony?' she asked in French, as if it hadn't been a year since she'd last seen her. Katie nodded fervently, and off they went together, running around the side of the château to see the horses.

D'Artagnan was there too, of course. He stood on the terrace watching us.

When Jules and I finally stopped hugging each other, she took a deep breath and looked at him. 'So, Guy.' She tilted her head slightly to one side and I flinched inwardly, thinking, *Shit, that's Jules' 'and now you shall die' look*. But I saw that there was a smile trying to make its way onto her mouth and I breathed out again.

'Juliette,' purred D'Artagnan. 'How are you? You look very beautiful as always.' He stepped forward, his arms poised to do Kissies.

'I'm very cross with you,' she said, not moving.

He blinked, confused. 'Why, Juliette?'

'Because you didn't talk to Nicole about what you were going to do, about reversing the vasectomy! Surely you realise you had an obligation to discuss it with her first?'

Big Gallic shrug. '*Bah*... You know, Juliette, Nicole she worry about everything. I do not want her to worry about this too.' He paused before stepping forward and touching her shoulders gently. 'And Juliette, you know I am *le mousquetaire de* Nicole... If she want something, it is for me to make this thing that she want happen.'

Slightly bemused, Jules turned to look at me. 'My God, Nicky, he really does believe that shit, doesn't he?'

I raised my eyebrows high. 'Yep, he does. Wait until I tell you about the ancestors...'

She shook her head again before she turned back to D'Artagnan. 'Don't *ever* do that again, Guy. I understand that you thought it was okay, but it—'

'Juliette.' D'Artagnan's tone was slightly withering. 'I can't do it again. I can only do it once. So I do it, and now Nicole is pregnant and she is very happy. We are very happy.' He paused. 'Please, can you not be happy too?'

She bit her lips, but I could see that she was doing it to stop herself smiling. She leaned in and embraced D'Artagnan. As he gave her a big hug, he winked at me over her shoulder and I thought, *Phew, he got away with that quite lightly.*

Then she kicked him hard on the shin. When he exclaimed loudly, she put her finger in his face and wagged it several times.

'Consent, Guy! You need to understand this – it's *vitally* important!'

He glanced at me as he rubbed his shin and I did a little Gallic shrug. 'Could've been a lot worse,' I said.

He grinned ruefully and turned to Mark. '*Bienvenue,* Mark! Are you ready to kiss like real French men?' He held out his arms in welcome, pursing his mouth, fluttering his eyelashes.

Mark snorted, took one of D'Artagnan's hands firmly and they exchanged a solid, manly handshake, eye to eye. When they'd finished, D'Artagnan grabbed him around the neck and hugged him anyway and Mark just laughed. I realised I had a really stupid smile on my face as I watched them.

We had a wonderful week together. The decibels when two seven-year-old girls and one ten-year-old boy are added to a big body of water were occasionally ear-splitting, but when they became unbearable we just shouted at the kids to shut up and they did for a while. Mostly, though, it was a joy to hear them, to have a swimming pool full of joyful children.

D'Artagnan, of course, was incapable of chilling by the pool. He needed something to do; he needed a project. The new project apparently involved bastard chainsaws again.

I stared at him over the lunch table. It was a lunch with lots of fresh salads, firm new potatoes from the Ile de Ré and *merguez* sausages for the meat eaters. And no sardines, no rice.

He shook his head at me. '*Mais non,* Nicole, you cannot eat any more sardines and rice. You need to eat something else now. I make you some salmon. It is completely *bio* and it's from the Pyrenees. It is full of all of the good vitamins, no antibiotics, so you try this today, please, *mon ange*, with the little *pomme de terres* from the Ile de Ré. Please, Nicole – I cannot... *Merde!* I *cannot* make any more sardines!'

He'd spent some time explaining to Jules that I had eaten, '*Mais rien,* Juliette, *rien du tout que ces foutues sardines et de riz depuis le mois de mai! Mais c'est fou*!' A big eye-roll while Jules laughed at him.

'And honey,' I added.

She made a slightly disgusted face at me. 'Honey? With sardines?' Her eyes were huge.

I nodded. 'Yep. They go really well together.'

She laughed. 'No, Nicky, they really don't. That's like ... *disgusting*!! Sardines and honey ... eeeeuurrgh!'

D'Artagnan nodded vehemently. 'You see, Nicole? I tell you this is not normal.'

I gave him a little smile and said, '*Your* baby, D'Artagnan.'

He made a face at me and pushed the plate of salmon and Ile de Ré new potatoes towards me. '*Allez, mon amour*, try it. It's good, I promise.'

I tried the salmon very gingerly; I mashed it up with the firm, divinely-flavoured potatoes and actually it was really tasty. I smiled at him and he smiled back, relieved. And I only put honey on the slightly blackened roasted broccoli because that was *non-negotiable*, and that was divine.

Juliette shook her head and blinked repeatedly as if she were being forced to watch a particularly bad horror movie about food. D'Artagnan rolled his eyes at me as he watched me eat. I blew him a kiss, gave him a slow wink which he returned. His eyes were soft as cashmere as he gazed at me and I was momentarily sorry that it wasn't just us, that we weren't completely alone, D'Artagnan and I.

Then he mentioned the new project. The one with the bastard chainsaw.

I frowned at him across the table. 'The last time that you engaged with a chainsaw, dear heart, it was all rather traumatic. Now that you're going to be a father again, I'm not very thrilled that you're planning to muck about with another chainsaw.' I narrowed my eyes. 'It really won't be at all helpful if you try to remove another limb just before I give birth. There's liable to be conflict in the pain stakes.'

'Last time was ... *bah*, it was an accident, Nicole.' His voice was only slightly imperious. 'This time I will be very careful. And also, Mark is going to help me.'

'Well, my angel, I'm very pleased to know that this time Mark is going to drive you directly to the hospital. But perhaps if you didn't touch a chainsaw, everything would be a whole lot simpler. Cause and effect, all that stuff.'

A hard stare now, fully imperious. 'Don't argue with me about this, Nicole. I am going to make a *parcours* for Nina. We already talk about this, Nina and me. I will have to cut down some trees to make the *parcours* – not a lot trees, but some.' He broke a piece of bread in half and popped it into his mouth, pouting even as he chewed, not once taking his eyes from mine.

Nina grinned at him, her mouth full of potato salad as she kicked her legs back and forth under the table. She had become very brown during the summer, despite my slathering her in factor-thirty suntan lotion at every opportunity, even though D'Artagnan told me there was no need to because, 'Nina is from the Mediterranean *mon amour*, she take the sun easily. The sun kiss her, it does not bite her.'

He waved his hand dismissively when I explained about sun damage and skin cancer, but I continued to apply suntan lotion to Nina. Her dark, almost black hair was now lit in places with lighter brown highlights that set off her green eyes, making them even more luminous.

'What's a *parcours*?' I asked.

'*Bah* it's a ... *piste*. A run. A *chemin*.'

I turned to Jules, frowning. 'Translation?'

She shrugged. 'It means like a pathway. A trail, I think.'

'Why does Nina need a *parcours*?'

'For me to ride on with Hermès.' My daughter turned those luminous eyes on me. 'Papa said he can make a long ride all around the château so that it's more fun to ride. With jumps!'

I stared at him. 'Jumps? Is that safe? Where around the château, exactly?'

'Around the inside of the château boundary, Nicole.' Slow blink. 'So that Nina can ride Hermès on the *parcours* because she is bored just to ride around the paddock. She want to do something more exciting.'

I looked at him hard, looked at Nina. More exciting sounded more dangerous. 'What does Camille think about this?'

'She think it is a very good idea.' D'Artagnan nodded firmly and Nina, sitting next to him, nodded equally firmly. Both of them looked very serious as they nodded in tandem.

'I already ride him around the château, Mama. I ride around all the paddocks but I am bored now of riding in the paddocks and Camille says I am a good rider, so she and Papa talk about making a *parcours* for me and Hermès. It will be very good, and when Espiritu is better we can ride together on it.'

I looked at D'Artagnan. 'Is it safe?'

He nodded lazily. 'Of course it is safe, Nicole. I make it safe. And it is inside the château wall, so Nina does not have to go out on the road at all.'

'But the gates are always open at the end of the drive, Guy. What if something happens – if Hermès spooks or something, and gallops off down the drive? There's nothing to stop him going into the road.'

'*Bah,* Nicole, I put a chain across the entrance. Hermès will not cross a chain – he is a good horse.'

It was Nina's turn to frown at him. 'Papa, Hermès is not a horse, he is a pony.'

He made a contrite face; apparently, he was capable of being contrite for Nina if not for me. '*Désolé, Nina, ton poney.*'

While Jules and I lay by the pool, D'Artagnan and Mark got on with making a *parcours* around the inside of the château boundary. We could hear the chainsaw occasionally, but I was comforted that Mark was with him; he was unlikely to do anything too outrageously stupid if Mark was there.

Jules and I lay in the sun some of the time, and we lay in the shade when the sun was too hot. In the late afternoon, when it was peak-heat, we lay on the top step of the pool and sipped cold, fresh watermelon juice that I'd whizzed up in the blender and we chatted a bit, and we read a little, and we kept an eye on the children.

It was the most wonderful week, a week that I would never, ever have dared to imagine, lying there in our swimming pool in the grounds of our château, watching my daughter playing with her friend, and spooning cool water over my gradually enlarging belly next to my best friend Jules.

***

The vet came again at the end of the following week. After she'd examined him, she said that Espiritu could trot around the paddock. '*Mais très doucement,*' she said. 'Once around the paddock in trot, then again in walk, then change direction and do the same. Not more than that.'

I bit my bottom lip, brimming with excitement.

'Not you, Nicole,' said D'Artagnan. 'Camille can do this, not you.'

I made a face and rolled my eyes at him. 'Yeah, whatevs. I'm doing it.' I took Espiritu's halter rope from the vet, gazed into his blue-black eyes and put my mouth against his ear. 'You're allowed to trot today, gorgeous Espiritu!'

'Nicole!' D'Artagnan's voice was sharp.

I ignored him as I walked alongside Espiritu along the paddock rails. Gradually I started to walk faster and faster, then I broke into a little run and so did he. He arched his neck and flicked his tail in the air, and the next thing he'd changed gait into canter. It was the smallest, neatest little canter, a canter that matched my slow run, but a canter so full of joy that I started laughing delightedly

And then he bucked. The vet exclaimed loudly and Camille was suddenly beside me, gently prising the halter rope from my hand. D'Artagnan was just behind her, scooping me up and holding me against him, but I ignored them all and watched Espiritu continuing to trot around the paddock while Camille ran alongside with the halter rope held lightly in her hand.

He slowed to a walk when she slowed and they did another circuit, then changed direction and he trotted again. It was so beautiful as I leaned against D'Artagnan and watched my spirit animal, now almost fully healed, trot around the paddock.

***

And then Xavier called. He sounded really chilled, really laid-back. Really ... happy. I kind of missed him. I missed hearing his low, gentle laugh.

D'Artagnan put my phone on mute and glared at me. 'Nicole, stop flirting with Xavier! *Merde*!'

I gave him the full benefit of my very accomplished Gallic pout and unmuted the phone. 'We can come in next week, Xavier, to run through the pre-trial briefing. Wednesday afternoon maybe, or Thursday?'

Pause. Paper shuffling. 'Not Wednesday. Virginie and me, we are cycling then. Thursday morning, that would be good. At 11am, this will give you time to drive from Cognac.'

'Virginie? The journalist who interviewed me?'

Slightly embarrassed cough. 'Yes, Nicole. The same Virginie.'

I grinned then, a big grin, and I felt really happy for him, for them. 'That's so cool, Xavier. I'm so happy for you. Please give her my love.'

I could hear the smile in his voice. '*Mais bien sûr,* Nicole. Of course I will tell her.'

***

No-one had told Xavier that I was pregnant, so he was completely shocked when he saw me. 'But ... but, you say that it is not possible, Nicole.' His grey eyes were wide as he stared at my belly, then into my eyes, then at my belly again. He blinked those luxuriantly long eyelashes several times.

'Well, y'know, Xavier that's what I thought. But it turns out that Guy had other plans.' I gave a little shrug and turned to look at D'Artagnan. He was smirking.

'But you say, you tell me that—' He glanced at Guy.

'Yup.' I nodded. 'Turns out vasectomies are reversible. I did not know this.'

Xavier grinned and started laughing and looked directly at D'Artagnan. '*Mais*...Wow! *Impressionnant* !'

That made D'Artagnan smile very smugly. They shook hands in a manly way and D'Artagnan was not at all bothered when Xavier gave me congratulatory Kissies. And as we did Kissies, I caught a whiff of Bleu de Chanel and felt that frisson, the edge of that little fantasy, intrude into my mind again, and I wondered what would it have been like having sex with Xavier.

The ones that get away, huh?

When Xavier handed me the document containing our formal statements in the case against Satan, I noted that only Léa and Elodie's names were on the front page with mine. I frowned. 'What happened to the woman in Geneva? I thought you took a formal statement from her?'

He made a face, blinked at me a couple of times. '*Bah*... Nicole, I did not tell you because I did not want *que tu t'inqueite* again but the woman in Geneva – I don't know what happen. We have a meeting in Geneva and she tell me what Guillaume do but then – no more. Nothing. She refuse to take my calls afterwards.

So I don't know. I cannot force her to testify. Maybe she decide it is too traumatic, it is too public.'

'Is that normal?'

'Sometimes.' A glum little smile. 'Not everyone is determined like you, Nicole.'

I paused. 'Or he got to her first.' I frowned. 'You know, that bastard Guillaume.' It was an effort to say his name out loud.

Slight Gallic pout. 'It's possible.'

'And the witness in Italy? In Milan, one of the dressers – the one that said she heard him backstage talking to the make-up artist that night – what about her?'

Xavier looked down. 'She also decide she is not going to say anything, Nicole. I am sorry.'

I stared at him. 'He's still all over this, isn't he, Xavier? He may as well not be locked up. He's controlling all of this from inside prison, isn't he?'

D'Artagnan was very quiet, seething quiet. His elbows were on the armrests of his chair and his hands were clasped in front of his face. His eyes were narrowed when I glanced at him.

Xavier sighed. 'It is very difficult to control what is going on in Italy when we live in France. And Guillaume have lots of people he know in Italy. I am not very surprised, Nicole, like I say before.'

'But this woman in Geneva? How did he get to her?'

He frowned. 'No, you must not think this is definitely what happen. This woman can easily have changed her mind on her own. Or she can have accepted some money from Guillaume. We don't know. Like I say, we cannot force her to testify if she don't want to.'

'Can he do that? Can he offer her money to keep quiet?'

Big shrug. '*Mais bien sûr* – of course he can, Nicole. It is not legal to do in France in a criminal case, but it happen. It happen a lot.' He had been leaning back in his chair; now he sat forward, put his long, slender hands flat on the desk. He fixed me intently with his clear grey eyes.

'Nicole, it is not for you to worry about how I prepare the case, about the witnesses, about what Guillaume is doing or is not doing. This is for me to worry about, not you. You need to trust me, okay? This is not your problem.' He smiled a little smile at me, a smile with soft eyes.

I *felt* rather than saw D'Artagnan's frown.

Xavier definitely saw it because he abruptly cleared his throat and said gruffly, 'But I think it will be very useful if you can meet with Léa. Next week we have a video call with Elodie, too. We can talk about the procedure so that everybody can understand how it is going to ... *se dérouler*. How it is going to happen, okay? Can you do this?'

'Of course I can, Xavier. I can do any day after Tuesday next week when Nina goes back to school.'

He smiled. 'The adoption, it go okay? You have adopted Nina?'

I nodded happily. 'Yes, in early July. She's our daughter now.'

He gave me a lovely, sweet smile. 'I am so pleased for you, Nicole.' Then he corrected the smile quickly so that it was more formal. 'I am so pleased for you both.' He turned back to his screen and frowned – but only to appear more professional, I thought. '*Bah*, maybe for me next Thursday? This is good for you?'

I turned to D'Artagnan to check he hadn't scheduled any emergency surgery or holidays or just general obtrusiveness that day. He shrugged, nodded. I could see that he was rather bristly around the edges.

I turned back to Xavier, smiled sweetly. 'That's fine for us, Xavier.' Wondered what would happen if I added 'darling' after that. Grinned inwardly.

Xavier nodded, all professional now. 'I consult with the others, Nicole. I get back to you.'

'Great!' Pause. 'So Xavier, tell me. How long have you and Virginie been, y'know, an item?'

At which D'Artagnan did an epic eye-roll and fixed me with *the* most disdainful look. I ignored it and focused on Xavier, all soft grey eyes and curly dark hair and three o'clock stubble, and he laughed, a bit embarrassed. He admitted that they had 'kind of' been seeing each other since the interview, that Virginie loved Bordeaux (who wouldn't?) and that she was thinking of moving there from Paris.

When we finally left his offices, D'Artagnan stopped in the street outside and wrapped his arms around me. He was careful of the bump but he held me tightly and I melted into him because it always felt so wonderful to be held like that.

His voice was slightly strangled as he whispered in my ear. '*Mon dieu,* Nicole, I cannot believe how close I come to losing you.'

I leaned away from him and looked him firmly in the eye. 'No, Guy, it was never that close. Xavier was just a diversion.'

His smile was sad. 'Nicole, it was very stupid what I did. I am so sorry. *Je t'aime, mon ange.*'

I said softly, '*Et moi, je t'aime plus, mon ange.*'

A slow smile then, and an even slower lick from those dark brown eyes. We kissed a soft, soft kiss, and then another, less soft, more intense, and then it became hungry and I wished, not for the first time, that the distance between Bordeaux and the Duchess wasn't quite so far.

When we stopped, Guy held my face in his hands and murmured in my ear, 'Apartment?'

Although that was what I really wanted to do, I shook my head. 'No, we can't. I promised Camille we'd be back by 2pm. She can only look after Nina until then.'

He nodded slowly but did not let me go. 'I know many quiet roads in the forest if we take the slow way home... '

I started laughing. '*No,* D'Artagnan! We are not shagging in the car on the way home like desperate teenagers!'

He moved my hair away from the side of my neck and fastened his lips, his teeth, deliberately on *that* place, the place that makes me dissolve every time. This time was no exception. '*Bah,* Nicole, you know you are just a desperate teenager really.' His mouth against my ear. 'And so am I. I am a *very* desperate teenager, *mon ange.*'

***

But when we were on the road, all thoughts of teenage misbehaving instantly evaporated because Camille called. She was crying, hysterically.

I could hardly understand anything she said, but my phone was on speaker in the car so we could both hear her. Guy understood what she was saying a couple of seconds before I did. 'No, it's not possible Camille,' he said firmly, calmly.

He reached for my hand, squeezed it and gave me a quick smile that was meant to comfort me. 'She must be there. She's just fallen off, that's all. She'll be there. She's just a bit hurt, but she's there, somewhere near the *parcours*.'

An agonized sob. 'No, Guy, you don't understand! She wasn't riding Hermès – I didn't let her ride on her own. She was just walking him, just walking beside him!'

I tried to swallow but my throat felt blocked. My heart was beating fast and I couldn't take my eyes off Guy's face.

He was watching the road. '*Bah*, Camille, maybe she just fell down. Maybe she had a little fall while she was walking him. When did this happen?'

'Half an hour ago, a bit more. Hermès came back into the courtyard on his own, still with his halter on, still with the lead on. The lead rope was over his neck like it had been put there. I've searched the *parcours* twice, Guy! I've searched the grounds, I've searched the château, I've searched everywhere and I've called and called and I can't find her – I can't find her anywhere.' Another sob. 'She's just ... disappeared. Nina's not here, I'm telling you.'

A freezing cold, evil hand slithered under my ribcage and grasped my heart tightly, squeezing it very firmly, very cruelly, until it ached. I knew instantly what had happened. I tried to breathe in but my lungs felt like they were shutting down; they were going on strike, setting up a blockade to prevent air going in or out. My upper lip was buzzing as if it were being electrocuted, and my heart was banging so loudly against my ribcage that it was drowning out Camille's voice, Guy's reply.

My body was in full, familiar panic mode, something that hadn't happened for over a year now. The last panic attack I'd had was when I'd realised that Guillaume was the creature from the Marble Villa in Hell.

While I tried desperately to breathe, to force a tiny bit of air into and out of my lungs, to not pass out, I knew that this was Satan's work. He had come for the one person he knew I cared about more than anyone. He had come for my daughter.

Even in my near-unconscious state, I was aware of the speed as Guy accelerated. I was aware that we were flying past other cars on the autoroute, that the vegetation at the side of the road was flashing past at a phenomenal speed. When I managed to turn my head, which was pressed back against the headrest by the gravitational force, I saw that Guy's jaw was set, his eyes narrowed.

He knew it was Satan, too.

Chapter Fifteen

By the time we skidded to a halt in front of the Duchess, I was managing to breathe in short gasps. Guy had looked at me only once on the way and said gently but very firmly, 'Nicole, you need to breathe. Think about the baby.' I had made a Herculean effort; I had cradled the child in my belly, concentrated on her, and decided that my body, my lungs, my heart were not going to damage her. I was going to breathe.

I also decided that I would give Satan whatever he wanted; I didn't care anymore. I didn't care what he asked me to do, what he wanted me to do. I would do anything to get our daughter back.

Unharmed.

That last thought made me want to die inside all over again.

Guy, Camille and Gabriela, who had also by now arrived at the château, searched the grounds thoroughly again. I searched the house; I searched every room, every cupboard in every room, under every bed. I went down carefully into the cellar and I searched there, too, calling Nina's name quietly, trying to keep my rising hysteria under control. The only way I could dominate it was to stop every now and again, lean against a doorpost or a wall and hold my belly. I concentrated on the child I was carrying, imagined her distress at my distress, and that helped to keep a lid on the hysteria.

All the while I bargained with Satan. It was a very simple bargain: give me back my daughter unharmed and I will drop every single charge against you. I will walk away from you as if I never existed, as if we never met. I will say it was all lies, that the night in the Marble Villa in Hell never happened. I will happily go to prison for as long as they want for perjury, for false accusation, for anything, if he would just give me – give us – our daughter back. Unharmed. Please God, unharmed.

Guy came to find me when they'd finished searching. I was sitting in Espiritu's stable on the upturned bucket in the corner where I often sat while Nina groomed him, or where Nina sat while I groomed him.

Espiritu was standing quietly, munching on the hay in the corner. I was utterly devoid of emotion by then. I was eviscerated, completely eviscerated, and I didn't even bother to look up when he came into the stable because I knew they hadn't found her.

Guy crouched down in front of me and took my hands. 'Don't worry, Nicole. We will get her back.'

I raised my eyes to his. It was an effort. 'You know it's Satan, don't you?'

He nodded slowly and took a deep breath. 'I take a call, Nicole. They call my phone. They tell me they have her, that she is fine.'

I stared at him. 'Why didn't you tell me? When did they call? Where is she? How do you know she's fine?!'

'Shhhh, shhh. *Calme-toi, mon amour.*' He stroked my hands with his thumbs. 'I talk to her very quickly. She sound okay.'

I started crying then; I couldn't help it. 'But Guy – I want her back, I want her back right now! You need to call them back, tell them I'll do whatever they want. I don't care! Whatever they want – seriously, call them back! Or call the police. You need to call the police, Guy. The police need to check the roads. She can't be that far away – it's only been an hour and a half, two hours at the most!'

He fixed me with his eyes; they were intense, dark, very focused. 'No, Nicole, we can't call the police. If I call the police, it put Nina in danger. So no, I cannot call the police. But—'

'Well, just call them back and tell them I'll do what they want! I'll call Xavier right now, tell him I'm dropping the charges right now, today!! Tell them I'll do it. Just please – please...' I was overcome with sobs. 'Please bring Nina back. Please tell them to bring my daughter back. *Please*, Guy!'

He held my hands very tightly, his own eyes bright with tears. 'Nicole, listen to me. I do something better, already. Something better than the police.'

It was hard to focus on him crouched there in front of me through the tears streaming down my face, to listen to him through my sobbing gasps.

'I call Francesca, Nicole. And Francesca is going to help us find Nina. Francesca's family have a lot of experience with this.

When Francesca is ten, she is kidnapped. She is going to help us, *mon amour*. Trust me. She has people who know how this work. Francesca is always very, very careful about what happen with her children. You need to believe that she will help us, Nicole.'

I carried on staring at him. 'Francesca has children?'

'Yes,' he said very softly. 'Francesca adopt two children from Haiti after the earthquake in 2010. She adopt two sisters.'

That just made me cry even harder. I felt so stupid. I had got Francesca so wrong as well. It hadn't occurred to me for one moment that she might also be a mother, that that was the reason she'd revealed where D'Artagnan was when I'd pleaded with her. That she had been stolen away when she was a child and that she spent her life protecting her children from the same thing.

And I was also crying because I knew she would help us. It was not just *us* against Satan, not just D'Artagnan and his impotent anger and my willingness to prostrate myself before Satan and drop all the charges.

When I finally managed to get the sobs under control I asked, 'Can she really do this, Guy? Do you really believe she can find Nina and bring her back?'

I had never, *ever* been so grateful to see Zeus appear in D'Artagnan's gaze then. The Lord of all the Gods blinked at me, took a deep, confident breath and said, 'Yes, Nicole, I believe she can do this. Francesca's family is very powerful, much more powerful than Guillaume's family. You must trust her. She is very strong, very determined. She is so shocked at what I tell her today, but she tell me she will find Nina and she will find her quickly. She know people who can do this. She already have people on this.'

I think I collapsed then, fell off the upside-down bucket into his arms. He held me tightly, stroked my back, my hair. 'Nicole, you need to come inside, drink something, eat something. You need to think about the baby now. We will get Nina back and she will be fine. Please don't worry, *mon ange*.'

I resisted the very strong urge to vomit over his shoulder at the idea of eating anything, but I did feel a tiny bit of tension leave my body as he held me.

***

It took less than twenty-four hours for Nina to be back in my arms, but they were the worst, the very worst hours of my life. Every single second of every single minute of every single hour was agony. They made the night in the Marble Villa in Hell and all of the subsequent twelve years seem like a picnic in comparison. But finally, it was over.

***

Two men in an innocuous grey transit van with the side and rear windows blacked out pulled up quietly in front of the Duchess just before midday the following day. The side door slid open and a woman unbuckled Nina's seatbelt. Nina leapt out and ran towards us. As she ran into my arms, I gathered her up and held her tightly against me, then D'Artagnan lifted her up and hugged her even tighter.

She was sobbing and I was sobbing. She put one arm around Guy's neck and one arm around mine and held us as tightly as her skinny arms could manage.

The door of the van slid shut quietly and the van drove off. There was no other exchange, verbal or otherwise.

***

'I want fucking *fortress* gates on the entrance and electrified barbed wire on the tops of the walls, Guy. And a full-on alarm system on the château. *Now.* Today. Tomorrow at the latest. We need to call someone!' I said the next morning, while I watched Nina going to fetch Hermès from the paddock.

It was clear she had been very frightened but D'Artagnan had spent the previous afternoon with her baking complicated little cakes in the kitchen and gently teasing out information at the same time.

She had not been harmed and it didn't seem that she had been mistreated. She had been walking Hermès along the *parcours* near to the chain across the gates when she'd heard something behind her. Then she felt an arm around her, a compress being pressed over her face, and the only thing she'd thought important to do before she lost consciousness was to throw Hermès' halter rope over his neck so that he didn't stand on it.

That made tears well up in my eyes as I leaned against the kitchen counter. Our seven-year-old daughter was so responsible and sweet that her only thought while she was being kidnapped was the wellbeing of her pony.

I held out my arms to her. 'Come here, Nina, my gorgeous girl. Come and give me a hug. You were so, so brave. I'm so proud of you.' She crossed the kitchen, flung her flour-covered hands around me and pressed her face against my side.

Then she leaned back a little and lifted her eyes to mine. 'Did the baby know that I was gone?'

I nodded. 'Yes, she did. She was very worried, but she knew you'd be back soon. I told her that we would get you back very quickly.'

She tilted her little head back, frowning. 'Does she know my name?'

'Yes, of course she does.' I smiled at her. 'She knows all about you!'

She grinned the gap-toothed grin. 'What's her name? Did she tell you her name yet?'

'Uhhh... Her name is Honey, of course.' I smiled back at her.

D'Artagnan stared at me from across the kitchen, a starey-frown that said, *Really? We haven't discussed this yet.*

Nina made a face. 'Uhnee?'

'No, Honey. With an "H". Remember Nina, we talked about the letter "H". How we say "h" in English. It's not "uh" like in French, it's "huh". We breathe out from the back of the throat, like this – "hhhhuh".'

'Uuuuhh,' Nina breathed out.

I glanced at D'Artagnan. He was watching us, grinning.

I tried again. 'Hhhhoney. Like that. Close the back of your throat, make the air vibrate as you breathe.'

She made the faintest 'h' sound. I repeated it to her and she repeated it back to me, her green eyes focused on my mouth as I repeated the word until, after the fourth time, she said 'Honey' perfectly. Actually, she said 'Hhhonnee' with an emphasis on the 'hun' and an extension at the end, but I let that go because it sounded rather nice; it sounded like honey is, silky and sweet.

D'Artagnan made a face. '*Uhnee.*' He blinked at me. 'This is not a traditional French name, Nicole.'

I blinked back. 'It is now, D'Artagnan. It just became traditional in this house.'

He shook his head, then he shrugged and smiled. He crossed the kitchen to kiss me, his beautiful eyes creased softly at the edges. 'Okay, *mon amour. Uhnee* it is.'

I didn't think about it much because in my mind I was seeing the word 'Honey' in English. I was so focused on the 'H' that native French speakers struggle to pronounce that I wasn't listening to what Nina and D'Artagnan were actually saying as they pronounced Honey's name in their French-accented English.

***

We did not get new gates. We did not get electrified fencing on top of the château walls.

'The squirrels and the birds will be electrocuted, *mon amour.*'

'I don't care,' I said.

He stared at me. 'But Nicole, you love all the little animals!'

'Guy, I need my daughter to be protected! We need protection, lots of protection!'

'Nicole, we are going to be protected. And we are going to be very, very careful about Nina now, until the trial is finished. Do not worry, *mon ange*. I take care of this.'

He hired armed guards instead.

'Armed guards?!' I squeaked. 'Armed with what? Guns? Real guns?'

He shrugged. 'I ask Francesca what she do. She recommend some men.'

I stared at him. 'Is it safe? I mean, guns are never safe Guy. What if they see something and shoot without looking properly? What if they shoot at one of us by accident?'

Condescending blink. 'Nicole, *mon ange*, these are very professional men. They work for Francesca's family some time. They don't do anything stupid.'

Mostly we didn't see them but I knew they were there. We had to explain to them – well, D'Artagnan had explained in Spanish because they were from somewhere in South America – who was who, who came to the château and when. He showed them pictures of Camille and Gabriela from the Bastille Day lunch. Angelique and Jean-Paul came once a week – Angelique more in theory than in reality, which was starting to annoy D'Artagnan to the point that he was actively trying to find another cleaner. Apart from the occasional delivery, which we had to warn the guards about, there wasn't really anyone else that came to the château.

Bérengère and Stephane came once, though, for lunch on the third weekend in September. She raised a lazy eyebrow when I told them to park outside the (non-existent) gates and came down the drive to meet them. She swept the thinning trees with her penetrating gaze. 'I see one of them.' Pause. 'Your Satan, Nicole, he is a very bad, very dangerous man.'

I shook my head, eyes narrowed. 'Not mine. *Never* mine, Bérengère.'

She smiled a little smile at me and said, '*Bah, oui* Nicole, he is yours. You hold his fate in your hands.'

'Yes.' I nodded. 'I suppose that is true. I do hold his fate. And in ten days' time, he's going to prison for a very long time – I hope for the rest of his life.'

Because it really was only ten days until Satan's trial.

***

Xavier had been horrified to hear about Nina's kidnapping. His grey eyes had widened enormously and he'd been genuinely shocked. When I told him Francesca had stepped in and Francesca's 'people' had found Nina, he was even more wide-eyed.

D'Artagnan frowned at me as I told Xavier. He murmured, '*Mais* Nicole, you should not speak of this. What Francesca do for us, this is not something we share.'

I frowned back at him. 'Guy, Xavier is my lawyer. Lawyer–client privilege.' Turning back to Xavier. 'Isn't that so?'

'Absolutely, Nicole. This is absolutely private. I can never speak of this.'

'*Oui, mais quand même...*' D'Artagnan's eyes were half closed, suspicious. 'Nobody can know this, Xavier, this is very, *very* secret. Francesca does not want this to be known.'

Xavier shifted his gaze to D'Artagnan; it was his turn to do the withering look and he did it rather well. 'Guy,' he said patiently, 'I am a lawyer, a criminal lawyer. I keep all of my clients' secrets. I keep this secret, like I keep all of the others.'

'*Ouais, mais...*' D'Artagnan continued his little protest.

I put my hand on his leg. 'Let it go, dearest, please. I trust Xavier implicitly.'

Eye roll. Little shrug. Testosterone re-routing.

***

I asked D'Artagnan if I could meet with Francesca to thank her.

'*Oui, bien sûr*. After the trial, we can do that.'

'Why not before?'

'Because that would not be *discret.* Everything about Francesca, her family, Nicole is very *discret.*'

I pondered for a while what it must be like to live in Francesca's world. Sure, there would never be a moment's worry about money, but to live permanently with the fear, the chance of someone that you cared deeply about, that you loved, being under threat?

I wanted to ask what had happened to Francesca when she'd been kidnapped as a child. How had that affected her? Was it one of the reasons she was so titanium-tough? I knew that the children of wealthy European families were always potential targets, and I couldn't imagine how it was possible to live with that constant anxiety on a day-to-day basis. Maybe that was what made Francesca seem so hard when she was actually a kind person, an empathetic person. She had empathised with me when I'd begged her to tell me where D'Artagnan was sulking, and she'd empathised with us when Nina was taken. She had pulled God alone knows what strings to get Nina back when she need not have done anything at all. Once again I felt ashamed of the caricature of her that I had painted so gleefully, so spitefully.

D'Artagnan drove Nina to school every day and picked her up afterwards. One of the armed guards always accompanied him whilst the other one stayed at the château.

Espiritu continued to improve. He was now allowed to trot several times around the paddock in either direction, and I could walk him up and down the drive and let him graze on the front lawn under D'Artagnan's watchful eye. Sometimes Espiritu did a little dance; he arched his beautiful, gleaming neck and he danced as if he were a little exasperated at having to walk, as if he had forgotten about his accident.

Each time he did that, I touched his cheek gently. I didn't tighten the lead rope; I let him dance a little but I asked him to be careful. I whispered that if he was careful like I was being careful, we would both be well enough to run about and to be ourselves again soon.

He seemed to listen to me and slowed down; he stopped dancing and he breathed out. Sometimes he snorted, blowing huge breaths out of his nostrils several times, but then he walked quietly beside me again and I scratched his neck, my fingernails under his mane on the arch of his thick, beautiful neck.

***

And then the day finally arrived. GTBSD. Get That Bastard Satan Day.

I wore grey. Xavier suggested I should wear something soft and feminine. 'You should wear something ... '*Bah*, with flowers, Nicole. A dress to show that you are very pregnant. This would be good for the jury.'

D'Artagnan frowned for a minute then gave one of his rare nods of agreement with Xavier.

I wore grey because I didn't need flowers. I wore a tailored grey, light-wool dress and a jacket, perfectly tailored to match. It was obvious that I was pregnant – there was no hiding that. I wore my hair up in a neat bun from which some strands persisted in escaping. I wore the Cartier necklace that Guy had given me all those years ago, on that night when I had finally accepted that he had fully, completely seduced me, the night when I realised that I was incapable of resisting him. I wore my most demure Louboutins, the ones I'd worn to his mother's funeral also all those years ago.

It was my war uniform. I was finally going to war with Satan.

***

I stared at Guillaume from the witness box, the Fuck-You box. I fixed my eyes on his hard, dark, horrible eyes. My jaw was tight, my face was tight. I held my head high and at no point did I drop my chin, drop my head, even when the tears were flowing freely from my eyes.

I answered all the questions his lawyer flung at me, batted back all the accusations. I brushed aside all the insinuations, and when the judge questioned me more gently after Satan's lawyer had finished challenging me I told him clearly and concisely exactly what Satan had done, what his friends had done.

I couldn't keep the emotion from my voice as I told everyone in the courtroom how I had struggled to deal with the repercussions for twelve years of my life, how that one night had led me to become a heroin addict and how I had overcome that. How Satan's revelation eighteen months previously had led me to relapse, and how I had overcome that as well.

Satan had refused to disclose the names of his little gargoyles in return for a reduced sentence, but Francesca's 'people' had made enquiries because D'Artagnan had asked her if she would. It was Francesca who later filled me in on the reasons for Satan not disclosing any names. According to Francesca's sources, one of the gargoyles was already dead. That made me feel both angry and happy: angry that he would never be brought to justice for what he'd done, and happy that he could never assault another woman. She didn't go into detail about the how or the why or the when, but she intimated that it wasn't entirely surprising that he was dead given the underworld in which he moved.

She hesitated a little when I asked her if she knew who the other one was.

'He is Russian,' she said, her pale-blue eyes fixed on mine. 'And if you can, it is really for the best if you forget about this man Nicole. You are never going to bring him to justice. And Guillaume will never dare to speak his name because if he does, he will also be dead very soon.'

I nodded slowly and gave a resigned shrug. I had no actual memory of him; there was nothing specific that my subconscious had recorded about him. After what had happened to Nina, I was willing to accept that bringing Satan, the ringleader, to justice would be sufficient. If Satan was afraid of the Russian, there was no way I was going to expose my family to any more risk.

I didn't wipe the tears from my face while I gave evidence. Once or twice, I blew my nose, but I blew it in a business-like way, put my tissue back in my jacket pocket and waited for the next question.

Finally, the judge invited me to stand down from the witness box. His voice was gentle. I took a moment to look across the courtroom at Satan and there was a long silence as I stared at him. I waited until he finally raised his eyes sullenly to mine and stared back at me, and then I mouthed very clearly, 'Fuck you.'

Despite the language barrier, I don't think anyone in the courtroom that day had any problem understanding what I had just said. Guillaume's horrible black eyes narrowed and he looked away because he knew that, after my testimony, that was exactly what he was. Fucked.

That made me feel powerful but also utterly exhausted. I wanted the floor of the courtroom to open up and swallow me, welcome me into its voluminous innards. After all those years, I had done everything I'd set out to do. I had nothing more to give.

I was so tired, but I made sure that when I sat down at Xavier's side my back was straight and my exhaustion didn't show. And then I felt D'Artagnan's hand on my shoulder; he was sitting behind me and he gave my shoulder the gentlest squeeze followed by the softest brush of his fingers against my neck. I reached for his hand on my shoulder and held it very tightly.

Guillaume was convicted of rape and sexual assault by six of the eight jurors and all three judges. Xavier later said that he thought Guillaume's family had got to at least one of the jurors who had voted against his conviction. He was sentenced to fourteen years in prison, just over thirteen including the nine months he'd already spent in custody. He could apply for parole after eight years. The thought that for a minimum of eight years women everywhere would be safe from Bastard Satan was pleasing, even if I would have preferred him to stay there permanently. Or be dead. The latter was preferable but hey, one can't have everything.

***

We hosted the Toussaint lunch again that year. By then, having made up with his son, Stephane had returned from Berlin. I'd shown him the photograph album when he returned in October and he'd asked if he could take it away with him.

It was a slightly smaller Toussaint lunch this time. Benoit and Veronique hadn't joined us, and I was almost eight months pregnant and starting to feel rather frustrated. D'Artagnan, of course, thought it was marvellous and insisted on taking photos of my ever-enlarging belly every week.

Nina was fascinated by the noises Honey made and spent a lot of time with her ear pressed against my belly, giggling. Once Honey kicked her and she thought that was the most hilarious thing ever; she doubled-over and gasped with laughter, which made me laugh too. Then I farted, which made us laugh so much I had to sit down.

But I'd be lying if I wasn't dreading what the stretch marks were going to look like. I'd spent the last three months doing a lot of yoga and following a strict diet that Sylvie recommended. D'Artagnan was very happy to massage the argan oil she'd also recommended into my abdomen every night ... and most nights didn't stop at my abdomen, which usually ended very pleasantly for both of us.

It was late afternoon and the autumn sun was low in the sky when we finished lunch. We were having coffee and digestifs in the salon. I asked Stephane what he'd learned from the photograph album. Nina was outside with Bérengère, giving the horses their hay ration for the night, and D'Artagnan was talking animatedly to Françoise and Pascal about the new development that he and Francesca had started in Biarritz.

'Did you find out who the young girl and the old woman in the photographs are? The ones dressed in beekeepers' costumes?' I asked.

Stephane nodded. 'Yes, Nicole. I know who they are and I know who the old woman is. It's very interesting because I've never seen a photograph of our great-great-great-great grandmother before.' He paused. 'Her name was Sophie-Anne Josephine du Beauchamp, and she was born here in the château in 1779.'

I stared at him. 'Was she the *duchesse*?'

'Yes, but she never really used her title. All titles were abolished in 1790 during the Revolution. Our family escaped from France in 1789 and went to England until 1810.'

'So she was never at Versailles?'

He gave a little smile 'No, I very much doubt she ever went to Versailles. Her mother died when she was young and that was why she inherited the title of *duchesse*.'

I felt a bit bad then for having spent all that time imagining the Duchess swanning her way around Versailles.

'She was a very accomplished woman,' Stephane continued. 'When my family returned to France, she spoke perfect English, Dutch and German, and she knew Latin. She was very curious, very intellectual – and she loved a party, loved to dance. My family had an apartment in Paris and when she was in her twenties, she immersed herself in Parisian life. She held soirées with many of the French intellectuals at that time.'

He paused again. 'She married late, when she was in her late twenties, after pressure from her father. Our family owned about forty hectares of land around Cognac, and her father arranged her marriage with the son of a wealthy local family who owned a lot of land and a prestigious Cognac house.'

D'Artagnan, Françoise and Pascal had stopped talking and were now listening.

Stephane paused and took a sip of his Cognac. 'So, she married and returned to live here in the château. I suspect she wasn't very happy about it, leaving her intellectual pursuits behind, but she did seem to love her husband.'

I frowned 'How do you know that?'

He smiled as he placed his glass down on the table. 'Well, her granddaughter wrote a letter to her own mother in 1865, in which she talks about her grandmother losing the locket with a miniature of her husband and a lock of his hair in the garden. They searched all day for it and finally, just as dusk was coming, they found it.' He paused again. 'She writes about how happy her grandmother was to find it.'

'Oh!' I realised I had tears in my eyes. 'How wonderful – I'm so glad she found it.'

He nodded. 'Yes, she would have been, uh—' he raised his eyes while he calculated '—she would have been eighty-five then.'

'That's the old woman in the photograph?' Françoise asked. 'That's Sophie-Anne, our great-great-great-great grandmother?'

Stephane glanced at me 'Or the Duchess, as Nicole likes to call her, I understand.' He gave me a little wink and I opened my mouth to say I didn't know the Duchess was a real person, it was just a nickname I'd given the château. Then I shut it again. It was too complicated to explain.

'And the young girl standing in front of her in the photograph, is that her grand-daughter?' I asked instead.

He nodded. 'Yes, one of them. She had three children, but two of them died when they were very young. Only our great-great-great-grandfather survived. But she had five grandchildren. The child in the photograph, the one who's standing by the beehives – that was her favourite grandchild. She's the one who wrote the letter, and she's the one who our great grandmother taught about beekeeping.'

A chill ran down my spine and I shivered. D'Artagnan turned to me and slipped his arm around my shoulders. 'Okay, *mon amour*?'

I gave a little nod, then turned back to Stephane. 'Was she a beekeeper, the Duchess?' I asked.

He nodded, smiling. 'Yes, she was quite a famous beekeeper. She studied the history of beekeeping, and she designed a new beehive that she had made, a beehive so that the honey could be easily removed without the bees being harmed. Apparently her bees produced wonderful honey. Maybe it was the way she looked after the hives, or maybe it was because she had studied beekeeping in Ancient Greece and Roman times. She was very knowledgeable on the subject.'

He took another sip of his Cognac. 'And, of course, the château was surrounded by a forest of chestnut trees, and hazelnut trees and walnut trees, and she grew honeysuckle and wildflowers, so the bees had a varied diet and were very healthy. Because she still knew lots of important people in Paris, word got back to Napoleon III about her wonderful honey and he used to send a carriage—'

He smiled at us all. 'Yes, it's true. Louis-Napoleon really used to send a carriage all the way from Paris to the château here in the Charente to collect the honey that our great-great-great – ' he paused, gave a little frown, continued ' – great-grandmother took from her hives.'

'Amazing,' breathed Françoise. 'I'd heard a bit about this from Grandmama, but I never really believed it was true.'

D'Artagnan squeezed my hand. When I turned to look at him, his eyes were very soft. I gave him a little smile before turning back to Stephane, who opened the album again to the page with the photograph of the Duchess and her granddaughter standing between the bee-hives.

Françoise and Pascal leaned over and studied it. 'When were they taken, these photographs?' she finally asked.

'I think it was probably in 1858 – she would have been in her late seventies then. It's a shame we can't really see her face because of the veil,' Stephane replied.

'What about the little girl, her granddaughter? How old was she then? Did she carry on keeping bees after her grandmother died?' I asked.

He narrowed his eyes as he looked at me. 'Why are you so interested in this young girl, Nicole?'

I shrugged. 'I don't know. I just get a weird feeling whenever I look at that photograph.'

He took a very deep breath. 'She is probably about eight or nine in that photograph. And yes, she continued to keep bees after her grandmother died. She was also very passionate about bees and honey.'

I stared at him. Finally, aware that my voice was very faint, I asked, 'What was her name?'

He tilted his head to the side. 'Her name was Anne, but she was always called Annie.'

And that was when I heard it. I didn't hear 'Annie', I heard 'Uhnee', which is the way the French pronounce the English word 'honey'. In French, 'an' is not pronounced like the English 'ant' or 'another' – it's pronounced 'uhn'; in other words, 'Annie' in French sounds exactly like 'Honey' when pronounced by a French native.

I continued to stare at him, mesmerised, aware that my heart was suddenly beating very fast. My mind whirred through everything that had happened that year, starting with Nina's imaginary friend Annie, then my nearly falling down the stairs, then Nina informing us that Annie had gone away but would be back at Christmas, and then my deciding on the spur of the moment that my daughter's name was going to be Honey. And as that last little piece of the jigsaw slotted into place, I realised both my eyes and my mouth were wide open.

'Nicole?' said D'Artagnan softly. 'What is wrong?'

I turned to him, shaking my head slowly and didn't – couldn't – say anything for a while. I realised his brother and sister and Pascal were all also watching me, so I quickly shook my head and said, 'Nothing, nothing's wrong, I'm fine. It's just – really interesting to know some of the background to the house and to the photographs in the album.'

But my heart was pounding.

I glanced at Stephane as he picked up the album again and opened it to the photograph on the first page. He held it out to me and pointed to one of the children in the photograph of the family posed in front of the château. 'There she is, the smallest child on the right – she would have been about six in this photograph.'

I took the album and stared at the little girl. She wasn't smiling and her head was slightly tilted as she gazed towards the camera as if she found it curious.

'And about four pages on, there's another one of her with her sister. She's a bit older then, a teenager, perhaps.'

I turned the pages until I found it, aware that my hands were shaking. It was a photograph of two young girls in long white, dresses standing side by side in front of the château. I knew instantly which one was Annie because her head had that little tilt again, and there was a slightly calculating smile playing around the edge of her mouth that I recognised immediately. It was a smile I'd seen so often on D'Artagnan's face.

I stared at her for a long time, aware that my heart was no longer beating as rapidly, aware that the longer I gazed at the photograph, the calmer I began to feel. And I also felt – although it's hard to describe it – a sense of wellbeing, contentment.

'Did she live a long life?' I finally asked.

'Oh yes.' Stephane smiled. 'She lived until she was ninety-eight, and she had a very happy life. She continued keeping bees until she died.' He paused. 'It's a shame none of her children continued with the tradition but by then the land that the family owned began to be divided and sold off and the family gradually moved towards Bordeaux, where we were born.'

***

D'Artagnan spent a long time massaging my back that night as I lay on my side, unable to sleep, cradling my unborn daughter and thinking about everything I'd just learned. I couldn't stop thinking about the Duchess and her favourite granddaughter out there with the bees, the bees that they'd sent to save me, to save my daughter. I was struggling to absorb the fact that the Duchess did not dislike me after all; in fact, the Duchess was completely on my side, my ally rather than my enemy. It made me laugh quietly to myself.

Although D'Artagnan stirred a little when I laughed, a minute later his gentle snoring into the back of my neck continued and his arms held me against his warm body.

Now I knew what I was going to be doing for the next phase of my life in France. I owed it to the Duchess, and I owed it to Annie.

***

Our daughter was born naturally on the fourth of December, not by caesarean, which Doctor D'Artagnan had spent a lot of time telling me I would need to have because, 'You have the 'ips that are too narrow, *mon ange*. It will be very difficult. You must have a *césarienne.*' Rather annoyingly, he was backed up by Sylvie but I ignored them both.

I had researched very thoroughly, done lots of yoga and Pilates and watched a lot of videos on YouTube. I was determined that my body would not let me down, and it didn't. It helped that Honey was slightly early; she was born in the thirty-sixth week and she wasn't a big baby – she was only just three kilograms – but she was perfectly, beautifully healthy, and my labour was less than four hours. Nevertheless, I said many very nasty things to D'Artagnan during those four hours and my fingernails dug into the back of his hand so hard that I actually broke the skin in two places.

'*Césarienne,* Nicole, you should have accepted to have a *césarienne* like I tell you,' he said the next day as he cradled Honey tenderly in his arms. There was a plaster across the back of his hand.

I was still tired, but not so tired that I couldn't raise my middle finger at him from behind Nina, who was sitting next to me on the hospital bed.

He saw it and grinned. 'But you do a very good job, *mon amour*. She's very beautiful, *petite* Honey – don't you think so Nina?' He sat down on the bed next to Nina, who had been showing me a video Guy had taken that morning on his phone of her jumping Hermès in the paddock.

Nina turned and looked at Honey. 'She's very small,' she said finally. 'I think it will be difficult to find a pony that's small enough for her.'

We exchanged a glance over her head. 'Maybe we should wait until she's a little bigger to find her a pony,' said D'Artagnan sagely.

Nina nodded. 'Yes. I think that would be better.' She carried on gazing at Honey, who had started making snuffling noises in D'Artagnan's arms. 'And she doesn't have a lot of hair,' she continued thoughtfully, reaching out and stroking Honey's head very gently with her fingertips. 'But she feels very soft.' She turned back to me and smiled. 'I like her.'

I smiled back at her. 'I like her too, Nina. Are you happy to have a new baby sister?'

She nodded firmly. 'Yes, I'm very happy. I've never had a baby sister.'

I squeezed her hand and tried to blink away the tears that were clouding my eyes. D'Artagnan's eyes were glassy too, so I knew it wasn't just the post-birth hormones.

He mouthed '*je t'aime*' at me, and I mouthed '*je t'aime également*' back at him.

Everything felt raw. The amount of happiness I felt in that moment felt so enormous it was almost painful.

***

That Christmas, D'Artagnan bought me another wonderful present.

He insisted that I was blindfolded before he and Nina led me carefully out of the dining hall, through the salon and out the front door onto the forecourt. I shivered a little; it was a cold, clear Christmas day and I was only wearing the usual four sweaters and the fake Patagonia jacket. Nina's hand was gripping mine very tightly and I could feel the excitement in her body as she jiggled from foot to foot. D'Artagnan let go of my hand and walked away.

I heard him before I saw him, heard his hooves on the gravel.

D'Artagnan said, 'Okay, Nicole, you can take it off now. You can look.'

He was standing beside Espiritu as I lifted the blindfold off my face and Espiritu had an extravagantly thick, red-velvet ribbon with a big bow tied around his gleaming neck. He was showing off a bit, doing a little dance in the cold wind that was lifting his mane off his arched neck.

'*Joyeux Noël, mon amour.*' D'Artagnan smiled the loveliest smile as Nina fizzed with excitement next to me.

'But...' I stared at him. 'But Camille? Did she...?'

He nodded, still smiling. 'We buy him from Camille for you. She didn't want to sell him, but she know that you save him so she agreed to sell him – but only to you, not to anyone else. Nina and me, we know how much you love Espiritu, so Espiritu now belong to you, Nicole. He is your horse.'

My hand flew to my mouth as I stared at him and then at Espiritu. My chest ached with joy.

'Are you happy, Mama?' asked Nina.

I leaned down and hugged her tightly against me, whispering, 'I'm very, very happy. Thank you, darling, Nina.' Then I let her go and embraced D'Artagnan, slipping my arms tightly around his neck and kissing him on the mouth. 'Thank you so, so much my darling, wonderful musketeer. It's like a dream come true.'

He held me tightly against him and said, 'For you, Nicole, I do anything to make all of your dreams become real.'

I took the halter rope from him and stood next to the most beautiful horse in the world, then put my hand underneath his forelock and gave him scratchies with my fingernails on his forehead. His blue-black eyes started to close with pleasure and I laughed at the goofy expression on his face. I was utterly blown away at the thought that he was mine, that the most beautiful horse in the world now actually belonged to me.

***

In late May the following year, D'Artagnan insisted that we go, just the two of us, to San Sebastian for a couple of days. I didn't really want to at first.

I was lying against him on the chaise longue in Heaven, breastfeeding Honey. I could not stop gazing at her, could not get over the sense of wonder I felt as I watched her. She was the most beautiful baby I had ever set eyes on, and I loved her so much that my heart actually felt slightly painful when I picked her up and held her against me.

'Nicole.' D'Artagnan was twisting my hair about on one of his fingers, his voice mild but slightly cajoling. 'I tell you about this before Honey is born. We need to take some time sometimes just for us. Without Nina, without Honey, just us two, *mon ange*. Françoise promise we can leave the children with her and Pascal in Bordeaux on the way to San Sebastian. She is very happy to do this. You know how much she love Honey and Nina. She *want* to do this, Nicole.'

I sighed, laid my head back against his shoulder and gazed up at him. His eyes were dark, liquid. He kissed my mouth softly. 'I need you, *mon amour*.' He blinked that slow, lustful blink. 'And I think also that we need to take some time to make a baby brother for Nina and Honey, because all little girls should have a baby brother. It is very important that they have a baby brother to boss around.' He smiled the lazy, sexy smile. 'Remember, you tell me in the beginning when we first meet Nicole, that you always want two girls and a boy? So, it's time to make a baby boy now. Before I am too old, *mon ange*.'

I lifted my free hand, slipped it behind his head and caressed the back of his neck. I let myself dive into his beautiful, sensual eyes and I thought... *Y'know, I'd quite like that.*

***

So we went to San Sebastian, Zeus and me. We took a suite in our favourite hotel, and I wore the dark-blue Balenciaga evening gown that I'd worn on the night he formally proposed to me in London. Although it was rather tight across my breasts, I was thrilled that it still more or less fitted me.

After dinner in the grand old-style ballroom, there was a band, a proper formal band with violinists and a cellist and a marvellous baritone. They played mostly tango music, all sweeping passion and drama. When we finished our dinner, D'Artagnan made a little signal to the band leader, then took my hand, led me onto the dance floor and took me in his arms just as the cellist played the very first, deeply melancholic chords of 'La Soledad'.

It was *our* song, the song he'd sung to me, his lips soft against my ear on that night in San Sebastian that felt like both yesterday and a thousand years ago; the night in the very beginning when I'd finally allowed myself to be seduced. The night I'd begun to fall in love with D'Artagnan.

***

Our son was born by caesarean. He was *not* small and Sylvie was *not* in a mood to be negotiated with and neither was Doctor D'Artagnan. We named him Valentin, because he was born on St Valentine's Day. Of course he was.

Duh, it's Zeus.

I was not allowed to name him Peanut even though that was all I wanted to eat while I was pregnant with him: peanuts, raw, grilled, salted, sweet; peanuts in every salad; peanut omelettes; peanut butter; peanut butter with cheese; peanut-butter with roasted broccoli...

D'Artagnan drew the line there; Peanut was apparently not an option as a first name.

I still call him Peanut, though, and D'Artagnan calls him Tintin because he has a little tuft of hair that sticks out from his forehead above his green eyes. Honey has D'Artagnan's eyes, although they are slightly lighter, more amber than dark-chocolate brown. She has his long, dark eyelashes too, and so does Valentin.

I've been fascinated to learn that the slow blink that D'Artagnan does so masterfully really *is* hereditary. Honey does it to me sometimes when she's happy and sometimes when she's disdainful, too. She has very expressive eyes. Peanut doesn't do disdain, not yet anyway, but he also does the slow blink.

Nina adores her little siblings and she is a wonderful older sister to them. She's now a very accomplished *cavalière* and has collected lots of show-jumping rosettes over the last two years, but she's getting too big for Hermès. She has reluctantly agreed that he will become Honey's pony in the future and we're actively looking for a new pony for her.

Nina and I have the most wonderful rides together in the forests and the vineyards around the château. When we ride out with Camille, we race each other up the long, gentle hills, each in our own row of vines, but we don't tell D'Artagnan about that anymore because he *vehemently* disapproved of it the one time I stupidly told him that Nina had nearly beaten us in that day's race. I never ask Espiritu to jump though – his ligament has healed well and he is pain-free, but both the vet and I don't think it's worth chancing anything by putting extra strain on it.

He's an opinionated little horse and quite highly strung; I have to keep a clear head while I'm riding him because if something bothers him, he can become very stressed very quickly, and that usually means some very brisk cantering on the spot, often while spinning in a circle with his neck in full Spanish arch. Nina says it's impressive to watch. I have very good inner thigh muscles, thanks to Espiritu.

***

We spend some time in the summers with Françoise and Pascal and her family in Pyla, and we always go down to Biarritz for a day or two to stay in Francesca's palace that sits on the cliffs, high above Biarritz and the Bay of Biscay. We're good friends now, she and I. Although her girls are older than Nina, they are kind to her and they love playing with Honey and Peanut.

Francesca still teases me about Xavier in front of D'Artagnan, but it's just to wind him up. It almost never fails; he gets that pouty look when I sigh wistfully and say things like, 'Ah, Francesca, I shall never know...'

Then I give D'Artagnan lots of little kisses until he stops pouting.

Speaking of Xavier, Virginie and he were married shortly after Valentin was born and she's expecting their first child any day now. We don't stay in touch with them as much as I'd like to, not because D'Artagnan is obstructive but just because our lives seem so much busier, so much fuller now. We only manage to stay in the apartment in Bordeaux for a couple of nights each month, and never in the summer, but we do try to meet up with them for dinner once or twice a year.

Stephane went off to Tibet just before Peanut was born and Bérengère joined him there while her niece stayed in her house and looked after her animals, but she came back on her own.

She frowned at me and rolled her eyes when I said I was sorry that they'd broken up. 'Nothing is broken, Nicole,' she said. 'Everything is fine between Stephane and me. Why do you say we are broken?'

'Well, it's just that you're uh, here, and he's y'know, there? Far away? Didn't he want to come back with you?'

She shrugged. 'I don't know, I didn't ask him. He seemed very happy. If he comes back then that will be great. If he doesn't – well, that's also great.' She put her hand on my arm and smiled at me. 'I don't need to have Stephane close to me to care about him.'

I saw her in the street in Cognac a week or so later, walking near the public gardens with her arm around the neck of a gorgeous woman with short blonde hair. They seemed quite intimate and I thought, *So even though she does still care about him, it seems perhaps theirs is a slightly more open relationship than the one that D'Artagnan and I have.*

Summers are marvellous at the Duchess. Jules and her family come for at least a week in August, and D'Artagnan's children and siblings and nieces and their children all come at various times, and we live on salads and food from the barbeque and everyone pitches in with the cooking and the shopping. It's total chaos. It's wonderful to watch all of the kids playing together in the pool, even if one begins to wonder just how far off the health and safety register the decibels really are.

Fish and Chips are fully grown now and Honey is their number one fan; when I can't find her, the first place I look is in their beds in the laundry room and she's invariably there, fast asleep with her thumb in her mouth and her head pillowed on one of them. Mr Muffin has decided that they are not quite as terrifying as he originally thought and likes to sit on the dining hall chairs and swipe at them as they walk past. Mrs Muffin still does not approve of them, and on the rare occasions when she deigns to take a break from her self-appointed role as Peanut's nanny, she hisses at them if they dare to come too close to her.

It's a really lovely laid-back, sun-drenched way to spend the summers, and Gabriela and Camille are starting the renovation of one of the big old barns out the back next autumn to create a two-bedroom gite so that we have more space for everyone to stay without having to queue for bathrooms.

I know the Duchess is very happy that the château's thick stone walls are once again ringing with the sound of childish laughter and shouts, and I'm pretty sure she approves of the four beehives I've had installed at the far end of the paddocks. When I'm out there with the bees I'm always aware of her presence, and this year we have had the most sublime honey imaginable. It tastes of all the meadow flowers I've planted in front of the château and behind the stables where the horses can't graze.

I'm pretty sure I caught her smiling at me from her usual position on top of the enormous stone mantlepiece in the dining hall when I nipped downstairs in the moonlight the other night to get another bottle for Peanut. After I'd fed him, and as I climbed back into bed, D'Artagnan stirred and woke. He reached out and pulled me into the curve of his warm body, burying his nose behind my ear and murmuring sleepily, 'Where did you go, *mon amour*?'

'Just to get Peanut another bottle. He's gone back to sleep again.' I paused. 'I saw the Duchess down there tonight,' I whispered. 'She smiled at me this time. I think she likes me quite a lot.'

He gave a sleepy snigger. '*Bah*, Nicole *mon ange...* You and *ze furking Duchesse...*'

And they all lived happily ever after!

They really did; fairy tales *do* still exist, even for adults – hell, we need them to! I hope you enjoyed reading the D'Artagnan trilogy as much as I enjoyed writing it and, as ever, I would be so very, very grateful if you would take just a moment to review it on Amazon or Goodreads or indeed anywhere that you might have bought it from. You don't even have to write a review – just clicking the stars makes a difference to my visibility.

You can find me at fiwhymsauthor on Instagram, and Fi Whyms, Author on Facebook, and my website is at fiwhyms.com – I'm relatively good at posting on the first two, and I have a blog on my website which I promise to update more often now that I've finally finished the D'Artagnan trilogy. It's also where I'll tell you about my next book which I'm *very* excited about...!

It only remains to say an enormous, heartfelt thank you to: SC and KH who have guided, advised and bolstered me when I'm feeling down; my wonderful, tolerant, lonely OH; and to those of you who've taken the time to tell me, both publicly and privately, how much you've enjoyed reading about Nicole and D'Artagnan –

Merci mille fois!!

Printed in Great Britain
by Amazon

26634427R00139

Índice

Ilustraciones: Tesa González
Edición: Celia Ruiz Ibáñez

Campezo s/n – 28022 Madrid
Tel.: 913 009 100 – Fax: 913 009 118
Impreso en la UE

LEE con Gloria Fuertes

Nanas para leer en la cama

Ilustra: Tesa González

Un cuento para dormir feliz

Te contaré un cuento

**Mañana te contaré un cuento
de un viejecito
que tenía un huerto,
y allí un arbolito;
el arbolito
tenía un nido,
la pájara se había ido,
y un huevecito dejó;
el huevo solito llora...
–¿Quieres que te lo cuente ahora?
Lo siento...**

Mañana te contaré el cuento
del viejecito
dueño del huerto,
y allí un arbolito...

¡Si te has quedado dormido!
Pues ya no te cuento el cuento
del viejo dueño del huerto,
ni el cuento de la pastora
que se la comió la loba,
ni el cuento del dragón verde
ni el de la vaca que muerde
ni el cuento de la princesa
dentro del «balleno» presa.

No, por haberte dormido,
ya no te cuento los cuentos
que soñando he aprendido.

Nanas para dormir a niñas y muñecos sin sueño

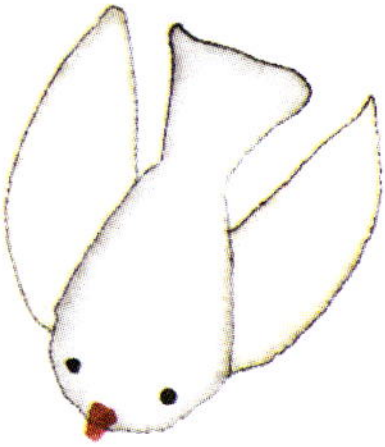

Son-nana

Cu, cu, Palomita,
Paloma, cu, cu.
¡Qué blanca mi niña,
Palomita, tú!

Y las madres negras,
¡qué pena y dolor!,
porque ellas no pueden
cantar este son.

Cu, cu, Palomita,
Paloma, cu, cu.
¡Qué blanca mi niña,
Palomita, tú!

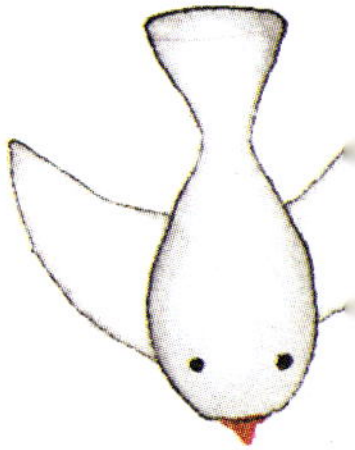

Nana para dormir a los muñecos

Tengo dos muñecos
y una muñeca,
se llaman Canutillo,
Marmolejo y Rubipeca.

Les tengo que cantar
para que se duerman.
He inventado tres nanas,
aprendedlas.

Duerme, Rubipeca,
que ya son las ocho,
ni una oveja bala,
ya duerme Pinocho,
hasta el río
se ha quedado dormido,
encogido en el pozo.

Duerme, Marmolejo,
que ya son las nueve,
ni un pájaro pía
ni un árbol se mueve,
hasta el viento
se ha quedado dormido
porque ha visto que llueve.

Duerme, Canutillo,
que ya son las diez,
ni una rana canta
ni queda un ciempiés,
hasta el grillo
se ha quedado dormido,
dormido de pie.

Nanas para dormir a animales y monstruos despiertos

Nana de la abuela lirona

(El lirón es un animalito
que se pasa la vida dormidito.)

El lirón careto
es un animalito poco callejero.
Vive en el campo,
come en silencio.
El lirón careto
es así...
entre ratón y conejo.

En vez de dormir como nosotros
–quedarse todas las noches dormido–,
¡duerme seis meses al año, todo seguido!

Se acuesta en noviembre
y se despierta en abril.
Duerme como un tronco
bajo el tronco
envuelto en la raíz.

–Ponte el gorro, lironcito,
ponte el pijama,
de cama,
que ya el invierno se asoma
–dice la abuela lirona–.

Después le canta una nana
muy dulce, con este son:

–Duérmete, orejudo mío,
duérmete que ya no hay sol.
Duérmete como lo que eres,
duérmete como un lirón.

Canta la abuela lirona.
Ronca el abuelo lirón.

Nana

Duérmete, mi gata Chundarata,
se han dormido los juguetes
y tú sigues dando lata.

Duérmete, que ya es la una.
Duérmete, mi cascabel
–queda poca noche–,
duerme mi doncel,
que ya son las tres.

Duérmete, gatita, duérmete,
que los piececitos se te ven.
Duérmete, castaña, duérmete,
que la luna apaga su quinqué.

Duérmete, pingüino, que al dormir
se te quita el frío en la nariz.
Duérmete, pequeña, encógete,
que los piececitos se te ven.

Duérmete, mi gata Chundarata,
se han dormido los juguetes
y tú sigues dando lata.

Duérmete, que ya es la una.
Duérmete, mi cascabel
–queda poca noche–,
duerme mi doncel,
que ya son las tres.

Nana de mamá mona

–Duerme, mi mono bonito,
eres más guapo que tu abuelito.

¡Ay qué bonito es mi monito!
¡Ay qué monito más bonito tengo!
Monito bonito duerme,
que si no el lobo te muerde.
Tu mamá mona está contigo,
para protegerte del enemigo.

El enemigo lobo,
la enemiga serpiente,
se quedarán perdidos en el puente.

Mamá mona te acuna en la cuna,
de la rama más alta por el puma.

Mamá mona te acuna,
y te canta la nana
con la luna.

–Duerme, mi mono bonito,
eres más guapo que tu abuelito.

Nana al Coco

Duérmete, Coco,
que viene el niño
que lleva a los Cocos
que duermen poco.

Ea, ea, ea,
que si el Coco no se duerme
se me marea.

Duérmete, Coco,
que viene el niño
y despierta a sus padres
y a su vecino.

Ea, ea, ea,
que si el Coco no se duerme,
se me marea.

Nana del ogro

Duérmete, coco,
que viene el niño
a asustar a los cocos
que duermen poco.

Nana de la ogra

Duérmete, pequeño,
que si no te duermes
te doy con un leño.

Fin